FREE LISONA

A PROPHECY BOUND BY BLOOD AND FIRE

TRISH MARTINEZ

Οἶκος Δράκων

HOUSE DRAKON

First Editi

ISBN: [97982982403

Dau Fantasy Romance Publishi

Cover by: Cover art generated using AI (Open AI tools), bas

On author-provided prompts and vision. Final design layout a

Formatting by Trish Martin

Interior design by: Tesia Gar

Printed in the United States of Amer

Table of Contents

Prologue

I was born on Earth, yet destined to reign as the Empress of Lisona, a realm far removed from my birthplace. My name is Aundrea, a name that would one day echo throughout the cosmos. I have long black hair that curls slightly at the ends, cascading to the small of my back—a striking feature that, along with my height, sets me apart. At five foot eleven, I tower over most ladies and have a slender yet strong physique bearing the unmistakable mark of both worlds. In Lisonian culture, women come of age at eighteen, when they are considered ready to take their place in the world.

My father, Expodus, was a being from Lisona—powerful, majestic, and king of Earth, a modern world he had conquered centuries ago. A place so advanced, yet so different from Lisona's raw magic and ancient ways. My mother, Arissa, was his unlikely love—a mortal woman with skin as white as snow and hair as black as the night sky. She stood tall for a human, at five foot ten, while my father towered at six foot two. Her beauty was captivating, and her memory still haunts me—especially since fate tore her from my life when I was only fourteen years old.

In a universe where interspecies unions were taboo, my father's love was a rare exception. Lisonians lived for twelve hundred to fourteen hundred years, wielding power across generations, while mortal lives flickered briefly—merely one hundred to one hundred and fifteen years. This disparity had far-reaching consequences for dominance on both Earth and Lisona.

My life on Earth with Father lasted until I came of age, when duty called. A portal shimmered into existence—an oval of swirling silver and violet light, humming softly as if alive. The air around it pulsed with energy, raising goosebumps on my skin. This was my passage to Lisona, a one-step journey that would carry me across galaxies to my predetermined fate: marriage to Emperor Jasino.

Scientists had discovered an intriguing phenomenon—humans who lived on Lisona enjoyed extended lifespans, ranging from two hundred to two hundred and fifty years. The reason remained a mystery, but researchers pursued answers with tireless fascination.

Given my half-Lisonian heritage, everyone assumed I would defy mortal limitations and live a remarkably long life.

Emperor Jasino embodied power incarnate. I felt dwarfed by his presence, and I wasn't alone—everyone trembled in his shadow. Fear mingled with intimidation; his life had been a seamless tapestry of getting everything he desired. How could I possibly compare?

***

Back on Earth, my brother Johnny—also half-Lisonian like me—awaited his own destiny as heir to our father's throne. He resembled Father more closely, inheriting his tall, slender stature and black hair.

A painful memory lingered—Mother's tragic death. She had slipped from a cliff overlooking the river that wound past our home and into Lake Wawona, all while fleeing Father's control. A harsh reality faced me: women in our world held little power. We lived under our fathers' rule until deemed suitable for marriage, then transferred to our husbands' dominance—a bleak echo of ancient Earth's patriarchal past.

In Lisonian culture, women's subservience was ingrained—a timeless norm. My mother suffered terribly under this expectation. She feared my father, Expodus, with good reason. He demanded obedience not only as her husband but also as her king. Expodus was a monster, abusive in every sense. His rule was absolute; defiance meant punishment. My mother's spirit refused to be crushed, and she paid dearly for it.

The day she attempted to escape, she begged me to flee with her. I regretfully stayed behind. Father had imprisoned her in her chambers for months prior, enraged by her secret visits to a serene lake near our manor—her peaceful sanctuary. But he discovered more: she had a companion, a young man with whom she shared laughter and conversation, though never intimacy. This wasn't her first transgression. "Years earlier, she had slipped away to a forbidden gathering—an illicit evening of mingling with men and drinking spirits not meant for women. Such behavior would have meant imprisonment for a commoner. But as queen, my mother endured my father's brand of justice—savage beatings and cruel confinement."

His abuse was twofold—physical blows and emotional manipulation. She lived in constant terror and emotional withdrawal. I watched her spirit slowly shatter, piece by piece—and now I fear I may inherit that same silent suffering, drifting into emotional distance with Emperor Jasino.

Although Father's abuse scarred Mother, he spared my sister Alissia and me from physical harm. Our betrothals to powerful men protected us—I to Emperor Jasino, and Alissia to his brother Jasper. Father feared Jasino's dark reputation: violent past and mastery of magic. Crossing him would be unwise. Instead, Father punished us by confining us to our rooms whenever we disobeyed. Alissia recently joined me on Lisona, uniting with Jasper in marriage. Though we haven't met yet since her arrival, I've heard she has blossomed into a stunning woman—five foot six with long black hair adorned with captivating highlights she loved to add.

Her beauty rivaled mine yet differed elegantly. My husband, Emperor Jasino, preferred my natural look—"beautiful just the way you are," he said before our marriage. His words were charming then; now I wonder if control motivated them. Alissia's love story with Jasper touches my heart—everything a girl dreams of. Jasper, Six foot tall with a stronger build than Jasino's lean physique, adored Alissia. He courted her devotedly on Earth before she relocated to Lisona. Their bond seems genuine—do I dare hope love like theirs exists for me too?

A rare gift marked my existence—the ability to heal. On Lisona, only a handful possessed this power, and among half-breeds like myself, it was virtually unknown. Only four living cases existed in Lisonian bloodlines currently, making my skill a captivating anomaly. Father claimed Emperor Jasino chose me because of this unique gift, saying, "You're special, Aundrea." But I knew the truth—our union was arranged, like most marriages for women in our world. Fathers selected husbands, and daughters obeyed.

My husband, Emperor Jasino... stunningly handsome, even to my unwilling eyes. Standing Six foot three inches with a lean, athletic build, his bronze skin glowed against jet-black hair, perfectly layered with subtle texture. Most Lisonian men paled in comparison—but beauty hardly mattered in my loveless prison.

Nearly two years of marriage, yet our union remained unconsummated. I slept alone in my chambers every night, rarely seeing Jasino beyond fleeting visits. He'd enter my room, exchange only a few words, then leave again—making me wonder if ruling Lisona alone was his true passion, not me.

Our conversations were rare and hollow, and any trace of intimacy—whether of the heart or the body—had long since vanished. Was this truly the life Father promised was my destiny? Marriage to Jasino has been a disconcerting reality—he shows little interest in me as his wife. Conversations between us are awkward and strained, like two strangers forced into an uncomfortable silence. I rarely leave the palace walls that feel more like prison bars.

Life in the palace often feels isolating—my moments with Jasino are fleeting, as though I exist in the shadows of his world rather than within it. He insists I remain inside, claiming it's for my protection, but a part of me, shaped by years under my father's rule, wonders if there's more beneath the surface. At times, I sense an intensity in Jasino that burns low and steady, like embers waiting to flare. His gaze sharpens when another man lingers too long in conversation or stands too close. I've learned, perhaps unnecessarily, to avert my eyes in public—not from fear of him, but from habit, from stories etched into me by a past I can't easily shed. Even so, I remind myself: I am not a prisoner. I was born to be, Empress, born of royal blood, and I have not forgotten who I am. I understand that life as royalty comes with its share of restrictions, but I never imagined this isolation would stretch on for centuries. My dreams of life with the emperor were filled with grandeur and partnership—not this lonely existence. Loneliness haunts me relentlessly.

Over the past few years, I've attempted to escape his grasp three times—desperate bids for freedom from my gilded cage. Escaping the palace is nearly impossible with guards watching my every move, yet desperation drives me—my husband's distance suffocates me.

Jasino confuses my heart utterly: His actions scream indifference, but his eyes... oh, his eyes whisper love and adoration. I glimpse it deep within his soul, a spark that contradicts his cold behavior. Those wide blue eyes, soft and pleading like a puppy's, undid me completely. I melted beneath his gaze, my resolve slipping away. But experience had taught me a bitter truth: even puppies have teeth, and bites can hurt.

My husband is far from shy—he rules Lisona with commanding presence—yet around me, he freezes. Words seem to fail him, leaving awkward silences. I empathize; I'm equally tongue-tied.

Our conversations are unhinged, as if we're dancing around the truth—scrambled, like thoughts tangled in our minds—and distant, like two people living parallel lives under one roof.

I've started to wonder if Jasino feels this disconnect as deeply as I do—if his heart races like mine when our eyes meet. Does he lie awake at night, questioning our failed conversations and loveless marriage like I do?

His gaze still haunts me, a lingering whisper of what could be... if only we could bridge the chasm between us. Do I dare hope that beneath his reserved exterior, Jasino harbors feelings for me—feelings he struggles to express, just as I do?

My attempts to escape have been futile so far, but perhaps the greatest escape I need is from the fear of uncovering his true emotions... and my own.

I heard that a family member he loved with all his heart was enticed by dark powers. Whatever horrors unfolded during those shadowed days left an indelible mark on him. They say he was never the same after—his spirit fractured.

Another person that I consider family: Michelle, My lady-in-waiting.

Michelle's life was forever altered when tragedy struck her wealthy family's estate in a devastating earthquake, claiming her parents' lives. By virtue of her family's social standing, my father, Emperor Expodus of Earth, graciously accepted her into our household as a lady-in-waiting for me—a title that would barely scratch the surface of our bond.

Michelle arrived at our manor on Earth about a decade ago, just eight years old, though originally slated to join us at age fifteen. My father made a rare exception, welcoming her into our home immediately. Years passed, and Michelle grew into an indispensable companion—my best friend.

When I left Earth to marry Emperor Jasino, I requested a special favor; permission for Michelle to remain by my side as my lady-in-waiting. Jasino granted my wish. Michelle is stunning—five foot seven inches with gorgeous red hair that cascades down her back in loose curls, usually tied up in a playful braid.

Her presence has been my salvation; she has kept my sanity intact during the darkest times. We shared everything—laughing together during singing lessons, twirling as partners in dancing class, studying side by side, quizzing each other on history and literature. Michelle's spirit is infectious—warm, vibrant, and full of life.

She is, without doubt, the greatest friend I have ever had; my confidante, my partner in mischief, and my sole comfort in this loveless palace. Now, I wonder... will she be the one I turn to when I need escape from Emperor Jasino's grasp?

That was my life, but this is where my story begins...

HOUSE DRAKON

Chapter 1

A Chosen Bride

The night was shadowed, a heavy shroud suffocating the sky—darker than usual, as if even the stars feared to twinkle. I stood alone by my bedroom window, my gaze lifted toward the heavens, searching the blackness, praying the gods themselves might shatter the emptiness inside me. My heart felt lost, a solitary drumbeat echoing in my chest. I whispered pleas into the silence, begging to discover who I truly was, but only echoes replied— haunting reminders of my isolation.

Footsteps whispered across the chamber floor, announcing my husband's approach. The door creaked softly behind him as he entered my sanctuary—or prison, depending on my mood. He moved toward me, his presence commanding attention without demanding it. I turned my head slightly, our eyes meeting.

"My Lord," I said, my voice barely above a whisper. "Why must I remain captive behind these palace walls? I've asked countless times, yet your answer never comes."

His gaze met mine, intense and piercing. He reached out, his warm hand settling on my hip, sending a gentle shiver down my spine. Those captivating blue eyes, windows to a soul I once admired, held mine fast.

"Captive? You are my wife. Outside these doors, men would die to have you," he said, his low tone laced with something deeper—fear, perhaps.

My heart swelled with emotion, the weight of it creeping into my chest like a tide of sorrow. I didn't want anyone else—not truly—but doubt had become a poison neither of us could ignore. He turned me fully toward him, pulling me closer, his hands firm around my hips until our bodies nearly touched. His breath ghosted across my skin, but the warmth of it couldn't thaw the distance forming between us. Anger simmered beneath my surface, a slow-burning flame. I knew who I was—daughter of a troubled mother, wife of a powerful emperor—but I refused to be defined by either title. Hiding my frustration behind a calm facade, I said evenly,

"While you were away, your brother Jasper visited to check on me. I asked if I could see my sister tomorrow, and he mentioned taking her to a ball." My voice carried a note of curiosity. "I wondered, my lord, if you would escort me, so I could visit with her?"

His expression shifted, a flicker of annoyance crossing his face like a candle flame in the wind. He stepped back, his eyes narrowing slightly.

"Jasper should not have spoken to you... but yes, we can attend."

I watched him carefully, noting the tension in his posture. Confusion clouded my features. "I thought you sent him to check on me during your absence. Was he not supposed to ensure my well-being?"

Jasino's gaze dropped, his shoulders sinking slightly, shaking his head slowly while staring at the floor. "Yes. He should have only... looked in on you. Nothing more."

My voice softened, gentle yet probing. "My lord, Jasper is your brother—married to my sister. You shouldn't worry about him speaking with me."

His response was firm. "Sweetheart, my concern is not jealousy of my brother... but that he intruded on our private life."

I turned away, my gaze drifting back to the window, the night swallowing my sigh. "If you'd rather not take me to the ball, I understand."

His hands found my hips again, gentler this time as he stepped closer, his breath brushing against my ear.

"Oh, but I do want to take you, my love... Jasper simply ruined my surprise."

My heart skipped a beat as I turned to him, wondering if he truly would have taken me—regardless of my conversation with his brother. The answer came not in words, but in the quiet assurance of his smile. It softened his entire face, and something in me exhaled. I wrapped my arms around him, pressing close, grateful for the warmth of his embrace. He held me gently, one hand cradling the back of my head, his lips brushing my hair with a tenderness that made my chest ache.

He began to move toward the door, calm and composed, his voice a soft hum in the air as he offered the time of our departure—midday, well before the ball. It struck me as early, and curiosity stirred again, but he said no more. He reached the door, one hand on the handle, seemingly trying to end our conversation.

"I want to escort you out of the palace before the protests begin. They gather near the gates in the late afternoon."

Alarm sparked inside me. I moved quickly, catching him before he exited.

"Why?" I asked, my voice barely audible. "Why outside our gate?"

He opened the door, stepping through it without turning back. His voice trailed behind him, low and unnerving.

"They protest for you."

The door closed behind him, leaving me stunned. My mind reeled. Why would anyone protest my presence, or protest for me? A chill settled in my chest, mingling with the excitement I had felt about tomorrow's outing.

Later, as I settled into bed, thoughts of the ball and seeing my sister offered a welcome distraction. I sat there for a while, savoring the idea of escaping the palace walls, but fatigue crept in. I wrapped myself in soft, comforting sheets, willing myself to drift off to sleep.

Just as I began to relax, my husband reappeared.

Every time he visits my room this late, unsettling emotions stir within me. We've been married two full cycles of the moon, yet intimacy remains elusive. I worried about his intentions.

He walked to my bedside and leaned over, gently pulling the blanket up to my shoulders as if to tuck me in. Then he pressed his warm lips to my forehead—a gesture that soothed me, but only briefly.

Straightening, he said, "I'd love for you to wear the red dress to the ball. The one I admire so much."

I replied cautiously, "The long one with the low back? That dress intimidates me... it feels overly daring and too revealing."

"Could I wear the satin royal blue one instead? The one with the V-neck and lace-up back? Please? I know the red one is your favorite, but people stare at me when I wear it."

He looked at me with disapproving eyes, clearly unaccustomed to being questioned.
"No, sweetheart. The red one."

Jasino's gaze lingered on mine, and he let out a soft laugh. "You're adorable when you pout."
His amused tone eased the tension between us—but only for a moment. He turned and walked out without so much as a backward glance.

I lay there in darkness, an ache blooming deep within my soul. My longing for real love haunted me like a ghostly whisper, always reminding me how alone I felt. Sleep did not come easily. My mind tangled with desire, unease, and nervous anticipation for the ball. Eventually, exhaustion overpowered my thoughts, and I drifted into restless slumber.

***

The next morning, anticipation buzzed through my veins. Today was the ball.

I sat up just as Michelle, my loyal lady-in-waiting, entered with a breakfast tray—a bowl of fresh fruit and a steaming cup of coffee that filled the air with its rich aroma. After savoring my meal, Michelle guided me to a warm bath she had prepared, delicately scented with rose petals.

"Tonight, I had two goals: to make the evening enchanting and to prove to my husband he could trust me."
I felt like he had never truly given me the chance to show

who I really was. I wasn't reckless, not like he seemed to believe.

Michelle laced my corset and slipped the stunning red dress over my head. The dress left my back bare, a stretch of skin exposed and vulnerable. My hair cascaded in soft curls, carefully styled to frame my face, and a touch of rouge warmed my cheeks.

"Natural beauty is always the best," he often said. I agreed with him, actually; less was often more— especially at my age.

When Michelle finished the final touches, I stood before the mirror, admiring my reflection. The red dress hugged my curves flawlessly. A faint shudder of wind grazed my skin, raising goosebumps and stirring something deep within me.

Michelle curtsied gently behind me. "You look breathtaking, milady. Your husband will be enchanted."

I smiled nervously, hoping she was right. Tonight felt pivotal—my chance to connect with Jasino beyond our formal roles.

A soft knock at the door broke the quiet. Michelle opened it to reveal one of Jasino's guards.

"The emperor awaits milady's presence in the grand foyer."

My heart skipped a beat. It was time. I followed Michelle through the palace, the red dress swishing behind me like a whisper of silk. The guard escorted us down winding corridors until we reached the grand foyer.

There he stood. Just outside of the doors.

Jasino waited, dressed in elegant black formal attire, his gaze fixed intently on me.

As we stepped outside, he was standing near the carriage, speaking with Sabion, one of his guards. The moment he noticed me, he broke away and approached, taking my hand with unexpected tenderness.

He looked at me with a warmth that lingered just a moment too long, his gaze drinking in every detail. The admiration in his eyes was unmistakable—genuine, even flattering—but it stirred something uneasy in me. That red dress, bold and unforgiving, had clearly been the right choice. And yet, beneath the thrill of being seen, a shadow of discomfort crept along my spine.

A slight chill passed over my shoulders. "It's a little chilly, my lord," I murmured.

He smiled and gently draped his cloak around me, pulling me close. "Better?" he asked, his breath warm against my ear.

I looked up at him, my voice barely above a whisper. "Yes, thank you, my lord."

His fingers traced softly along my jawline, stirring a tremble beneath my skin.

With a soft nod, he extended his arm, his gaze steady and unwavering as he invited me to follow. I nodded, and he led me to the carriage waiting beneath the arched palace entrance. Its velvet curtains had been drawn back, revealing plush cushions inside. He opened the door himself—a gentlemanly gesture that surprised me—and offered his hand as I stepped up.

I sank into the soft seat, the rich fabric comforting beneath me. He climbed in after, sitting so close that our thighs nearly touched. The door shut with a quiet creak, enveloping us in intimate silence. He reached for my hand, his fingers intertwining with mine as the carriage began to move.

"Alone with you at last," he whispered, his voice brushing my skin like velvet.

His words sent a tremble through me. The carriage wheels creaked beneath us, rolling gently down the palace drive.

From outside, Sabion called out, "The protest crowd is smaller than expected, Your Majesty."

Jasino's grip on my hand tightened ever so slightly at the mention of protests. I looked up at him, my brow furrowed with curiosity, but he only smiled and pulled me closer.

The carriage rolled through the gates and out onto the main road, where we passed a crowd gathered with raised banners and swatches of cloth. Though their shouts were muffled by the thick windows, their intent was unmistakable—
White veils for mourning.
Red sashes tied around wrists in defiance.
A black silhouette of a woman painted on linen, arms chained.
And in several hands, dolls cloaked in crimson—
representing me.

My heart dropped. Confusion and fear tangled in my chest. Two protests—one crying out for women's rights, the other determined to silence them. The crowd was split, but I was the common focus.

Jasino's expression darkened, his jaw tense. His eyes locked onto mine, guarded, as if he held back truths he feared I would uncover.

He leaned in close, his voice like a command wrapped in velvet.

"You are exquisite, Aundrea."

My cheeks flushed. I could barely meet his gaze.

"Thank you," I whispered.

He reached up, his hand gently resting on the back of my head, guiding me to rest against his chest. I felt the slow, steady rhythm of his heart beneath my palm. For a moment, time suspended.

Then he released me, his right hand cradling my cheek. His touch ignited warmth beneath my skin, but my thoughts spun with questions.

He brushed a strand of hair behind my ear, leaned in, and kissed me—softly, slowly, lingering just long enough to leave me breathless.

Unprepared for the intimacy, I pulled back slightly, shifting toward my seat.
"I'm sorry, my lord."

His expression faltered. He sat upright and turned away, as though my subtle rejection had pricked his pride. I sensed the night teetering on the brink of ruin unless I found a way to soften the moment. I slid closer to him, gently resting my head on his shoulder. He raised his arm and wrapped it around my back, pulling me near.

"Already forgotten, sweetheart."

We rode for nearly an hour and arrived at a majestic building bathed in soft, golden torchlight, its elegant architecture overlooking a serene, breathtaking lake.

He stepped out of the carriage and walked to my door, opening it with a gallant flourish and extending his hand.

"Will you join me, my love?"

I placed my hand in his, and he helped me down. Standing beside him, I felt graceful—cherished. People nearby turned to stare, likely due to my husband's royal presence, but I kept my focus fixed on him. He wrapped his arm around mine, escorting me toward the building's entrance where a long corridor awaited, lined with elegant candelabras glowing softly.

Inside, we entered a smaller chamber adorned with exquisite ancient artwork. A dignified man stood behind a polished wooden stand, impeccably dressed in black with a bold red sash wrapped around his waist, its silk glinting softly in the candlelight. He bowed deeply—first to my husband, then to me. "Right this way, Your Highness," he said with reverence.

He led us to a wall of towering windows that offered a breathtaking view of the lake's tranquil surface. Tables lined the windows, each set with fine crystal imported from the caves of Crimson Spine Mountain.

My husband pulled out a chair for me, his gaze locked on mine in a gesture of rare intimacy. As I approached the seat, the steward stepped forward.

"May I take your cloak, milady?"

He glanced at Jasino, who nodded in subtle approval. The steward lifted the cloak from my shoulders, and I could feel Jasino's eyes tracing my exposed skin as the fabric slipped away. I sat down gracefully, acutely aware of his attention.

Jasino gently pushed my chair in, then took the seat across from me. The steward disappeared with my cloak as my husband picked up a leather-bound parchment listing the kitchen's specialties and scanned it briefly. When his eyes met mine again, they sparkled with warmth.

Soft music filled the room, mingling with the hum of gentle conversation—but my attention was wholly on him. In our two years of marriage, we had never shared a romantic evening like this. Every moment felt precious, unfamiliar.

He set the parchment listing down and reached across the table, his hand covering mine.

"Tonight, I wanted it to be just us," he said softly.

My heart skipped a beat. What did he mean by those words?

His thumb stroked my hand gently, sending a familiar shiver down my spine. I searched his eyes, aching to understand what had inspired this sudden tenderness.

"Is everything... alright, my lord?" I asked softly, my voice barely audible above the music.

He smiled faintly and leaned in closer.

"Call me Jasino tonight," he whispered. "Not 'my lord.'"

My heart raced. I nodded slightly, unsure of my voice.

His gaze held mine—warm, vulnerable, unguarded.

"Tonight, I want to be your husband," he said, "not your emperor."

He spoke my name with unexpected softness. "Aundrea... do you want to look at the parchment listing the kitchen's specialties, or shall I order for you?"

Considering the ego I'd bruised earlier, I chose caution.

"I'll have whatever you decide, Jasino."

A soft smile played at his lips as he glanced down again. After a moment of quiet, he looked up, his eyes searching mine.

He reached for both my hands across the table.

"Aundrea, my hope tonight is to reshape our path together," he began, his voice low and sincere. "I've given you time and space to glimpse the man behind the title. Yet I've seen fear in your eyes since the day you became my wife."

His gaze did not waver—intense, longing.

"Tonight marks the beginning of our new life... a new direction."

I felt my breath catch. After two years of distance, two years of being strangers under the same roof... what did he mean by "beginning"?

My voice came barely above a whisper, weighted with the uncertainty I felt. "I want that too."

My cheeks flushed with heat. I meant the words— but I also feared what they might invite.

He opened his mouth to respond, but footsteps approached—our steward returning. I glanced up, then back to Jasino, captivated again by his quiet confidence as he ordered for us with graceful command.

Once the steward bowed and stepped away, Jasino's gaze returned to mine—still warm, still searching. He leaned in slightly, his voice intimate.

"Tell me, Aundrea... what did you think our life together would be like when you became Empress?"

His question caught me off guard. It pierced right through the armor around my heart.

Was he finally ready to hear the truth?

The soft murmur of voices surrounded us—quiet conversations and stolen glances, likely inspired by our presence. I noticed a woman behind Jasino whispering and pointing. My curiosity flickered. Were they admiring us... or questioning our bond?

Jasino's gentle voice pulled me back. "Would you like to stroll along the lake after lunch?"

"I would very much like that, Jasino," I replied, my heart fluttering at his tenderness.

Speech came in tremors, like a melody trying to find its rhythm. We seemed to live in separate worlds—his consumed by ruling and politics, mine centered on quieter pursuits: reading, studying, singing, drawing, and writing. My life often felt dull in comparison.

He looked at me intently and asked, "What do you desire from our life together, my love?"

The question again caught me off guard. I paused, glancing around before replying, barely above a whisper, "I don't know."

He chuckled softly and encouraged, "You must have some idea. Do you wish to become a mother? Or study new subjects?"

My uncertainty deepened. I looked at him hesitantly.
"I suppose I'm destined to bear your children, Jasino. But what use is learning new things... if I'll never experience them freely?"

My voice trailed off. I gently shook my head, my gaze dropping into my lap as a sigh slipped from my lips. The table seemed to blur as emotional vulnerability surged within me.

Then his hands reached for mine—warm and steady. He placed his left hand, palm up, beneath mine, and gently rested his right hand on top.

"Look at me, Aundrea," he whispered, his voice low and intimate. "Why are you so conflicted in your happiness? One moment I see my beautiful wife... the next, an injured soul."

I met his eyes, confusion and sorrow swimming in them.

"Because of the life I was forced into," I said quietly. "Because of our marriage."

His expression shifted—first to surprise, then to a deep sadness. He leaned in closer, his voice husky.

"Was it only the marriage you were forced into, Aundrea... or was it me?"

My lips parted, but words failed me. Tears welled up, then spilled down my cheeks as his eyes searched mine. His question pierced deeper than any blade—uncovering the truth I could no longer hide. I nodded slowly—just a fraction—but he saw it.

His face fell, stricken. He released my hands, though his eyes never left mine, now filled with pain and vulnerability I had never seen before. His voice, low and broken, whispered a single word:

"Why?"

Tears streamed freely now as I watched the emperor falter... and the man underneath begin to unravel.

"I did not choose you," I murmured. "You chose me."

His eyes shimmered with tears—an image that shattered me further. He leaned back slowly, as if my words had physically pushed him away.

"I've tried for two years to reach you," he said, his voice raw. "Yet you still push me away. What can I do to make you understand? I love you deeply, and I yearn for more between us. It's not enough for me to love you alone. I want your happiness—and your heart—to desire mine in return."

My voice trembled. "Jasino, I'm lost... I know your desires, and I long to fulfill them, but I don't know how. I fear your anger. Your disappointment. I just... I don't know what you want me to say."

Jasino's eyes locked onto mine. His grip on my hand was firm yet tender.

He sat up straighter, emotion thick in his voice. "Tell me what I can do to bring you a little happiness."

Taking a deep breath, I whispered, "I want to be with you more often. Share your life. Leave the palace sometimes. Even just walks in the garden would bring me joy."

My voice cracked. "I don't want to be so alone."

His expression softened. He rose from his seat, walked around the table, and knelt beside me, taking my hand again.

His eyes burned with intensity. "Danger lurks outside these walls, Aundrea. There are hearts filled with evil who would harm you. My protection is my only motive."

He gently lifted my chin until our eyes met. "My love... I promise change. Garden walks together. Inclusion in my daily life. Freedom from solitude. Will this bring you happiness?"

A single tear fell. He wiped it away with his sleeve.

My heart raced. "I would very much like that, Jasino," I whispered.

He leaned in and brushed his lips against mine, holding me close. My entire body ignited—stomach, chest, knees... everything tingling with sensation.

He pulled back, his eyes searching mine. "I love you, Aundrea."

I nodded slowly, still sobbing softly. But inside, a storm raged.

I wanted to love him. I truly did. But fear and intimidation had ruled my heart for so long... How could I love someone who inspired both awe and terror?

Jasino gently returned to his seat with a warm, almost fragile smile. My thoughts still swirled when footsteps approached.

The scent of Lisona's blooming nightshade flowers wafted through the air as the steward approached, his gentle smile a warm contrast to the formal atmosphere. He placed each dish before us with precision: steaming seafood that released a savory aroma, fresh garden salads that glistened with dew, and warm, crusty bread that filled the air with the fragrance of fragrant herbs. The soft clinking of silverware against fine china accompanied the steward's movements.

As another steward stepped in, the gentle gurgle of liquid meeting glass filled the air. He poured steaming tea into my delicate china cup, the scent of starpetal and moonbloom rising to greet me. "Whiskey over ice?" he asked Jasino politely, his voice low and respectful.

The first steward's query broke the silence: "Will there be anything else, Your Highness?" Jasino's gracious shake of his head was accompanied by a soft smile.

The stewards' bows were mirrored by the soft sway of the crystal lanterns beyond the veranda, their forms fading into the melodic hum of soft music and the gentle lapping of the lake's waves against the shore. The music seemed to match the rhythm of my heartbeat as Jasino's hand covered mine, his touch warm and reassuring.

His eyes searched mine, concern and gentle affection mingling in their depths. A lump formed in my throat as I struggled to find my voice. "I'm just... overwhelmed, my lord." I whispered, the words barely audible over the music.

Jasino's squeeze on my hand was soft, comforting. "No titles tonight," he reminded me gently. "Call me Jasino, Aundrea. " His voice sent a shiver through me, the sound of my name on his lips like a caress.

I nodded, my voice still barely above a whisper. "Jasino." The word felt intimate on my lips, a secret shared between us. His smile deepened, the corners of his eyes crinkling as he heard his name spoken in my soft tone. "It's music to my ears, hearing you say my name like that."

His thumb brushed softly over the back of my hand, and the lake view behind him faded from my awareness. I saw only him.

"Why tonight, Jasino?" I asked. "Why the sudden desire to change everything between us?"

I stared at the unfamiliar dishes before me, confused and curious.

Jasino noticed, amusement flickering in his eyes.

"What's wrong, Aundrea?"

I gestured to the small plate. "What is this?"

He chuckled. "Escargot, my love."

My blank stare prompted more explanation.

"Escargot is a delicacy from Earth—France, specifically. It's... a snail. I thought you might enjoy something from your home world."

My eyes widened. I looked from the plate to him, my voice a horrified whisper. "This is those slimy slug things?"

He giggled, clearly entertained by my reaction.

"Do I... have to eat this?"

Still grinning, he set down his spoon, picked up the small escargot fork, and prepared a bite.

"Here—try it, my love," he said, coaxing, as he held the bite out to me.

I hesitated, then slowly opened my mouth and let him feed me.

The texture was strange—soft, chewy, slightly gelatinous. But the flavor, enhanced by rich garlic butter, wasn't terrible. I chewed slowly, watching his amused expression.

"Well?" he asked, smiling. "Did you like it?"

I thought a moment. "I don't know... The texture is very strange. It's not horrible, but I'm not sure I want to eat it again."

He leaned back, nodding with understanding. "That's fair. You don't have to eat it if you don't want to."

Relieved, I turned my attention to the next dish. "What's this food?"

He laughed softly, clearly amused by my eagerness to move on.

"This is pan-seared Lisonian salmon—a local favorite from our island waters."

His eyes sparkled. "And no slimy creatures involved, I promise."

I giggled at his teasing tone, already feeling more at ease.

I picked up my fork and took a tentative bite of the salmon...

The flavors exploded on my tongue—delicate, flaky, and utterly delicious.

I looked up at him, surprised.
"This is amazing!"

His face lit with a warm smile.
"I'm glad you like it. Shall we talk while you eat, or would you rather I answer your question from earlier?"

He leaned in slightly, his gaze locked on mine.
"About why tonight is different... why I want things to change between us."

My heart skipped at his reminder. I swallowed the salmon and set down my fork, my hands fluttering slightly in my lap.

"Yes... I want to know. Why tonight, Jasino? What made you realize you wanted more from our marriage?"

His expression grew thoughtful. He leaned back in his chair, steepling his fingers.

"Many things," he said softly. "But mostly... watching you sleep last night."

Curiosity bloomed within me, and I leaned in.
"What do you mean?"

He smiled faintly, his eyes distant and nostalgic.

"You looked peaceful... truly happy for the first time in years. But not because of me. That realization hurt, Aundrea. It showed me how much distance there still is between us."

His voice dropped, raw with emotion.
"I wanted to wake you and ask... am I just your husband? Your emperor? Or could I ever be your love?"

My breath caught. Our eyes locked, and I felt tears prick the corners of mine.

"Jasino... why do you want my love so badly?" I asked, my voice barely a whisper. "Our marriage was arranged."

He reached for my hands again, gripping them tightly.
"Because, Aundrea... without your love, my empire is empty. My power, meaningless. Every conquest, every victory—hollow—if shared with only a wife, not a partner. Not a soulmate."

His thumbs brushed my skin, His words touched a tender spot in my heart.

"I've lived two hundred and thirty-five years," he said, "and ruled this empire for one hundred and ten. But until I met you... I had never felt my heart truly beat. You were supposed to be a strategic match, a union to secure Lisona's future. But one look at you, Aundrea... and my strategy shifted to obsession. To making you mine."

His voice cracked with emotion, his eyes burning with intensity.

***

After lunch, we stood by the lake, admiring the golden light rippling across the water. Beneath the surface, glowing stones shimmered in shades of violet and pale blue, their soft luminescence flickering like trapped starlight. Tiny threads of silver-veined metal coiled through the sand at the shoreline, pulsing faintly as if the lake itself breathed magic. It was a beauty unlike anything I had known on Earth—untouched, ancient, alive.

The air was still, holding its breath as Jasino stepped closer. His fingers brushed mine, then slowly rose to cup my cheek. I met his gaze, and for a moment, the world quieted. There were no titles, no thrones, no wars—only his eyes, searching mine.

Then he kissed me.

This kiss was not soft or cautious—it was deep, consuming. His mouth moved over mine with aching reverence, as though trying to memorize me. My knees weakened under the weight of it, under the truth it carried. My hands gripped his tunic, clinging to the warmth and strength of him. A low hum resonated through my chest, as if love was the answer to a question I hadn't dared to ask, a solution to a loneliness I hadn't fully acknowledged, a beacon guiding me into his embrace. Something opened inside me.

I wasn't sure when it happened—whether it was the moment his lips claimed mine, or the way his hands held me like I was something sacred—but something shifted. I felt it in my bones, in the shiver that rolled throughout my body, in the ache blooming in my chest. Was this love? Or the edge of it? I didn't know. I only knew I did not want him to let go.

He lingered close, his breath warm against my skin, reminding me that even in the beauty of stolen moments, the world still moved around us. "Come, Aundrea… the ball awaits."
His voice held a playful lilt, but his eyes remained tender, still tethered to the magic we had just shared.

**

As we rode to the ball, I leaned my head on his shoulder, feeling both vulnerable and trusting. His arm wrapped behind my back, holding me close. We rode in silence—no words, just quiet affection. My heart fluttered with hope.

When the carriage finally slowed, I sat up, turning toward the window with wide-eyed wonder. The torch-lit spires of Lisonian Hall shimmered like golden dragons' teeth against the fading sunset—utterly magical.

Jasino exited the carriage and opened my door, smiling slightly as he offered his arm.

"Walk with me. Your sister awaits."

As we stepped through the towering double doors, I gasped in awe at the grandeur around us. And then—I saw her. My sister. Her eyes locked onto mine, and euphoria surged through me.

I turned quickly to my husband. "Can I go to her? I haven't seen her in so long!"

He chuckled softly and released my arm. "Yes, Aundrea. Go hug your sister."

I rushed forward, overwhelmed with joy, and embraced her tightly. Tears welled in my eyes, the reunion nearly breaking me. Jasino approached his brother, Jasper. "Brother, it's good to see you again." Then he turned to me. "Come, Aundrea. Let's take our seats."

Jasper and Alissia followed closely behind. The crowd parted respectfully, every head bowing as we passed—the royal family's presence acknowledged with reverence.

My sister and I sat side by side, catching up on lost time. Behind us, Jasino and Jasper stood tall, scanning the room as they spoke quietly. My husband's hand rested lightly but possessively on the back of my chair.

He leaned forward, his eyes gleaming. "Would you dance with me, my love?" My heart fluttered at the gentleness in his voice.

Alissia smiled knowingly at me, then looked at Jasper before glancing back—her silent blessing obvious.

I slipped my hand into Jasino's outstretched palm, and he helped me to my feet.

The room fell silent—every face turning toward us in anticipation. He led me to the center of the grand hall where musicians waited. At Jasino's subtle nod, the music began—a haunting, elegant melody that seemed to echo the rhythm of my heart.

He turned toward me, eyes burning, and placed one hand gently at my waist.

His breath warmed my skin. "Aundrea," he whispered, "I want to live in this moment."

My cheeks flushed. I placed my hand on his shoulder, feeling the strength beneath his formal attire. We swayed together, moving in harmony with the music. His gaze never wavered—intense, steady, filled with something I hadn't seen in him before.

I felt like I was drowning in the depths of his eyes, my heart fluttering with every press of his hand at my waist. The grand hall faded into a blur. In that moment, it was just the two of us.

He leaned in close, lips brushing my ear. "Tonight, Aundrea... I feel like I'm finally dancing with my wife."

***

Chaos erupted.

Screams echoed from the entrance as the massive double doors burst open. My heart jolted. People surged into the hall like a dark tide, panic spreading like wildfire.

My grip tightened on Jasino's arm.
"Husband, what is happening?" He pulled me gently to the side, stepping forward and shielding me with his body. His eyes scanned the room, cold and focused—deadly in their intensity.

Jasino's gaze snapped to the entrance, his body tensing beside me. A flicker of disbelief crossed his face—then hardened into something darker. I instinctively tightened my grip on his hand, feeling the shift in his energy, the storm rising beneath his skin.

Guards surged forward, wrestling intruders to the ground in a flurry of steel and shouting—but one man walked untouched through the chaos, as if cloaked in shadow and command.

From across the hall, Jasper appeared—blade half-drawn, his expression fierce as Alissia clung to his arm, eyes wide with alarm. He moved to stand between us and the advancing stranger, protective instinct clear in every motion.

Then I saw him. The approaching man looked exactly like my husband—every line of his face familiar, except for a thin scar above his left brow. The resemblance was uncanny, chilling.

Jasper stepped forward, sword raised—but Jasino lifted a single hand in silent command. A warning. A gesture to stand down.

The air seemed to thrum with tension as he approached, a sly smile stretching across his face.

"Brother," the man said, voice smooth and sharp. "It's been a long time."

Jasino took a step forward, his voice low and lethal. "Why are you here, Ravon? You were exiled by our father—never to return. He chose me to take the throne, not you."

My heart pounded as Ravon's laughter echoed through the chamber, cold and mocking.
"Our realm?" he sneered. "I am the rightful heir. I will reclaim the throne—and the bride that should have been mine. Your time, brother, is almost up. I've returned... and I will take back everything you stole."

His words hung like a curse: My rightful throne... and the bride that should have been mine. What did that mean?

"Jasino's grip on my hand tightened briefly before he released it, signaling his guards—all while keeping himself between me and the looming threat." They moved in instantly, surrounding Ravon with practiced precision.

"Arrest him," Jasino spat. His voice dripped venom.

The guards grabbed Ravon's arms. He did not resist—instead, he grinned darkly as they dragged him backward. "You cannot hold me, Jasino. My magic is too powerful."

Jasper slowly lowered his sword, his wary eyes never leaving Ravon's. The tension remained, thick and taut, but the danger—for now—had passed.

Jasino placed a firm hand on Jasper's shoulder. "Thank you, brother. I'll see you back at the palace." Jasper gave a curt nod, still shielding Alissia with his body.

I stepped closer to her and whispered,

"I'll see you soon, sister." Her worried eyes met mine, but she nodded, squeezing my hand.

Then Jasino's fingers slid gently into mine, his grip warm, steady. With a soft tug, he led me away from the crowd—away from the ghost of the past that had just resurfaced.

***

We climbed into the carriage, its doors closing with a soft thud, sealing the chaos behind us. A heavy silence hung between us as the carriage rolled into motion.

I finally broke it with a quiet question.
"Jasino... I did not know you had a brother. He looks just like you."

He turned toward me, his expression grim. "I don't. At least... not anymore. Ravon was exiled by our family years ago for dabbling in the dark arts. He has no place in our lineage. Twin or not—he is no longer my brother. No longer family."

I stared down at my hands clasped in my lap, mind reeling. Dark arts...

How could someone so powerful be drawn to such evil? I looked back up at him, curiosity overriding my fear. "What did he mean when he said he has come to take his rightful throne... and bride?"

Jasino's expression darkened, his voice dropping low. "Aundrea, my brother was born a heartbeat before me. That made him the traditional heir to Lisona. But he was found to be a tyrant—consuming souls instead of ruling with compassion. You were promised to the heir of Lisona..." He paused, eyes sharp. "He believes my throne belongs to him. That my wife belongs to him." He exhaled, jaw tight. "My brother is evil."

The rest of the ride passed in silence. I stared out the window, the shadows of trees and torchlight blurring past while my thoughts tangled in knots.

***

When we arrived at the palace, Jasino and I returned to my bedchamber. He said nothing as he closed the door behind us. Then he stepped toward me.

He wrapped his arms around me, pulling me into a quiet, firm embrace, his lips brushing against mine—then softly kissing my cheeks... my forehead.

"Tonight," he whispered, "I sleep at your side, my love."

The words hung in the air like a promise, taking my breath away. For two years, our beds had been empty of each other. The distance had been our constant. But now... he held me as if afraid to let go.

He lay down beside me, his arm tight around my waist, his breath warm across my skin. His face rested inches from mine, and for the first time in our marriage—I felt safe. I felt seen.

As I drifted off in his arms, exhaustion from the night faded into something deeper...

A quiet belonging. For the first time, I fell asleep not as his obligation, or his empress—but as his wife.

Chapter 2

In the Emperor's Eyes

Morning sunlight danced across Jasino's face as he gazed at me, his eyes burning with desire. My skin still tingled from last night's whispered promise. Jasino's fingers traced slow circles on my skin as he whispered, "Good morning, my wife."

My eyes, drawn to him, gently opened. "Good morning."

His hand glided slowly beneath the covers, landing softly on my hip. He pressed his warm lips to my forehead, gradually trailing to my eyes. I trembled with passion, devoured by a longing that pulled me closer. Again, his lips returned to mine, igniting a storm of new emotions.

The air sizzled with desire and unspoken words. His hand slipped under my gown with a silent promise of something more—something deeper. I caught my breath as his touch sent shivers down my spine. I held my breath but only for a moment, savoring the exquisite pain that mingled with a burgeoning pleasure, a symphony of sensations that promised a love both fierce and tender, a connection that transcended the physical and touched the very core of my being.

The world outside was fading into a distant hum as our souls intertwined, creating a tapestry of shared vulnerability and increasing passion that I knew would forever bind us together. We moved together, the world fading away. In binding rhythm, our movements were poetic—a testament to my undying attraction. We were as one.

Under my breath came a silent gasp as an unfettered power overtook me. His gaze locked with mine as he drew back, his hand gently threading through my hair before his lips pressed to mine again. He pulled me closer, his chest rising with gentle breaths. For a moment, I felt a part of me leave my body, as if my soul leaned forward to touch his. My lungs forgot air. My heart forgot rhythm. A shattering blast possessed every inch of me—a violent beauty of sensation exploding through my entire being. Time suspended. My breath vanished. It was a seismic explosion that claimed my soul.

"You're mine now," he whispered. "Completely mine, and I've wanted this moment for so long."

I snuggled deeper into Jasino's arms. "I never knew," I said, taking a deep breath. "I never knew it could be like this. I never knew I could feel so..." My voice trailed off.

His eyes consumed mine as I smiled softly. "You're smiling, my lord. Why?" I traced his lips with my fingertip.

"I wonder how I got so lucky finding you. You're even more beautiful now than you were before." His words felt like a conversation between our souls, devouring every part of me.

"My lord!" I interrupted, lying back beside him, placing my arm over his chest and pulling him close.

"Call me Jasino. Or husband, my love. We are united now."

That seemed so foreign to me. Reluctantly, I continued, "Husband, I've never called you anything else in two years. That might be difficult." I chuckled.

He moved his lips close to mine and whispered, "Hearing 'husband' from your lips may be breaking all the rules, but it feels so right. Two years of hearing you say 'my lord'..." He traced my lips with his fingers. "How long until 'my love' becomes natural too?"

Looking down with a bashful smile, I wondered: Love, is this love? What am I feeling?

I leaned deeper into his arms, burying my face in his chest. "I want to make you happy. I do. I just don't know how."

He gently placed his fingers under my chin, tilting my head toward him. "You already do." His lips brushed mine, and he held me tight again. "But if you want my heart to skip beats while we're alone in each other's arms—say my name. No title. Just Jasino."

I smiled and let out a small, gentle laugh. "Jasino, my husband, I thank you for the last few days."

He smiled slightly, embraced me tighter, and kissed the top of my head.

"As much as I want to stay with you here in this moment forever, I have things I must do—and a kingdom to rule."

He brushed his lips softly against mine one final time before slipping out of bed and pulling on his clothes.

"You're still glowing," he whispered, his eyes crinkling as he smiled at me.

I blushed, feeling my heart skip a beat. "Thanks to you," I replied, my voice barely above a whisper.

With one final glance, he headed for the door, then turned around one last time. "I love you, sweetheart," he said, his voice low and husky. "I'll see you later tonight. I'll be taking you for a walk under the starlight—just us."

"My favorite kind of night," I said softly, my soul soaring.

He chuckled. "Mine too. Today, duty calls me away from you, but soon, you'll rule by my side—as my Empress, my partner, my everything."

A wave of gratitude washed over me, and a radiant smile spread across my face. 'Forever with you is all I want,' I whispered, my heart full.

***

I sat on my bed for what seemed like an eternity, waiting for Michelle to bring my breakfast, thinking about everything I had experienced in the last few days. My world was changing.

Michelle walked into my room with a tray in her hand. She set it down—a pastry and some fresh strawberries.

"His Majesty instructed me to ensure you rested and ate well today. He seemed different this morning. Happier." Her eyes sparkled with curiosity. "If I may ask, milady— what changed?"

I looked at her as my eyes began to well with tears. "I finally became his wife."

Michelle's eyes widened with surprise, then softened into a warm, loving smile. "We've waited so long for this day." With a graceful curtsy, she acknowledged who I was. "Congratulations, my Empress."

She stood up, her voice filled with admiration and excitement. "Would you like me to prepare your chambers for joint occupation tonight?"

My face lit up as I agreed. On a whim, I asked her to prepare me a rose-petal bath. With Michelle on board, I polished off my food, luxuriated in a bath, and prepared myself for the day ahead.

As I sat at my vanity, gazing into the mirror and pondering the mysteries of the night and the uncertainties of my future, Michelle approached and spoke. "Would you like me to lay out the velvet dress your husband gifted you on your naming day?"

Grinning, I replied affirmatively, adding that I believed he would be pleased with the idea.

In the mirror, I caught Michelle's tender smile as she carefully arranged my gown. It was a royal blue masterpiece—my absolute favorite. The fabric was long and incredibly soft, and the back featured an elegant crisscross design.

I rose, allowing her to help me into the dress, then settled back into my seat at the vanity. Michelle's gentle fingers worked through my tangled hair as I gazed into the mirror, lost in thought about what had transpired that morning.

She chatted softly while styling my hair, but my responses were blunt. My heart still raced from this morning. With each stroke of the brush, I felt a sense of calm washing over me—yet my thoughts remained tangled. Just as Michelle's brush glided across my scalp, the door creaked open. Jasino's piercing eyes locked onto mine in the mirror. My heart skipped a beat as the room fell silent, then I heard his low, husky voice: "May I interrupt?"

Michelle's hands paused mid-stroke as he walked closer. Jasino stepped behind my chair, his hands finding my shoulders as he leaned in. A soft kiss landed on the top of my head before he turned to Michelle, asking for a moment alone. She eagerly left the room.

He continued, his hands slowly tracing down my sides. Still, a flicker of awareness prickled at the base of my throat—a sensation I couldn't quite place. He kissed my eyelids, then my cheek, whispering, "You're stunning"— words he had spoken countless times before, yet today they felt, almost perfectly rehearsed. I moved my hand into his and whispered, "I thought you had things to do."
But instead of answering, he leaned in and kissed my hand... then my wrist.
Something stirred inside me—a whispering sense that something wasn't quite right.
But I did not question it. I silenced it.

Was this the silence that had foreshadowed every past word, every hidden truth, every unspoken fear that had ever lingered between us? In his arms, logic faded, and doubts were muffled—but for the briefest moment, my soul whispered: This love feels like him...but does it feel like his heart?

His embrace was my solace, my happy place—yet, for a fleeting instant, my heart hesitated to fully surrender, as if sensing a subtle discord beneath his familiar touch, before love silenced my doubts with his kiss.

He lifted me onto the bed with firm gentleness, his eyes gleaming. He removed his attire with swift efficiency, then lifted my dress with a cold intimacy. His touch lacked the warmth I had experienced before. He moved in—his body closer, yet somehow distant. The moment between us was fleeting—awkward, almost calculated.
It vanished before any true emotion could take root, leaving

behind only hollowness.
I did not examine the emptiness; my mind was just numb.

I rolled over, seeking comfort, as he held me close—his embrace tight but lacking tender pressure. He looked into my eyes, his gaze piercing yet unfamiliar. "Aundrea, my love," he whispered—his voice low and husky, yet off, like a melody sung in the wrong key. "We will be together soon. I promise."

His words hung in the air like a vow.

He rose from the bed and dressed with rapid precision. Before turning to leave, he asked, "Will you be waiting for me?"

His voice sent shivers—not of love, but of something else.

"Yes, yes, my lord," I said, my reply barely above a whisper, my heart wondering why I hadn't said "my husband." He turned and left, the door closing behind him like a seal on a secret.

I shook off the lingering unease, attributing the hollow sensation to my limited experience with physical love. I told myself this must be what marital intimacy felt like—ordinary, inconsistent. I convinced myself the emptiness I felt was just my own innocence.

I called for Michelle.

She entered the room, her heart still racing from witnessing our moment in the mirror. She forced a calm smile onto her face, though her mind was ablaze with curiosity. What had transpired between Jasino and me? Her loyalty belonged to me, but her fascination with our love story had grown.

Had I truly surrendered to his charms?

Michelle's eyes narrowed slightly, remembering the encounter before leaving the room—his piercing gaze still locked on me. The sharp angles of his face seemed more defined. His smile dazzled—but just a fraction cooler, less uniquely him, than when he had first stolen my heart.

What secrets lay behind those smoldering eyes?

As I sat across from her, my heart still reeling from the encounter, I noticed a subtle shift in her expression. Her eyes, usually bright with warmth, now held a mix of happiness for what she believed was my bliss... and a trace of curiosity.

I sensed the question behind her gaze: Is the passion I've found with him truly worth the risk of heartache?

Her loyalty to me was palpable—as if she wanted to shield me from pain.

Michelle's thoughts swirled behind her calm eyes as she poured me a cup of tea. Her hands moved with practiced ease—a comforting routine amidst the tension within me. She handed me the cup, her fingers brushing mine, grounding me in the moment.

"Milady, you seem... distracted," Michelle said softly, her eyes locking onto mine with gentle concern.

I took a sip of the tea, buying time to gather my tangled thoughts. The warmth spread through my chest, but my mind remained a maze of emotions. "It's just... everything feels different now," I replied vaguely, unsure how much to reveal about the hollow sensation still lingering inside me.

Michelle's expression turned intrigued, her eyebrows rising slightly as she sat beside me on the couch.

"Different in a good way, milady?" she asked, her voice gently probing, as if sensing there was more to my words.

I hesitated, unsure how to articulate the emptiness that had followed his intense gaze and passionate touch. My heart still raced from the encounter, yet my soul felt... unconnected.

"I'm not entirely sure," I admitted softly, looking down at my hands cradling the teacup.

Michelle's hand covered mine, warm and reassuring. "Tell me what you do know, milady," she whispered.

My eyes met hers, and I felt a surge of trust—I decided to confide in her.

"It just didn't feel... like him," I whispered, my voice barely audible. "The way he touched me, looked at me—it was intense, but somehow... off."

Michelle's expression turned thoughtful, her hand still covering mine. "I am a maiden," she said gently, "but I imagine not all your encounters with your husband are going to be the same. Passion can ebb and flow like the tides."

Her words were logical, yet my heart remained uncertain.

"Do you think that's all it was?" I asked, searching her face for reassurance.

Michelle's eyes sparkled with curiosity again before she replied, "Milady, did he say anything unusual to you?" she asked softly.

I thought back to his whispered promise: We will be together soon...

"Yes," I replied hesitantly. "He said we would be together soon... it sounded almost like a promise, or a warning."

Michelle's expression turned thoughtful again.

"It's likely a fluke, milady," she reassured me. "Lord Jasino loves you dearly—his words were probably just romantic musings. He intends to see you tonight."

Michelle smiled pleasantly as we walked together.

"I'll wait for you in your sitting room, milady," she said. "You might want to... refresh yourself before getting ready for your walk tonight."

I nodded, knowing exactly what she hinted at—my hair was likely tousled, and my complexion still flushed from the intimate moment with... Jasino.

"I'll just take a few moments," I replied, heading toward my bedroom.

Michelle's gentle voice followed me. "Take your time, milady."

I closed the bedroom door behind me and leaned against it, my mind replaying Michelle's reassuring words, but my heart still harbored doubts.

"Lord Jasino loves you dearly..."

The man who held me earlier seemed... different.

I pushed off from the door and began to refresh myself, my fingers tracing the path his lips had touched on my skin.

I opened my dresser drawer and a piece of paper tucked inside caught my attention—a small note hidden beneath my jewelry box.

My heart skipped a beat as I unfolded the parchment, recognizing Jasino's handwriting instantly.

My beloved Aundrea,
As I watched you sleep tonight, moonlight dancing across your face, I felt my heart swell with gratitude for every moment with you. You are my forever sunrise, my safe haven, my everything. Tonight, under the stars, I want to hold you close and whisper promises of our future together.
Yours always,
Jasino

Tears pricked at the corners of my eyes as I read.

I finished reading the letter. The words danced on the page like Jasino's gentle touches—loving, sincere, and utterly him. The contrast between this tender letter and the intense, almost stranger-like encounter earlier struck me deeply.

Could Michelle be right—was I overthinking everything?

I folded the letter, pressing it against my lips, feeling a surge of love and reassurance.

Just then, I heard a soft knock at the door—Michelle's voice followed.

"Milady, are you ready?"

I opened the door to Michelle, the letter still clutched in my hand, a soft smile on my face.

"Michelle, come in—I need to show you something," I said, my voice filled with emotion.

Her curious eyes widened as she entered, and I handed her the letter. She read it silently, her expression transforming from curiosity to surprise to warmth.

"Oh, milady..." she whispered, looking up at me with tears in her eyes. Then she corrected herself. "...You're going to kill me for calling you that when we're alone."

I laughed, and she continued.

"This letter is beautiful. Lord Jasino loves you dearly."

My heart still soared from the romantic words.

"It's from Jasino—he must have written it while I slept," I explained.

Michelle handed the letter back, her face gentle with relief.

"I told you—Lord Jasino loves you dearly. This letter... it explains everything. Your doubts were just nerves."

I nodded eagerly, feeling my earlier fears dissipate.

"Yes, exactly—this letter fixed everything..."

But Michelle's expression had shifted to something closer to relief than celebration.

"What's wrong, Aundrea? You look worried." Michelle sensed hesitation—or maybe a glimpse of something more—coming from me.

"Nothing..." I sighed. "I'm just nervous about tonight."

Tonight was supposed to be perfect, and Jasino's letter had promised our future together. Yet doubts were creeping back in.

***

It was time. Michelle gave my hand a gentle squeeze, her smile offered silent comfort.

"You look breathtaking, Aundrea. Shall I walk you out to Emperor Jasino?"

I nodded, my heart racing with anticipation and a hint of nervousness. Michelle offered her arm, and I took it, comforted by her loyal presence beside me.

We glided out of my chambers and into the grand corridor, lined with towering candelabras and portraits of Jasino's ancestors. The soft glow of candles danced across the polished marble floor as we passed:

– The Library of Eldrid, its doors slightly ajar, releasing whispers of ancient parchment
– The Music Room, where the scent of jasmine lingered, reminding me of Jasino's favorite flowers
– The Gallery of Heroes, where brave knights' armor stood guard, their empty helmets seeming to watch us pass

Michelle and I turned a corner into the main palace hallway. The sound of gentle laughter and soft music drifted from the entrance hall. My pulse quickened; We were close.

The massive wooden doors of the palace entrance came into view, adorned with Jasino's family crest. Michelle squeezed my arm gently before releasing it. I took a deep breath as she nodded discreetly to the servant standing beside the doors.

The servant bowed slightly and pushed open the heavy wooden doors, their hinges creaking softly. A warm golden light spilled in, illuminating the entrance hall behind me, and my heart skipped a beat as I saw him.

Lord Jasino stood beneath the palace portico, dressed impeccably in a black tailcoat with silver embroidery, his eyes locked intensely on mine. His gaze sparkled with affection and anticipation, and for a moment, my doubts faltered—he looked like my Jasino.

He bowed low, his voice low and husky as he said, "Milady… you dazzle me."

Michelle curtsied behind me, then discreetly retreated into the palace, leaving us alone.

Jasino straightened, his eyes never leaving mine, and began walking toward me...

I extended my hand, and he kissed it softly, his lips brushing against my skin like a whisper.

"Milady... you dazzle me," he repeated, his eyes locking onto mine with adoration. His touch made me tremble, and for a moment, my doubts seemed foolish.

He straightened, still holding my hand, and then wrapped his arms around my waist, pulling me close. His chest was warm against mine, his heart beating in perfect sync with my own racing pulse. I breathed in deeply—his scent was familiar, comforting.

"You look so beautiful under the sunset of the sky, my love."

His eyes burned with affection, and for a moment, I thought I saw the deepest spark of love I'd ever known from him. He leaned in again, his lips brushing mine in a tender, exploratory kiss—as if reacquainting himself with my skin. My doubts flickered... then dissolved like mist in sunlight.

But he wasn't done—he deepened the kiss, his mouth moving slowly, passionately against mine. Time suspended. Everything faded away.

This kiss... it was Jasino's soul kissing mine. I felt his love, his heart, his everything aligning with my own. All uncertainty, all fear, all doubt—annihilated.

I melted into him, my arms wrapping tightly around his neck as he lifted me slightly, holding me closer. When he finally broke the kiss, gasping softly, I smiled up at him—my heart forever his.

"My love," I whispered, voice barely audible.

"My forever," he replied, eyes shining with tears of joy.

In that moment, I was home—in his arms, in his love, forever entwined. His eyes sparkled with tears of joy, and mine shone with tears of doubt—finally laid to rest.

Chapter 3

Whispers and Warnings

Weeks had passed. As the day's quiet reflection faded, a deep longing lingered within me. Jasino entered our room, swept me into his arms, and spun me until my feet gently touched the ground—his smile utterly captivating.

"Tonight will be perfect, my love," he murmured, his eyes lit with longing. "Walk with me in the gardens again?"
I leaned into him, resting my head against his chest, his heartbeat synchronized with mine. I savored the embrace for a moment before reluctantly pulling away.

***

The night air greeted us like an old friend as we walked hand in hand down the corridor, leaving the palace behind. Moonlight spilled over the stone path as we entered the gardens. We paused together, kneeling near a rosebush. I reached out to touch a velvety petal, its beauty drawing me in, the flower's sweet fragrance weaving around us like a memory.

Jasino took my hand once more, guiding me to a pavilion at the garden's heart. He gently pushed me against the open doors, his gaze intense.
"The garden is beautiful, my love, but it pales in comparison to my beautiful wife," he whispered before his lips met mine in a tender but passionate kiss.

Slowly pulling away, he wiped a tear barely forming at the corner of my eye.
"What troubles you, my love?"
I gazed up at his striking face, a warmth spreading through

me.

"I'm just so happy we've finally found each other," I confessed, my voice soft. "I love you, my lord."

A small smile barely formed on his lips as he replied,
"When we're alone, call me Jasino. Formal titles aren't needed. Aundrea."

He reminded me again, and I nodded—a silent agreement sealing the intimacy of the moment. Jasino's lips met mine again in a kiss both tender and passionate. Our hearts raced in unison, but the moment was shattered by a stern voice in the distance.
"Emperor Jasino, forgive the intrusion," a guard said with a slight bow. "Riots have erupted in the city square. Your presence is required immediately."

Jasino reluctantly broke free from our embrace, his eyes still locked on mine.
"Aundrea, please return to the palace," he said softly.
My hand instinctively gripped his arm.
"No. Jasino. I want to come with you."

His expression turned guarded and conflicted. He was still not used to being questioned, concern etched on his face.
"Aundrea, it's not safe. Please, for my sake, return to the palace."
But I stood my ground. "I'll be safer with you. I am always safer with you."

Jasino's jaw clenched, then he gave a brief nod, knowing that saying no to me would only cause friction between us.

***

"Very well," he said. "But stay close to me." He turned toward the guard. "Let's move."

As we followed the guard through the winding streets, the air thickened with tension and smoke. Torches flickered wildly, casting eerie shadows on buildings as angry chants grew louder.
"Justice now! Justice now!"

Jasino's grip on my hand tightened, his eyes scanning the crowd with growing unease.

Sabion, my husband's head guard and most trusted advisor, approached rapidly and out of breath. "Your Grace," he said. "Your brother. Ravon, has escaped his confinement. He broke free and to be honest, we really don't know when.".

My husband interrupted, "How did he escape and you are just finding out about it?"
Sabion replied, a hint of fear in his eyes, "He used dark magic to make the jailors see him when he wasn't there. I went in to check on him, and he was gone."

I could see rage consuming my husband.
"Find him! I must deal with these riots," he declared, his voice edged with steel.

Sabion bowed low, then turned and quickly walked away, clearing the path. We pressed onward to the center of the riots, the ominous sounds from beyond growing louder and louder with each step.

Suddenly, we emerged into the center of the city square. As we walked up the stairs. I saw a sea of faces, torches, and banners surrounding us. My heart raced as Jasino pushed me slightly behind him, his protective instinct flaring.

Jasino stepped forward, his commanding presence drawing all eyes to him. His voice echoed across the city square as a hush fell over the crowds.

"People of Lisona. I, Emperor Jasino, stand before you today to address your grievances. I've been informed that your protests over the past months have extended beyond taxation and food distribution. An extension of our protection laws, now branching into calls for full equality—while others still fight to preserve our traditions" He continued,

"My wife…" Jasino turned toward me and grabbed my hand, pulling me gently to his side. "My wife stands beside me, a symbol of the progress we are making. Yet clearly, more work remains."

Cheers erupted from the women in the crowd, their voices rising like a tide around us. But through the swell of sound and celebration, I saw the men—scattered among them, silent, their faces etched with unease and something darker.

Jasino's silent plea pressed against me, heavier than the roar of the crowd. Fear twisted in my gut. He wanted me to speak? To stand before them and say what? I knew nothing of laws or rights—only pain, survival, and silence. What words could I offer that wouldn't crumble the moment they left my lips?

Releasing his hand. I took a tentative step forward.

"People of Lisona," I began, my voice trembling slightly, "I know that you are hurting right now. But perhaps we can start with something small, with my husband's approval. Let's begin with marriage… with women having the right to choose their own husbands, instead of their fathers choosing for them…"

A wave of anger surged through the crowd. Husbands, brothers, uncles—men from every corner of the square erupted in fury, their shouts rising like thunder, fists clenched, eyes ablaze. They turned on the women beside them, voices laced with betrayal and disbelief.

My breath caught. The world spun. I stumbled backward, heart racing, the roar of the crowd closing in like a storm. Hands flew up, voices cracked, and I couldn't tell who was shouting or who might strike.

Blindly, I turned and collided with my husband's chest, my hands clutching his robes for balance, for protection, for something solid in the madness.

"I'm sorry," I gasped. "I thought it would…"

He cut me off, voice steady and unshaken. "It's okay, Aundrea. You want it to be law, so law it shall be."

Jasino stepped forward, his presence commanding, instantly seizing control. "People of Lisona, you will stop and listen. My wife has spoken. This law shall be upheld, and let no one dare challenge it."

A hush fell over the crowd, broken only by the sobs of several women who lay on the ground, victims of the sudden violence.

A man emerged from the crowd, leading a faction of men who sought to have total control over women.

"Your Grace, what will this accomplish?"

Jasino turned and stepped back towards me, offering a nod of approval. Trembling, I found my voice. "If your wife marries you for love, you'll have a better marriage. She will feel safe and happy. If you continue in a loveless marriage no one will be happy…"

The man sneered at my words. "Love and happiness are fleeting weaknesses, Your Grace. Women need discipline and guidance, not a choice of freedoms!" He spat on the ground near my feet.

The insult hung in the air like a slap. In an instant, several of the royal guards surged forward, swords drawn and raised with deadly intent, forming a protective wall between me and the offender. The air crackled with restraint.

But Jasino lifted one hand — a small, deliberate gesture — and the guards froze. With practiced discipline, they lowered their blades, though their eyes burned with indignation.

The message was clear: disrespect toward the Empress of Lisona would not go unanswered. Not now. Not ever.

I took a step backward, then stood tall, my eyes blazing with conviction. "Discipline without love breeds resentment and rebellion—which is why we are standing here today. Our mothers taught us that love and respect are intertwined, so why would we deny our daughters the same?"

The man's face burned with rage. "ENOUGH OF THIS NONSENSE!" He raised his fist, and suddenly men surged forward, attacking women in the crowd again.

Screams and cries erupted from the city square. Women fell to the ground, critically injured. My eyes widened in horror.

Jasino's face twisted in fury as he leapt into the chaos, his powerful arms sweeping men aside like rag dolls, his guards joining the fray. I stepped back, frozen, watching in fear. The men wanted control. The women only wanted choice. What else could I do?

I watched in horror as people were violently slammed to the ground. My husband swept through the crowd, unfazed, until he stopped—standing tall, his voice thundering across the square.

"ENOUGH!"

The fighting ceased instantly. Men stumbled back in fear. Jasino's piercing gaze locked onto me, his eyes burning with urgency.

"Aundrea, heal them. Now."

He turned to the crowd, raising his hand for silence. "My wife possesses a gift that only a few Lisonians possess. She will save those injured. Dare not harm her, or face my wrath. And lay not your hands on another woman here."

I moved slowly toward the injured. I had never healed so many people before. This ability was a gift, but this would take more time than I had. Some would surely die.

A warm sensation engulfed me. My skin shimmered with an illuminating glow, and light flickered from my palms like nascent flames. I extended my hands toward the crowd, arching my neck back to gaze at the heavens. The air crackled with unseen power as I felt energy surge from above, mingling with the raw, untamed force rising from the ground beneath me.

Then—suddenly—a release. A blinding blast of light and a gust of wind swept over the crowd, carrying a promise of renewal. I had only ever healed one person at a time—never an entire crowd like this. No healer had.

I did not know how this came to be. My hands usually had to touch the individual that I was healing. But at this moment, something changed. Something inside of me was growing.

When the surge subsided, all my strength had been spent

From across the square, my husband watched in awe as women who had been critically injured rose to their feet, their wounds mending before his very eyes. I had healed every single person at once—a feat of unimaginable power. Then, I collapsed like a puppet with her strings cut.

My husband ran to my side, his face engraved with concern. I had passed out, and all strength in my body had been depleted. He gently lifted my head, cradling it in his lap like a precious treasure. Jasino's brother, Jasper, rushed to our side, his eyes wide with worry.

"Is she okay?" Jasper exclaimed, his voice laced with panic.

"She is breathing, brother," Jasino replied, a mix of relief and apprehension in his voice. "Just weak, I think."

My eyes fluttered open. I searched his familiar, comforting gaze. "Jasino…"

He smiled and placed a tender finger over my lips. "Shhh. Rest, my love," he whispered, his voice gentle and soothing.

I tilted my head, noticing everyone standing around. A loud cheer rose from the crowd. I turned again, gazing back into my husband's eyes.

He turned to Jasper, instructing him to call for a healer, his tone firm but gentle.

Then I saw a dark figure emerge from the corner of my eye.

"I am a healer," the man announced.

He got down on his knees and placed his hand on my forehead—and then, darkness claimed me once more, pulling me into its velvety embrace. My eyelids fluttered open, and I gazed up at Jasino's worried face. I tried to speak, but my voice barely escaped as a dry croak.

"Jas...ino..."

Fear crept into my eyes as I shifted my gaze to the healer beside Jasino. My heart sank, overwhelmed with emotion. I knew that face—those eyes. It was Ravon.

My pupils dilated in terror. I tried again to speak, but only a faint gasp escaped my lips.

Jasino leaned in, the shadow of concern tightening his features. "Aundrea, what's wrong?"

My gaze shot to the healer's.

"She will be okay; she just needs to rest now," he said calmly. "She needs a drink of water to replenish her energy, and after a night's rest, she'll recover."

He retrieved a glass flask from his satchel, the leather wrapping creaking softly in the tense silence. With a quick tug, he pulled free the cork and pressed the cool rim against my parched lips. Fear coiled within me, a venomous serpent whispering doubts.

What was truly in the water?

Suspicion gnawed at me, and I choked, spitting the liquid from my lips in a sputtering spray. His eyes—dark and piercing—held mine, sharp as a blade beneath velvet.

"Your Highness, I promise it's okay," he said, his voice a soothing balm against my rising panic. "You just need to drink some water." He repeated, "It's just water," in a calm, low tone meant to reassure—but it only deepened my unease.

Just then, Sabion appeared. He had heard the healer speak—"I promise it's just water." Without hesitation, he snatched the bottle from Ravon's hand and took a long drink. He paused, eyes narrowing as he examined the bottle, then handed it back, seemingly convinced the healer had spoken the truth.

Sabion had always been cautious—he'd tested drinks for my husband many times before. He offered the bottle again, and despite my apprehension, I succumbed, allowing a small amount to trickle down my throat.

Almost immediately, a strange numbness crept through my limbs, stealing my strength and clouding my mind.

It wasn't just water. I knew it in my bones.

He had used a potion, concocted from dark magic, to manipulate my power and restore my body—for his own twisted purposes. He had no intention of harming me, but his use of dark magic to heal me would prove to be a stain on my soul. I sensed something more, deeper, something more sinister. A warmth bloomed in my chest—wrong, unnatural. My pulse quickened not with fear, but with something dangerously close to affection. For him. For Ravon.

I recoiled inwardly, panic scraping against the edges of my thoughts. Was it a spell? Had the drink twisted my mind? What did he give me? Why didn't it affect Sabion.

Desperate, I struggled to form words, to warn my husband of the betrayal. "He… Ravon…" I gasped, the name barely escaping my lips. But the darkness surged—an irresistible tide crashing over me.

My husband listened closely to my words but didn't understand why I had said Ravon's name. I tried to speak again, but the haze reclaimed me, dragging me back into its suffocating embrace. After my eyes fluttered closed, he rose slowly, scanning the square. But Ravon was nowhere in sight. He turned to the healer, extended a hand, and said, "Thank you."

The potion was strong—I could feel it brewing deep within my bones. Sabion, untouched by its influence, stood in sharp contrast to the calculated grip that was slowly consuming me.

With a surge of protective fury, he scooped me into his arms, his strong embrace a stark contrast to the night's terrors. He carried me back to the palace, his footsteps echoing in the silent corridors, each stride a promise of safety.

Gently, he placed me upon the bed, the soft linens a welcome haven after the night's ordeal. As I lay there, still unable to speak, the weight of exhaustion pressing down, I knew this night of terror had finally come to an end.

Meanwhile, Jasper, ever the loyal brother, remained behind, ensuring that every soul who had braved the night's dangers returned home safely, his vigilance a silent vow to protect those under his care.

Chapter 4

Shadows in the Palace

I slowly opened my eyes, blinking away the haze. A warm, gentle light filled the room, and I was met with Jasino's loving gaze.

"Good morning, my love," he whispered, his voice low and soothing.

I tried to sit up, but a gentle hand pressed me back onto the pillows.

"You need to rest," Jasino said softly. "You were exhausted after everything that happened yesterday."

My mind was foggy, but fragments of memory began to resurface: the garden, the riot, the healing, the crowd... but something was missing. There was a nagging sense of something just out of reach.

"What... happened after I healed everyone?" I asked, my voice barely above a whisper.

Jasino's expression turned thoughtful before he replied. "You don't remember? A healer came from the crowd and helped you rest. You've been asleep for hours."

My heart skipped a beat. Healer... Something about that word felt off.

Jasino leaned over me and pressed his warm lips to mine. "I love you."

Smiling, I placed my hand on his face and replied, "I love you too, husband."

His eyes sparkled with delight as he deepened the kiss slightly, then pulled back to gaze at me.

"You're feeling better, I see," he whispered, his voice low and husky.

I nodded, my heart still racing. "Much better... I feel much better, thanks to you," I said softly. My hand

lingered on his cheek, and I felt a sudden urge to share a secret I had kept.
My fingers traced the curve of his jawline. "May I show you something?"

**

Intrigued, his eyebrows rose slightly, curiosity dancing in his eyes.

"What is it, my love?"

I threw off the covers and swung my legs over the side of the bed.

Jasino watched with interest as I struggled to pull the vanity away from the wall, revealing a hidden compartment in the back. My fingers slid into the narrow space, and I retrieved a small, hand-carved box.
I opened it and pulled out a small stone, glowing with ancient power, and I held it in the palm of my hand.
Jasino's face went utterly still—shock and panic washing over him simultaneously. He rose from the bed like a man drawn by invisible strings, his eyes fixed on the stone as if mesmerized.
"By the gods…" he breathed, barely above a whisper.
He stepped closer, reaching out to touch the stone, but hesitated.
"How…" he stammered, eyes locked on mine. "How did you touch it without being consumed by its power?"
I blinked. "What do you mean? I did not even know what it was, let alone why it would consume me."
Jasino stared between the stone and my face. "That… that's a Dragon Stone. Only two exist in our world. One belongs to the Drakon, and the other to the Divine One—part of the prophecy of the Emerging Drakon. Where did you find this?"

Looking down at the stone, then back at my husband, I said, "A year ago, when I ran away... the night I was missing. I stayed in a cavern carved into the side of a mountain. It was the only shelter I could find to stay warm. I laid down with my head resting against a rock when I heard a sound coming from deeper inside. I saw a faint light and followed it, my heart pounding. The tunnel grew brighter. Then, I found a box—light spilling from around its edges."

I paused, holding Jasino's gaze, noting the quiet concern etched in the lines of his face. The memory unfolded as curiosity stirred within me. I had opened the small box, drawn out the glowing stone, and slipped it into my pocket, uncertain of its meaning but captivated by its beauty. Sleep had come soon after, and when morning arrived, I'd reached for my pocket to be sure it hadn't been a dream. Sabion found me not long after and brought me home. Since then, I had kept the stone hidden in my vanity, untouched but never forgotten—a secret I wasn't yet ready to surrender.

Jasino's eyes burned into mine, his voice low and reverent. "Aundrea, the Dragon Stone you hold… it's one of two sacred artifacts tied to the prophecy."
He stepped back, collecting his thoughts. "My family always believed I was the future Drakon—the one destined to wield immense power and bring balance to the world."

His eyes drifted back to the stone. "For years, I searched relentlessly for one of them, terrified Ravon would find it first and try to claim the title. I've even hesitated, doubting myself, fearing the darkness and his ambition."
His gaze snapped back to me. "But now… everything makes sense. You, Aundrea. You are the Divine One. You already hold the power to heal—and you've done what no

healer ever has. You healed an entire crowd. That power...
it's part of the prophecy. You're the missing piece."
He stepped closer, his voice trembling with revelation.
"The stone chose you, my love. Randomly, yet perfectly.
My heart, my destiny—everything... it aligns."

I gently placed the stone back into the box and
returned it to the hidden drawer. As I struggled to push the
vanity back toward the wall, Jasino stepped forward to help
me.
I giggled, teasing, "Well, that was easy for you... since I
helped."
Jasino chuckled, brushing his fingers across mine. "Indeed,
it was, my clever wife."
He leaned in, his voice lowering to a whisper. "Now that
the stone is hidden again... we have more pressing
matters."

His warm breath danced across my skin, it stirred a
tremor within my soul. Then he straightened, his tone
turning serious again.
"The prophecy, Aundrea... we need to understand what it
means—for us, for the kingdom, for Ravon's next move."
Jasino leaned in, gently taking my hands in his. "The
prophecy speaks of the true Drakon—one who will merge
with the Dragon Stone to shield our lands from a darkness
unlike any we've ever known."

I met his gaze, questions rising in my chest. "Then
why can't you merge with the stone I found?"
He answered with a soft kiss, his lips brushing mine like a
promise. "Because that stone has already chosen you. If I
were to touch that stone, it would drive me to madness. The
Dragon Stone selects its bearer... never the other way
around. We must travel to the Bivarian Mountains past
Firefly Valley and meet with the Seer. She may know how
to find the second stone. She may hold the answers we

seek."
I nodded in agreement to Jasino's plan.

He immediately summoned Sabion, instructing him to prepare the horses and gather the necessary supplies for our journey. He leaned into me, his hand tracing my cheek. "Do you feel okay to travel?"

With a small nod, he turned back to Sabion. The Bivarian Mountains were inaccessible by carriage; the terrain was far too rugged, choked with dense, untamed brush. Our trip would take several days, if not weeks, that we would have to spend camping under the open sky. Sabion bowed deeply to my husband, acknowledging the command, before departing to fulfill his duties.

Following Sabion's exit, Jasino called for Michelle, tasking her with preparing my personal belongings for the trip. He emphasized the need to pack only the essentials and to select clothing suitable for the difficult journey ahead. After relaying these instructions, he pressed a tender kiss to my cheek, promising to return shortly before leaving the room.

I watched as Michelle efficiently began packing, her movements precise and practiced. Seated on the edge of the bed, I allowed my mind to wander, replaying all the explosive events that had transpired over the past few weeks. The weight of it all settled heavily upon me. "Does he mean for me to pack trousers for you, Aundrea?" Michelle inquired, her voice laced with a hint of curiosity. I couldn't help but giggle at the thought. "No, not trousers," I replied. "But a loose-fitting dress paired with leggings would be appropriate, I think."

With the single bag packed to satisfaction, Michelle left the room to deliver it to Sabion, ensuring it was properly stowed with the rest of our gear.

I dressed with urgency, tugging on soft leather leggings that clung to my skin, then slipping into a royal blue travel dress, its fabric both durable and elegant, flowing around my legs like whispered resolve.

The cool touch of the embroidered collar brushed my throat as I fastened it, grounding me with its familiar weight. Then I pulled on a pair of black leather boots, their worn soles molded to the shape of my feet, firm and ready for the road ahead. Moments later, my husband returned, his eyes filled with concern and anticipation.
"Are you ready, my love?" he asked softly.

I smiled up at Jasino, feeling a flutter in my chest at his gentle tone. "Yes, I'm ready," I replied, rising from the bed to stand beside him. He offered his arm, and I slipped my hand into the crook of his elbow, feeling a sense of comfort and security.

As we walked together toward the door, he leaned in close, his voice low and husky. "I'm glad you are coming with me, Aundrea. I need you by my side. All I want to do is keep you safe from whatever dangers are lurking in our future."

"Husband, is Jasper and my sister coming with us?" My voice was soft and even. I leaned in, my head against his chest.

His eyes locked onto mine, filled with emotion. My unanswered question lingered. Sabion appeared in the doorway, a hint of a smile on his face. "Everything is ready, Your Highness. The horses are saddled, the supplies packed, and the carriage escort awaits outside." He bowed slightly, his eyes flicking to Jasino before returning to mine. "Shall I inform Jasper and the guards to prepare for your departure?"

Jasino nodded, his arm still wrapped around mine. He turned to me, his voice dropping to a smoldering murmur. "Shall we begin our adventure, my love?"

My husband looked at me with a curious gaze.

Just then, Sabion appeared again, and his face turned grave. "Your Highness, my scouts reported Ravon's spies lurking near the palace gates this morning."

My heart skipped a beat as Jasino's grip on my arm tightened.

"They're getting bolder. We need to leave now." Jasino's eyes narrowed thoughtfully as he considered Sabion's warning—and my last question before Sabion entered.

"My love, I think it would be beneficial for Jasper and your sister, Alissia, to remain at the palace."

Then, turning his attention to Sabion, he said, "A decoy—send your men out to distract Ravon's spies from our true departure route."

I looked at Jasino curiously. "Husband, I would like to say goodbye to my sister before we leave."

With a firm voice, my husband answered, "No, Aundrea. Time is short, and we need to get on our way."

He started to lead me toward the back of the palace when I stopped, pulling away from him. Set in confusion, Jasino stopped and turned toward me.

"I won't leave without saying goodbye to my sister, Jasino."

My words pierced his armor, leaving him momentarily stunned and defiant.

"Aundrea," he said with a sharp but commanding tone. "We need to go. Now."

He started to reach for my hand, and I pulled away from him.

"Our journey may be dangerous, and we do not know what

to expect. I will not leave without seeing my sister. What if it is the last time?"

Tears trembled on my lashes as a single tear ran down my cheek. I knew that challenging my husband this way was like pushing him to the edge of his patience. I knew that defying the emperor would be a risk and a public embarrassment, but I needed to see my sister.

Jasino's face darkened, his eyes blazing with a mix of anger and hurt pride as he took a step closer to me. My knees weakened with panic.
"Aundrea, do not test my patience further," he growled low in his throat. "You're questioning my judgment as Emperor… and my love for you." His voice dropped to a whisper, sending a chill down my spine. "Do you think me incapable of protecting you?"
He paused, his chest heaving slightly with restrained emotion.
"Answer me, wife."

Jasino's eyes dug in like daggers, his voice icy. "You're pushing me to choose between kingdom and family, Aundrea. Between duty and love."
His words cut deep, and for a moment, I saw a glimmer of hurt behind his anger.
Sabion stepped forward, his voice calm and measured. "Your Highness, perhaps we can find a

compromise? A brief farewell to Lady Alissia, under guard, before departing?"

Jasino's gaze never left mine, but he considered Sabion's suggestion.

Then, his eyes flashed back at mine, intense and unyielding. But before he could respond,

Jasino's face turned red with rage, his voice thundering through the palace corridors. "Enough, Aundrea! You dare suggest my love for you is conditional on your sister's presence?!"

He once again closed the distance between us, and fear gripped my heart. "Am I nothing to you without Alissia by your side?!"

His anger hung in the air like a challenge, but I stood firm, tears streaming down my face. Then, my body betrayed me—sobbing profusely, I collapsed to the ground, overcome with emotion.

Jasino's expression froze, his chest heaving with restrained fury… but as he gazed down at me, shattered and sobbing, his fierce ego began to crack. His face softened, eyes filled with anguish. He dropped to one knee beside me, gently lifting my face to his.

"Aundrea, my love," he said, his voice just above a whisper, his anger replaced with tender concern. He helped me to my feet, his arms wrapping tightly around me. "No more than a breath of time. That is all I can give you."

He turned toward Sabion. "Secure the area. Retrieve my brother and his wife. We will wait here." Sabion bowed and rushed off.

Jasino pulled me against his body, his eyes fixed on mine. In a low and teasing voice, he said, "You're a bit feisty today, my love." A soft giggle escaped his lips, and my tears began to dry. My voice softened. "Forgive me, husband. I never meant to defy you… especially in front of our guards. My heart races with fear for our uncertain future—and the thought of leaving my sister without saying goodbye…"

My voice trembled as my eyes swelled with tears once again. "I love her..."

Looking down, I wiped the tears from my cheek. "It's unbearable." Jasino once again placed his hand under my chin, lifting my face until our eyes met. "Don't be sorry, my love. I understand. Sometimes, I just need to listen." He leaned over and kissed my nose, then my forehead. "I love you, Aundrea."
My arms wrapped tightly around him, and I replied, "I love you too, husband."
We were interrupted by a familiar voice. "Brother, I am sorry for interrupting."

Alissia was standing beside him, her eyes wide with worry. Jasino explained the plan, and Jasper nodded gravely while Alissia ran into my arms and clung to me. Tears fell as we hugged each other tightly.
"Everything will be okay, sister," I whispered, trying to reassure her.
Alissia pulled back, her voice trembling. "Be careful, Aundrea... Ravon's madness scares me."
Looking into her fearful eyes, I said, "Alissia, I love you. Pray for us."
We walked to a nearby bench and sat down.
Jasper placed a hand on Jasino's shoulder. "Return safely, brother. We'll hold the palace."
They shared a quick embrace, and then my husband approached me, palm extended.
"It's time, my love."

I stood and took his hand, turning to Alissia, exchanging a lingering gaze. We began walking down the corridor. Tears streamed down my cheeks as I looked back. Alissia stood in Jasper's arms, watching us disappear into the passage.

***

As we walked swiftly through the dark passage, Jasino's head swiveled around, his senses on high alert.
"What is it?" I whispered.
"Something feels off," he replied in a low voice. "The passage seems… disturbed. Like someone's recently passed through."

Letting go of my hand, he drew his sword silently. Sabion followed his lead. As we walked further, Jasino's instincts screamed warning. Suddenly, three figures burst from the shadows. One grabbed me from behind; a glinting knife pressed against my side. Jasino's blood ran cold. The other two men drew swords, eyes locked on Sabion and Jasino. Without hesitation, Jasino launched himself at the man holding me, his sword flashing in the dim light. He grabbed the man's wrist, twisting it until he yelped and released me. I stumbled forward, gasping, my heart nearly bursting from my chest.

Sabion charged into battle alongside Jasino. Swords clashed and sparked in a deadly rhythm. The attackers fought fiercely, but Sabion and Jasino were better trained, better in sync. I backed away, narrowly missing the clash of two swords beside my head. Pressing myself to the corridor's cold stone wall, I watched.
One by one, the attackers fell. At last, all three lay motionless.
Jasino rushed to my side, sheathing his sword, pulling me into his arms, scanning me for injuries.
"Are you hurt?"
Trembling, I tried to speak. "I…"
"Speak up, wife. Are you hurt?" he said, firm but concerned.
Catching my breath, I managed, "I... I am okay, husband."

He pulled me close, one hand behind my waist, the other cradling the back of my head against his chest. "You're safe now, my love. I've got you."

The trembling slowly began to subside, as hope began to bloom.
Sabion cleared his throat, a quiet reminder that we needed to keep moving. My eyes found my husband's. "I... was so scared."
He held me tight for one last embrace and kissed the top of my head.
"You were never in danger, my love. We need to go."
We continued walking through the corridor for a heartbeat longer, and finally emerged into the crisp air outside the palace walls, horses saddled and ready. Guards loaded our supplies while Sabion stood watch, eyes scanning the horizon.

**

Jasino turned to me, his face inches from mine. "One last moment alone with my wife before danger finds us again." His lips brushed against mine softly. His touch lit a spark that rippled through my entire being. "I love you, Aundrea,"

he proclaimed, his voice resonating with an intensity that mirrored the depths of his piercing eyes. A warmth spread through every part of my body, replaced with desire chasing away the lingering shadows of doubt and fear.
"I love you too," I whispered softly, the words barely parting my lips, yet filled with profound sincerity.

He gently took my hand. A flutter stirred deep within, cascading like stardust along my skin. With his tender strength, he helped me into the carriage, ensuring I was settled before joining me.

We would start with the carriage, and then, when the carriage could not move any further, we would ride horseback.

The leather of the seats was cool against my skin, a stark contrast to the heat that still lingered in my cheeks. As the carriage lurched forward, I found myself drawn to the window, my gaze fixed on the world outside. The sky was a canvas of washed-out blue, where clouds lingered like forgotten dreams. They danced and shifted, their forms ever-changing, mirroring the uncertainty that still swirled within me. I sat in silence, lost in thought, the rhythmic clatter of the horses' hooves carried on the wind.

Jasino's gentle hand found mine again, his fingers intertwining with mine as he broke the silence.

"My love, your thoughts are miles away... What troubles your mind?"

His voice was low but soothing, his eyes firmly locked onto mine with tender concern.

The carriage slowed slightly as we navigated a gentle curve, and Jasino's fingers began tracing gentle circles on the back of my hand.

"I'm scared of what Ravon will do... if he finds out about the prophecy or the stone..."

He interrupted, "My brother knows, Aundrea. He knows about the prophecy and the stone. I imagine he has been searching for the stone for years. He just hasn't found it yet—nor have I."

He continued, "I know it has to be close because you have one of the stones... destiny is reaching out to us."

I turned to him, fear gnawing at the edges of my soul like a shadow with teeth. The prophecy haunted my thoughts—if the Dragon Stone chose its bearer, what danger could possibly remain?

But Jasino's gaze held a weight I didn't yet understand, the kind that came from ancient knowledge passed through generations. My understanding was still so limited, and he knew it.

He explained what my heart already feared—that Ravon, in his arrogance, believed he could bend the Dragon Stone to his will. That he could wield its divine power, twisting it into a weapon for the dark. The very thought made the air around me feel heavier, colder.

But the stone was not his to claim. If he tried, madness would take him—ravenous, uncontrollable, the kind that devoured reason and tore through the mind like wildfire in dry fields. A destruction no one in our world had ever witnessed... and no one could stop.

I studied his soft and caring eyes. "Jasino, what does the prophecy say about the Divine One?"

My eyes searched his, filled with vulnerability.

Jasino's expression softened, his eyes burning with intensity. He pulled me closer into his arms, inches from my face.

"It says, 'The Drakon will share life and power with the Divine One," he whispered into my ear.

"You are safe with me, Aundrea." His warm breath sent trembles through my skin.

He continued, "Ravon will never have you. I swear it on my life, my kingdom, and my love for you."

His arms wrapped tightly around me, holding me close as the carriage swayed gently forward. I practically dissolved into his comforting embrace.

A soothing heat spread through me, chasing away the cold dread that had been my constant companion.

Buried in his arms, the steady thump of his heart was a hypnotic rhythm, and I drifted off into a deep, dreamless sleep.

***

When I awoke, Jasino was gone. My head rested on a small, fluffy pillow, and his cloak was draped over me like a protective shield. The scent of him clung to the fabric, a silent promise of safety.

I sat up and gazed out the window, mesmerized by the sunset blazing across the horizon. A dense forest loomed in the distance, its shadows hinting at the hidden mysteries and unknown danger that lay ahead.

The carriage came to a sudden halt, and I eagerly stepped out, my boots crunching on the gravel beneath my feet.

Jasino rode up beside me atop Vandros, his magnificent grey-and-white steed. The stallion's silver mane rippled like silk in the wind, and his hooves struck the ground with the weight and rhythm of thunder. Muscles rippled beneath his dappled coat, each movement a display of restrained power.

As they approached, the scent of leather and fur mingled with the crisp morning air.

Jasino's smile—confident and radiant—could have melted glaciers, but it was Vandros's proud snort and arched neck that made the moment feel truly regal.

"Sleep well, sweetheart?" he asked, his eyes sparkling with affection.

"Why have we stopped, Jasino?" I mumbled, still half-lost in slumber.

He dismounted, his gaze softening with love. "The horses need food and water, and we have to leave the carriage behind now because the forest is too dense ahead."

Sabion appeared, offering me a flask with his usual reserved grace. "Drink, Your Highness. It will be a long ride before we camp for the night."

I gratefully accepted the flask, the cool water soothing my dry throat.

As I returned it to Sabion, I watched Jasino load supplies

onto two spare horses, balancing the weight with practiced ease. My heart pounded with anticipation as we prepared to enter the forest.

Finally, Jasino turned to me, his eyes locking with mine. With a tender hand, he helped me onto Vandros, ensuring I was secure. Then, he swung up behind me, his strong arms encircling my waist as he took the reins.

His presence was a comforting reassurance, a shield against the unknown, as we plunged forward into the depths of the dark forest.

THROUGH SHADOW, POWER
HOUSE RAVON

Chapter 5

The Wolf in the Forest

As we rode deeper into the forest, the trees seemed to close in around us, casting long, ominous shadows on the ground. We wandered the forest for weeks trying to find our way through the thick and dense forest. A mist slithered across the ground, curling around our legs and leaving behind a chill that gnawed at my nerves. The silence pressed down like a weight, broken only by the rustling of leaves and the occasional snap of a twig beneath the horses' hooves. We rode silently, the tension between us as tight as a drawn bowstring. High above, birds cawed in alarm, their cries carrying an eerie warning.

Then came the sound that made my blood run cold—a sharp, piercing howl that shattered the quiet and sent a tremor through our mounts. Vandros trembled beneath us, hooves dancing anxiously. My husband's arms tightened protectively around me.

"Easy, my love," he whispered into my ear, his voice calm but alert. "It's just a wolf pack."

He dismounted with fluid grace, calling out to Sabion, "Ready the guards."

Jasino drew his sword, its edge gleaming in the dim light. Sabion followed suit, barking orders to the men. My husband handed me the reins with urgency.

"Control Vandros but stay back, Aundrea."

I nodded, gripping the reins tightly as guards took position around us. The howls multiplied, echoing through the forest like ghosts. I looked ahead and caught a glimpse of two small, glowing yellow eyes. The wolf's mottled grey fur blended seamlessly with the shadows, making it nearly invisible until it moved. Then I saw more—eyes were everywhere, circling us like silent predators.

My heart pounded. There were at least a dozen of them. Their massive forms padded silently between trees, each movement fluid and predatory. Their teeth glinted with anticipation as growls rose from their throats, deep and primal.

Suddenly, Vandros reared back in panic as the wolves lunged. One leapt toward us, its jaws wide, fangs gleaming. I yanked the reins, spinning the horse aside just in time. Sabion swung his sword and slashed the creature's flank, but it wasn't enough. It turned back, snarling, ready to strike again.

Before it could, Jasino drove his sword straight through its heart, and it crumpled to the ground with a guttural snarl. Two more wolves lunged toward them, and the fight exploded around us—swords clashing, snarls ripping through the air, the guards locked in a ferocious battle.

I tightened my hold on the reins. Then I saw it—a beast far larger than the others. Its coat was black as midnight, shaggy and thick with muscle rippling beneath. Its eyes were molten gold, fixed on me with terrifying focus. Its lips curled back in a low, guttural growl.

My heart leapt into my throat. I looked down at my husband. He was fighting off three wolves, his blade moving in a blur. Sabion was in a similar struggle. I turned back to the monstrous wolf creeping toward me.

I pulled the horse around and kicked off in a full gallop, leaves scattering in my wake."

The enormous wolf gave chase. I could hear it—each breath a ragged snarl, its claws tearing into the ground behind me.

The sounds of battle faded behind me, swallowed by the pounding of hooves and my own pulse. Vandros's mane whipped my face. The wolf was gaining on us. Its breath hit my back like steam, the sheer heat of its body unnerving. I felt a nip at my dress and then another, tearing the material next to my leg.

***

Then—an arrow whistled through the trees, striking the beast squarely in the heart. It crumpled with a pained yowl, skidding across the dirt. I yanked the reins, my horse slowing. Vandros danced around its lifeless body. My gaze flew to the hill ahead.

There, standing tall and half-shrouded in the afternoon mist, was a lone rider. My breath caught. I stared, heart pounding in my chest, a strange pull anchoring my gaze. For the briefest flicker of a moment, I thought it was my husband—his posture, the shape of his jaw—but as the mist thinned, clarity shattered the illusion. It wasn't him. It was Ravon. He stared straight at me, gaze burning with terrible intensity, as he descended the hill, leading his horse with slow, measured steps.

"Aundrea, my beautiful Aundrea... I've saved your life. Why do you shy away from me?"

Fear rooted me to the saddle. He approached my horse, reached up, and gently pulled me down. His hand brushed my cheek. I recoiled, pressing against my horse's flank.

"Why do you run from me, my love?" he asked, his smile smug and amused.

He stepped closer. "I saved you from the wolf's jaws. Are you not thankful?"

My voice broke free. "Ravon, you are my husband's brother. Why do you pursue me? I do not love you. I want Jasino."

Ravon reached for me, one arm snaking around my waist, the other curling behind my head. He pulled me in with forceful grace, his lips crashing onto mine in a deep, possessive kiss. I twisted in his grasp, trying to break free—but his mouth was warm, commanding, and a flicker of heat ignited deep within me.

Desire flared—unbidden, unwelcome—burning through my confusion. For a heartbeat, I leaned in, returning the kiss, lost in the haze of it.

Then something cracked inside me.

A pang of guilt struck like lightning across my chest, tearing through the fog surrounding me. I wrenched myself back, breathless and shaking. My hand flew on instinct, striking his face with a sharp, echoing slap.

Ravon staggered slightly, more shocked than wounded.

I turned toward Vandros without another word, the sting of my palm still tingling, my heart thudding with shame and fury.

I grabbed the mount, struggling to climb back up. My dress caught in the stirrup as Ravon laughed.

"Really?" he murmured. "A young lady mounting her horse in a dress without help. You amuse me."

I sat tall on Vandros, glaring down at him. "I do not love you, sir. I never will."

His smile twisted into something darker.

"Your words only fuel my love for you. Jasino doesn't deserve you. He doesn't love you. He just wants to possess you. He is blind to your fire... your spirit. I saved you because I want to be the one you burn for."

His eyes glowed with fierce longing. "You say you don't love me, but I saw it in your eyes—the flicker of surprise when I kissed you. That means deep down... you wonder."

A moment's hesitation flickered inside me. He did not seem evil.

No. I shook my head. "I trust Jasino. I will not yield."

I kicked the horse into motion, galloping back through the trees, hoping to retrace my path. His laughter echoed behind me.

"Aundrea! Your resistance only delights me..."

Hooves thundered behind me—he was following. His voice, laced with desperation, cut through the wind.

"Jasino trusts no one... least of all you, my love."

He drew up beside me. I cried out as he seized my reins, forcing our horses to stop.

"You're not going back to him," he said, his voice low, almost tender. "You belong with me."

I stared at him, trembling. "I don't even know you, Ravon. How can you love someone you do not know?"

He reached out, wiping a tear from my cheek, his gaze never leaving mine. "You know me better than you think, Aundrea." He let out a sinister laugh.

"Don't you remember the day after the ball? You wanted me then, my love. And when I came to you at midday, you did not reject me." A smile spread across his face, clearly amused by his own words.

I stared at him, disbelief flooding me. "That was you? How? You have a scar above your eye. I clearly saw no scar. You lie."

He moved closer, lifting his palm to cover the scar. A faint blue glow shimmered under his hand. When he removed it, the scar was gone. "You mean like this?"

Fury and fear surged within me, betrayal clawing at my insides. "I thought you were Jasino... you! No! It can't be."

My shock seemed to delight him. He leaned in again. "Yes, it was me. Jasino was indisposed that day." His lips brushed my ear, a cold dread slithered through me. "You trembled beneath me, my love. You called me 'my lord' and whispered, 'Take me deeper."

I yelled out in anger, "I did not! You were cold, Ravon!" His fingers gently traced my face. "Did you truly think Jasino could ignite such fire in you, I am the one you truly burn for?"

I thought about the moment, the memory fresh in my mind, Fire, no! He was cold and distant, and I knew then, that something was wrong. His lips hovered close to mine. I recoiled in outrage, yanking my reins from his hand and driving Vandros into a full gallop. Only the pounding of hooves filled the air.

Then I heard Jasino and Sabion yelling my name in the distance. Behind me, Ravon's laughter faded into the trees. He had vanished into the forest shadows, leaving me burning with shame and fury.

***

As I rode into view of my husband and Sabion, both on horseback and rushing toward me, I leapt from Vandros before he stopped, tumbling to the ground. I scrambled up and ran into Jasino's arms, sobbing uncontrollably. He embraced me tightly, his warmth grounding me.

Jasino didn't know about the wolf… about Ravon…he didn't know about the kiss… and especially not about that terrible day. I wept, clinging to him. Somehow, I would have to tell him. But not today. I feared what he would think, what he would feel, if he ever found out.

He held me close, his breath soft against my ear. "Aundrea, my love, what's wrong? Your tears are killing me. Are you hurt?"

I took a breath, choosing my words carefully. "It was Ravon."

His eyes locked on mine, intense. "What about Ravon?"

"A wolf chased me… He saved me from it, but his words… they were twisted and cruel."

Jasino's arms tightened around me, his body tense. "What did he say to you?"

I hesitated, omitting the worst of it. "He implied you don't truly care for me… that I'm just a possession to you."

His face darkened. "That monster lies. You're my everything, Aundrea." He pulled back slightly, wiping away my tears with his thumbs. "Do you believe him?"

My heart ached. "No… I know you love me, Jasino."

But guilt echoed louder than my voice. He kissed me—deeply, with a passion that stole my breath. His lips were warm, insistent, searching for the part of me that hadn't been broken.

I trembled beneath the weight of it, torn between love and shame. My hands clung to his tunic, fingers curling with longing, even as guilt burned behind my eyes. "Forever mine, Aundrea, Ravon's lies will never come between us."

I wanted so badly to confess the truth. But fear held my tongue. I remembered Jasino's struggle with jealousy, his pride. I just couldn't do it.

I melted into his arms, searching for safety in his embrace while my mind raced with hidden truths.

Sabion cleared his throat. "Your Highnesses, perhaps we should press on to camp just outside Firefly Valley? Nightfall approaches."

Jasino nodded. "Yes, Sabion. Lead the way. We'll follow shortly."

As Sabion rode ahead, Jasino turned back to me, eyes narrowing slightly. "Aundrea, is there something Ravon said that you're not telling me?"

My heart stuttered. He sensed it. He saw the shadow in me. I forced a smile. "No, my love. Just… his cruel words still echo in my mind. For a moment, I thought I'd never see you again." My words to him were truth, his words did echo in my mind, but not the ones that I told him about.

His gaze lingered, searching my soul. Then he nodded slowly. "Very well. But know this—my love for you is unwavering."

Guilt churned inside me.

Jasino helped me onto Vandros and climbed up in front of me. My arms wrapped tightly around his waist as we rode toward camp, my secret still gnawing at my heart. Upon arriving at the camp, tents were already being set up. Sabion approached us. "Your Highness, we've reached a suitable campsite, and the men will finish setting up for the night. But I must mention… strange tracks were found nearby, leading into the woods."

Jasino's eyes narrowed, his hand instinctively going to his sword. Sabion's expression turned grave. "They appear to be fresh horse tracks. But with an unusual symbol carved into the ground beneath us."

My heart sank as Jasino's gaze locked onto mine. "A symbol, Sabion? What kind?"

Sabion's voice lowered. "A raven's claw mark, Your Highness."

Jasino's face darkened, his jaw clenched. "It seems my brother has been tracking us."

He gave orders to the guards to patrol the perimeter, then pulled me close, whispering, "You're safe with me, Aundrea. Ravon's obsession will end. I won't let him near you again."

His breath grazed my neck, a soft exhale that made me feel safe, rooted, and entirely his.

Sabion interrupted, his voice low and urgent. "Your Highness, should we prepare defenses for the night? Ravon rarely travels alone, and since your wife has already encountered him, he is likely close by. His followers are ruthless and well-skilled in the dark arts."

Jasino's grip on me tightened, his eyes scanning the surrounding woods. "Sabion, I agree. Double the guard detail on the perimeter."

He turned back to me and, with a low and gentle voice, said, "Aundrea, go with Sabion to our tent. I need to oversee preparations for the night."

***

As I turned to follow Sabion, a twig snapped nearby, echoing through the forest. I froze, and terror consumed my body like a tidal wave. I began to shake, something was off, something was extremely close. My husband and the guards all drew their swords.

"Who's there?" he called.

There was no answer. With a tense expression, Jasino's eyes locked onto mine. "Get behind me, Aundrea. Something or someone is here."

His body tensed, sword raised defensively, as he pushed me gently backward. Suddenly, the campfire flames danced wildly, casting eerie shadows on the trees. I could hear the fuel from the flames exploding as the flames danced higher into the dark black sky. Sabion rushed forward, sword clashing with a hidden assassin's blade.

I scanned the camp. A terrifying number of assassins flooded into the campsite, swords drawn and surrounded by a strange purple haze. Then the battle erupted.

I tried to stay close to my husband, but chaos tore us apart. Swords blazed all around me. Sabion yelled, "By the Emperor's guard!" as he fought off multiple attackers. Guards rushed to aid him, steel ringing out as chaos unfolded.

Jasino spun, fending off assassins closing in. I crept closer again, cautious of the deadly blades wailing around me.

"Aundrea, stay back!" he called.

I stumbled backward, nearly tripping. From a fallen tree, Ravon emerged, his figure cold and shadowed.

Caught in the middle of the fighting, I moved behind a table and crouched low. As I peered around it, my eyes locked with Ravon's. He raised his hands, and a vibrant purple glow erupted from his palms.

I screamed, "Husband! Ravon is here!"

Jasino sprinted toward him, sword flashing in fury. "Ravon, no magic will touch her!"

His blade met Ravon's dark spell.

From the corner of my eye, I saw a guard collapse. I rushed to his side, kneeling.

Urgently, I pressed my hands to his chest, trying to draw on my power to heal him. But something felt wrong. An invisible barrier blocked me. He was gone. A sinister purple haze drifted from his body—Ravon's magic.

I rose slowly, devastated, unaware of the danger. Suddenly, I was seized from behind. Panic exploded in my chest as I kicked and screamed. "Help me, Jasino, help me!"

Ravon's man dragged me toward the trees. Jasino's face twisted in anguish.

"AUNDREA!"

He charged toward me, sword slicing down anything in his path. From the shadows, a voice echoed, "You'll never have her, Jasino. She'll be mine."

Jasino shouted to Sabion, who was locked in battle. "SABION, CUT HIM OFF FROM THE TREES!"

Sabion and the remaining guards closed in, but the man dragged me deeper into darkness. "JASINO!" I screamed.

Suddenly, the man's grip faltered. Jasino's sword flashed inches from my face. I broke free, and he grabbed me, shielding me with his body as he fought.

"Aundrea, I've got you!"

But the attacker recovered and blasted Jasino back with dark energy. "Away from her, false emperor!"

The blast tore me from his arms. "NOOO!"

Sabion struck the man from behind. "You will never have her!"

He landed a final blow. The man dissolved into mist—a conjuration of Ravon's dark magic.

***

Jasino regained his footing, his breath still ragged from battle. The fury in his eyes softened the instant they found mine—relief flooding his features like sunlight breaking through a storm. Without hesitation, he closed the distance and swept me into his arms, holding me as if the world itself might try to steal me away.

"You're safe, my love," he whispered, his voice rough with emotion.

My tears spilled freely, soaking into the fabric of his tunic, which was still damp with sweat and the scent of steel and smoke. My fingers clutched at him, desperate to feel the solid warmth of his body anchoring me back to reality. "I thought I was going to lose you," I choked, my voice breaking.

He pressed a kiss to my forehead, his lips trembling against my skin. I trembled in his embrace, the remnants of fear clinging to me like a second skin.

"Jasino…" I sobbed, burying my face in the curve of his neck. "How can he say he loves me… and still terrorize me?"

His lips remained at my brow, his voice low and deadly. "Ravon's obsession is with power, not you. He pulled back slightly, his thumbs wiping the tears from my eyes. "He wants to own you, Aundrea, body and soul—but you'll never be his. You're mine." His arms wrapped tighter around me, holding me close as if shielding me from Ravon's evil reach. "I'll destroy him for touching you…"

Sabion approached quietly, respectfully giving us space, but Jasino still sensed his presence and glanced up. "Sabion, summon Lyra, the healer of Firefly Valley. We have a fallen guard to mourn and prepare for burial."

Jasino's gaze returned to mine, his voice softening. "First, I need to make sure you are safe." I leaned over, clutching my stomach as the contents of my stomach erupted onto the ground. Jasino's hand gently found its way back to my back, and I could feel the weight of concern pressing through my dress.

"Are you ok Aundrea?" he asked, his voice laced with worry.

Slowly, I straightened up, the cool air brushing against my face.

"Yes, husband," I replied, my voice still trembling slightly, "I am just a bit overwhelmed."

Sabion brought me a flask filled with water, so I could rinse the foul and bitter taste from my mouth. I leaned into Jasino's chest. His arms enveloped me tighter, lifting me off the ground as he walked toward our tent. The flickering campfire lights danced across his face, illuminating his gentle smile.

***

"Finally, alone with you." He pushed aside the tent flap with his shoulder and carried me inside, laying me down on the soft furs. Then he joined me, wrapping his body around mine, holding me close as if never letting go.

"Aundrea, my heart almost stopped when Ravon's man took you…" His lips barely brushed against my ear, my breath caught as something electric danced beneath my skin. "Promise me you'll never scare me like that again."

I turned my head, my lips meeting his in a deep, passionate kiss. Pausing then for a moment, I murmured, "I'll try, husband…" Jasino's heart fluttered closed, deepening the kiss as his arms tightened around me. Then his lips gently broke away and he whispered softly, "Sleep, my love. You're safe now. I've got you."

His hands started gently stroking my hair, soothing my frazzled nerves as his chest rose and fell with calming breaths. My eyelids grew heavy, trust and love overcoming my fear. As I drifted off to sleep, Jasino's whispered promise echoed in my mind: "Ravon will never have you, Aundrea. I swear it."

Suddenly, Jasino's body tensed slightly. He was still awake, watching over me. I jolted awake, a scream caught in my throat, and Jasino's strong arms immediately pulled me closer.

"It's alright, Aundrea. I'm here," he murmured, his voice a soothing balm against my terror.

Tears streamed down my face, a torrent of fear and guilt. Jasino believed my distress stemmed from the brutal attack on our camp, the trauma Ravon had inflicted. But my tears held a darker truth—two secrets I dared not speak. One born of a kiss I should have rejected, the other whispered in the throes of a day I thought belonged to my husband... but didn't.

My dream had twisted into a nightmare, my husband's loving embrace morphing into Ravon's predatory grasp. How could I confess that I had unknowingly betrayed Jasino with his own brother? Would he ever forgive me? Would he forgive me for the stolen kiss?

The fear was a suffocating weight, crushing me with the certainty that I would lose Jasino. And the thought of Ravon... it filled me with a paralyzing dread.

I buried my face deeper into Jasino's chest, continuing to cry. Why was this so emotional for me? Why was it so hard? Fear grasped my soul for just a moment as I shuddered at the thought—I could be with child. Still too early to know, but the fear was growing.

Jasino's arms tightened around me, his voice low and gentle. "Aundrea, my love, what's haunting you? Your tears... they're not just from Ravon's attack, are they?"

He pulled back slightly, his thumbs wiping away my tears, his eyes searching mine with deep concern. "You can tell me anything, my love. I'm your husband—your shield."

I looked into his eyes, my thoughts choking the words before they could fully form. "Ravon... he kissed me."

Tears streamed down my face as Jasino pulled me into his arms, holding me as if he could shield me from the memory. His hands trembled slightly as they caressed my hair, but he said nothing at first. Just held me.

"I wiped that stain away," he whispered into my ear, voice low and tight. "It's gone now."

But his silence said more than his words. I felt the way his breath hitched, the way his jaw tightened against my temple. He suspected the truth was deeper—darker.

And he wasn't wrong.

Even with his warmth around me, I couldn't stop crying. The kiss was not the only secret I carried. I had let Ravon touch me. I had let him near. I had fallen under his illusion, just for a moment—but long enough to shatter everything.

He kissed me like he owned me. And I let him. The shame clawed at me, and though Jasino wiped my tears, he could not erase what Ravon had whispered in the shadows of that day—the day he violated me, stealing something that was never his to take: my dignity.

He held me tighter, as if my silence spoke the truth. "There's more, isn't there? Whatever it is, Aundrea... we'll face it together. I'll fix it for you." His expression softened further, filled with tender alarm. "Aundrea, you're trembling… and your tears… they're laced with fear of something more. What is it, my love?"

Tears blurred my vision as I gazed into my husband's eyes, the weight of the unspoken truth pressing down on me.

"No, I can't! I cannot tell you, husband," I choked out, the words in a strangled whisper. Uncontrollable sobs wracked my body, each one a painful reminder of my hidden transgression.

I pushed myself up in the bed, the movement jerky and desperate. "Why?" I called out, my voice thick with anguish, gasping for air as I looked toward the heavens. "Why me? I've never done anything to hurt anyone!

My sobbing had become intense. Jasino, still lost in the shadows of my nightmare, now sensed the presence of a dark secret—a truth I was terrified to reveal.

He offered words of comfort, his voice laced with concern. "Please, my love," he gently coaxed, lifting my chin until our eyes met. "It's okay. There's nothing you can say to me that will make me leave you. Tell me."

I put my hand on the side of his cheek, gently caressing. "I can't… I cannot tell you. I don't know how…"

I leaned forward and put my head back onto his chest, trying to bury the memory.

Jasino knew it wasn't the time. He knew I wasn't ready to tell him yet, but he also knew that whatever the secret was, it was torturing me—and that bothered him deeply. He wanted so much to help, but he couldn't. And out of fear of saying the wrong thing, he told me it was going to be okay.

He leaned forward, his lips close to my ear, and whispered, "Sleep, my love. It will all be okay. You don't have to tell me tonight."

He kissed the top of my forehead, tightening his grip on me. He knew I was hurting inside, and he felt completely helpless. He knew that Ravon must have done something to me—but he just couldn't figure it out. Jasino's arms enveloped me tightly, holding me close as if shielding me from the darkness of my own secret. His chest rose with a deep breath, and I sensed his inner turmoil. He spoke just above a whisper, "Know this, my love, whatever Ravon did to you, it's eating away at your soul and mine…Not being able to fix it for you is killing me." His lips brushed against my forehead, a soft, reassuring kiss. "You're not alone in this darkness, I'm here. I'm here when you need me."

It wasn't just a matter of having a spark of love for Ravon; a fierce hatred burned within me. What he had done was an unforgivable violation, a deep wound that festered with the passing of time. My self-reproach was just as potent. How could I have been so blind, so naïve? It wasn't a simple matter of blame. It was a time of heightened passion, of reckless abandon. I had willingly submitted, lost in the moment. I hadn't known who he truly was; I had believed him to be my husband. Ravon took advantage of that moment. A war raged within me, a battle between the desire for truth and the paralyzing grip of fear.

I was trapped, caught in a web of my own making. How could I confess this to my husband? The shame was a suffocating weight. How could I even call it assault when I had been a willing participant? Would he ever understand the depth of my violation—the way Ravon had stolen something precious under false pretenses?

Consumed by a turbulence of emotions, I sank back onto the bed, reaching for my husband. I nestled against his side, burying my face against his chest, and wept until sleep claimed me, offering a temporary escape from the torment.

Jasino's eyes remained open, burning with a mixture of confusion and devastation. As he held me close, his chest rose with a slow, anguished breath. Whispering into my ear with boundless emotion, "What did he do to you, my love?"

He lay there for hours with his face tucked closely to mine, his touch remaining tender despite the turmoil brewing inside him. Hours passed before his exhausted body finally succumbed to sleep.

Chapter 6

Tethered Hearts

My eyes fluttered open, the world slowly coming into focus. I pushed myself up from the bed of furs, a symphony of sounds drifting in from outside the tent, voices mingling with laughter and playful giggles. My husband's side of the bed was empty, the indentation in the furs a silent testament to his absence. A wave of nausea washed over me as I crawled across the bed, grabbing a bowl left behind sometime in the night. I spilled my empty stomach into the bowl with a mouthful of bitterness left behind. I reached for my bag tucked snugly in the corner. I felt utterly wretched, my body craving the soothing relief of a bath.

With trembling hands, I pulled out my hairbrush and began the task of untangling the knots from my hair. After what felt like an eternity, I managed to corral my hair into a simple balance of order, clipping it back into a soft braid.

Next, I rummaged through my bag, selecting a fresh dress and a pair of leggings, eager to shed the clothes that clung to me like a second skin. Once changed, I hesitantly emerged from the tent, still feeling grimy and unclean despite the fresh attire. Still, I felt guilty about my burning secrets.

My eyes immediately found my husband, who stood near the crackling fire. He met my gaze, a knowing understanding in his eyes, and extended his hand toward me, an unspoken invitation to join him in the warmth of the firelight. He took a step closer to me as I approached, his hand still extended, voice low and gentle. "Aundrea, you look beautiful. Did you sleep okay?" His finger brushed against mine as I placed my hand in his. It was like starlight had kissed every nerve. "I think so, husband, but I'm not feeling very good."

He closed the gap between us, his voice low but gentle, "Last night… we did not finish our conversation. I was hoping with a good night's sleep we could talk about it." He led me closer to the fire, the comfort enveloping us as he turned to face me fully. "Aundrea, we cannot build our relationship on secrets, and it kills me to think that whatever is bothering you is eating you from the inside out." His hand gently stroked the back of my hand, his eyes burning with intensity. "Do you feel ready to face this fire with me, my love…?"

Suddenly, a soft voice interrupted from behind us. I turned to look. "Your Highness, breakfast is ready… would you like it here or in your tent?" It was Michelle, my loyal servant. She had arrived with a group of new guards sometime in the middle of the night.

Jasino's gaze never left mine. I squeezed his hand gently. "Yes, Michelle, bring it here but give us a moment." Michelle curtsied and backed away, a discreet smile on her face. "As you wish, Your Highness."

Jasino watched her leave, then turned back to me, his eyes still burning with intensity. "Alone again… finally." He gently put his hand under my chin, lifting me out of a soul-crushing thought. "Where were we, my love?" He handed me a steaming cup of coffee and continued, "Ah yes… secrets." His thumb continued stroking my hand. "You were about to tell me… or at least, I hoped you were." He paused, studying my face. "Your eyes still hold a thousand unspoken words, Aundrea. What are you afraid to say?"

Suddenly, his expression softened further. "Is it something that could change everything between us?"

Tears welled up in my eyes, blurring my vision. "Yes!" I choked out, my voice thick with emotion. Sobs wracked my body, each one a painful reminder of the secrets I held within.

He gently placed his hand on my shoulder, his touch a silent offering of comfort. I looked up into his eyes, searching for reassurance but finding only my own fear reflected back at me. "I'm afraid you're going to be so angry at me that you'll leave, or... you'll hurt me. I'm frightened."

Jasino's eyes softened, his gaze filled with curiosity and unwavering assurance. "There's nothing you can say to me, my love, that would make me hurt you. I've never hurt you before. Why would you ever think I would do that to you? There is nothing that could ever make me leave your side. My love burns for you."

My fear wasn't rooted in him—it was rooted in the past. In the way my father had treated my mother. In the way love had once looked like control, and tenderness had always come with pain. That history clung to me like a shadow, twisting what I felt, poisoning what I trusted. Even now, in the arms of someone who had never hurt me, I couldn't always tell the difference between safety and threat. Between love and fear.

I looked away for just a moment to collect my thoughts, then returned to his eyes again. Tears streamed into the cup of coffee I held in my trembling hands. I sniffled, wiping away the ones that clung to my cheeks. "I know I have to tell you," I said, my voice laced with desperation. "It's just so hard. There's something else that I'm afraid of, which makes it even harder."

Just then, Michelle approached, carrying two trays laden with food. Though I knew I should be hungry, the sight of it turned my stomach. My husband gestured for her to place the trays on the table behind us. Michelle bowed gracefully and retreated, leaving us once more in our fragile bubble of intimacy. A couple of guards began to walk toward us, but my husband subtly waved them away, signaling our need for privacy. They obeyed, their footsteps fading into the background.

"Aundrea," my husband tilted my chin once again, forcing me to meet his gaze. "It's time. I need to know, and I cannot allow you to continue tearing yourself up inside. Just tell me."

I closed my eyes for a brief moment, gathering the courage, then sniffed and wiped away a final tear. "Husband," I began, my voice trembling, "the day after the ball, in our bedchambers... I slept with your brother."

Fresh tears poured down my face, each one carrying the weight of my shame and regret. "I thought he was you. We were just together, and I thought you came back to me. He had no scar above his eye. He tricked me. I didn't know how to tell you...can you ever forgive me?"

As the words left my lips, I saw a change come over Jasino. Whatever affection had flickered there vanished, leaving only a frostbitten stare. Lines of age seemed to etch themselves into his face, his skin becoming gaunt and pale. A wave of fear washed over me. I backed away from him slowly, dropping my cup to the ground, my body trembling uncontrollably.

Jasino's face remained frozen in shock, his eyes wide with a mix of horror and betrayal. Time seemed to stand still as he processed my words, his chest barely rising with slow, deliberate breaths. Then, his gaze dropped to the ground, where my cup lay shattered, coffee spilled everywhere. A perfect reflection of his shattered trust. His voice, when it finally came, was low and frighteningly calm. "Aundrea, my wife…" He paused, swallowing hard as if choking back emotions. "You slept with my brother?"

Fear consumed my body as he took a step closer to me. "Ravon, my… my brother." Jasino's eyes wide with horror, he takes a step back, as if physically recoiling from my words. "Aundrea, no… this cannot be happening." He paused, struggling to compose himself. "You told me that there was another devastating secret… You slept with my brother thinking he was me... Are you…" He looked at me in the moment, unable to look away. "Are you…with child?"

My heart left my body for a moment, and I was unable to speak.

My mind was shattered. My heart was dead. He stood tall, eyes blazing with intensity. "Tell me Aundrea, do you still love me? Or has Ravon's deception destroyed that love too?"

"No, Jasino!" I cried, my voice cracking with a sob that wracked my body. My hands flew to my face, attempting to shield him—and myself—from the raw emotion spilling out of me. "I don't love Ravon! It's you I love." But even as the words escaped, a treacherous whisper echoed in my heart, a secret I dared not utter. His kiss, … I hadn't pulled away. For one breathless moment, I had leaned in, craving something I didn't understand, something forbidden.

It was true; a flicker of something had stirred within me for Ravon. Yet, it was a mere shadow compared to the blazing inferno of my love for my husband—fleeting, a momentary lapse that left me drowning in guilt. How could

I confess such a betrayal, however unintentional? Especially after Ravon's vile actions. I hated him… or did I?

Stumbling backward, I nearly fell, my foot catching on the uneven ground. I reached out blindly, grasping the edge of a nearby table, knocking both trays of food to the ground below. Finding my footing, tears consumed me, blurring my vision as I looked at my husband. A primal urge to flee overwhelmed me, and I turned and ran. I did not know where I was going, passing several guards, left astonished and daring not to interfere as Jasino followed close behind.

Blindly I ran through the trees, jumping over logs and dense brush. Each step was fueled by a desperate need to outrun the pain, the confusion, the shame. Bursting from the trees, I found myself in Firefly Valley. Still I ran, as fast as I could, oblivious of my surroundings. I could hear the sound of my husband's desperate cries behind me. Jasino's voice echoed through Firefly Valley, his words torn apart by anguish. "AUNDREA! MY LOVE! COME BACK TO ME!"

His footsteps pounded the ground behind me, gaining speed as he chased after my fleeing form. "No matter what secrets you've hidden… NO MATTER WHAT RAVON DID... MY LOVE FOR YOU REMAINS UNBROKEN!" He burst into a clearing, his chest heaving with exertion, eyes scanning wildly until they locked on mine as I looked back at him.

"Aundrea… stop. Please… talk to me." His voice cracked as he took slow steps closer, hands outstretched, palms up.
I stopped, throwing my hands over my swollen face, as if trying to shield my shame.
"I've faced wars, battles, enemies… even my brother's evil.

But losing you—that's the only defeat I fear." He dropped to his knees in the soft valley grass, eyes pleading. "Tell me… is there still a chance for us to be happy together?"

Still gasping to catch my breath, I fell to the ground, my tear-filled eyes scanning the glowing valley. There were fireflies everywhere, surrounding us but parting to make room for us in their circle of light. My hands, clasped tightly together in my lap, trembled uncontrollably, mirroring the turmoil within, barely holding my body upright under the weight of my guilt and despair. I couldn't bear to meet his gaze; couldn't face the pain I knew I was inflicting upon him.

Summoning a sliver of strength, I forced myself to meet his eyes. Apology swelled in my throat, thick and aching. Guilt coiled through every breath as questions tore at my spirit—how could someone as broken as I had become be chosen as the Divine One? How could I claim to fulfill a prophecy when I had betrayed the very man I loved most? The words spun like thorns in my chest. I wasn't worthy of him. I couldn't be who they believed I was. Not after this.

In the distance, along the tree line, the royal guards began to assemble, forming a respectful perimeter around us. Their silent presence was a stark reminder of who we were—who I was supposed to be. But instead of comfort, their watchful stillness only deepened the shame burning in my chest. I had humiliated him in front of them all. The weight of it pressed down on me, heavy and suffocating. I didn't feel divine. I didn't even feel worthy to stand at his side.

Jasino's face contorted in agony as he watched me collapse. He scrambled to my side, still on his knees, gathering me into his arms as if holding together shattered pieces of his own heart. "No, Aundrea, my love… don't say such things."

His lips brushed against my forehead, tears streaming down his face as he whispered, "You are the Divine One. The prophecy chose you because of your heart… not despite your flaws, but because of them."

His voice faltered as he drew me into his embrace, the weight of his emotions trembling beneath each breath. The warmth of his hold told me more than words—he saw in me a heart still capable of love, of forgiveness, of feeling deeply… and to him, that was my worth.

His fingers lifted my chin gently, guiding my gaze to his. In his eyes, a fierce intensity burned—not of anger, but of truth. Ravon had not just betrayed me; he had betrayed him. And through all the deception, my heart had never truly left the one it belonged to.

Then, like a veil falling away, his expression shifted, revealing a vulnerability so raw it nearly unraveled me. This wasn't just about destiny or prophecy. It was about fear—his fear of losing me not to fate, but to a world where our hearts no longer beat in unison. He clung to me not with desperation, but with the quiet ache of a man who knew that without me, his soul might not endure.

I held my breath as the next secret clawed its way to the surface. Ravon had pulled me into his arms and kissed me—right after the wolf attacked. That moment had haunted me ever since. The guilt twisted deep within me, but the thought of hurting Jasino any more than I already had was unbearable. So I left it at a truth he already knew, swallowing the rest like poison. I hadn't pulled away. I had leaned in. Just for a moment… but long enough to know that something inside me had responded. And that truth, however fleeting, was almost too heavy to bear.

The guards remained frozen in respectful silence, witnessing our intimate moment…

My sobs began to quiet, the storm of anguish giving way to a trembling stillness as I searched his eyes for the truth I so desperately needed. In that gaze, I found no hesitation—only sincerity, unwavering and raw. His arms wrapped around me, strong yet tender, anchoring me to the moment. I buried my face in his chest, where the steady beat of his heart calmed the ache in mine. He held me as though I were made of fragile glass, one hand gently stroking my hair in comforting rhythm. There was no need for words—his love enveloped me, an unspoken vow that even betrayal and prophecy would not sever our bond. He pressed a kiss to my forehead, a silent promise that healing would come, and that whatever darkness Ravon had unleashed, we would face it together.

I spoke, my voice barely rose above a whisper. "What if… what if I'm carrying his child? Will you still want me?"

Jasino's body tensed in my arms, the sharp intake of his breath cutting through the stillness like a blade. For a moment, he said nothing—only held me tighter, as if anchoring himself in the storm. Then, slowly, he exhaled and drew back just enough to look at me. There was anguish in the depths of his expression, but beneath it burned a fierce, unyielding devotion that reached for me like a flame desperate not to be extinguished.

"Aundrea… if you are carrying his child, I will still want you. But the question is…" his voice dropped, rough with vulnerability, "will you still want me?"

My tears streamed freely now, blurring the edges of the world as I nodded, voice shaking. "Always, Jasino. My love for you has never wavered."

Even as the words left my lips, something twisted inside me—a fire of guilt too hot to contain. I wasn't the kind of woman who could mask the truth behind comfort. Not even for him.

I gently pulled away, his arms loosening without resistance. Sitting upright, I folded my trembling hands into my lap, the chill of honesty settling over me. I had spoken the truth of my heart—but not the whole of it. Not yet.

"Husband, I do love you with all my heart. I don't want you to think anything different, but I have something else I need to tell you. I cannot live with the guilt." Jasino's eyes locked onto mine, a mixture of relief and apprehension swimming within them as he gently wiped the lingering tears from my cheeks. His voice was low and husky. "What is it, my love? You've already confessed the unthinkable to me… what could possibly be worse than Ravon's deception, his assault on my wife or the possibility of his child."

His grip on my hands tightens slightly, as if bracing himself for another blow. "Tell me, Aundrea. Free yourself from the guilt. I swear on my crown, my honor as a warrior… and on my love for you, that my heart will remain unchanged." He leaned in closer, his breath whispering against my skin. "Is it… something about Ravon? Did he stir something in you that still lingers?"

My heart skipped a beat as I realized he was closer to the truth than I wanted him to be. My face burned with shame as I gave the slightest nod. I pulled my hands free and covered my mouth, as if I could trap the confession before it escaped. But it trembled at the edges, begging to break free.

Jasino watched me, the hope in his eyes dimming with each passing heartbeat. I could feel his world crumbling under the weight of my silence. He stepped closer, gripping my arms, his voice low and shaking. The question he did not want to ask hung in the air between us.

I turned away, pressing a hand to my forehead, unable to meet his gaze. His grip loosened, then shifted— one hand wrapping around mine again, desperate for clarity.

And still, the words came like a storm. Not in full sentences, but in fragments torn from the chaos inside me. I didn't know what I felt. Or maybe I did, but couldn't bear to name it.

A scream tore from my throat. It wasn't just an answer—it was everything. The shame, the confusion, the unbearable tension that had coiled inside me.

Something dark had been stirred deep inside—a force so compelling it clouded my thoughts and blurred the lines between truth and manipulation. Ravon's voice, his promises, still lingered in my ears like a curse. He whispered poison about Jasino just as often as Jasino had warned me of his lies. Each voice trying to rewrite the truth of my heart.

And worst of all… I still felt something. Not love, not exactly—but a tether I hadn't yet cut. It made me sick, made me weep even as I admitted it. I didn't forgive him for the horrors he'd inflicted. I couldn't. But that did not undo the damage. He had twisted my will, ensnared my feelings, and led me into choices I never would have made of my own accord.

And now, standing before my husband, I felt the full weight of that betrayal pressing down on me—body, heart, and soul.

My sobs intensified, wracking my body with each convulsive breath. Despite the chaos within, a flicker of clarity emerged, guiding me toward the only choice that felt right.

"My husband," I pleaded, my voice barely able to function.

"Despite the shadows he left in me, despite the life I might carry, my heart is yours. Tell me I haven't lost you… please." The words hung in the air, heavy with desperation and hope, as I waited for his response, my fate hanging in the balance.

The weight of everything crashed into him at once. Grief and relief twisted across his face, his shoulders trembling as he braced himself against the ground. When he finally looked up at me, there was no armor, no mask—only raw, unguarded emotion.

He reached for me, hands resting at my hips, forehead pressing into my stomach as if grounding himself in my presence. His tears warmed my skin, a wordless confession pouring from him with every shaking breath. I felt his anguish, his need, his gratitude—for my choice, for my love, for surviving everything that had tried to tear us apart.

When he finally met my gaze, the fire in his eyes wasn't just love—it was a vow.

I cupped his face, wiping the tears from his cheeks, then pulled him into a kiss—deep and steady, arms circling his neck like a lifeline. He wrapped his arms around my waist and lowered me gently onto the soft grass, as if afraid I'd shatter.

Above me, his voice broke through the quiet. A low promise carried on the wind: Ravon would pay. For everything. Our lips met again, this time with desperate passion, sealing that vow with fire.

Then he stood and helped me to my feet, his hand never leaving mine. The guards waited at the edge of the trees, silent and still.

***

"We need to find Lyra," he said, his voice low but steady. "She'll know if you carry a child."

I hesitated, unsure. "Isn't it too soon to tell?"

He stopped, turning to me with certainty etched in every word. "Not for Lyra, my love."

As we reached the edge of the trees, a sudden wave of nausea overwhelmed me. I broke free from Jasino's embrace, dropped to my knees, and braced myself against the soil. Dry heaves racked my body until a bitter stream rose from the hollowness within me, splattering the forest floor. There was nothing left to bring up—only bile and sorrow. The retching came in waves, fierce and punishing, as if my body was purging more than just sickness. I trembled, breathless and raw, my hand instinctively pressing against my stomach—half in fear, half in desperate protection.

This was the third time, a cruel reminder of the possibility of life growing within me. I looked up towards Jasino, my eyes searching for reassurance, for answers. "I believe you are with child, my love." He let out a small giggle, kneeling on one knee placing his hand on my back. As I held my position waiting for more to come, I could feel my husband's hand softly rubbing my back. I sat down on my knees, feet behind and gathered myself. My husband stretched his arm out offering his hand and helping me to my feet.

We continued walking back to the camp and he put his arm around me. I looked towards him while continuing our pace. "I am hungry, Husband. I still haven't eaten anything today."

My husband let out a soft chuckle, his voice low and husky. "That, my love, is how I know you are with child. If you were simply ill, food wouldn't be the first thing on your mind."

I laughed lightly as we entered the camp. My husband signaled for Michelle, who hurried toward us.

"Please prepare something to eat—my wife is hungry," he said with a playful but warm authority.

Michelle curtsied and stepped away to fulfill the request. Jasino then took my hand again and said, "In the meantime, let's go see Lyra."

We walked toward the healer's tent, and he gently nudged me through the flap. Inside, Lyra sat at a table. Jasino pulled out a chair for me, and I eagerly slid into it. He sat beside me, taking a deep breath before speaking.

"Lyra, I believe my wife is with child. Can you confirm if she carries a child within her?"

I glanced nervously at Jasino and Lyra. She offered a tender, reassuring smile.
"It's a pleasure to finally meet you, milady," she said gently. "I've heard much about you."

Her eyes widened slightly as she reached for my hand, then turned to a nearby shelf to retrieve a small bottle of herbs. "I'm not just a healer," she added as she selected a vial containing a thick black substance. "I've begun training in the mage arts—still early in my journey, but the Gods have been generous."

She gently wiped the balm across my forehead, its scent sharp and herbal. Then she took my other hand between hers, and her palms began to glow with a soft warmth. She looked skyward, silently calling upon the Gods.

A comforting heat spread through my body. She was a healer like me, yet older—wiser—with centuries of knowledge woven into her touch. But beyond her healing, I sensed the flicker of something raw and untamed: the quiet force of elemental magic still learning to bend to her will.

Slowly, Lyra opened her eyes, returning to the present. She looked first at Jasino, then at me.

"Milady," she said gently, "congratulations. You are with child."

A single tear welled in my already-swollen eyes. My mind swirled with thoughts of the uncertain future. Jasino's voice trembled slightly as he spoke. "Is the child mine, or…" He stopped, unable to finish the question. Lyra's expression showed mild surprise. "The stars whisper many secrets, Your Highness, but that one remains beyond my grasp… for now."

Jasino stood gently, taking my hand and helping me to my feet. As we exited the tent, he turned back for one final word. "Nothing spoken here today will ever pass your lips, Lyra."

She gave a solemn nod and a gentle smile. "Of course, Your Highness."

Jasino escorted me to a nearby table, where a small feast had been laid out. I sat down, and he joined me. We ate in silence, the weight of our thoughts settling heavily between us.

After just a heartbeat, Sabion approached. "Your Highness, once you've finished your meal, we should continue our journey. We still have a few days ahead of us, and the daylight is fading."

Jasino nodded. When we finished eating, I walked slowly around the camp, my hand resting lightly on my belly while the others prepared for our departure. What a cruel pain I carried within me. A life was growing inside of me… and I feared the possibility that it was Ravon's child.

What would this mean for my future? And for the future of my child?

Chapter 7

The Lake within the Lie

The soft glow of Firefly Valley wrapped around us as we rode through its heart, tiny lights flickering like stars brought down to Lisona. Their gentle dance should have brought me peace—perhaps even a sense of homecoming. Instead, it only deepened the ache in my chest. I leaned into the warmth of Jasino's hand as it closed around mine, steady and reassuring.

He studied me for a breath, as if reading something between the lines of my silence, concern softening his features. "The fireflies seem to be welcoming us home," he murmured, his voice like a balm against the ache I carried.

I managed a faint smile, more out of gratitude than ease. He could still see it—the residue of pain I hadn't yet shaken, not from secrets, but from the sheer weight of what we'd survived. And yet, he didn't press. His hand stayed with mine, a silent vow that we would face whatever came next—together.

"Is everything well, my love?" he asked, his voice low and probing. "You've been distant since dinner."

My mind raced with fear I'd barely dared to think aloud. Does this life belong to the man I love… or the monster who violated me. Ravon's twisted words still echoed in my mind like a haunting curse. I glanced around at the terrain, the fireflies' twinkling lights mocking my inner darkness. Michelle rode behind us, chatting quietly with Sabion, oblivious to my silent struggle.

The memory of Ravon's encounter weighed heavily on my heart, stirring up a mix of fear and anxiety. The possibility that he could be the father of my unborn child haunted me. My love for Jasino was boundless, and I yearned for the child to be his. But the uncertainty surrounding the child I carried cast a shadow over my joy, muddling hope with fear.

As I grappled with these thoughts, a wave of terror washed over me—not just for my own life, but for my unborn child as well. Suddenly, a surge of nausea gripped my body, demanding my attention. Instinctively, I pulled back on the reins, halting Vandros in his tracks. Leaning as far to the right as I could, I succumbed to the queasiness, my body convulsing with each wave of sickness.

In an instant, Jasino dismounted with agility, concern etched on his face. His presence was a comforting reassurance amidst the turmoil within me.

"My love, what's wrong?" Jasino's voice was laced with alarm as he reached up to support my waist, holding me steady against the horse. I felt tears prick at the corners of my eyes as another wave of nausea overtook me. Michelle and Sabion reined in their horses behind us, their faces etched with worry.

Jasino gently helped me down from the horse, leading me a few steps away to a small clearing surrounded by fireflies, still glowing innocently around us. He supported my forehead as I bent over, his other hand rubbing soothing circles on my back.

"Aundrea, speak to me… is it the baby?" His voice trembled slightly, revealing his deep concern.

I nodded weakly between gasps for air, still trying to catch my breath after the intense sickness. As I stood up straight, I was filled with a mix of fear and love.

"Do you think… could something be wrong?" he whispered.

Hesitating for just a moment before answering, I gained control over the lingering nausea and looked up at my concerned husband. "It's alright, Jasino. Just morning sickness, that's all."

I managed to make a weak smile as I slowly straightened, steadying myself. At that moment, Michelle rode her horse closer, offering a loaf of freshly baked bread—a remedy known to soothe the stomach.

Jasino, ever attentive, stepped forward, accepting the bread from her hand with gratitude. Michelle returned to Sabion's side as Jasino broke off a piece of warm bread and handed it to me with tender care.

"Here, my love, eat this. It will make you feel better."

I took a bite, and the comforting taste and aroma worked their magic, calming the queasiness within.

Once I had finished, Jasino signaled to Sabion for another mount, then gently helped me onto the horse. After making sure I was secure, he mounted Vandros and took up the reins, riding close beside me."

"In case you feel sick again, my love, we'll ride next to each other…" I nodded with approval.

***

We rode for hours, the serene landscape undisturbed, until Sabion suggested we find a suitable place to camp for the night. After another hour of riding, my husband, ever the vigilant protector, rode ahead to scout the area, leaving me in the company of Sabion and the guards.

He soon returned with news of a perfect spot nestled amidst the trees, ideal for setting up camp. The night passed uneventfully, and after a satisfying dinner, I drifted off to sleep in Jasino's strong, protective arms, feeling safe and cherished.

***

When I awoke the following morning, Michelle brought breakfast to the tent, but the scent of the meat on the tray immediately triggered a wave of nausea. Jasino, noticing my discomfort, waved off the tray and gently instructed her to bring fresh fruit and sweet bread instead, explaining that it would be better for the baby if I could keep the food down. After a light breakfast, and with everyone packed and ready to depart, Jasino helped me onto my horse with his usual care and attentiveness.

As we continued our journey, Firefly Valley began to give way to a denser, more verdant landscape, with trees and shrubs enveloping us on all sides. We stopped briefly at a stream, where Sabion signaled for us to follow him. With his exceptional tracking abilities, he led us through the dense foliage until we emerged into a breathtaking clearing, revealing a beautiful lake shimmering in the sunlight.

The sun hung low in the sky when Jasino, ever attentive to my condition, insisted I take my rest. He carefully selected a spot amidst the trees, close to the lake, to set up camp for the night. Once everything was arranged, he suggested that Michelle and I take the opportunity to bathe in the lake—a refreshing respite after our long journey. He led us through the thick brush, his eyes constantly scanning the surroundings for any signs of danger.

When we reached the edge of the lake, he gently placed my bag on the ground and turned to me, his voice filled with love and concern. "My love, I'm going to leave you here with Michelle so that you can bathe. I'll return to the camp and keep a close watch on the perimeter, ensuring your safety. If you need any help, just call out. I'm close enough to hear you. I love you."

He leaned in and captured my lips in a long, passionate kiss, his hand gently cradling the back of my head, before turning and heading back to the camp, leaving Michelle and me to enjoy the tranquility of the lake.

Michelle smiled warmly as we watched Jasino disappear into the dense foliage. "He's always so attentive to your needs, Aundrea. You're truly blessed."

I returned her smile, feeling grateful for Jasino's love, but my mind wandered back to the unspoken fears lingering within me.

The lake's gentle waves lapping against the shore created a soothing melody as Michelle began to undress. I followed suit, my eyes scanning the surrounding trees instinctively—a habit formed from past encounters with danger. As we waded into the cool water, Michelle chatted with me about a crush she had. We laughed and giggled for a moment until I teased, "Who is it, Michelle?"

"Sabion, she giggled, I think he is so brave and brilliant and handsome…"

I cut her off with a laugh, supportive but playful. Then I went silent as emotion flooded my mind.

"Aundrea, is everything okay? You've seemed distant lately…"

My heart skipped a beat as I hesitated, unsure if I should confide in my friend. Michelle's concerned eyes locked onto mine—open, inviting trust. I took a deep breath, the lake's serene surface was a stark contrast to the turmoil inside me.

"Michelle… there's something I need to tell you. And it might change everything." My voice dropped, barely above a whisper as I pressed on. "Before I made it back to camp—when the wolf was chasing me—Ravon found me. He saved my life. And… he kissed me." She interrupted. "You cannot trust Ravon, Aundrea."

I looked at her, my emotions a tangled knot I couldn't unravel, then lowered my gaze to the reflection staring back at me from the still surface of the water. She doesn't know everything.

There was more—so much more.

The memory clawed its way to the front of my mind. The morning after the ball… when Michelle had been brushing my hair, unaware of what I was about to endure. It hadn't been Jasino who slipped into my bedchamber.

It had been Ravon.

That fevered afternoon had unfolded in a blur of deception and shadows. I had been wrapped in his arms, lost in a haze I hadn't understood until it was too late. It wasn't my husband between the sheets. It was Ravon who violated me—who left me shattered, stripped of my dignity, and cloaked in shame I hadn't yet found the strength to fully name.

Tears welled in my eyes, blurring the forest around me as I recounted the tale to Michelle. She leaned forward, drawing me into a comforting embrace.

"Sweet Aundrea," she whispered. "It wasn't your fault. He tricked you; he tricked us both. I thought he was Jasino as well." She paused; her voice laced with sorrow.

"Your husband loves you. He will never blame you for his brother's evil."

* * *

Michelle gently wiped away my tears, offering a fragile moment of solace—but it shattered with the sharp crack of snapping twigs behind us. Ravon stepped into the clearing, his presence slicing through the stillness like a blade. He turned toward the camp and raised his hand. A beam of violet light burst from his palm, scorching the air. Chaos ignited. Screams rang out as his dark followers descended in a frenzy of violence—an orchestrated diversion to keep the guards occupied while he came for me. Ravon's gaze locked onto mine, and I froze, paralyzed by fear. As I choked out a desperate cry for my husband, Ravon's voice cut through the air, laced with cruel amusement.

"My dear Aundrea, unless you want me to kill my brother right now, I suggest you do not call out for him again."

His words hung in the air—a chilling promise of the devastation he was capable of unleashing.

Michelle's arms tightened around me, but I pushed her away, my eyes fixed on Ravon's menacing figure across the lake. His purple glow illuminated the surrounding trees, casting an eerie light on the chaos unfolding behind him.

Jasino's voice echoed through the forest, clashing with Ravon's evil tone. "AUNDREA!"

But Ravon's threat hung like a dagger over his brother's life.

I felt Michelle grab my hand, her grip desperate as she whispered, "Don't go to him, Aundrea!"

But Ravon's words had already enslaved me with fear; fear for Jasino's life, and fear for my unborn child.

Slowly, as if trapped in a nightmare, I began to wade toward Ravon through the lake's calm water, now a terrifying pathway to doom.

Ravon's cruel smile spread across his face as he held out his hand, beckoning me closer. "Come, Aundrea. Let us resolve this family matter alone." I felt an unnatural pull like a doll being drawn with strings.

Michelle's panicked cry followed me. "Aundrea, NOOO!"

But I was already under his control. I had my mind, but my body was like a puppet moving to his whim. I emerged from the water, my bare skin exposed to Ravon's intense gaze. He removed his cloak, draping it around me with a possessive gesture. I felt control return to my body as I began to quiver with uncontrollable fear.

He leaned in, his lips hovering tantalizingly close; yet holding back.

"I don't want to make you love me, Aundrea," he murmured, his voice a transparent threat, "but I will have you." Michelle was desperate to reach me, wading through the water, but Ravon reacted with terrifying speed. With a flick of his hand, she was suspended mid-step, frozen in place, encased in a swirling purple haze of dark magic. Her naked body was exposed, her voice silenced, her eyes wide with horror.

"Please, don't hurt her, Ravon," I begged, tears streaming down my face. "She is my best friend, and I love her."

His sinister voice cut through my pleas. "Then I suggest you listen to me, Aundrea."

I nodded, the weight of my powerlessness crushing me.

"Aundrea, you are mine."

His voice curled around me like smoke as he cupped my face, drawing me closer. Lips brushed my forehead, then hovered at my mouth before he kissed me— long, possessive, and burning with twisted affection. My knees weakened beneath the weight of it. Anguish and guilt warred within me, but I didn't pull away. A forbidden longing stirred in my chest, rising like a tide I neither fought nor welcomed. I leaned into him, hands slipping up to his shoulders, trembling.

But then—he stopped.

Ravon drew back, eyes widening in stunned recognition. His gaze dropped to my abdomen, and a low, delighted murmur escaped him: You are with child, my love.

A cruel smile crept across his face, stretching into something monstrous. He laughed, the sound cold and triumphant as it echoed over the water.

In his mind, the child was his.

He spoke of ruling Lisona, of heirs and thrones, already claiming what I hadn't even accepted myself. My terror spilled out like a wave, and for the first time, he hesitated. A flicker of uncertainty crossed his features, as if my fear might harm what now belonged to him.

Then his voice returned, laced with both promise and threat. "I will come for you soon… you will join me. Not today. But I will return—for you, and for our child."

His hand hovered over my stomach—his touch not tender, but possessive. Obsessive. As if he had already bound us together in a fate I hadn't chosen.

And then he vanished, leaving behind only the chilling echo of his vow.

As the haze around Michelle faded, silence settled over the trees. She ran to our bags and pulled out a towel, quickly wrapping it around her trembling body. I remained motionless, still cloaked in Ravon's garment, tears slipping silently down my cheeks as the weight of it all pressed down on me.

***

Suddenly, the underbrush rustled. My husband emerged from the trees, flanked by Sabion and several guards, their faces tense and battle-worn. They had broken free—at last.

Jasino's eyes found mine. "My love…" His voice cracked as he rushed toward me, gaze flicking over my face, then down to the cloak that still clung to my shoulders. Fury and heartbreak collided in his expression.

Sabion and the guards quickly closed in, forming a protective ring around us, hands resting on their hilts. Michelle clung to me, her tear-filled eyes wide with confusion and pain.

"Your Highness… he used dark magic," she whispered.

Jasino approached slowly, his voice low and trembling. "Aundrea, my love… what happened?"

I felt like I was breaking apart. I reached for him, trembling. He caught my hand, his touch igniting a sob from deep within me.

"I'm going to kill him," he growled.

A chilling dread crept through me. Without the Dragon Stone or the Seer, Jasino was vulnerable.

"Jasino," I said, choking on my tears. "Ravon… he knows about the baby. He believes the child is his."

The confession shattered something in both of us. Jasino's reaction was swift and fierce. He barked a command to the guards, who spun to form a tighter circle, turning their backs to us. His jealousy burned hot, eclipsing everything else. He tore Ravon's cloak from my shoulders and flung it to the ground, then draped his own cloak around me, as if to erase Ravon's touch.

The discarded garment lay there—a symbol of Ravon's intrusion.

"What happened, Aundrea? Did he…" He couldn't even finish the question.

I met his gaze, shame twisting in my stomach. "He kissed me… but nothing more," I whispered, my eyes on the ground.

"I felt like a puppet being drawn in," I whispered again, "then he released me. What has he done to me?"

Michelle stepped forward. "It wasn't her fault, Your Grace—she—"

Jasino lifted a hand, silencing her without looking away from me. His eyes pierced through me, demanding answers I wasn't ready to give. Jasino's questions hung in the air, "Did you feel anything for him? Did you pull away?"

The weight of it crushed my chest. My heart pounded like a drum of guilt. I swallowed hard, but the truth refused to stay buried. Tears streamed freely down my cheeks as a single, damning truth took shape within me—I had felt something. Just a flicker, a moment—but it was enough to unravel everything.

Jasino's expression twisted with pain. He stepped back, as though my silence alone had wounded him. Behind me, Michelle began to sob, her anguish folding into mine, but I couldn't turn away from him. Couldn't breathe. Couldn't fix what had already shattered.

With pain flickering in his eyes, he breathed the words like a final hope—"Do you still love me?"

I froze. No words would come. No answer could undo the damage.

He needed something—anything.

But all I could offer was the truth written in my actions. I dropped to my knees before him, hands trembling as they reached out—not in apology, but in surrender.

"Yes… I love YOU," I cried, my sobs tearing free. I crawled to him, clinging to his feet. "Forgive me, my love. I was weak… blinded by fear and deceit. You are everything. My protector. My soulmate."

He stood frozen, trembling with the weight of everything. Slowly, his hands reached for me, lifting my face.

"No," he said, his voice thick with emotion. His grip was firm as he pulled me up. "You are my wife. You do not belong at my feet. Ever!"

He lifted my chin, forcing me to meet the anguish in his eyes. The unspoken truth was etched across his face—I had betrayed him. Pain clung to every breath he took, but beneath it, something fierce and unwavering still remained. Love. Raw and burning, tangled with fury.

Then his attention shifted to Michelle. The change in his posture was sharp, his authority sudden and cold. Without a word, the command was clear—this moment was over. We were to dress and prepare ourselves.

Michelle bowed her head and quietly obeyed, pulling her clothes back on. I reached for my own garments, fumbling through tears, my fingers clumsy as I tried to gather the fabric. Sobs spilled from me as I struggled to cover myself, shame wrapping tighter with every motion.

Jasino turned back to me, his expression softer, but fire still burning in his eyes.

"When we get back to camp, you'll eat. Then you'll rest. You have more to think about than yourself now, Aundrea. You have our child growing inside you." I nodded, my body still trembling from the encounter with Ravon. A swirl of guilt and conflict tore through me. I knew, deep down, that I was vulnerable when alone with him—but my heart belonged solely to Jasino.

His anger was a tangible thing, simmering beneath the surface like a storm barely restrained. He needed me to understand that I had crossed a line, that my actions had consequences. I knew he would never stop loving me, never stop fighting for me—but he would make certain I understood the gravity of my failure. He did not blame me for Ravon's actions, but he did hold me accountable for my own.

Tears continued to fall like rain as Jasino's gaze bore into my soul. His fury pulsed with every heartbeat. He saw the difference between Ravon's violation and my response—and it was the latter that wounded him most.

"You betrayed me," his words still echoed in my mind, hollow and devastating.

My heart was heavy with shame, I reached out and placed my trembling hand against his chest, my palm pressed flat against his armor. "Jasino, I understand... I crossed a line. But my heart still belongs to you."

He covered my hand with his own, his grip tight—a blend of possession and restraint. "We will speak of this when we are alone, Aundrea."

Michelle now stood beside me, fully dressed. Sabion and the guards waited in silence behind her. I wrapped both arms around Jasino's, leaning my head gently against his shoulder, hoping to feel even a shred of forgiveness.

He pulled slightly away, though his fingers still held mine. His rejection wasn't harsh—just tense, distant. The air between us was thick with hurt.

Michelle fell into step behind us. Sabion and the guards formed a protective barrier as we moved. Only the crunch of gravel and leaves beneath our feet filled the silence. I dared not look up at Jasino, afraid of what I might see in his eyes.

***

As we neared camp, the comforting scent of roasting meat and fresh bread drifted in the air. Jasino released my hand and spoke in low tones to Sabion, instructing him to increase patrols tonight. His eyes flicked to mine for just a moment—brief, unreadable.

Michelle brushed my arm gently, whispering, "Are you okay?"

I gave a small nod, still avoiding eye contact with Jasino.

He turned toward me again, his voice firm and commanding. "Aundrea, go to our tent. Eat something. Then rest. We will talk soon."

I nodded wordlessly and walked toward our tent, the soft fabric rustling as I stepped inside. Michelle followed, helping me ease onto the furs and plush blankets spread out across the floor. She handed me a steaming bowl of broth and a small piece of bread, but my stomach churned at the sight.

"Aundrea," Michelle said softly, "try to eat. For the baby's sake… if not for yours."

I took a sip of the broth. The warmth slid down my throat and into my chest, soothing me just enough to break off a small piece of bread. Another sip followed. Michelle sat quietly beside me, her hand holding mine until I gently squeezed it—asking her for space.

I continued eating. The bowl was half-empty, a little bread gone, when I finally pulled the blankets closer and curled in on myself. Knees bent, arms wrapped around them, I rocked gently, whispering into the darkness, "What have I done? What if Jasino never forgives me?"

The tent flap rustled.

A single candle slipped through the opening, its glow soft and low. Then came Jasino's voice—low, gravelly, familiar. I looked up, meeting his eyes with my own, raw from crying, and gave a small nod.

Tears slipped down my cheeks again, a quiet cry catching in my throat as he stepped inside. He sat beside me, his presence heavy with emotion. His eyes searched mine, and though he said little, I could feel the storm inside him.

He was angry—betrayed. The hurt lingered in every breath he took. Forgiveness wouldn't come easily, and I knew that. But love still lived in him. He hadn't abandoned me.

I sobbed again, quieter this time, clinging to each silent message between us. He lay back on the bed of furs and extended his arm without a word.

I crawled toward him, slowly, cautiously, and curled into his chest, letting the steady beat of his heart ground me. My voice cracked under the weight of everything I carried as I whispered my sorrow—words he barely needed to hear. I loved him. That much had never changed.

Jasino said nothing, but I knew he heard me. Despite the turmoil, despite the betrayal, he knew my love for him remained. But I also knew he would never rest—not until Ravon was gone. He would journey to the cave, seek the Seer, and find the second Dragon Stone if it meant protecting our love. Our future depended on it.

He kissed the top of my head—passion and desperation wrapped into a single touch.

"Sleep, my love," he whispered. "I won't let my anger make you fear losing me." He kissed me again, his arm pulling me tight, strong and protective around me. Though his anger still simmered, he would not let it control him. I closed my eyes, tears still leaking as I drifted toward sleep, listening to the rhythm of his heart. It used to calm me completely. But tonight, it barely touched the storm inside.

Just as sleep claimed me, I felt Jasino's lips brush my forehead one last time. "I love you, Aundrea," he murmured.

Chapter 8

Truth In the Cave

I woke up to Jasino's gentle stirring, but his eyes told a different story—the anger from the night before, still simmered just beneath the surface. He sat up, his voice firm but clipped as he began issuing instructions. "Aundrea, rise. We break camp within the hour. Michelle will help you pack."

I threw off the blankets quickly and stood, obeying without a word, hoping my promptness would somehow bridge the gap between us. As I reached for my dress, Jasino added, "Eat something. You need strength for the journey ahead."

I nodded silently, continued to dress, and then made my way to the campfire, where Michelle handed me a bowl of porridge and a piece of bread. Her empathetic glance told me she sensed the tension between Jasino and me. I ate quickly, feeling the weight of his gaze on me. Every time I looked up, his expression remained stern.

Sabion approached him, discussing the route to the Seer's cave. Jasino's responses were brief, but his focus was solely on me. When I finished eating, I rose to help Michelle pack the remaining supplies.

"Aundrea, come here," Jasino called out.

My heart skipped a beat as I hurried to his side, wondering if this was my chance to talk—maybe plead for forgiveness. But he only said, "Ride with Sabion today. I need to scout ahead." His tone tightened. "And I need some space from you."

I nodded obediently, masking the hurt that stung like a fresh wound. As I walked toward Sabion's horse, he glanced at me with concern etched across his face.

"Milady," he said gently, "shall I help you mount?"

I accepted his hand and climbed onto the horse, grateful for his kindness amid Jasino's coldness. Sabion mounted behind me, his arms loosely around my waist for stability. We fell into line behind the guards, with Jasino visible in the distance, scouting ahead alone. Michelle rode beside the supply wagons, casting occasional worried glances my way.

The silence between Sabion and me was comfortable at first, but as the hours passed, I finally spoke. "Sabion… do you think he'll ever forgive me?"

His gentle squeeze around my waist conveyed empathy before he answered. "Yes, milady. Jasino loves you deeply. This pain—it's because you were hurt. He feels he failed to protect you."

He spared me the harsher truth—that part of the pain stemmed from my own actions.

"Thank you, Sabion," I whispered, wiping away a tear that the wind had already begun to dry. After a pause, I asked again, "Do you think he still trusts me?"

Sabion paused in thought. "Honestly, milady… I think that trust was wounded. But his love remains unwavering. Only time will heal trust."

I nodded slowly, absorbing his words as I glanced ahead. Jasino stood on a distant ridge, his eyes fixed intensely on me before he turned to scan the terrain once more.

I turned to Michelle, riding beside the wagons they'd acquired in a nearby village, and beckoned her closer – Sabion slowed our pace for her horse to draw near. Michelle rode up beside us, her expression etched with concern. She reached over, brushing her fingers lightly across my hand in a gesture meant to comfort. I offered a quiet sigh in return—there was no need for words. I was hurting, and she could see it.

She tried to ease the heaviness with a soft, teasing comment about the physical distance between Jasino and me, but her voice faltered when Sabion cast her a disapproving glance. The playfulness vanished. She whispered an apology, but I gave a slight nod, letting her know I wasn't offended.

Still, Michelle wasn't ready to fall into silence. Her voice, gentle now, spoke of what she had seen—Jasino pacing outside the tent the night before, visibly tormented by what Ravon had done to me. The image pierced something in me.

Guilt swelled in my chest. I hesitated before speaking, unsure if I even wanted to voice the thought. Was I foolish… to respond to Ravon, even if only for a moment?

Michelle's gaze turned solemn, thoughtful. Not foolish, her eyes seemed to say. Just vulnerable. Ravon had preyed on my fear, twisting it into something I couldn't understand in the moment. Had I even been given a choice?

I looked down, the whisper in my mind barely audible even to myself. Maybe if I had fought harder…

Michelle leaned in, her eyes searching mine. "Are you actually in love with Ravon? Did anything else happen that Jasino doesn't know about?" Before I could respond, Sabion's firm voice sliced through the air. "I'm not sure your husband would appreciate his wife speaking to a another lady about whether or not she is in love with another man. That's a little disrespectful, Aundrea."

My face burned with shame. Michelle's eyes widened, but she said nothing. I looked down, my voice barely audible. "You're right, Sabion."

The conversation died instantly. Michelle guided her horse back toward the wagons, leaving an awkward silence behind. I felt exposed and chastised, Sabion's words echoing with the gravity of my secret thoughts.

Jasino reappeared ahead, this time closer, his eyes narrowing slightly as if sensing the shift in mood. He fell in beside us, his gaze fixed first on me, then sharply on Sabion.

The horses moved steadily beneath us, hooves crunching against uneven ground as we wove between scattered trees and distant hills rising like watchful sentinels. A breeze stirred the branches, but the tension between us hung heavier than the air.

Jasino's voice cut through the quiet, sharp and cold. "What is going on, Sabion?"

I started to answer, but he didn't even glance my way.

"Nothing, Husband. Michelle and I were just talking," I offered, trying to steady my tone.

But his gaze remained fixed—unyielding—on Sabion.

"I wasn't speaking to you," he snapped. "I was speaking to Sabion."

Sabion cleared his throat, his voice low but steady. "My lord, Lady Aundrea was discussing certain sensitive topics with Michelle earlier, and I informed her it was not appropriate to do so with her Lady." Jasino's jaw clenched. His eyes snapped back to mine, sharp and cutting. "What topics, Sabion?" His voice was dangerously calm.

Sabion hesitated for only a moment. "Whether her feelings for Ravon were genuine… and whether there were other things you did not yet know."

The air turned to stone. Jasino's gaze burned into mine, his face darkening as anger and hurt battled for control.

Michelle, sensing the escalating tension, slowed her horse to a stop near the supply wagons, watching anxiously from a distance. Jasino's voice, thick with venom, sent tremors down my back.

"Aundrea, we need to talk. Now."

He signaled for Sabion to let go of me and then slid off his own mount. Grasping my elbow firmly, he pulled me down beside him, with a firm yet gentle grip. We stood alone on the dusty path, his eyes blazing with accusation. Sabion, retreated back towards the wagons meeting with Michelle.

"Do you have feelings for my brother—still, even now?" he demanded, his voice cracking with emotion.

I shook my head vigorously. "No, Jasino. Only fear and confusion."

He searched my face intensely, trying to discern truth from lies. After a moment, he stepped back, his expression still thunderous.

"What you discussed with Michelle was unacceptable, and highly inappropriate. Matters of our marriage are not to be shared with anyone—least of all a servant."

His words cut deep, slicing into wounds that hadn't even begun to heal. But I was done swallowing pain. The burden of new life, betrayal, and abandonment surged like fire through my veins, threatening to consume me whole.

I snapped. "I understand you're angry with me—and you have every right to be! But how dare you judge me when you shut me out! You left me drowning in silence, with no one to confide in but Michelle—my lady, my friend, not some faceless servant you command."

My voice echoed through the trees, startling even the horses. Rage roared in my chest, wild and unfiltered. I was trembling, but I didn't back down.

Jasino's eyes widened, stunned by my outburst. For a single breath, pain flickered across his face—but it vanished beneath something far more volatile. The Emperor rose within him like a tidal wave. His jaw clenched, and without hesitation, he lunged toward me, stopping just inches from my face. His breath came hot and ragged, every line in his body drawn tight with rage.

This wasn't just a husband scorned. This was a ruler whose authority had been challenged—publicly, by the one who was meant to stand beside him.

Fury radiated off him in waves, suffocating in its intensity.

"I am the Emperor—and your husband," he thundered, voice sharp enough to split stone. "Don't ever raise your voice to me like that again. Get back on that horse. Now."

The words cracked through the air like a whip.

Around us, the guards stiffened. Sabion tensed. Michelle's eyes brimmed with fear. I stood frozen, trembling—caught in the space between defiance and dread. I had crossed a perilous line, and everyone knew it.

Embarrassed and aching with guilt, I stormed off toward Sabion's horse, needing help to remount. My legs felt like lead, my heart heavy with dread. Sabion assisted me silently, his expression full of concern, not judgment. Michelle turned away, trying to compose herself after witnessing our explosive argument.

As I settled onto the horse, I could feel Jasino's glare burn into my back. The silence between us had turned toxic, heavy with unspoken threats and shattered trust.

Jasino wheeled his horse around and dismounted beside Sabion. With a gentleness that contradicted the fury in his eyes, he reached for me again. Carefully, he lifted me from the horse, mindful not to harm the unborn child I carried. Gripping my hand, he tugged me toward his own mount, his frustration simmering just beneath the surface.

He hoisted me up, then swung onto the saddle in front of me. Capturing my hands, he guided them around his waist—a possessive gesture, both tender and forceful. With a sharp command to his steed, we surged forward, leaving Sabion, Michelle, and the guards trailing behind.

I sensed the deep frustration boiling inside my husband and chose my words carefully, hoping to soothe rather than stoke the flames.

"I'm sorry for speaking to you that way," I murmured, my voice barely audible over the rhythm of hoofbeats.

Jasino's anger, though still burning, had been tempered by something deeper—his instinct to protect me, and likely, to scrutinize Michelle's role in all of this.

"I truly don't wish to address this right now," he interrupted, his voice tight. "Please... don't speak, my love."

His words hung heavy between us; an uneasy truce cloaked in silence. I obeyed, pressing my cheek to his back as we rode. The steady rise and fall of his chest was the only comfort I allowed myself.

The Seer's cave was close now. Sabion had estimated we'd reach it by midday. I wondered if the ancient wisdom held within would mend what was breaking—or unravel it further.

Jasino let out a deep breath, finally breaking the silence. "We'll stop soon to rest and water the horses. Then we'll see what the Seer reveals... about Ravon—the prophecy and hopefully more."

I didn't respond. I only leaned my head against his shoulder, wishing for peace, for closeness, for forgiveness.

He called out to Sabion. "Ahead."

Jasino led us into a serene clearing near the cave entrance, surrounded by silver-leafed trees that shimmered softly and thick brush that rustled with every gentle breeze. Above, birds sang sweet melodies across the sky, their trills harmonizing with gentle water bubbles rising from the spring. We dismounted beside the crystal-clear spring. The guards began watering the horses, while Michelle sat on a nearby rock, her eyes cast downward.

Jasino helped me down, his touch gentle but brief. We stood together for a moment, gazing out at the peaceful landscape—a stark contrast to the storm between us.

"The Seer awaits," he said. "The ancient one sees beyond what mortals can. Hopefully she'll reveal Ravon's plans… and maybe other truths."

His gaze found mine, and I knew he feared what else might be revealed—about me. I could see the pain welling up in his eyes. Michelle approached cautiously. "My lord… may I speak with you for a moment?"

Jasino's jaw tensed. "Briefly. Aundrea, wait here." I nodded, watching them step aside, their low voices carried by the wind. I could only hear parts of their words. "The nights, your influence. My wife… questionable… loyalty…Wrong."

My heart sank. He was confronting her. I saw the insults land on Michelle's face like slaps. "You're nothing but a servant—beneath me, beneath my family's notice!" I heard him yell as it traveled on the wind. Michelle's eyes welled with tears. She tried to speak, but Jasino cut her off. His words got louder, and I started to piece them together. "Your loyalty is questionable. Your discretion, nonexistent. You'll be dismissed from our service and returned to your humble origins, back on Earth."

Horrified, I stepped forward. My voice was firm but cautious.

"Jasino, stop! Your anger is misplaced. It's directed at me, not Michelle!" He spun to face me, fury blazing in his eyes. "This is because of your secrets with her!" his irritation and fury building inside. "No; this is because of my secrets from you!" The guards and Sabion shifted uncomfortably, sensing the real root of his fury. Michelle, seizing the moment, slipped into tears and headed toward the horses. Sabion's eyes shifted towards Michelle's, and I could see the concern in his eyes. My focus remained on my husband. Jasino's chest heaved, his expression slowly shifting from fury to realization.

"You're right," he finally said, his voice quieter but still heavy. "My rage is with you, Aundrea... not Michelle." The cave loomed behind us, an ancient, silent witness to everything that had just unfolded.

I glanced toward Michelle's escape route, worried about her well-being after Jasino's harsh words. "She didn't deserve that," I said softly, turning back to Jasino. "Her loyalty has always been to me... and to you, through me."

Jasino's expression remained solemn, but he nodded slightly in acknowledgment. I stepped closer, searching his eyes for any lingering anger or buried love. His gaze met mine—intense and complex—emotions still simmering beneath the surface. My heart skipped a beat as he reached out, his fingers brushing my cheek in a gentle, tentative touch.

I looked up at him, uncertainty still clinging to the edges of my heart. The question hung between us—unspoken but understood. Was there still a path forward for us? Could we face the seer together, or had too much already shattered?

Jasino's hand slowly fell to his side, but his eyes never wavered. In them, I saw something steady. A vow not yet broken. Despite everything, he still wanted to face whatever truths awaited—with me. For our marriage. For our child. For the fragile hope of the world we might still save.

Something warm stirred in my chest. Not peace—but the promise of it.

Sabion approached quietly, keeping his distance as he awaited instruction. With a silent nod, Jasino gave his answer. But then, his focus shifted, and with a firm gesture, he made it clear—we would go in alone.

Sabion bowed deeply and stepped back. Together, Jasino and I turned toward the cave's entrance, the air around us thick with uncertainty and resolve.

Together we stepped into destiny. I followed alongside Jasino, ready to face the seer's revelations. Then I whispered, "Promise me one thing—promise me we will face whatever the seer says with no secrets, no matter what." Jasino looked into my eyes giving me a reassuring nod.

Finally, I looked back to make sure Michelle was okay. She stood near the horses, watching us with a mix of concern and hope. Sabion nodded discreetly toward her, as if ensuring her safety. With one last glance, I turned back to Jasino and nodded to proceed.

***

We entered the cave together, the air inside thick with anticipation and ancient magic. Ravon was forbidden to cross these sacred grounds; the elders had warned that the darkness within him would shatter beneath the seer's pure sight—exposing evil to a force even he could not control.

Torches lined the path, their flames flickering wildly, casting eerie shadows that danced along the stone walls. As we moved deeper, the air grew colder, tighter. The only sound was the crunch of my footsteps on the uneven ground—until I slipped my hand into Jasino's.

I clung to him, my fingers trembling, fear curling in my stomach like smoke. The unknown ahead pressed against me, suffocating in its weight. Without a word, he drew me closer, his arm wrapping protectively around me, shielding me not from danger, but from my own fear. His warmth steadied me. Even after all we'd endured, I still found refuge in his presence.

Suddenly, a low, mystical voice echoed through the cavern. "Emperor Jasino and Lady Aundrea. I sense turmoil, love, and deception. Come forth."

The Seer emerged from the shadows, her eyes blazing with inner fire as she beckoned us closer. Jasino grasped my hand tightly, his palm damp with tension.

The Seer approached me, her presence both commanding and ethereal. Gently, she placed her hand on my shoulder, and with mechanical grace, I sank to my knees. My eyes began to glow blue, light pulsing through my fingertips.

Instinctively, Jasino moved to help me, his protective instincts flaring—but the Seer raised her hand in a silent command that stopped him mid-step. Trust wrestled with his concern as he paused, eyes locked on me, feeling both distant and near.

As the Seer withdrew her hand from my shoulder, the luminous glow remained, casting an otherworldly light across my face. She turned to Jasino, her voice grave.

"Your wife is under a powerful spell. It emanates from within; cast by evil. She will be unable to hear your words. The enchantment prevents it. Even if you or another tells her, she will not comprehend."

Jasino's brow furrowed, worry contorting his features. "What is it? What spell?" he asked, his voice trembling.

The Seer's tone darkened. "There was a time when Aundrea was vulnerable. Ravon approached her, disguised as a healer. You saw him as an old man with white hair—but it was Ravon. Your wife, weak and unable to speak, tried to warn you… but you could not hear her. He offered her a flask of water, but within it was a potion—one that ensnared her heart and made her love the Dark Lord."

She paused, her voice growing gentler. "Your wife is the Divine One. She holds a power Ravon did not anticipate. She fights even now to remain loyal to you, unaware she is locked in a battle for her very soul. Her kiss, her betrayal—was not hers. It was Ravon's."

Jasino staggered back, his hand flying to his chest, as if feeling the weight of his guilt press down on his heart.

The Seer raised her voice, urgent. "You must move past your rage and shield her. The worst is yet to come. The Dark One will take her, and you will be powerless to stop it." She turned slowly, lifting a small, ornate box carved with ancient runes. As she opened the lid, a soft hum filled the room—a sound that seemed to vibrate through the walls and into my bones. Inside, nestled in velvet, a glowing stone rested. Its surface swirled with hues of deep sapphire and violet, like a storm captured in crystal.

"This Dragon Stone," she said, her voice low and reverent, "is your only hope."

Jasino froze. His breath caught, chest rising and falling with the weight of a thousand thoughts. The firelight flickered across his face, casting shadows of doubt—but also resolve.

He stepped forward, slowly, as if approaching something sacred. Jasino understood the weight of what he held. The Dragon Stone's power was no mystery to him—he knew what would come with the merge. And though a shadow of hesitation flickered in his eyes, it did not last. He trusted the stone. Trusted the legacy it carried. Because of that, the union between them was seamless. No struggle. No resistance. Just purpose… and fire.

When his fingers brushed the stone, a warmth surged through his arm—alive, electric, and ancient. The stone pulsed in his palm, radiating not just heat, but memory. Light spilled between his fingers, chasing away the gloom around us. It was more than power. It was legacy. It was fate.

The stone's legacy was etched into his family's ancient bloodline. He knew about the formidable power of the Dragon Stone. Jasino closed his eyes and clutched it to his chest. He knew and trusted its energy. His father had merged with a Dragon Stone, centuries ago. The stone crumbled into glittering dust, its essence sinking into his skin. A surge of raw power erupted within him. His limbs elongated, his skin shimmered with Silver and golden scales. Then great wings of flame burst from his back.

He became the beast—magnificent and mighty—his scales the color of Lisonian skies. And yet, this was more than a dragon. He had become the Drakon. A thunderous roar burst from his lips, reverberating beyond the cave's mouth, carried for miles by the wind. As the roar echoed outward, Sabion's head jerked up, his eyes fixed on the dark cave entrance. He let out a roar so loud it shook the cave and ground below, awe and fear threading his voice. The guards exchanged nervous glances, hands resting on sword hilts. Michelle, still shaken, felt a flicker of hope ignite within her. Could that roar belong to Drakon? She strained her ears, every nerve on edge, as the sound seemed to vibrate through every cell in her body. It was unlike anything she had ever heard—primal, powerful, unmistakably Drakon.

Drakon unleashed a second deafening roar, his head snapping toward the tunnel's exit as a torrent of flame erupted from his maw. The seer approached, her touch gentle as she brushed his snout. "Protect your wife," she intoned, her voice echoing with prophecy. "Much remains unwritten in your future. You are Drakon now." As she spoke, the dragon's form receded, revealing Jasino once more—though forever changed. His skin shimmered with a bronze hue, a testament to his new form. Mastery over the transformation still eluded him. An ancient power and newfound purpose awaited.

"Your wife carries your unborn child, Drakon—a child born of love, not Ravon's deceit. This child will inherit the mantle of Drakon." The seer's words hung heavy with importance. "Ravon draws near, seeking to claim her for his dark palace. You must find the Death Stone. If Ravon possesses it, darkness will consume Lisona, and your wife will be lost forever. She must not know the child is yours, for her pure heart would betray you."

With a final desperate question, Jasino asked, "Can I prevent him from taking her?"

The seer's gaze did not waver. "No. It is written. Take your wife immediately to the riverbed at the base of the hill. Let no one follow. I have a loyal servant waiting— to give her the Dragon Stone that she hid in your palace. Tell her to keep it in her pocket, close and concealed. If Ravon knows she has it, he can block her from becoming a part of it. She cannot absorb the stone's power until she trusts it fully. Remember, she must not know the truth of the child's parentage, and she will not comprehend that she is spelled. The Death Stone lies in the Crimson Spine Mountains. Locate it, and destroy it." With those final words, she dissolved into nothingness.

***

I stirred, confusion was clouding my eyes. I saw the radiant glow surrounding my husband. "Jasino!" I cried out, rushing to his side.

"No," he replied, his voice resonating with newfound strength. "I am no longer Jasino. I am Drakon, bound to the Dragon Stone." I embraced him, my voice was trembling. "The seer… where—?"

"She is gone," he answered, cutting me off.

"What do we do? Was the child yours?" Questions invaded my mind, one after another. Burdened by the seer's warning, Drakon was struck with remorse. He had promised no secrets, but now he must keep one. He cupped my face, his gaze brimming with sorrowful love.

And the only words he could offer me was, "I forgive you, my love, with all of my heart. You will never hear of any betrayal from me again." Though suspicion lingered in my eyes, I accepted his embrace. And together, Drakon stepped out of the cave beside me, ready to face the trials ahead.

I stood frozen, still glowing with eerie blue light, as the seer's revelations shattered Drakon's world. He shut down, his emotions locked away, secretive. Drakon took my hands, and turned towards me, and planted a passionate kiss that lingered in the air.

"We must go to the riverbed at the bottom of the hill. Alone."

I trusted Drakon completely, following him without question. As we walked, my curiosity began to stir. "What's happening, my love? What did the seer say?"

Drakon's eyes met mine, brimming with love, concern, and secrecy. "The seer revealed much," he said quietly, "but for now, let's just say our situation is... complicated."

I studied his bronzed skin and asked, "And your skin—it's changed. What caused it?"

"The Dragon Stone transformed me into Drakon," he replied, his voice hushed. "In this form, I am forever."

I reached out, gently touching his warm, slightly electrified skin. He suddenly stopped, urgency flashing across his face.

"Aundrea, the seer gave me instructions. I must retrieve something to bring back to you."

His eyes scanned the riverbed, locking on a young man partially hidden among the trees. Drakon leaned in, kissed my forehead, and whispered a reminder of his love before descending toward the shadowed figure.

I waited patiently, watching him approach the man hidden beneath the trees. My mind spun with questions about the mysterious events unfolding around us.

***

After a stretch of silence, Drakon returned... The man vanished into the forest, and a small box was clutched tightly in Drakon's hand.

"This was the box you hid in the palace," he said urgently. "The seer said it contains your Dragon Stone— you had hidden behind your vanity."

He opened the box to reveal the glowing stone. "Take it, my love."

I reached out, feeling its warmth pulse in my palm.

"She said to keep it close and hidden, in your pocket," Drakon warned. "Ravon must never know you possess it."

I slipped the stone into a hidden pocket in my dress and sealed it tightly. Together, Drakon and I walked back toward Sabion and Michelle. My husband, needing to speak with them privately, asked me to remain by the fire next to the guards. As he approached Sabion and Michelle, they immediately recognized him as Drakon, Emperor of Lisona. Knees buckling in stunned devotion, they fell before him. Drakon's commanding hand waved upward, bidding them to stand. A low, guarded tone escaped his lips, tension coiling within him like a snake. The seer's haunting words replayed in his thoughts, his eyes never leaving my anxious gaze.

Michelle's face paled, her eyes welling up with tears as Drakon, sworn to secrecy, wrestled with the fate that awaited me. Sabion nodded gravely, his expression resolute. He spoke just above a whisper, "I will protect these secrets to my dying breath if needed."

Drakon moved swiftly back to my side. He leaned in close, his voice low and hastened by urgency. "Ravon could arrive any moment, my love. We must prepare to leave for Firefly Valley. Ravon's dark magic is weakened there."

Something else flickered behind his eyes— something he wasn't saying. I couldn't stop the questions rising in my chest: What had he seen in the cave? What truth had the seer shared that he couldn't speak aloud? Why so much secrecy? And why was he so certain Ravon would come?

He glanced at Sabion, then Michelle, and finally back at me—as if weighing what could be said, and what still had to remain buried.

Sabion and Drakon carefully, yet swiftly, lifted me onto a horse. Drakon mounted Vandros, securing me first. With a snap of the reins, Sabion urged his horse forward, bolting into a fierce run. Hooves pounded the ground, sending clouds of dirt flying as Michelle, Drakon, and I raced behind. The rest of the guards formed a protective escort, flanking us and trailing close behind.

Suddenly, Ravon materialized—a solitary figure standing defiant in our path. Drakon, his face carved with fear for me, seemed to realize the seer's prophecy was unfolding. I would be taken, and nothing he could do would prevent it. Urgency surged through him, and he spurred his horse forward, his hooves dancing in place.

Jasino turned to Sabion, "Watch my wife, Sabion. Don't take your eyes off her for a moment."

Sabion's nod was grim with agreement. Drakon jumped from his horse, approaching Ravon slowly, sword drawn, maintaining a cautious distance. "Ravon, why are you doing this?" he called out.

Ravon's gaze locked onto Drakon's. "I see you have become one with the Dragon Stone, brother," he said, a sinister laugh escaping his lips. "No matter. You still don't have the power to defeat me... and you never will. I've come to claim my prize. Aundrea carries my heir, and I will not leave her in your grasp a moment longer. You are poisoning her heart against me!"

Disbelief washed over Drakon as he retorted, "Ravon, you cloud yourself with delusion. Aundrea is my wife. She loves me. I am the Emperor not you!"

Ravon's anger flared. "Give her to me willingly, brother, so the baby goes unharmed. She is my rightful bride. Walk her into my arms, or I will kill you, and all of your men, and take her anyway."

Sabion pulled my horse gently closer to him, horror unfolding before my eyes like a nightmare. Ravon's sinister laugh echoed through the air; his gaze fixed on Drakon.

I could hear the growl of the dragon through Drakon's vibrating chest. "I'll die before surrendering her to you, brother."

Sabion urged Michelle, closer to me, his voice firm. "No matter what happens Michelle, protect the Lady Aundrea, do not leave her side."

Michelle nodded, her face deathly pale with terror, eyes locked on the menacing figure before us.

My voice rose, fierce and trembling, echoing across the landscape as I stood my ground.
"Leave me alone! No one knows who this child belongs to—but I don't want to go with you! I don't want you!"

Ravon's face turned purple with rage as he thundered back, "SILENCE, Aundrea!" His dark magic swirled wildly around him, echoing his fury. Michelle grabbed my arm tightly, whispering urgently, "Aundrea, we must flee!"

Sabion spurred his horse forward slightly, preparing to gallop. Drakon took advantage of Ravon's momentary distraction and charged forward, drawing his sword. The guards followed Drakon's lead, clashing with Ravon's emerging dark followers.

Uproar erupted as swords clanged, horses screamed, and dark magic exploded into the air. Sabion yelled, "Hold tight, milady!" and kicked his horse into a frantic gallop.

Michelle clung close to me as we rode wildly away from the battle scene, the chaos still echoing behind us. Sabion charged forward, blade drawn, rushing to aid Drakon.

The wind tore at our hair and cloaks as our horse galloped through the trees, hooves pounding against the ground.

Michelle shouted over the thundering rhythm, her voice laced with panic and clarity. "We have to get back to the seer's cave! He can't follow us there—Ravon can't enter!"

I looked back, my heart racing with dread. "Is Drakon still fighting? Is he safe?"

My blood ran cold at the devastating sight before me as I took one last look. Every soldier—ours and Sabion's alike—was trapped, suspended in a shimmering haze of dark purple magic. They stood frozen mid-motion, expressions locked in fear and confusion. Then I saw him. Drakon. My heart shattered. He was caught too—his sword raised mid-strike, his body unmoving, his eyes fixed on me with a helpless terror that stole the air from my lungs. Tears welled in my eyes as dread crushed down on me like a wave.

I stopped! Dead in my tracks, swinging my horse around in fear of Ravon killing my husband. I rode with determination as Michelle's screams echoed behind me, "Aundrea. No. Don't do it. Drakon wouldn't want this!" Ravon's attention shifted to me, his dark eyes alight with triumph. I dismounted, sliding down the horse's side, my boots catching in the shrubs beneath my feet. "Ravon, stop!

Please, just stop! Don't hurt them!" I cried, my voice cracking with desperation.

Ravon's triumphant scream pierced the air. "YOU ARE MINE, AUNDREA!" He surged forward, a storm of black haze swirling around him. His breath was ice against my ear as he whispered, "The child you carry will seal your eternal bond... to ME."

Despair crushed me. I glanced back—my beloved husband bound by Ravon's magic, frozen in torment. Tears streaked my face, hopelessness seeping into every inch of me. Michelle jumped from her horse, sprinting toward me, but with a flick of his wrist, Ravon trapped her in a twisting column of dark smog. My heart splintered, the sound of it breaking as sharp as steel on stone.

Ravon's voice slithered against my ear. "You and our unborn child will soon forget him forever..." I tried to appeal to the sliver of mortality, I once thought existed in him. "Ravon, stop! This is madness! You were once Drakon's brother—his family. What darkness has consumed you so..."

He laughed, cold and cruel. His grip on my wrist tightened. "That weakness is dead. Power and love for YOU have reborn me."

I struggled. I searched his expression for any hint of hesitation—but none came. Why didn't he just take me already? Why linger?

"I'm going to kill your husband," he breathed, eyes wild with delight, "and all of his people here."
"No, wait!" I reached for his chest, my hand trembling. "Take me with you. Don't kill them, and I will go willingly."
His eyes flared with triumph. He drew me closer, his breath

hot against my ear. "That's all I needed," he whispered. "One willing word, and the pact is sealed."

His fingers gripped tighter, voice dark and reverent. "The ancient law binds me as surely as it will bind you. A soul cannot be claimed by force—not fully. The old magic demands choice, spoken aloud. It craves surrender, not struggle."

I felt his lips graze my neck as he added, "They call it the Binding Rite—formed in shadow, sealed in word, and eternal once spoken. Your vow just saved them... and damned you."

His cloak wrapped around me. His arms tightened. Darkness swallowed everything. We vanished into the void, leaving behind Michelle's desperate screams, Sabion's furious cries, and Drakon's heart-wrenching pleas.

Ravon's magic faded from the valley, a whisper of shadow vanishing into silence.

Shouts erupted, footsteps thundered across the ground. Sabion and Drakon had broken free of Ravon's binding. They sprinted toward one another, Michelle close behind, the guards quickly surrounding them for direction.

Drakon's roar tore through the heavens. He fell to his knees, arms raised toward the sky. "AUNDREA! MY LOVE, WHERE HAVE YOU GONE?! NO!"

But his pain did not stop him. Collecting himself with effort, he exchanged a determined glance with Sabion. Without speaking, they mounted their horses.

Drakon leaned toward Sabion, voice low and urgent. "Firefly maps indicate the Death Stone lies hidden near Crimson Spine Mountains and the seer confirmed it was there."

Drakon's eyes burned like fire as he drew his sword. "We ride for Crimson Spine Mountains—alone." He turned to Michelle. "Stay in Firefly Valley, near the lower basin. There's a village nearby—warn them. Ravon's darkness spreads."

Michelle, pale and shaken, nodded slowly. "I'll warn them, Your Highness." Tears welled up in her eyes. "Please... bring Lady Aundrea back."

With that, Drakon and Sabion galloped off, their silhouettes swallowed by the horizon. Michelle, accompanied by two guards, turned toward Firefly Valley—her figure small and resolute as she disappeared into the shadows, her desperate plea lingering like a haunting promise.

The wind whipped through Drakon's hair as he rode, Sabion close beside him. He would find the Death Stone at Crimson Spine Mountains and destroy it. Drakon's sword glinted, and his heart burned with one vow—he would reclaim me... and Ravon would fall.

SHADOWFORT CITADEL

Chapter 9

Chains of Fire

A week had passed in suffocating silence. One more click echoed through the chamber as the door locked again, and tears welled in my already swollen, red eyes. I buried my face into the eerie black pillow, stifling my sobs against the silky fabric.

The air in the room was thick and stale, clinging to my skin like a shroud. I tried to sit up, my body trembling. The bed beneath me was surprisingly soft, in stark contrast to the cruel cold of the stone walls. It made everything feel more surreal—like the luxury here was meant to mock my pain.

I had seen no one except for the silent servants who came and went without a word, leaving trays of food behind. Not Ravon. No guards. No one.

The room was elegantly furnished, far too elegant for a prisoner. A vanity sat just outside the adjoining washroom, its gilded mirror catching the flicker of the distant torchlight from the hall. A wardrobe lined the far wall, black wood etched with more of those strange crimson runes. None of it offered comfort.

I wrapped my arms around myself, rocking gently, trying to breathe. The echoes of Ravon's words haunted me, like thorns pressing against my ribs. My stomach churned—not just from fear… but from the lingering magic I could still feel crawling under my skin—his touch. That vile touch had wormed into my very blood. I could still feel its effects clinging to the corners of my mind like cobwebs.

I stood, unsteady on my feet, and approached the vanity. My reflection stared back—pale, gaunt, and bruised by exhaustion. But beneath the weariness, there was still a spark. A flicker of something Ravon hadn't taken yet. A part of me he hadn't shattered.

My hand moved to my stomach. A subtle flutter stirred within me—soft, barely noticeable, but real.

Life.

My child.

I did not know if the father was Drakon… or Ravon... But I knew one thing with absolute certainty: I had to protect this child, no matter the cost. Even if it meant enduring this nightmare longer than I could bear.

A knock echoed at the door. I flinched, my heart pounding. Then the lock clicked. The heavy iron door creaked open. A cloaked figure entered, perhaps a servant, with a tray in hand. The smell of roasted meat and herbs wafted into the room. My stomach twisted again—not just from hunger, but from dread. I backed toward the corner.

The servant set the tray on a small table near the bed and bowed slightly. She spoke no words, keeping her hood low as she turned and exited without a glance.

I waited until I was sure she was gone before approaching the tray. My throat ached with thirst. There was a goblet of water—clear and still—and a plate of food that looked freshly prepared. My eyes locked on the goblet. Is it safe?

My hands trembled as I reached for it, hesitating. My body cried out for hydration. Too many days and nights had passed in silent protest, rejecting nourishment. I had to think of the baby now. I could not risk losing my unborn child—he was all I had left.
I sat down on the edge of the bed, nibbling on the food, and stared at the locked door. I could feel him on the other side

of it, like a storm waiting to break. Ravon wanted a queen. He wanted my child.

But I would give him neither. Not willingly.

And Drakon... wherever he was, I prayed to the gods he would come. I prayed he would find me. Before it was too late.

I knew what Ravon's intentions were—lock me away in isolation, bitter loneliness, so that I would beg for his company. I knew the tactic. I knew it well. I remembered my father using it on my mother. And it worked.

But Ravon would never break my spirit.

The silence in the room was broken only by the muffled sound of my own sobs. Through the bars of the thick iron door, I could hear Ravon's breathing—slow and ragged, still thick with restrained passion and rage. His palm rested against the cold metal as he leaned closer, and his voice slithered through the bars like smoke.

"Tonight, Aundrea," he whispered, "your tears will fall for a different reason."

Footsteps echoed down the stone corridor. A loyal servant approached, his voice low. "My lord," Valtor said, bowing, "the feast preparations are complete."

Ravon's mouth curled into a menacing smile. "Ensure Aundrea is bathed and dressed in the black gown with crimson lace I selected for her... She will make a stunning bride-to-be."

Valtor entered cautiously, head lowered, his voice hesitant. "Milady, Ravon has ordered that you prepare for tonight's feast."

Hatred flared in my eyes. "I'll never dress for my own captivity," I spat. "Tell Ravon he'll have to drag me there naked before I do anything he desires."

Valtor flinched. "Milady… please. He has threatened my family's life if you are not perfectly prepared." For a moment, my defiance faltered. Innocent lives should never be the cost of my resistance. My voice dropped, cold and sharp. "Tell him… his threats ensure only one thing. I'll wear the damn dress. Nothing more."

Valtor gave a slight bow and hurried to the washroom, drawing a bath and laying out the gown on the bed before quietly slipping out again.

Though the bath was perfumed and tepid, the silence pressed in, making the water feel as hollow as I did. My skin prickled from the cold stone walls, my body shivering as I stepped out and dried myself. I stared at the black gown—lace like blood tracing the hem, velvet like midnight. I slipped into it, struggling to fasten the buttons in the back, an impossible task. I gave up, then crossed the room to the vanity.

My fingers closed around the brush, and I began pulling it through my damp hair, each stroke deliberate, mechanical.

The vanity was black-lacquered wood with gold leaf detailing along the edges. A strange symbol was etched into the top of the mirror, glowing faintly in the low torchlight. It formed a single word—kórax: raven. I scanned the room again. Everything here was shadows and secrets. Black and gold dominated every surface, suffocating any hint of life or color. I moved back to the bed, the gown brushing against my bare ankles, and laid down, exhausted. My thoughts swirled, and eventually, sleep overtook me.

Not long after, Ravon's voice echoed elsewhere in the fortress.

"Valtor," he said with quiet command, "send riders through the rift to Firefly Valley. Bring back Michelle, Aundrea's loyal servant… alive!"

***

Hours passed, before the door creaked open again. I sat up quickly. Scooting myself to the head of the bed. Michelle was thrown through the doorway like a discarded doll, her face bruised and stained with tears. I rushed to her and knelt beside the bed, gently helping her climb onto it. My hands cupped her face gently.

"Michelle! What did they do to you?"

She clung to my gown, sobbing against my chest. "They said… they said if you didn't obey Ravon, I'd suffer worse…" Her voice cracked as she spoke.

My arms wrapped around her instinctively, protectively. I looked up—Ravon stood in the doorway, his eyes cold and full of power. I held Michelle tighter.

Valtor threw one last sneer in our direction. "Don't defy him again, milady." He spat on the floor at my feet, then turned and left. His words rang false—he had no remorse. Only a hunger for Ravon's approval. Valtor had a hint of the same darkness lingering inside him, that I saw inside Ravon's eyes. His story about Ravon, threatening his family, clearly a lie to manipulate me.

Ravon stepped into the room. "How touching," he said, voice slick with malice. "Aundrea's loyalty can be bought… with Michelle's pain."

My fury boiled over. "You're a monster, Ravon! She's a young girl—fragile and human. She has no weapon, no power. And you call yourself powerful for hurting someone who can't even fight back?"

He smiled as if my hatred were his favorite flavor. "Guilty as charged. Now, the choice is yours: dine with me tonight as my willing future queen... or watch me make Michelle suffer."

My voice trembled. "Ravon... What guarantee do I have that you'll spare her?"

His smile widened, cruel and slow. "For now, Michelle will remain here. A convenient hostage. I do not... trust you completely, Aundrea."

Michelle gripped my arm, her voice a breathless whisper. "Aundrea... Drakon will come for us. Don't cry." Her words steadied me.

Before I could say anything, Ravon's fury exploded.

He stormed to Michelle, striking her across the face. She cried out, crumpling on the bed. My heart shattered.

Ravon towered over her, voice low and deadly. "Never speak my brother's name again, or I'll find torments that'll tear your soul apart."

Michelle's eyes met mine, terrified. Tears streamed down her cheeks as she nodded quickly. I threw myself between them, arms around her like a shield.

"Stop! She won't say it again—I swear it!"

Ravon's gaze met mine. His face softened, but not with mercy—only obsession. "Good, Aundrea. You're already learning to protect what belongs to me."

He stepped forward, prying my arms away from Michelle and pulling me to my feet. His touch was gentle, but his eyes blazed. "You'll swear obedience so easily for her sake... Will you swear it for your own?"

I raised my hand and struck him across the face. A deep sting flared in my wrist. Ravon didn't flinch. He let out a low chuckle, taking my injured hand in his own and flipping it palm-up.

"Are you hurt, my love?" he asked softly, and amused.

A chill of disgust crept across my body. His thumb traced the skin on my hand, slowly, pressing his lips against the palm of my hand. For a brief moment, I felt a flicker of passion burning inside my soul…and then nothing but dread.

"You should be more concerned about the pain I will cause you," he murmured.

I narrowed my eyes. "You'd never hurt me, Ravon."

He studied me. For a heartbeat, he looked almost normal.

"I may not hurt you… but I will cause your pain," he said darkly.

I stiffened.

"Why do you think I brought Michelle here?" he asked, his voice like ice over a blade. "To ensure your obedience. That was just the beginning."

I stared at him, eyes burning. A single tear slid down my cheek.

He reached up and brushed it away, his touch deceptively tender. "Every tear she sheds, Aundrea… every bruise she bears… will be the price of your defiance."

Behind me, Michelle's broken whisper trembled in the air. Ravon smiled in its wake, like a serpent basking in triumph.

Ravon pressed his hand to my shoulder, pushing me gently down onto the bed. I dropped into a seated position, stiff and alert. His attention turned to Michelle, who whimpered softly as he seized her by the arm, dragging her roughly to the far corner of the room. His grip was merciless.

"Sit!" he ordered, his voice sharp and demeaning— like he was commanding a dog.

Michelle collapsed onto the cold stone floor, her knees drawn to her chest, her face hidden in her arms. Her shoulders trembled with quiet sobs that tore through me.

Ravon turned back, his expression shifting into a false gentleness. He sat beside me, one arm draping over my shoulders, trapping me against the hard bedframe. I flinched, my entire body tensing with fear. His breath ghosted against my cheek as his fingers traced my jawline.

"I will never hurt you, my love… you do not need to fear me like that." He lingered on the word "you," chilling me to the bone. The implication was clear—others weren't as lucky.

Michelle's muffled cries continued, a haunting counterpoint to his whispered lies.

Ravon noticed the back of my dress was still unfastened. He gently pulled me to the edge of the bed, brushing my hair forward over my shoulder. His fingers moved with eerie care as he buttoned each clasp at my back—slowly, deliberately.

The sensation was unbearable—unwanted and twisted—and yet, my body responded with a forbidden shiver that I despised.

Ravon lingered a moment, studying me with dark fascination, then stepped away.

"Tonight then," he said simply, turning toward the door. "I'll be back shortly."

The door closed behind him with a solid thud, followed by the unmistakable clank of the lock. I was trapped again.

***

I wasn't without hope. My heart pounded as I remembered something—tucked away in my gown. I darted to the washroom, sinking onto the cold floor, fingers digging through the pleats of the fabric.

There. I pulled it out: the Dragon Stone.

Tears burst from my eyes. Drakon had warned me—never let Ravon find it.

Clutching it to my chest, I raced back into the chamber, eyes scanning the walls. I spotted a loose stone near the far side of the room. I pried it loose with shaking hands, the scraping sound echoing ominously. Clearing space, I tucked the glowing stone deep within the wall, shielding it from view. Michelle's eyes were locked on my every movement.

It pulsed briefly—brilliant and alive—before dimming, hiding itself with a magical hush.

Turning, I found Michelle still curled in the corner, her arms wrapped tightly around her knees. Her face was tear-streaked and ghostly pale, the bruises standing out like ink on parchment. She looked so small—so fragile—like a doll left in the rain. My heart ached for her, the weight of her suffering pressing against my chest.

I crossed the room, every step, echoing with guilt, and knelt beside her. The cold stone seeped through my skirts as I settled on the floor. I reached out, resting a hand gently on the back of her head. Her hair was damp with sweat and tangled from where she'd been trembling.

"Michelle," I whispered, my voice barely audible over the silence. "I need to tell you something."

She lifted her head slowly, as if even that movement cost her strength. Her battered face was taut with pain, her eyes rimmed red from crying, but behind the exhaustion, I caught a flicker of something else, fear... and maybe a question she wasn't sure she wanted the answer to.

She looked into my eyes, her battered face drawn tight with pain.

"There's a stone hidden in this room. You must never tell Ravon about it. Ever. He'll try to separate me from it, and I... I cannot let that happen."

Michelle blinked through her tears, trying to process my words. She tried to speak, but fear consumed her voice, like a predator stalking breath in the silence of the night. Her lips trembled, parted—but nothing came out.

Then suddenly, a sharp ringing noise filled the air, high and metallic, like a scream only the magic could hear. The wall behind me shimmered with a pale glow as the stone embedded within it pulsed—once—then dulled to stillness, leaving behind a strange pressure in the air, like the aftermath of a storm.

My body stiffened as an icy chill burrowed deep into my bones. I turned back to her, heart pounding now. "Michelle, do you understand? You cannot tell him where it is."

She stared at me, her eyes wide, the fear still there—but now clouded with something else: confusion. Her brow furrowed slightly, as if trying to grasp something just out of reach.

"Understand… what?" she asked, her voice a soft, with a cracked whisper.

My breath caught.

Her gaze, once so sharp with understanding, had dulled, like a flame smothered by ash. The flicker of recognition I'd seen only moments ago was gone, replaced with a blankness that hadn't been there before. Like something had been severed.

The stone had erased her memory.

I felt relief crash over me like a wave. She wouldn't remember. For now, that absence of memory was her shield—and the secret of the stone lay veiled behind the fog of her mind.

I gently placed my hand against Michelle's battered and swollen face, the heat of her skin trembling beneath my fingertips. A golden light began to pulse from my palm, seeping into her bruises and burrowing through the layers of pain. I closed my eyes and tilted my head toward the heavens, summoning the well of power deep within me. Warmth surged through my chest, then down my arm—a radiant current that flowed like sunlight into her. As the last of the energy slipped from my fingers, I opened my eyes to find Michelle gazing up at me, her lips curled into a soft, grateful smile. "You'll be okay, Michelle," I whispered, still catching my breath, but certain—I had healed her.

***

Just then, heavy footsteps echoed beyond the door. I froze. Ravon lingered just outside, pacing. I could feel his thoughts bleeding through the stone—his mind fixated, obsessed.

I looked back at Michelle and placed a hand over hers. "Don't worry," I whispered. "Drakon will come for us."

Outside the chamber, Valtor approached Ravon, carrying a tray with flickering candles and a decanter of wine.

The door opened. Ravon stepped inside, his eyes locking on mine. "Emotional reunions are touching, my dear," he said coolly, "but our dinner awaits." He looked down at Michelle, a dark, ominous laugh curling from his lips—low and venomous. His eyes gleamed with recognition, and I knew in that moment he had realized: I had healed her.

I wiped the tears from my cheeks and sat up straighter, rebuilding my composure. Michelle clung to my hand like a lifeline. Her eyes were distant, her spirit dulled by everything she'd endured.

Ravon gestured for Valtor to approach.

"Take her to the adjacent chamber. Aundrea and I will dine alone."

Clutching Michelle protectively, I leaned forward—not to comfort her, but to face him. My voice dropped low, meant for Ravon alone.

"Lord Ravon, make sure she is treated gently," I said, "And give her something to eat."

Ravon gave a slight chuckle, the sound low and mocking. "Lord Ravon," he mused. "My servants call me that, Aundrea. You will address me by my name only."

Then he added with a more indulgent tone, "I've already instructed Valtor. She will receive a warm bath, soft blankets. A comfortable bed. Roasted meats, fresh bread… Her every comfort provided. So long as you uphold your end of our agreement."

Valtor gave a slight bow and helped Michelle to her feet. She leaned against him, weak legs, gaze never leaving mine. But his eyes weren't on me, they were on her. His gaze into Michelle's face softened, the hardness in his features flickering. For a fleeting moment, I saw something almost civilized. Empathy. As if, in her pain, he saw someone else… someone he had once loved. Michelle resembled his wife—I could see it in the way he looked at her, haunted and tender, like a ghost had stirred in his memory.

Her eyes were pleading. I forced a soft smile to reassure her, though it felt as fragile as she looked. Valtor eased her toward the archway connecting our chambers, his steps slow and careful. I stood still, heart aching, as she disappeared into the adjoining room. The door whispered behind her.

Ravon turned back to me, extending his hand. "Shall we dine, my queen?" We stepped through the doorway, my mind racing with ways to escape for a future rebellion. Ravon glided beside me with sinister elegance, his fingers extending like skeletal branches as he moved toward a wall adjacent to the thrones. No opening! Just the hard stone wall, empty. I swept the room with my eyes, searching for a crack, a passage—anything that might offer escape. But the walls held only silence.

With a subtle flick of his wrist—a cruel gesture that reeked of dark magic—the air rippled and distorted, as though reality itself bowed to his will. A low, ominous grind echoed as the stone seams parted like dark lips, revealing a hidden chamber.

I shivered at the raw, unsettling power he wielded.

Inside, a long table stood illuminated by flickering candlelight, casting twisted shadows against the stone walls. A lavish feast was laid out across the table, and in the far corner I spotted a velvet couch beside a carved serving cart adorned with gleaming goblets and decanters. Ravon's eyes blazed with unbridled obsession as he stepped forward, beckoning me into his private lair. The wall, slid shut behind us with a deafening crash, sealing us into that hidden room, where only the flickering flames and his burning gaze lit the space.

He approached the table, pulling out a chair with a mockery of grace. His hand slid to the small of my back, sending an unwelcome jolt through my spine as he guided me into the seat. Leaning in close, his voice low and composed, he whispered, "Your heart is the only dowry I desire, Aundrea. Yet circumstances demand our union sooner rather than later. Our child will arrive within eight moons. Marry me willingly before then or become my bride by force. The outcome is yours... for now."

My blood ran cold. Speech failed me beneath the crushing weight of his threat. Eight moons. That was all the time I had to find an escape—or succumb to a lifetime of darkness.

I forced myself to take a bite of food, the taste clashing with the bile rising in my throat. My gaze met Ravon's across the table. "Ravon, I... I don't know how to be your wife after living so long as Drakon's." I lowered my eyes to conceal the lie behind my words. "But I'll try."

His satisfaction was immediate. He leaned back in his chair, fingers steepled, a sinister smile spreading across his face. "Time," he repeated, "I'll give you that, Aundrea. But you have three moons to forget Drakon's touch, his kisses, his name. I am your future—you and our unborn child."

He reached into a velvet-lined box and produced a black-gold ring adorned with a crimson stone. "During this time, you will dine with me nightly, wear this token of our bond… and give me your loyalty." His words oozed control.

My eyes flicked to the ring, my breath catching as I recognized it for what it was—a symbol of bondage disguised as a gift. I dropped my gaze to my lap again, hiding my revulsion.

Then he asked it—the question that made my heart seize.

"Do you think, Aundrea," he said softly, "that Drakon will still want you after you share my bed?"

A sob burst from my throat before I could contain it. The guilt stabbed deeper than any blade. I twisted the ring on my finger—Drakon's ring. A symbol of the love we'd built, now destined to be erased.

Ravon watched me crumble. His dark triumph filled the room. My sorrow was his satisfaction. He rose from his seat, walking toward me with slow, deliberate steps. Reaching out, he wiped my tears with his thumb.

"Your tears," he murmured, "are the first vows of our union."

His fingers drifted down my cheek, cold and possessive. "Drakon will never again wipe away your tears… or touch your skin."

He knelt beside me, one hand braced on the chair, the other resting on my knee. "Do you really believe he'll recognize you after three moons with me, Aundrea?" His voice sank into my bones.

I gasped, his words stealing the air from my lungs. He saw the ring on my hand—Drakon's ring—and reached for it with chilling precision. His fingers wrapped around my wrist, malice in every motion, and slid the ring free. A faint purple glow shimmered over it before it vanished entirely, swallowed by his magic.

From the box, he plucked the replacement. The cold black-gold band with its crimson stone slid onto my finger like a shackle. His voice was thick with claim. "You are mine."

He lifted my chin with two fingers, forcing my eyes to meet his. "Before you answer, remember what I'll do to Michelle if you refuse. Will you become my wife?" He waited, already basking in his conquest.

I stared at him, terrified of what might come next. "Yes." I said as the word caught in my throat.

Ravon's smile deepened as he kissed my lips—soft and possessive. "Eat, my love. Our child needs nourishment."

My voice barely emerged, a whisper of horror. "What did you do with my other ring?"

He smiled, satisfaction curling his lips. "That ring belonged to a forgotten life. My ring is your destiny now."

I forced my trembling hands to lift the food once more, but each bite was heavy and bitter. He watched me with grim amusement.

"My reluctant bride eats for our child, yet starves herself of hope," he murmured. "After tonight, Drakon will never want you again."

I couldn't stomach another bite. Nausea surged violently, and I stood abruptly, clutching my stomach as I fled from the table, gagging. Burdened with new life, my body rejected the torment it had suffered.

Panic twisted across Ravon's face. He raised his hand, and with a pulse of dark magic, the far wall rumbled—stone grinding against stone as a hidden door revealed itself. A healer was being summoned. My stomach lurched, shame and sickness overtaking me as I staggered toward the nearest basin. Before the next wave hit, I looked up to Ravon's worried eyes, "It's just morning sickness "It's been getting worse lately."
Ravon's expression shifted—from feigned worry to fascination—as his eyes gleamed with twisted intensity. "Our child grows stronger every day..."

The door creaked open, and I froze.

He raised his voice. "Freyan, deal with her immediately!"

***

I recognized her at once. Freyan—once a revered healer of the realm, known for her grace and unmatched skill—had long since fallen into shadow.

A year ago, during one of the darkest moments of my life, I had run away—alone, lost, and in pain. I'd fallen from a horse and injured myself, helpless and surrounded by thick brush. And then... she appeared. Cloaked in silence and mystery, the woman had bowed, introduced herself as Freyan, and knelt beside me. Her touch was calm, practiced. She placed her hand over my swollen ankle, healing it with a warmth so unexpected it stole the breath from my lungs.

Before vanishing back into the woods, she murmured, "I have healed your body, but your true healing lies with the rightful heir."

At the time, I hadn't understood what she meant. But now... it was so clear.

Betrayed by a man she once loved, Freyan had turned away from the light and bound herself to Ravon in grief and fury. Whispers told of a pact she made with the dark god Zha'thik to deepen her healing gifts. And though shadows clung to her like a second skin, I sensed something more beneath it all. A flicker of warmth still lingered in her—buried, but not gone. She was a tattered soul. Not evil. Just broken. I saw the remnants of love still flowing somewhere deep in her veins.

Now, that same woman—once my savior, now Ravon's servant—rushed to my side, her gentle hands guiding me away from the basin.

"My lord Ravon," Freyan said softly as she led me to a nearby couch, "she needs rest and some ginger tea to soothe her stomach."

Ravon nodded, his gaze never leaving my pale face. "See to it, Freyan. Spare no comfort for my beautiful wife—she carries my heir."

Freyan helped me lie back on the couch, her cool hands brushing my forehead.
As I closed my eyes, a chill of dread rippled through me.

My gaze drifted upward toward the ceiling—a rugged vault of dark granite, its stone slabs fit together like the scales of some ancient beast, casting eerie silhouettes across the room.

Hearing a voice, I briefly glanced at Ravon still standing in the entrance of the door as if to trap my only escape route. I saw him talking to Valtor. I looked back at Freyan, whispering with great secrecy, "Please help me get out of here. The rooms have no exits until Ravon opens them. There has to be a way." Freyan gazed at me with sympathetic eyes, feeling my intense pain, "I am sorry, milady, I cannot help you." She grabbed a teapot on a table against the wall, pouring hot tea into a cup before passing it to me. "Drink this, it will make you feel better."

Ravon was still in the doorway, eyes fixed on me as I sipped the tea, feeling the nausea retreat. He waved off Valtor and approached me on the couch. His eyes blazed with fury as he towered over Freyan, "Freyan, leave us, now." She hastily set the tea tray down and backed away slowly, bowing, a last fearful glance at me before leaving the room. As she exited, the walls closed in, sealing the exit behind her.

Ravon's gaze snapped back at me, his expression twisted in rage. "So, you plot escape… and betrayal." He reached out, his fingers wrapping tightly around my wrist, pulling me up into a sitting position. He got down on one knee in front of me and continued, "A single moon hasn't even passed, and yet you beg others for freedom from me…" His breath hissed against my ear. "Do you think anyone in Shadowfort will dare help you against my will?"

My heart raced beneath his grip, pounding wildly against the fear tightening in my chest. Scared and shaken, I wiped at the tears streaming down my face, but they kept coming—rushing in like a tidal wave, impossible to contain.

How could he expect me to simply accept this? To be locked away, alone, as if my will didn't matter?

I lowered my gaze, unable to meet his eyes any longer. My trembling hands clutched at the hem of the black gown I wore, fingers brushing the lace trim. Cold. Lifeless. Just like this place.

"I just… Can I please just go to my room?"

Ravon looked at me and shook his head in defiance. "No, Aundrea. We are going to Michelle's room." Fear consumed me once again like a tsunami ripping through my heart. "No… Please don't hurt her." I put my hands on his chest, hoping for some glimmer of mercy Michelle would not find. My eyes locked onto him, pleading silently as my voice could barely whisper. "Anything but hurting her, Ravon… spare her pain and I'll give you anything."

Ravon's gaze burned into mine, his expression unreadable for a moment before a sinister smile spread across his face. His grip loosened slightly, surprised by the desperation in my voice. "Anything…" he repeated. "Aundrea, I already have everything I want."

Ravon towered over me, his eyes gleaming with malice as he lifted me to my feet. He strode towards the wall we had entered through earlier, his hand weaving a subtle pattern in the air. The stone seams trembled, then split open with a low, ominous grind, revealing the throne room beyond.

We walked through the dimly lit throne room, our footsteps echoing off the cold stone floors, and stopped at a door adjacent to my chambers. Ravon's fingers brushed against the rusty handle, and a faint spark of dark magic danced across the metal. The lock clicked open, surrendering to his power.

The door creaked inward, revealing a cramped, gloomy cell disguised as a bedchamber. Michelle lay across a narrow bed, her face pale and frightened. A tiny washroom clung to the side wall like an afterthought. The room was a bleak reflection of Michelle's lost hope. A black and red comforter suffocated the small bed. A single pillow seemed a cruel luxury. A miniature wardrobe stood like a sentinel, filled with black dresses that seemed to mourn her freedom. The space was barely large enough for us to stand without touching... a deliberate design to crush spirits.

Ravon's movement was swift and merciless. He seized Michelle, slamming her against the wall with enough force to knock the breath from her lungs. I screamed, pleading for mercy, as his hand struck her with a crack like breaking glass. Blood poured from her nose, dark and steady, like a river set loose. He pinned her to the wall, his eyes blazing with rage, her feet never touching the floor. "My bride has not learned yet that I will not accept betrayal," he hissed, his voice venomous.

Michelle was thrown onto the bed like discarded trash, crawling desperately to escape his grasp. Panic radiated from her in waves—her breath hitching in short, gasping sobs as her eyes darted around the room, wild with fear and disbelief. Ravon grabbed her by the leg, yanking her back and flipping her over to force eye contact. She froze, trembling, her face pale with helpless terror.

He pressed his hand to her neck, pinning her to the bed as her hands clawed at his arm, reaching for any chance—any sliver of air or mercy from his crushing grip. I dove forward, shoving Michelle's shoulder gently in a desperate attempt to create space, then tried to wedge my fingers beneath his hand, prying at his wrist. She was gasping now—her face turning a dangerous shade, eyes wide with panic.

"Please," I cried, my voice shaking, "she cannot breathe. You are going to kill her!"

I lunged at Ravon, grasping his dark cape with trembling hands and yanking with all the strength I had left. "Please, Ravon, please." I felt so helpless I could barely breathe, let alone form the words I needed to say.

For a moment, he didn't move. Then, with a frustrated exhale, he released her and turned to face me. "Never again. Say it, Aundrea."

I broke. My knees nearly gave out as tears spilled down my flushed, swollen cheeks. Shame clung to every word as I forced them past trembling lips.
"I won't do it ever again."

I covered my face—not just to block out the horror of what I'd just witnessed, but to hide the anguish his victory had carved into me.
I reached for her, placing my hands on her and calling forth my inner light.

"I won't allow you to heal her again," Ravon snarled, his voice sharp and venomous. The air around him thickened, charged with rising fury. Shadows clung to the edges of his form as he moved between us, yanking my hands from her battered body—his eyes burning with possessive rage.

Each word dripped with menace, as if he were casting a curse with his tongue.

I ran out of Michelle's room into the throne room; Ravon followed behind, shutting Michelle's door and locking it. He waved his hand in a symbolic motion on the opposite side of the room, revealing an exit. I turned toward the exit, which exposed the night sky. Valtor walked in and bowed to Ravon. "You summoned me, my lord."

Tears still consumed my face, but with calculation,

I never took my eyes off the door, but its edges were still glowing faintly from where the stone had shifted, and the night sky shined through. My breath caught every time it flickered, every time the silence stretched. Ravon stood beside me, watching my stillness with unnerving calm. With a sharp nod, he instructed Valtor to tend to Michelle. I barely heard the footsteps retreating behind me.

Then he moved closer, sliding an arm around my waist—and though the gesture mimicked affection, it carried no warmth, only power and possession. His touch burned cold.

He looked up at the stars with me, as if trying to remember what beauty was, pretending peace, pretending care. "It's a beautiful night, Aundrea," he murmured, his breath brushing my cheek like smoke. A sneer curled his lips as he continued, soft and cruel, "Would you like to leave now? Go…Go and don't look back."

I froze.

Was this real? Was this freedom? After everything—he was just letting me go, or was this some kind of trick?

I couldn't breathe. I couldn't speak. My tears had begun to dry on my cheeks, but now the sting of new ones pressed at the corners of my eyes. I turned to him slowly, searching his expression, looking for the trap.

"I can go?" My voice was barely more than a whisper.

"Yes," he said. "You can go."

I hesitated, heart pounding, then looked toward the narrow passage that led to Michelle's chamber. The thought of leaving her behind twisted something inside me.

"Can Michelle come too?"

His laugh was sharp and poisonous, echoing through the hall like a dagger dragged across stone. His entire body stiffened, his voice thick with possessive rage.

"No," he snarled, his eyes gleaming with satisfaction. "She belongs to me now."

He took a step back, but his gaze never left me. "Do you want to go, Aundrea?"

My shoulders sagged. All my strength drained from me in one breath.

I looked at him, the man who held my body captive and my soul hostage, my eyes hollow with defeat. "No, Ravon. I want to stay."

His eyes lit with satisfaction... He hadn't set me free to be kind. He wanted me to

choose this.

Choose him.

With a wave of his hand, the glowing exit vanished behind solid stone once more. And the tears came again, heavier now, soaking the remnants of hope I hadn't realized I was still holding.

"Do you see now, Aundrea? You are mine. My bride. Stop looking for escape. When you had the opportunity to save yourself, you decided to stay. If you ever leave, Michelle will suffer for all eternity."

Chapter 10

Cage of the Garden

The silence pressed in from all sides, heavy and unrelenting. Ravon was nowhere near me. A twisted form of punishment, he had isolated me from any hope of company, and the weight of that loneliness had begun to crush me from the inside out. The walls seemed to draw closer with every passing day, their silence louder than any scream.

But this day was different. After a servant brought a tray of fresh fruit and bread, she exited the room—without locking the door. No guards stood watch inside my room either—an unsettling surprise, though I understood why. There was no exit beyond the throne room.

My black gown from last night lay crumpled on the cold stone floor, its fabric wrinkled and twisted like a discarded shadow. In its place, a fresh one had been laid out across the bed—a replica of the gowns from before, dark and lifeless. The silk caught only the faintest shimmer of light from the wall torches. The sight of it chilled me. A uniform of submission. A bleak reminder that I was still a prisoner, even in elegance.

A week had seeped by, its emptiness echoing within me. As I closed my eyes, a lone tear broke free, tracing a solitary path down my cheek. Yet, amidst the desolation, a spark remained - my love for Drakon. I yearned for him to find me, to claim me once again. The weight of the world pressed down, a crushing reminder that Ravon held my body captive, but my heart remained unbroken, a fortress he could never breach. My thoughts drifted to Michelle, and the resolve hardened within me: I would keep her safe, no matter the cost. He might have me, but I would never let him touch her again.

I stood before the bed, my heart hammering as I lifted the fresh gown in my trembling hands. The silk felt cool and slick against my fingers, its weight deceptively light. I slipped it over my head and let it fall to cascade around my legs, then reached behind me to find the first tiny clip at the nape of my neck. My fingers fumbled, slick with sweat, grazing the smooth metal until I caught its edge. I pressed the two sides together, feeling the faint "slip" echo in the silent room.

Climbing each row of clamps—one, two, three— my arms ached from holding them aloft, the gown's fullness pulling at my wrists. I refused to call for help. Ravon's touch still burned on my skin, and I wouldn't let him touch me again. My breathing grew ragged as I leaned forward, struggling, feet steadying me against the icy floor. Behind the smallest hooks, I paused, my heart twisting. With a final push of my fingertips, they met—and fastened.

I straightened my shoulders, aching but my spirit was unbroken. The gown was secure.

I pushed open the heavy throne room doors, my heart racing with every creak. The chamber was dimly lit, torches flickering all around the room. I rushed toward Michelle's chamber, grasping the cold iron handle, but it refused to turn. "Michelle…" I whispered, speaking urgently through the bars. A faint response came from within. "Aundrea?"

I slid down beside the door, sitting on the chilly stone floor. Michelle mirrored my pose on the other side. I placed one hand on the door and my ear tucked gently against the icy metal, He was so brutal to you. Are you ok?" I took a deep breath before continuing, my words hardly above a whisper. "I think Drakon is coming for us. I feel it."

Michelle touched the smooth cell door, her voice trembling. "Shhh, Aundrea... please don't talk about him here. Ravon already warned me never to say his name." Her voice cracked with fear. "I'm so sorry, Michelle. I want to go home." Tears began to fall, one after another. The memory of last week's horror pierced my resolve.

As I leaned into the door, my voice barely above a whisper, I made a vow that sparked a glimmer of hope within me. "By the Gods, Michelle, I promise—I'll find a way out of here." For a moment, her trembling ceased, and her faint voice held a fragile light. "Aundrea... if Ravon finds out you're planning escape again... he might kill me." But as the words left her lips, the light extinguished, and a chill crept in, her voice dissolving into soft, muffled sobs. The fear that had been lurking in the shadows pounced, suffocating the hope that had momentarily flared to life.

Suddenly, the torchlight near her cell flickered, dimming as though disturbed by a presence. But no cell doors had opened. I scanned the throne room, every muscle tense, heart pounding in my chest. The air had shifted, heavy now, thick with something unnatural. I could feel it pressing in, cold and alive with dark power. Then, the far wall began to shudder, stone grinding against stone. Someone was coming.

Michelle's whisper turned cold and urgent. "Aundrea... go. Now." The stone wall parted, and Ravon stepped through, the sharp cadence of his boots echoing as he emerged from the shadows. His voice was smooth and sinister. "What are you doing, Aundrea? Discussing something intense with your friend?"

His gaze honed in on the cell, as if straining to hear Michelle's retreating sobs. I stood slowly, heart racing, and backed away from the door. "Ravon," I stammered, curtsying low. "Michelle and I were… praying."

His piercing eyes snapped to mine, doubtful. "Praying… in whispers? With tears?" He stepped closer, his hand drifting toward the cell door handle—dangerously close to the truth.

I panicked. Lunging forward, I gripped the fabric of his dark cape and pulled him close. Looking up into his eyes, I felt an uncontrollable fire rising within me—desperation or deflection, I wasn't sure. But as my lips brushed his, the moment took on a life of its own, a fire which felt uncontrollable. In a moment of my attempted deception, I felt as though I was losing myself.

Ravon's eyes widened with surprise, then darkened with desire. His hands—moments ago poised to unmask our secret—now wrapped around my waist, drawing me in. His lips crashed into mine, hungry and possessive, as he spun us, pressing me against the cold wall beside Michelle's cell.

The faint gasp from behind the door—Michelle's shocked silence—seemed only to stoke his fire. His hands roamed boldly, sending unwelcome trembles through every fiber of my being. Breaking the kiss for a moment, he whispered, "My clever bride… trying to distract me with your lips?"

His eyes danced with suspicion, demanding an answer. I stepped back, the haze of his touch lifting. My gaze fell to the floor. "I… I wasn't trying to distract you," I said shakily. "I was drawn to you. There is something…"

His expression darkened, voice curling like smoke around me. "Aundrea, don't play coy. Your lips were eager, but your eyes betrayed your fear. What. Were. You. Discussing. With Michelle?"

He tapped the door rhythmically—cold, deliberate. Michelle whimpered softly behind it.

"Tell me, my bride," he whispered, lethal now, "or Michelle will relive her previous agony."

Heart pounding, I forced my voice to tremble and let tears gather in my eyes. "Oh, Ravon, we… we were talking about what you did to her." My voice cracked, the lie slipping in like truth. "Michelle was still shaken, and I was trying to comfort her. She asked me… if you would ever show her mercy again."

His eyes narrowed, suspicion morphing into twisted curiosity. "Mercy?" he echoed. "She begged for mercy, and you think I showed her none?"

I nodded slowly, trembling. "No, Ravon. You showed me mercy. Your anger towards me, scared her more than the pain. You only stopped because of me."

He studied me intently, watching for deception. But my trembling hands and trembling voice convinced him. Something softened—dark admiration curling behind his gaze.

He turned toward Michelle's cell, his voice low, almost amused. "Fascinating. My brutality terrifies her less… than my anger toward you. Her love for you is strong."

His eyes burned with a fierceness that made me forget how to breathe. "You have influence over me, my bride. A power I've never granted anyone." I was surprised by his blatant admission. Sometimes, Ravon almost seemed to care.

Ravon locked arms with me and whispered against my ear, "My love, it is time to go feed my beautiful wife and our unborn child."

He waved his hand in a fluid, magical motion, and the wall obeyed him—splitting apart and revealing the passage beyond. I followed him in silence, each step echoing like a verdict. When we reached the dining room, he pulled out the same chair I'd sat in before and eased me into it. Then he leaned down and pressed a kiss to the crown of my head.

"I am sorry I cannot eat with you this afternoon," he murmured. "I'll send Valtor to escort you back through the wall to your room."

"Ravon," I blurted, desperation creeping into my voice, "Can… Michelle join me? I don't want to eat alone."

His eyes sparkled, clearly surprised by my request. Then they narrowed, calculating. "Very well. Michelle may join you. Valtor will bring her to you shortly. But be warned, my bride…" His voice dropped low, curling around me like smoke. "These walls have ears. Choose your words wisely."

His lips curved into a twisted smile as he leaned in one last time, his breath like frost on my skin. Then he turned and departed, in a swirling twist of dark magic, leaving me cloaked in silence and escalating dread, in a room with no exits, a tomb.

***

Moments later, Valtor entered, his eyes scanning the room like a hawk. My gaze dropped to his hands—and there it was. A black ring gleamed on his right hand, etched with the sigil of the dark god Ravon served. As his fingers brushed the ring, the wall behind him shimmered, its solid form rippling and dissolving.

That ring—it was more than jewelry. It was a key. A possible means of escape.

He guided Michelle inside gently, with a surprising softness that didn't match the man who had helped brutalize her. "Milady," he said, helping her into the seat across from me.

Michelle looked frail. Her eyes, once bright, were now dulled by trauma. But as I looked at her, something stirred inside me—my resolve hardened. I had to save her.

Valtor met my gaze briefly, his expression unreadable. Then he bowed. "I will return for you both shortly. Ravon's orders." He turned and placed his hand on the ring again. He walked through and the wall shimmered closed, resealing us in stone silence.

My eyes met Michelle's, our minds already weaving silent plans. I reached across the table and took her hand, gently wrapping my fingers around hers. My eyes held hers with fierce intensity, and I gave her hand the slightest squeeze—a message unspoken, but felt.

Michelle's haunted gaze flickered with a glimmer of understanding. Her fingers curled back around mine. We sat there in shared silence, hands clasped like a secret vow, the weight of Ravon's warning pressing down on me like a storm cloud.

Was Valtor the key? Was it the ring—or him?

Could Michelle distract him?

Could I manipulate Ravon's obsession?

Michelle's eyes searched mine. I leaned forward, voice soft as a prayer. "I love you, my friend."

I closed my eyes, the familiar hum of my inner light stirred, like the gentle buzzing of a harp's strings. I called upon its power, and a soft radiance seeped from my pores, infusing my hands with a warm, golden glow. The light danced across Michelle's battered skin, soothing her wounds as it washed over her. Her breathing steadied, and the tension in her body eased, like the first gentle rains of spring thawing frozen ground. A small smile crept across her face, and tears pricked at the corners of her eyes, shining like dew-kissed sapphires in the dim light. The air around us vibrated with the sweet scent of healing, and I felt Michelle's gratitude wash over me, a warm wave that crested and ebbed as her wounds began to mend.

I leaned in, my voice barely above a whisper.

"The roses are blooming early this year."

Michelle's eyes met mine, and she paused, her gaze searching for meaning. Then, her face softened, and she replied,

"But the frost still lingers."

The meaning clear,

The roses are blooming early this year: Drakon is coming for us soon.

But the frost still lingers; acknowledges the danger or challenges that still exist, showing she's understood the underlying message.

My heart pounded in my chest as I detected the faintest glimmer of understanding in her eyes. We sat silently, the unspoken words hanging between us like the delicate petals of the roses I'd mentioned, as we mechanically ate the meal before us. The taste was bland, but the connection with Michelle was a feast for my starved soul.

A sudden flicker of the candles and a soft breeze across the table meant that Valtor was returning. We turned our attention to the plates before us, acting as if time hadn't passed. I sipped my tea—ginger and mint, soothing the nausea that still churned in my belly.

The wall shimmered again, parting smoothly as Valtor stepped in. His sharp eyes swept over us.

"Did you get enough to eat, milady?" he asked. "Ravon asked me to ensure you were satisfied before I returned you to your quarters."

"Yes," I replied, keeping my gaze steady. He gave a curt nod.

"Time then to return you both."

His voice was deep and low, each word deliberate. He guided us from the dining room through the now-open corridor into the throne room. Michelle walked ahead of me, but before she passed through her cell door, she turned. Her eyes locked onto mine, brimming with unspoken fear.

Valtor paused. His eyes flicked from me to Michelle. Something strange flashed across his face, longing, almost. Desire.

Michelle's eyes widened, recoiling as that memory stabbed through both of us—Valtor's fists, his kicks, his cruelty. And now… affection?

It twisted in my gut.

He placed a gentle hand on her back and guided her inside. The soft clang of the door closing behind her was a dagger to my heart. The scrape of the lock followed, sealing her in once more.

I hated him.

Not just for what he had done to Michelle, but for the arrogance that clung to him like smoke. The way he looked at me—like I had upended his place beside Ravon simply by existing.

Valtor turned to me, his expression shifting into a smug sneer.

"Milady," he said, placing his hand against the small of my back and giving me a firm, guiding push toward my chambers.

I turned toward him, barely containing the venom in my voice. "Valtor," I said, exasperated and full of contempt.

"Do not touch me, unless you want me to tell Ravon."
Valtor didn't flinch. Unbothered by my threat, he merely sneered and stepped aside, opening the heavy door to my quarters. "Your turn," he said with a smirk, gesturing with an exaggerated sweep of his arm.

I walked past him slowly, then spun around and fixed my eyes on him. "Why lock Michelle's door and not mine?" My voice was laced with suspicion.

For a fraction of a second, the mask of arrogance slipped from Valtor's face. Surprise flickered in his eyes, quickly replaced by his usual smugness. He stepped partially into the doorway and said in a self-satisfied tone,

"Milady, Ravon's decision is based on his trust and affection for you."

My stomach twisted in disgust. "Trust, Affection?" I scoffed, letting out a bitter laugh. "Valtor, there are no exits. Where would I go? Where would Michelle go? He doesn't trust me, or I'd have one of those rings—and I could leave this awful place!" My voice trembled as rage overtook me. "Ravon disgusts me!"

As soon as the words flew from my mouth, I clapped both hands over my lips, heart slamming in my chest. I hadn't meant to say it out loud—not like that.

Valtor's entire demeanor changed. The fury that overtook him ignited like dry tinder, puffing up his proud stance, his chest rising with rage.

He raised his hand.

I shouted, my voice cracking as the words tore from my throat.

"What, Valtor What are you going to do?"

My heart slammed against my ribcage, and my skin prickled with sweat as he loomed over me, his eyes blazing with a lethal fire that seemed to sear the air between us. My muscles tensing in anticipation of the blow, my breath catching in my throat as his fury simmered just below the surface. For a heart-stopping moment, I genuinely feared he'd strike me, or worse, summon Ravon to unleash his twisted cruelty. The sound of my own ragged breathing was the only sound I could hear, until Valtor's voice dripped with venom,

"You'd do well to show some respect, Your Highness."

But then something shifted. His fury curled into something more venomous—jealousy.

Valtor's gaze darted around the room, his eyes lingering on every shadow as if ensuring we were truly alone. His voice dropped to a venomous whisper, each word laced with a toxic intensity. "You think Lord Ravon disgusts you?" he spat, his lips curling in disgust. "I find it revolting that he wastes his attention on you. You're nothing but a brittle, flawed thing, Aundrea – a pale imitation of the power and beauty that could be his." His words were a low, vicious hiss, and for a moment, his hand twitched, as if the weight of his palm against my face was a tantalizing prospect.

The air seemed to vibrate with the force of his restraint, his jaw clenched so tightly I could see the muscles flexing beneath his skin. His eyes burned with a bitter, almost possessive fury, as if Ravon's interest in me was a personal affront to him. "Lord Ravon could have anyone," he sneered, his voice dripping with contempt. "Gods, anyone. And yet he's fixated on you." The words seemed to choke him, and with a sudden, violent motion, he spun on his heel and stormed out, the door crashing shut behind him like a crack of thunder, the sound echoing off the stone walls.

Adrenaline surged inside me. I darted after him, yanking the door back open and storming down the corridor toward the throne wall. "You cannot lock me in these rooms alone!" I yelled, my voice echoing like a battle cry. "What's stopping me from following you through the portal?"

Valtor turned slowly, smirking. "Ravon," he said flatly, hoping the name alone would send me retreating in fear.

***

I sprinted forward, feet pounding against the stone floor as I lunged for the portal. My fingers clamped around Valtor's wrist like a vice, and I yanked myself upward just as the shimmering edge began to vanish. His reaction was swift—and brutal.

With a snarl that was almost animalistic, he spun me around and slammed me into the stone wall, my skull cracking against the unforgiving surface. The impact left me dazed, stars dancing across my vision as he pinned me in place, his fingers digging deep into my shoulders like talons. The pain was a searing brand, and I could feel the warmth of my own blood trickling down my scalp.

"You're either very brave... or utterly stupid, Aundrea," he hissed, his breath hot against my face, his eyes blazing with a fury that seemed to consume him whole.

But before he could say more, the thunder of Ravon's boots echoed through the tunnel, growing louder with each passing heartbeat. Valtor's demeanor transformed in an instant. He recoiled, his hands springing open as if I'd burned him, and stepped back, his face smoothing into a mask of calm, calculated servitude. Ravon emerged from the shadows, his eyes locked on me with an unnerving intensity. Valtor's voice was a silky whisper, a stark contrast to the violence that had just transpired. "Why did you try to escape again, milady?" His tone was detached, almost bored, as if he'd never laid a hand on me.

Ravon's eyes bore into mine, filled with restrained violence. Shoving Valtor out of the way, He came inches from my face, pushing me harder against the wall.

"Why try to flee, Aundrea?"

Terror welled up in my chest, constricting my breath. "I wasn't trying to escape, Ravon! I would never leave Michelle."

He glided to the other side of the passage, folding his arms and leaning against the opposite wall. Valtor stepped forward again, smug as ever. "Then why follow me through the portal, milady?"

I smiled bitterly, tilting my chin. "Because I could! You told me never to attempt escape, Ravon—not that I couldn't roam Shadowfort."

Ravon studied me with narrowed eyes, visibly irritated by our exchange.

Valtor's sneer deepened. "I don't believe you."

I spun back to Ravon, my voice escalating into a furious shout. "Ask Valtor why he burst into my room, his eyes blazing with hatred! Ask him why he slammed me into this wall, leaving me breathless and battered!" My gaze locked onto Valtor, my anger a palpable force. "You're so devoted to serving me to Ravon on a silver platter, aren't you? You're so eager to prove your loyalty."

Valtor's face went ashen, his confidence crumbling as he took a step back, his eyes darting towards Ravon with a flicker of fear. "Aundrea, tell Ravon what you said in your quarters, the words that—"

"ENOUGH!" Ravon's voice boomed through the tunnel, making the stones tremble beneath our feet. He turned to me, his eyes flashing with a cold, calculated fury. His hand shot out, his fingers closing around my wrist like a vice. I felt the bones grinding together as he yanked me forward, and I cried out in pain. "Ravon, you're hurting me!"

For a moment, Ravon's grip tightened further, his eyes flashing with a warning. Then, his expression smoothed, his grip relaxing slightly, though his hold remained firm. "Both of you will come with me." he growled, his voice low and menacing.

As we moved forward, Valtor trailed behind us, his eyes fixed on Ravon's back with a mixture of fear and wariness. Ravon swept his free hand through the air, and the wall ahead shimmered, revealing the narrow tunnel to the throne room. The air was heavy with tension, and I could feel Ravon's anger radiating from him like heat.

The torches within the throne room flickered violently, casting elongated shadows across Ravon's storm-dark face. He dragged me toward Michelle's cell. His grip crushed my wrist, surely leaving bruises. Valtor followed in silence, his expression unreadable.

Michelle's pale face appeared behind the bars, her eyes wide and horrified. "Aundrea…" Michelle whispered in a shallow and shaky voice.

"Silence!" Ravon's voice reverberated through the stone chamber. He turned to me, his fury palpable. "What is it, Aundrea, that you said in your room?"

Tears blurred my vision as I crumpled at his feet. "I… I didn't mean it, Ravon!"

He yanked me upright and grasped my chin, forcing me to meet his eyes. "What did you say, Aundrea? Do not make me ask again." My breath hitched as panic consumed me. I felt as though my knees would buckle under the weight of my body. "I said… he doesn't trust me…" My voice faltered. "Or I would have one of those rings… and I could leave this awful place!"

I dropped my gaze, unable to look at him.

Valtor's cold voice sliced in. "Tell him the rest, Aundrea."

Ravon seized my chin again, eyes drilling into mine. "What else, Aundrea, what are you trying to hide?"

My chest ached. Fear crushed me. I opened my mouth, the words trembling free like poisoned daggers. "I... said. You disgust me."

The weight of truth hit the floor with a deadly thud. I collapsed into my hands, sobbing uncontrollably as shame and fear tore through me.

Ravon's voice dropped low, frightening and final. "You are playing games with me, Aundrea. And now... you are going to learn the consequences."

Ravon's gaze settled on Valtor, and a dark purple light erupted in his hand, its raw power sparking like wildfire across his palm. The air seemed to vibrate with anticipation as he raised his hand, the back of it connecting with Valtor's face in a swift, merciless motion. The sound of the impact was like a crack of thunder, sending Valtor flying across the throne room. He soared through the air, his body arcing in a helpless trajectory, before crashing onto the stone floor with a sickening thud. The room was bathed in stunned silence as Valtor groaned, his limbs trembling like a puppet on a string. His face twisted in agony, his skin already beginning to bruise and swell.

Ravon's voice boomed through the room, the sound waves pounding against the stone walls like a tempest. "Never touch my bride with anger, and never threaten her again." The words hung in the air, heavy with menace, as Valtor struggled to rise, his pride shattered by the brutal display of power. He kept his gaze lowered, his voice barely above a whisper, his words laced with pain and submission. "Yes, Lord Ravon."

Ravon's eyes locked onto mine, blazing with an intensity that made my skin crawl. The memory of Valtor flying across the room, the sound of his body crashing onto the stone floor, still echoed in my mind, filling me with a creeping sense of dread. Ravon's voice cut through the silence, and my heart plummeted. What now? What unimaginable pain awaited Michelle this time? Panic set in, my breath coming in ragged gasps as I sprinted forward, positioning myself in front of the cell door. Tears streamed down my face, hot and bitter, as I shielded the cell with my trembling body.

"Ravon… what I said, it wasn't about you," I whispered, my voice barely audible over the pounding of my heart. My head bowed low, tears dripping onto the stone floor like a steady rain. "I was angry with Valtor. He's... so cruel to me..." My words tumbled out in a sobbing confession, each phrase punctuated by a ragged breath. "He torments me with his eyes... spits at my feet... whispers threats behind your back. I was rebelling against him... not you." My body shook with each sob, my hands covering my face as if to hide from the horror of it all.

Ravon raised his hand, halting Valtor mid-step, his expression frozen in stunned stillness. For a moment, it was as if time itself had stopped, the only sound was the quiet sobs from behind the iron bars. Even Valtor's sneer faltered, a flicker of shame dancing across his face as he realized the power I held over Ravon – the ability to manipulate his affections with a single, anguished word. Then Ravon's voice came, low and unexpectedly soft, a gentle breeze in the midst of a tempest.

"Aundrea… my love."

He stepped toward me, slipping an arm gently around my waist, the other brushing stray strands of hair from my tear-streaked face. "Are you afraid of Valtor?" His hand found mine, coaxing it away from my eyes.

His thumbs brushed along my cheeks, slow and deliberate, catching the warm trails of my tears. His skin was rough—calloused from war and power—but for a fleeting moment, his touch was careful, almost reverent. It lingered with a strange gentleness, as if he were trying to remember how to be civil, almost mortal. And in that breath of stillness, he almost felt like he was.

"Tell me, my bride," he said again, more firmly this time. "Are you afraid of him?"

I looked up at him, still crying, and seized that moment of manipulation with a hollow, confused sound. I shook my head.

"Not anymore… not now that I know you'll protect me from him. I just hate how he treats me. I know you'd kill him if he ever truly hurt me."

I gazed deeply into Valtor's eyes—a silent reminder of the power I held.

Ravon seemed to inhale the moment, his pride fed like a flame.

The darkness of Shadowfort seemed to press closer—but instead of shrinking from it, I fell forward into his embrace. My head rested on his chest, where I could feel the rhythm of his breath, the steady beat of his heart. It lulled me, pulling me deeper into his void.

I felt him tense slightly beneath me—then exhale. His arms wrapped tightly around me, protective and possessive. His voice rumbled through his chest, deep and steady. "Exactly... I would kill anyone who dared raise a hand to you."

He glanced at Valtor, and his gaze was venomous.

Then, his lips brushed my hair with delicate reverence. I stood stunned at the gesture—the softness from a man carved of shadow and pain.

Behind us, Valtor cleared his throat awkwardly, as if reminding himself to breathe. His eyes had narrowed, watching our intimate moment with something between loathing and confusion.

Michelle slid down against the wall inside her cell, her face pale, eyes wide. She listened to us silently, a strange mixture of fear and wonder flickering behind her lashes.

Ravon's hand gently stroked the back of my head. He whispered, "My bride, you've become my only light… in all this darkness." He drew back, searching my face. "Do you think you could ever love me?"

Still wrapped in a fog I couldn't explain, my thoughts felt distant—like trying to grasp smoke. Something inside me was shifting, dulling my clarity, softening my will. I did not know why. It felt as though the darkness was moving through my veins. My body leaned toward him again, responding without my permission, like a puppet pulled by unseen strings. But deep within me, something recoiled. A quiet voice—faint, but frantic— screaming for me to stop…

"I… think I'm losing myself," I whispered.

I pushed him away gently, hands trembling, desperate to draw a line, to hold onto something real. I took a few steps back, my eyes locking with his. Tears fell again, warm and relentless. "It's only a matter of time, Ravon…"

My voice broke. "This place is tearing me apart."

I looked at the cold ground beneath my feet, then raised my head again, pleading.

"I'm suffocating in solitude. Confined to my chambers, wandering only this throne room. No sky. No sun. Just shadows."

I flung my arms wide, laughing with bitter sarcasm. "And now, even Michelle's presence is rationed like water in a desert."

Ravon stepped toward me, calm but stern. "Aundrea, did I not allow her to dine with you this morning?"

I scoffed, frustration cracking my voice. "And what then? I'm supposed to count that as kindness, while I lose my sanity, moment by moment?"

***

Then—pain struck.

A jolt of agony lanced through my stomach, twisting deep and sharp. I doubled over, clutching my belly.

"Oh Gods… the baby!"

The pain spread like fire—radiating into my back, dragging me to my knees. I cried out, the terror, my voice raw with emotion. "Something's wrong, Ravon!"

Panic surged.

Ravon's arms closed around me like a lifeline, his warmth enveloping me as he cradled me against his chest. My vision blurred, and I felt myself slipping away, my voice barely above a whisper. "You have power... can't you help me?" I reached for him, my hands trembling as I clutched at his shirt.

Ravon's hands stilled against my skin, his voice cracking with emotion. "I'm not a healer, Aundrea... I'm sorry." His forehead pressed against mine, his breath coming in ragged gasps as he struggled to contain his own fear. He waved at Valtor, his gesture curt and commanding, ordering him to fetch Freyan.

As the pain seared across my belly like a knife twisting in my flesh, I felt my world narrowing to a single, terrifying thought: losing my baby. The agony was a living thing, consuming me with each passing moment. Blood began to saturate my dress, warm and sticky, a visceral reminder of what was happening. My hands were slick with it, the metallic scent filling my nostrils as I felt myself losing control.

Ravon's face was a blur, his eyes wild with concern as he held me close. His voice was a gentle whisper in my ear, "Aundrea, stay with me. Hold on." His words were a prayer, a desperate plea to keep me and my child safe. As the pain intensified, Ravon's grip on me tightened, his arms wrapping around me like a shield. He laid me gently on the bed, his eyes never leaving mine, filled with a deep concern for his bride-to-be and his unborn child.

In that moment, I heard footsteps echoing outside my chamber, approaching quickly from the throne room— the healer. Ravon didn't move from my side.

Freyan burst into the room, her robes flowing behind her. She knelt at my side, placing her hands over my blood-soaked dress.

Her magic pulsed faintly, but then—nothing. Something blocked her power.

"No..." she whispered. Her face paled. "I can't... I cannot reach the child."

I screamed, a guttural sound of pure devastation. "By the Gods! No, my baby!"

I clutched Ravon's hand with all the strength I had left. Blood soaked my gown, hot and terrifying. I locked eyes with him, silently begging. Save me. Save us.

I pressed my shaking blood-soaked hand to his cheek, and in a whisper I begged, "Please…" Ravon looked at me with utter devastation—and something he was unaccustomed to: helplessness.

Then I closed my eyes, diving beneath instinct, into a power no spell had ever taught me. Something ancient stirred within me. Divine. Hidden. I reached inward, desperate to heal myself… but nothing happened. This wasn't something a healer could fix—I knew that. No healer possessed magic that they could use to heal themselves. It just wasn't possible.

Still, I kept reaching. Deeper.

I felt something buried far beneath the surface, calling out to me. It wasn't power I'd learned. It was something only I could awaken.

And then, clarity broke through the haze—sharp, undeniable. I knew what I had to do. The words tore from my throat, fueled by the force now rising inside me… something ancient, something mine.

"BY THE POWER OF THE DRAGON, HELP ME AND MY UNBORN CHILD!"

My body began to illuminate with a golden hue. Ravon stumbled back, his face contorting with confusion and fear. His eyes locked on mine, wide with disbelief, just as the wall behind him erupted in a deafening blast. The chamber shook as stone shattered outward like a volcanic eruption. He ducked instinctively, debris whistling past his head.

From the chaos, it came.

The Dragon Stone—once lost, once hidden—soared through the air, aglow with burning light, its power unmistakable. And then… it found me.

It landed in my outstretched hand like it had always belonged there. The instant my skin met the stone, it disintegrated into dust, its essence pouring into me with a rush of heat, color, and fire. My body arched, glowing with blinding light, the sheer force of it making the air hum and crackle. It's light penetrating the depths of my veins.

And then—silence.

The light faded. I gasped, drawing in the first breath that truly felt like mine. I sat up slowly, my hands moving instinctively to my swollen belly. I cradled it gently, protectively, as tears surged into my eyes—not from fear, but from something far deeper.

Love. Fierce and eternal.

I could feel him—my child. Not just inside me, but around me. As if some part of him had awakened too, answering the call of the stone. It was as if I could already feel his tiny weight in my arms.

Across the room, Freyan stood frozen. Her eyes were wide, her mouth slightly parted, caught between reverence and dread. Something flickered in her gaze—not just awe, but recognition. And Ravon… he was still kneeling where the blast had thrown him, one hand braced on the scorched floor. He stared at me as if seeing a ghost. Or a goddess.

He didn't speak.

He didn't move.

Because in that moment, I was something more than he had ever imagined. And he knew it. He looked deep into my eyes., tears streaming down my face, as I whispered, "I healed the baby…" Ravon's gaze burned with mixed emotions, shock, anger, and deepened love. As realization dawned on him that I had kept a secret from him. I possessed the other Dragon Stone, and it was here, inside Shadowfort all along. He immediately knew that I had merged with the stone, claiming the rightful title of The Divine One, that had been prophesied for centuries. His knowledge of the stone was just part of his history. A reminder of what could come to pass.

Ravon knew this power had bound me to him forever. It had to—because now, I was a threat. I could never leave. I was still his captive. His bride. His obsession. He knew with chilling certainty Drakon would have to be annihilated if he dared try to reclaim me. Ravon's eyes burned with intense emotion. His love for me deepened, yet tangled with anger at my deception, an overwhelming relief that I, and our unborn child, were safe. His low, robust voice finally broke the silence, "You are even more mine now. I can never let you go."

Ravon's eyes seemed to devour every inch of me, his gaze burning with intense possession. Turning towards the door, Ravon dismissed Freyan. Without haste she left the room. He then turned his attention on Valtor, "Bring me a night dress for my bride, and something to eat, Aundrea needs to rest." With swiftness, Valtor left the room.

***

Ravon stepped into the washroom and murmured a command. Moments later, the sound of water being poured echoed softly as unseen servants filled the basin with steaming water, the scent of herbs drifting into the air. He returned to my side and offered his hand, palm up. "Come, Aundrea. Let the bath soothe you," he whispered, gently easing me out of the blood-soaked dress that clung to my trembling body.

Crossing my arms, covering myself, I stepped into the warm water, bloody rivulets streamed down my skin, clouding the clear liquid with a soft, eerie pink hue; like faded rose petals. I curled into a fragile ball, knees tucked tightly to my chest, arms wrapped protectively around them, my forehead pressed against my knees in defeat.

He kissed the top of my head before leaving me, gently closing the door behind him.
Ravon sat on the bed, elbows on knees, hands clasped behind his head—I could imagine his mind reeling with revelations: the Dragon Stone had been hidden in my chambers, secretly empowering me right under his nose; his unborn child saved by its ancient power—a debt he now owed.

Anger simmering inside him, betrayed by my deceit… yet gratitude warming his chest. The baby and I were safe. Had his obsession pushed me to this point, forcing me to take such desperate measures?

My mind reeled with thoughts of what he might do. How he would react.
Then came a soft knock, breaking the silence.
"Come," I heard Ravon say—his voice low, controlled.

Though I remained behind the washroom door, I could hear everything: the quiet scuff of boots on stone, the rustle of fabric, the soft click of a tray being set down. I imagined Valtor, always precise, entering first. He must have brought the gown—the one Ravon mentioned.

Black silk, embroidered with gold and threaded through with royal blue... my favorite color. That detail alone told me this wasn't just an offering—it was a message. A peace offering wrapped in elegance, chosen not for practicality, but to disarm me.

The servant girl had likely brought food. I caught the faint scent of bread, sweet fruit, and something savory—meat, perhaps. All meant to comfort me.

Moments later, I heard footsteps again, then the door shut quietly. They were gone.

Had Ravon watched them with that calculating stillness of his? Had he noted my silence behind the door? The thought made my stomach tighten. He was planning something. I just didn't know what.

Ravon stood up, moving to the bathroom door, his voice low and gentle. "Aundrea, the water must be cold by now. May I help you out?" Silence hung in the air, heavy and still, until the faint sound of splashing water broke the quiet. I was moving. He turned the handle gently and pushed the door open, and a tendril of steam swirled out around him.

"Aundrea, let me help you..."

He helped me step out of the bath, wrapping me in a plush towel, covering my exposed, naked body, then guided me to the bedroom. The black and golden nightgown lay invitingly on the bed. He picked it up, holding it open for me. I slipped into the gown, its royal blue sparks shimmering softly against my pale skin. Ravon's fingers brushed against mine as he smoothed out the fabric with his gentle touch.

He softly sat me on the side of the bed, grabbing a brush from my vanity against the wall. Calmly he brushed the tangles from my hair, in silence that filled the air. He set the brush down, picking up the tray and placing it gently on my lap, sitting down next to me as I ate the meal in silence. He brushed his hand against my hair, moving it out of my face.

Without a word, once I was finished, he took the tray and set it down. Then he turned and pulled back the velvet bedcovers, revealing crisp black sheets. "Into bed, my love," he whispered, helping me settle in. Then, unexpectedly, he slid in beside me, his body a warm presence in the darkness. Ravon gently wrapped his arms around me, cradling me close — his tender gesture from a man who wielded only power and fear.

My tense body slowly relaxed against his, but my mind and heart were still with Drakon. I nestled down further into the soft bed, as exhaustion won. His lips brushed my forehead, a soft kiss as he whispered, "Sleep." My eyelids drifted closed, trust fleeting across my face before sleep claimed me. Ravon held perfectly still, watching me sleep, his expression a tangled mix of obsession, possession, and something that almost resembled love.

***

I opened my eyes slowly, the flickering torchlight slicing through the shadows and piercing the quiet stillness. My body felt heavy beneath the black and gold covers. Ravon sat upright against the headboard, his eyes already fixed on me, unreadable.

"How are you feeling today, Aundrea?" he asked, his voice low but controlled.

I shifted subtly, inching away, needing to put some distance between us. My arms instinctively curled around my belly, as if shielding the child growing inside me. A tremor passed through me—was it Drakon's? Or… could it truly be Ravon's?

"You cannot keep me locked away here forever," I said softly, but with edge sharpening my words. "I'll go mad."

Leaning forward, I wrapped my arms more tightly around myself, protectively. "Will you at least allow me to see Michelle? Or walk in the castle gardens—anything beyond these walls of stone and silence. You do have a garden here at Shadowfort, don't you?" My voice cracked as I tried to steady it. "Is my surrender not enough to earn even a glimpse of freedom?"

Ravon's expression remained unreadable, but a flicker of surprise crossed his features. He steepled his fingers in front of him, elbows resting on his knees, eyes narrowing.

"Freedom is a generous term, Aundrea," he said, his voice cool. "You would call being my bride, mistress of Shadowfort… freedom?"

The question twisted something inside me.

"However," he added slowly, "I might allow you access to the gardens… and Michelle's company."

Hope stirred, rising from somewhere long buried—until he continued.

"On one condition," he said darkly. "The deception, the arguing, the escape attempts—end now. No more whispering to my courtiers. No more begging servants. Promise me, Aundrea."

I did not hesitate. I surged forward, laying my cheek against his chest, my arms wrapping around him. "Yes. I promise. I promise…"

He hesitated, then held me tightly, his fingers running softly along the back of my head. The other wrapped around my waist, firm but no longer threatening. He gently lifted my chin until my eyes met his, then kissed me—deliberate, possessive. I took a deep breath, as if it were my last, and surrendered to his touch, losing all sense of control. We slowly parted, our eyes still locked in the moment,

"Come, Aundrea," he murmured. "Let me show you something."

He rose from the bed and pulled his cloak from a nearby chair, draping it around my nightgown like a shield. I slipped my feet into the soft black and gold slippers that waited on the floor beside the bed. With a flick of his hand, shadows stirred—blue and purple sparks arcing through the air as a fresh cloak shimmered into existence around his shoulders.

He extended his palm, covering my hand with his other. His thumb traced the ring he had placed there—its stone absorbing streaks of glowing light, blue and violet tendrils curling inside the gem. Then he leaned in, brushing his lips against mine once more before pulling back, his eyes clinging to mine.

"Place your hand over the ring, Aundrea," he instructed.

I obeyed. The stone beneath my palm pulsed with dark energy. A low rumble shook the chamber as stones began to shift, grinding apart until a tunnel opened before us. Ravon took my hand and led me through the threshold, the wall closing silently behind us.

"The ring will only take you where I allow," he warned, his voice grave. "It grants you no freedom—only permission. But be loyal to me, and I will give you the world. Betray me…" He paused, then leaned closer. "You already know what happens when you make me angry."

My breath hitched as I stepped through.

The chamber we entered took my breath away.

A massive glass dome arched above us, light refracting in soft hues across its surface. Diamond panes shimmered like stars caught in daylight. Grand pillars surrounded the courtyard, sentinels standing guard over beauty imprisoned. There were no doors, no passageways—just this perfect illusion.

The garden beneath the dome was stunning. Native flowers from Lisona bloomed in colors that defied nature— deep sapphire, radiant amethyst, glowing roses. The air was thick with their scent, sweet and sharp and intoxicating. I moved slowly, pulling my hand out of his, absorbing it all—the scent, the breeze, the colors of my stolen home.

I turned in a slow circle, eyes wide, heart aching.

This was my soul.

This was Lisona.

Imprisoned.

Tears blurred my vision as I turned to Ravon, my voice a trembling whisper. "This… is a piece of my soul you've recreated here."

I took a step closer, pain flickering across my chest. "Lisona's beauty… trapped like me… beneath your dome."

Ravon's eyes did not waver, though a shadow of vulnerability flashed beneath the intensity. "Because I wanted you to feel at home," he replied. "Shadowfort is what I decide it will be."

I didn't know whether to thank him or curse him.

Then—

"Aundrea…"

Michelle's voice called softly. I spun around, my heart leaping from my chest.

She stepped out from behind a pillar, cautious but smiling. And behind her, Valtor stood in the shadows of a tunnel—only for a moment—before giving Ravon a silent nod and sealing the wall behind him.

My eyes darted to Ravon, silently begging. He gave a single nod and a wave of his hand. That was all I needed.

I ran to Michelle and threw my arms around her, clinging as though she might disappear.

Taking both of her hands, I led her toward the garden's center. "Isn't it beautiful, Michelle?"

She looked around, her expression caught somewhere between awe and dread.

"I could live right here for all eternity," I whispered.

Michelle's gaze locked onto mine—she could see it, even when I could not. The haze I was sinking into. The invisible strings beginning to pull, already playing their part. Her voice barely more than breath, she whispered, you might have to." Her voice trembled as she added something else, something important, but I couldn't make sense of it. The sound reached me, but the meaning did not. My mind wouldn't hold on.

Before I could respond—CRACK.

Ravon's hand struck Michelle with the back of his hand.

She dropped to the stone floor, a cry escaping her lips, blood dripping from her nose.

My heart screamed silently as the warmth of the garden suddenly vanished, leaving only the cruel frost of Shadowfort behind. I fell to her side, cradling her in my arms. Tears streamed down my cheeks as I looked up at Ravon, overcome with emotion. "Why…" I choked out, "Why do you have to ruin everything?" My voice cracked with anguish as Michelle's blood soaked into the fabric of my nightdress.

Ravon began to speak to Michelle, but their voices blurred together—sharp, heated, but distant, like a storm rumbling behind a closed door. Michelle's tone was clipped, desperate. Ravon's was lower, colder, laced with the kind of fury that settled in bones.

They were arguing. I knew that much. Michelle's eyes kept flicking toward me, wide with fear, her hands clenched at her sides. I could feel her anger, the way it trembled through the air like static. Ravon's face was tight with control, but his jaw twitched—barely contained rage or something worse.

But the words—the actual words—slipped through me like water through cupped hands. I heard them, but I couldn't hold onto them. Couldn't make sense of them. It was like trying to read a dream.

Why couldn't I understand?

I blinked hard, struggling to focus. My mind felt wrapped in cotton, my thoughts fogged and slow. The world around me felt too bright, too sharp, just wrong.

Michelle shouted something, voice breaking, and for a breath, I almost caught it. Almost. But it was gone again before I could grasp its shape. She was trying to tell me something. But I couldn't understand why.

Ravon's chest rose and fell with restrained fury, his eyes ablaze with warning. "She dared to suggest that my gift to you was a prison," he growled. Clarity returning from my clouded mind, He took a step toward us, but I shifted, shielding Michelle with my body.

"As if you hadn't already chosen to stay when offered freedom," he continued.

Freedom. The word stung like venom. In Ravon's twisted mind, he clung to a distorted version of love, calling it freedom while using Michelle as a hostage. Michelle let out a soft moan in my arms. I gently stroked her hair, her blood warm against my skin. My tears dripped onto her forehead. I placed my hand gently over Michelle's face, reaching deep inside myself to summon the hidden light. Warmth began to stir in my chest, rising toward my fingertips—but before I could release it, Ravon lifted his hand. A swirling haze of deep violet and electric blue crackled in his palm. With a sharp flick of his wrist, the dark energy lashed out like a whip, striking my hand with a force that felt like a stinging slap. The power I had gathered scattered instantly, ripped from my grasp as though torn by invisible claws. I recoiled, gasping, my palm tingling with the echo of his attack.

"Look at the monster you become," I said through clenched teeth, "when anyone dares suggest you don't own me, you wish them pain." My voice trembled, hoarse with heartbreak. "Is this the man I'm supposed to marry? The father of my child?" Ravon's face contorted, rage flickering against something deeper—pain, maybe, or guilt—but quickly buried beneath his anger. He raised his hand, summoning his dark magic. A haze of shadows swirled around us, thick and cold.

Then—darkness.

***

When the haze cleared, I was back on the floor of my quarters. Alone.

Michelle was gone.

My heart seized in panic. "Where did she go, Ravon?" I shouted.

He appeared behind me, his voice calm and cold. "She is with Valtor, in her cell." I turned away from him, fury boiling inside me. He reached out, placing a firm hand on my shoulder. "Why won't you let me heal her." I shouted, anger and guilt hovering in my voice.

"Michelle is a negative influence on you, Aundrea, she needs to learn her lesson." he said softly. "I will find you another friend… for now." My heart broke all over again. "You can't just replace friends, Ravon. You cannot choose them for me. Friends are loyal. They love you unconditionally." My voice cracked, each word falling like a stone into the silence between us, this was a concept that he could not reach.

A knock came at the door. Ravon didn't look away from me. "Come," he commanded.

Valtor entered, his face unreadable. "I apologize for the interruption, my lord, but your Seer is at the gate. She brings news of Drakon."

My breath caught.

Ravon turned to me, lifting my chin to meet his gaze. His voice softened again, but the fire in his eyes had not dimmed. "We will discuss this when I return, my love."

He pressed his lips against mine—soft, possessive. I tried to pull away, but he held me firmly, then released me and vanished in a swirl of black haze, Valtor close behind him.

***

I sank onto the bed, trembling. My hands clutched my belly, fear creeping in like a chill. Would Drakon come for me? Would he even want to?

Tears spilled again. I slid from the bed to the floor and knelt, folding my hands tightly in my lap. I reached inward, drawing strength from the spark buried deep within me. I let it rise—let it flow like wind through the stone walls of Shadowfort. A warm sensation bloomed in my chest, pulsing outward.

I closed my eyes and whispered into the darkness, praying my words would find him.

"Drakon... my love. I hope you're listening. I almost lost the baby. I had to merge with the Dragon Stone to save our child. Ravon saw it happen. He knows I'm the Divine One now. He saw me change..."

A sob escaped me. My voice cracked, raw and desperate.

"Please, don't leave me. I'm sorry for my betrayal. I don't know what's happening to me. I love you... I need you...please save me..."

Οἶκος Δράκων

HOUSE DRAKON

Chapter 11

Between Light and Blood

Nearly a moon ago… just after Aundrea vanished into Ravon's clutches, I made my choice beneath Lisona's burning sun.

I halted my horse, Vandros, abruptly, dust kicking up around his hooves. "Sabion, hold!" I called out, my voice firm and urgent. Sabion reined in his own horse, turning to face me with a questioning gaze.

"I need you to continue on to Crimson Spine Mountain," I instructed. "Locate the Death Stone and guard it until I come. But beware, Sabion—touching the stone with your bare hands will unleash a dark curse."

Sabion nodded gravely, his jaw tight with resolve. "I'll find it, Drakon," he said, his tone resolute.

"I'm going to Shadowfort," I continued. "To my brother's cursed palace. I must save my wife. I cannot leave her in his grasp."

Sabion gave a single nod, understanding the weight of our tasks. Without another word, he spurred his horse and disappeared into the horizon, riding hard toward the Crimson Spine.

Turning back to my remaining men, I raised my voice to rally them. "Men, we ride for Shadowfort— Ravon's dark lair! Our mission: rescue your Empress, Lady Aundrea, from his evil grasp!"

A roar of affirmation erupted from the guards. Steel rang out as swords were drawn, the scent of iron mingling with sweat and dust. We rode hard, hooves thundering against the dry ground, a battle-bound force with one purpose.

The sun blazed above us, merciless in its heat, as if Lisona itself scorched us in warning. The terrain changed as we pressed on—green hills giving way to blackened trees twisted by shadow. Ravon's corruption had leeched into the very veins of the land.

***

Days passed beneath the cloak of a grey, mist-choked forest. An uneasy silence clung to our column like smoke. My guards gripped the hilts of their swords tighter, every snapped twig echoing louder than it should.

By dusk on the third day, we reached a shrinking stream. We stopped to water our horses and to catch fleeting moments of rest. I paced along the stream's edge, haunted by visions of Aundrea—bound in darkness, eyes hollow with fear. The weight of it pierced my chest, sharper than any blade.

A voice broke through the noise. Thane, one of my seasoned veterans, approached quietly. "Your Lordship, we may have been spotted. Ravon's scouts could be watching us. We must prepare for ambush."

I nodded once, scanning the mist-shrouded forest. "Agreed. Split the men into three squads. Two will flank left and right to scout ahead. The third remains with me in center column."

Thane bowed his head and moved to relay the orders.

We pushed forward in formation, the air thicker now, charged with tension. Then, from the left flank, a rider galloped toward me—Viktor Asanfir, his face pale.

"Drakon, my lord," he said breathlessly, "I've encountered a woman... a Seer. She appeared out of nowhere and took hold of my arm."

I frowned, every muscle tensing. "What did she say?"

"She said Ravon holds Aundrea captive in Smiatin Ridge…
a volcanic place, far from Shadowfort."
I narrowed my eyes, fury creeping up my spine. "That's a
lie."

Viktor blinked. "But she was a Seer, my lord…"
"She was corrupted," I snapped. "Tempted by Ravon's
power, no doubt. He would never move Aundrea far from
his grasp, not while she still holds value to him. Shadowfort
is where she remains."

Though doubt flickered in my men's eyes, they
obeyed without question. They mounted their horses and
rode on, their loyalty unwavering despite the dangers.

***

A full moon passed in our journey. At last, we
reached a small clearing surrounded by towering, ancient
trees. A brook trickled through the grass, and I raised a
hand.

"Set camp here," I commanded. "We move at first
light."

Tents were pitched, fires lit. The air grew heavy
with anticipation. Men sharpened blades and murmured in
low tones. The smell of burning wood clung to my armor.
I walked among them, offering quiet strength. Thane
approached once more, his expression unreadable.
"Drakon… about the Seer. Do you think her warning held
any truth?"

I stared into the flames, the flickering light casting
shadows across my thoughts.
"She may have once been one of the Ancient Ones," I
admitted. "But the darkness has twisted her. Whether her
words were truth, a decoy, or a trap—we continue to
Shadowfort. With caution."

Thane gave a solemn nod, and we stood in silence as night pressed in around our camp.

Our campsite was aglow with warm fire pits, casting flickering shadows across the tents that circled the clearing. My men relaxed, their laughter carrying into the night air. Some whittled wooden trinkets, others sharpened their blades or lay resting, ready for dawn's march to Shadowfort. The forest beyond our perimeter loomed dark and menacing, trees like skeletal fingers reaching toward us.

***

Suddenly, branches snapped.

Ravon's dark army burst forth from the blackness—swords raised, eyes glowing like coals, their battle cries splitting the night like thunder.

My men scrambled to arms, the sudden clash of steel ringing out across the field. Chaos erupted in a blaze of motion—shields splintered, arrows hissed through the smoky air, and the scent of blood thickened with each heartbeat.

A shadow guard lunged at me, blade gleaming. I parried hard, the jolt of impact rattling down my arm. I pivoted, slicing across his chest—his scream lost in the roar of combat. Another came at me from behind. I turned, ducked, drove my sword upward through his ribs.

All around me, the battlefield burned. Flames from toppled torches danced across armor and flesh. Warhorses shrieked and reared. I fought with fury in my veins—cutting through Ravon's men like a storm given form. Each clash rang like a drumbeat of war, each breath drawn through smoke and blood. I was not just fighting for her. I was fighting to bring an empire back from the brink.

Just as I dispatched one attacker, another figure stepped

from a rippling rift in the shadows—a dark guard, his voice dripping with malicious intent. "I have a message from Lord Ravon," he sneered. "Aundrea was offered her freedom and chose to stay with him. Your pursuit is useless."

I responded with fire building beneath my breath. "You lie!" I bellowed, sword trembling in my grasp. The guard raised his hand, and a rippling, mirror-like portal opened beside him. Aundrea's face appeared. She stood in a doorway beside Ravon, her voice barely above a whisper. The words that followed shattered me. I watched, paralyzed, as she turned down freedom, her voice gentle but resolute.

It had to be a manipulation.
Dark magic.
The spell.

My eyes remained fixed on the portal, mind reeling from her devastating words. "No…" I whispered, then roared, "NO!" My sword arm faltered. The dark guard sneered again. "Seems your beloved's heart belongs to another."
Enraged, I regained composure, struck down another attacker, and turned on him. "That is not her voice. Ravon controls her!"

I stumbled backward, my breath shallow. A surge of dragon power rushed through me. The mirror vanished, but Aundrea's words still echoed in my mind.
My hands trembled—I looked down. They had transformed into claws.
Then back again.

A strange heat coursed through my veins. My skin still tingled with the remnants of dragon magic. I had shifted—partially.

Thane approached cautiously, his sword still dripping with enemy blood. "Drakon, my lord... what sorcery was that?" I shook my head, still stunned. "I... don't know. My shift is still weak."

My men formed a circle around me. Wary glances passed between them. Their leader had just revealed that he didn't understand his own power.
"I could feel my dragon heritage awakening," I said, voice rough. "But it faded as quickly as it came."
"We've had enough darkness for one night," I declared, regaining my strength. "Rest now. At dawn, we ride for Shadowfort—stronger and more determined than ever."

My warriors nodded grimly, tending wounds and sharpening blades. Thane spoke with me privately, his expression unreadable.
"My lord... do you think her words were truly her own?" I clenched my jaw. "You're asking if Ravon spoke through her?"

Thane did not answer, but his eyes said enough. "Could his magic be influencing you through your bond with her?"
The thought sent a chill through me.
"Thane," I snapped, more harshly than I intended. "Lady Aundrea is not in love with Ravon. She is under his spell. She doesn't know what she is saying. She is trapped in that dark palace—counting on us to bring her home."

Thane flinched. I continued, lowering my voice but not my conviction. "My dragon core senses no dark magic within me. If we abandon her, Ravon wins. And darkness will blanket all of Lisona. It is written. It is prophesied."
He bowed. "Forgive me, Lord Drakon."
"Rest now," I ordered gently.
He obeyed. My warriors watched in solemn silence as Thane withdrew, his expression now etched with

acceptance and renewed loyalty.

I walked through the camp, checking on each man, ensuring morale held. Torches cast flickering shadows on their determined faces. Every soul among us knew our cause was just.

I stopped at the camp's edge, gazing north. Shadowfort rose in the distance—twisted towers black against the moonlight. Even the stars struggled to shine through its veil. My heart burned with resolve. Aundrea would be saved. Ravon would fall. Light would return to Lisona.

Then, a breeze stirred the trees, and I heard it—a whisper so faint, so fragile, I nearly missed it: "Drakon... my love. I hope you're listening. I almost lost the baby. I had to merge with the Dragon Stone to save our child. Ravon saw it happen. He knows I'm the Divine One now. He saw me change... "Please, don't leave me. I'm sorry for my betrayal. I don't know what's happening to me. I love you... I need you... please save me..." My legs gave way.

I stumbled back, gripping a nearby tree for support, eyes wide with tears. "Aundrea..." I whispered. Her voice was real—familiar and unmistakable. A flood of emotion surged through me. Relief—she was alive. Rage—Ravon knew the truth. Agony—she had nearly lost our child. And love— undeniable, pure, and eternal. Thane and the others rushed to my side. "Lord Drakon, what is it?"

I composed myself, then repeated her haunting prayer aloud. "She carries our child, and Ravon holds her prisoner. To save the baby, she bound herself to the Dragon Stone... and now, she's reaching out—begging me to come." I scanned the crowd of loyal men and took a step towards them. "It was Aundrea," I declared, my voice steady and fierce. "I sensed the power of the Dragon from within. No dark magic could fool those senses."

The campsite erupted into murmurs of determination. I raised my hand. "We march at dawn."

My warriors' faces hardened with resolve. They were ready—eager—to bring down Ravon's darkness.

Thane approached me once last time. "May the dragons watch over us tomorrow, Lord Drakon."

I clasped his shoulder firmly. "They will, Thane. For Aundrea, for our child, and for Lisona's freedom."

With that, I retreated to my tent, but rest eluded me. I lay on my pallet, eyes wide open, haunted by the vision of Aundrea's face—her voice trembling, her plea raw with desperation. Our unborn child's safety hung in the balance. Ravon's downfall had to come tomorrow. My fingers tightened around the hilt of my dagger, the cold steel grounding me. Slowly, the adrenaline faded, replaced by exhaustion. My eyelids grew heavy… Tomorrow would bring battle. Tonight, restless sleep.

***

Dawn broke like a blade across the sky, slashing through the last shreds of darkness. Crimson and gold bathed our camp in fierce light as I stepped out of my tent, my eyes scanning for readiness. Warriors tightened armor, sharpened blades, and adjusted their shields—each marked with the soaring dragon of Lisona.

Horses snorted and pawed the ground, sensing the coming charge.

Thane appeared at my side, his gaze locked on Shadowfort's black silhouette.

I raised both arms high and shouted for all to hear, "Today we reclaim Lady Aundrea! For our unborn heir! For light

against darkness! CHARGE WITH ME!"
Our army roared in unison. Hooves thundered as we surged
toward Shadowfort's gates.
Arrows rained down. Ravon's soldiers not moving, just
standing at the gate.
But something else was wrong.

We burst through the haze—only to find ourselves
not at Shadowfort, but back inside our own camp. Chaos
reigned. Horses reared, confused. Arrows still flew. Shouts
echoed as men scrambled to make sense of it.
I reined in my horse and shouted to Thane. "Stop! We're
caught in a Shadowfort trap."

His face was pale. "Lord Drakon, what's
happening?"
I scanned the camp, watching my soldiers circle again in
confusion. "Everyone halt! We need to talk. Gather the
men!"

The noise ebbed as I raised my voice over the
clamor. "This is a shadow trap. It's magic—and it's a
riddle."
A younger soldier stepped forward, his face twisted with
doubt. "With respect, Lord Drakon… how do you solve a
riddle that doesn't ask a question?"
Fear flickered in the eyes of others. Doubt rippled through
the ranks.

I squared my shoulders, voice calm but
commanding. "Exactly. This trap doesn't present a riddle
with words. Ravon's magic defies convention. We must see
the riddle in the trap itself."
Thane rubbed his chin, his brow furrowed. "You think the
trap… is the question?"
"Yes," I said. "But it's not verbal. It's magical."
Thane's voice was uncertain. "Then how do we fight magic
we cannot see or hear?"

I stood in silence, then murmured aloud, "One and one."
Thane blinked. "A simple equation?"
I nodded. "We fight magic with magic."

I closed my eyes, drawing deep within myself,
summoning the ancient magic of my lineage. My body
tensed. I forced the transformation—claws erupted where
hands had been. Heat flared beneath my skin as scales
spread like glowing embers across my arms. My face
reshaped, dragon features rising—silver, gold, crimson, and
the sunlit hues glimmered in the morning sun.
Dragon senses ignited within me. The illusion shattered.

The camp revealed its truth: glowing magical auras
surrounding my warriors, tendrils of unseen enchantment
coiled around us. The dense miasma fog clung to
Shadowfort like a cursed veil. My eyes dropped to the
ground—hoofprints shimmered with magic, trailing
forward toward the gates... and circling back.
Apparitions of our charge played before me—ghostly
images of our men riding forward only to loop endlessly,
returning like echoes.

Thane's voice broke through. "What does it mean,
Lord Drakon? Why do we keep returning here?"
I turned to him, my dragon-scaled face set with grim
determination. "The answer is not forward... it's
backward."

We wheeled our horses around. Blades gleamed.
Silence fell—not from fear, but from focus. Then—
together—we thundered back the way we came.
As we neared the point of departure... the fog swallowed
us again.
And once more—we emerged in the same cursed camp.
Men dismounted in frustration. Some cursed under their
breath. Others simply looked at me, waiting.
I raised my hand. "Stand down. Let them rest, Thane. I

need to think."
He nodded and relayed the command.

Men slumped against trees, tended to horses, drank from the stream. I moved to a fallen log, its bark rough against my palms as I sat and stared into the flickering flames. My thoughts tangled like vines. What were the spirits trying to show me? What was the trap really hiding? The sky faded from gold to violet. Then violet surrendered to night. Stars emerged like watchful sentinels in the black above. I felt the dragon slip away, leaving my mortal form behind.

I stood up slowly, regaining my will. "Thane, make camp for the night. Shadowfort will wait. Darkness is Ravon's ally. We will not face him tonight."

Chapter 12

The Whispered Plea

Somewhere beyond these cursed walls, I felt him—
Drakon.
Like a whisper caught in the breath of the wind, his
presence stirred the bond between us. He was coming. I
knew it in my blood. But so did Ravon.

Valtor led Ravon through Shadowfort's secret
passages, their footsteps vanishing into the stone like
ghosts. Rising from the sumptuous armchair set by the
tapestries and pressed against the chill of the stone wall, my
heart pounded with an inexplicable urgency—as though
fate itself were on the verge of being sealed. Near the
eastern gate, the seer waited, a silent sentinel shrouded in
shadows and quiet, his presence as enigmatic as the shifting
tide of destiny.

"My lord Ravon," she intoned, her voice thick with
unseen power. "Drakon marches toward Shadowfort with
his army. He comes to reclaim the Divine One… your
bride."
Ravon's eyes darkened. "I tried to send him on a decoy, but
he saw through it—he senses the darkness surrounding
her."
He heard her cry, carried on the wings of the dragon.
He heard her prayer… through the bond." He growled.
The seer's confirmation only fueled his wrath. "He knows
Lady Aundrea has merged with the Stone. He knows she
used the power of the Divine One to save the baby… she
pleaded for him to rescue her."

***

My heart sank as I sat alone in my quarters, still reeling from that desperate prayer. I had clung to the faintest hope Drakon would hear me—some part of me believing the bond we shared might still reach across the void. But now, my mind was a storm of fear and uncertainty, every thought unraveling into dread.

Kneeling with my hands folded in my lap, I flinched at the sound of voices beyond the heavy door. Ravon and Valtor, were in the throne room speaking. Ravon's tone was sharp, venomous, each word striking like a blade.

"Summon the Dark Guard," he hissed. "The Endless Shadow Trap has already been set. He'll never escape now. Time is nothing to him—he'll wander in circles while the real world moves on."

A chill swept through me, settling deep into my bones. I wrapped my arms around myself, trembling at what I knew was coming next.

"And Aundrea," Ravon added coldly, "will pay for her betrayal… tonight."

Betrayal? I wondered. Does he know I tried to reach Drakon? If he does, what will he do?
I shivered violently. His rage seemed to seep into the very walls of Shadowfort, like the stone itself had absorbed his fury. My heart pounded against my ribs as I paced the floor, my feet tapping against the stone below. The weight of his looming presence was almost unbearable.

The door slammed open with a crash that echoed like thunder. Ravon stood in the doorway, his eyes blazing. I stumbled backward in a feeble attempt to move away. "You dared reach out to him," he hissed. His voice was low and guttural, more beast than man. I could see the haze of magic swarming his body. "How could you betray me like this, Aundrea… after everything I've given you?"

I froze, fear squeezing my throat. He stepped closer. I tried to move back further, but the wall had already staked its claim on me. I tried to speak, but my voice wavered. "Ravon… what do you mean?"

He spun on his heel, rage radiating from every inch of him. "Don't play dumb with me. You called to Drakon. I know what you did. Did you think I wouldn't find out?"

I raised a trembling hand in a silent plea. "Are you talking about what I said aloud earlier? When I sat on the floor, crying?" My voice cracked, tears slipping down my cheeks. "I wasn't trying to reach him. I swear it. I just whispered his name—I didn't know he would hear me."

Ravon's expression shifted. Confusion flickered in his gaze, then suspicion. "No. The seer told me otherwise. She said you called to him through the Dragon Stone… begged him to save you."

My tears came faster, panic welling inside of me. "That's partly true—but not how she made it sound." My voice shook. "She must've seen me praying. I was desperate, Ravon. I didn't mean to call him. I just wanted to be heard by someone. I'm part of the Dragon Stone now—you know that. But I don't understand the power of The Divine One. I don't know how to control it."

My voice cracked. "I wasn't trying to defy you. Please believe me. I almost lost the baby. I don't even know how I managed to save it. If it happened again, I… I might not be able to do it."

Ravon's rage seemed to falter, if only slightly. His eyes searched mine, his breathing uneven. He took a cautious step forward. "Aundrea… look at me."

I slowly lowered my hands, my cheeks streaked with tears. Our eyes locked. He stared deep, as if searching for deception.

Then his gaze drifted down to my belly, and something shifted in him. "The baby..." he murmured, placing a tentative hand against my stomach. His voice softened with a rare vulnerability. "Our child... almost lost to us..."

I swallowed, willing myself not to tremble. "I swear on my soul, Ravon. I spoke words aloud, but I didn't know he would hear them. I didn't mean to reach him."
He lingered there for a long moment, the fire in his eyes dimming. Then, in a hushed voice, he said, "Promise me... you will never speak his name aloud again. If you ever reach out to him, you'll regret it."
Relief swept through me, so intense it nearly knocked me to my knees. I nodded, desperate for this confrontation to end.

He placed his hands on my shoulders, his grip firm but not cruel. "There's something else," he said, voice lower now, but no less commanding. "I'm moving Michelle to another cell. I don't want you seeing her again—at least not for a while."
"What?" I asked, panic rising again.
"She is a negative influence. I saw joy in your face today in the garden. You twirled like a girl again... until she took that from you with a single phrase."

My heart ached with fear of our separation. He continued, "I'm assigning two servant women to chambers near yours. They'll tend to your needs. Perhaps you'll make friends with them—but do not conspire with them. They don't have a ring. They have no access to the garden. They have no hope of escape."

His voice dropped to a whisper, cold as death. "If you disobey... they will suffer. Don't make me prove it."
I felt a surge of fear as Ravon's grip on my shoulders tightened, his fingers digging into my flesh just enough to

deliver the warning with weight. His eyes bore into mine, demanding not just understanding but complete submission. I lowered my gaze, my heart racing, finally grasping the full extent of the prison that was Shadowfort.

He leaned in, his breath warm against my ear, a whisper both intimate and threatening. "You're beginning to understand the privileges of being my future bride... and the consequences of disobedience."

His lips brushed my earlobe, a feather-light touch that sent a ripple of guilt and desire, sparking throughout my body. I shuddered. His presence was smothering, and my thoughts spiraled—this was no longer just captivity. This was possession. I felt as if I was losing all control. Ravon pulled back, eyes scanning my face—fear, resignation, and a flicker of defiance still clinging to me. "The dark guard reports Drakon's army has reached Wysteria Valley," he said, a cruel smile tugging at the corners of his lips.

"As we speak, they walk blindly into my endless shadow trap. Time will have no meaning to him. Your former love will soon be mine to crush."

His words struck like a blow. I fought to keep my face still, but tears welled up, stinging my eyes. "What will you do to him?" I whispered, my voice so fragile it barely escaped my throat.
I recoiled, shivering, my tears falling like rain. "If you promise to spare his life, then I vow to stay here... with you, with our baby. You have my word."

My hands trembled as I pressed them together in a desperate plea. "I'll marry you, Ravon. Willingly. No tricks, no escapes. I'll be your wife, your companion... your everything."

I dropped to my knees before him, voice choked by sobs. "Just spare Drakon's life. Exile him, imprison him—just don't kill him."

Ravon's expression flickered with surprise, then fascination. For the first time, I could tell he believed me. "Aundrea… you would give up everything for him? And yet you offer me your surrender. Why?"

His eyes narrowed, sharp and searching, as if trying to pierce through the layers of my soul. The air between us thickened, taut with unspoken demands. He tilted his head slightly, a flicker of confusion buried beneath the cold certainty in his gaze. Love was foreign to him—an emotion twisted by power, not born from tenderness. He couldn't grasp the shape of it, not the kind that gave without conquering.

The silence between us stretched thin, vibrating with the weight of a question he didn't know how to ask—or perhaps, feared to understand. I could feel it, lingering in his stare like a blade poised at my throat: Was it only to save Drakon... or did some part of me love him?

I raised my hand to wipe the tears streaming down my face. "I cannot lie to you about my heart," I admitted. "Drakon has it. But when I'm with you, I feel something… intense."

I turned away, the torchlight casting our shadows across the stone wall.

Slowly, I turned back, locking my eyes with him—his face, so hauntingly like his brother's, yet colder. "Every day I look at you… I see him. And my feelings for you are tangled in those memories."

The tears returned, hot against my cheeks. "But maybe—over time—I could learn to love you."

My voice was soft, cracking under the weight of emotion. "Let him leave with his life… if he comes. Please, Ravon."

His voice was low and shadowed. "If he survives my trap, Aundrea… I will show him mercy. But he will not leave."

Relief collapsed my knees beneath me, tears still streaming, though now tinged with hope. "Thank you," I whispered, barely audible.

His gaze softened as he stepped forward, fingertips brushing my cheek. "Our bargain is sealed, Aundrea." He drew me in, wrapping his arms around my waist. "I love you."
Then his lips crashed into mine—not a kiss of tenderness, but a claim. It was fierce, unrelenting, a collision of mouths and breath. His kiss burned with hunger, demanding my surrender. I felt my body react, every nerve alight, trembling beneath his touch. His mouth moved against mine like wildfire—consuming, desperate, possessive. I raised my hands, holding his shoulders, as he pulled me in closer. I was being swept away, like a wave crashing down on my soul.
Finally, he released me.

"Aundrea, my love," he said softly, almost sweetly. "I need to move Michelle. I'll return later to dine with you. I'll also send Valtor to relocate Sarah and Dania to new quarters near yours."

His words were like silk draped over steel—calm, composed, hiding something cruel beneath. He turned toward the door, already halfway gone when the dread in my chest surged like a rising tide.

"No, wait," I breathed, but it barely left my lips.

Panic wrapped around my ribs like a vise. Michelle. The last flicker of familiarity in this hollow fortress. The only soul here who looked at me like I was still me. My heart thundered as the distance between us widened. He was taking her. Taking her away from me.

I couldn't move. I couldn't stop him. Where would he send her? Would she be hurt? Would he punish her because of me? The image of her alone in some shadowed cell made my stomach twist. I wanted to run after her, cling to her hand, beg him to leave her with me, but my body was betraying me. I was frozen under the weight of fear and helplessness. But in that moment, I snapped. I yelled out again,

"Please, Ravon," I added softly.

I needed him to look at me one last time. To see the truth in my eyes, the raw desperation, the longing that still flickered despite everything.

"Michelle is not good for you, my love," he said, his voice like a cold, hard stone. "And you have nothing left to bargain with."

My heart sank at his words, but I refused to yield. I followed him into the throne room as he turned to unlock Michelle's cell. I spoke out in desperation, pleading for him to see beyond his resolve.
"That's not true," I said, hurrying in behind him, my slender hand lightly grasping his arm, turning him toward me. My eyes locked onto his, brimming with tears, silently pleading.
Ravon's gaze narrowed, curiosity flickering within his cold stare. "What is it that you have to offer me, my bride?" His voice was low, menacingly gentle.

My grip on his arm faltered, my dignity collapsing beneath the weight of despair. I sank to the floor, my velvet dress pooling around me like a dark cloud. My face tilted downward, tears streaming silently as I whispered—a haunting admission of defeat.

Ravon turned to me, a low chuckle escaping his lips, laced with amusement at my desperate attempt to rescue my friend. He seemed to find twisted humor in my plea. Still standing, he squatted beside me, his fingers lifting my chin with gentle, yet commanding force until our eyes met. His gaze was intense—predatory—and it eroded at my soul.

"How about a compromise, my love?" he purred, his voice a silken threat.

"One moon… That is all you have. Marry me, and that is the day I return Michelle to you."

My eyes fell, my spirit crushed. I tried to pull my chin from his grasp, the almost imperceptible shake of my head betraying my inner turmoil. Knowing my fate was sealed, I whispered, completely defeated,

"…Okay."

Even a single moon felt like it could stretch into eternity. One moon under his control felt like a lifetime. I couldn't tell if, by the end, I'd still be me—or just the pieces he hadn't yet broken.

Ravon's eyes gleamed with triumph as he turned and strode toward the cell. The metal door clanged open, echoing through the vast chamber. Michelle huddled on her bed, knees drawn to her chest, her eyes wide with fear—of a trapped animal.

"Come, Michelle," Ravon ordered, his voice booming. She obeyed swiftly, her gaze fixed on the cold stone floor I sat upon. Ravon seized her by the wrist, his grip tight and possessive. I felt my heart aching as he led Michelle toward a shimmering portal he opened with a flick of his wrist. They stepped through, and the portal snapped shut behind them, leaving me alone in the heavy silence.

Darkness seemed to close in around me as I sat frozen on the hard stone floor, despair clinging to me like mist. My eyes remained fixed on the place where the portal had vanished, my mind reeling from the finality of Michelle's departure.

"One moon…" Ravon's words echoed in my mind. "The day you marry me is the day I return Michelle to you."

A cold dread settled in my chest. I was truly trapped now. The only sound in the throne room was the ragged rhythm of my own breath. Suddenly, the torches on the wall started to dance, and another portal opened. Valtor stepped through, accompanied by two women.

"Milady," he said softly, "Ravon instructed me to introduce Sarah and Dania, your new attendants."

I turned to them, forcing a faint smile—a mask to hide my shattered heart. But as I looked into their wary eyes, I wondered… would they become my allies or Ravon's spies?

***

Days passed, turning into weeks. The wedding drew closer. My beloved Drakon remained ensnared in Ravon's shadow trap.

Sarah came to help me dress for the day. She was outgoing, with a beautiful smile—tall and slender, and likely close to my age. There was a quiet grace in the way she moved, and she spoke with the ease of someone well-educated. She was the daughter of the Grand Duke—Lady Sarah of House Primston... Sarah's father was loyal to Ravon.

Dania was younger, quieter, and clearly broken. A fragile shadow of a girl. She was half human, like me, a quiet reminder of where I came from.

Sarah stood behind me, lacing my corset with steady hands. Her fingers brushed mine, soft and deliberate. When I looked back at her, her eyes sparkled with warmth. For a moment, I found myself wondering… could she be trusted?

Ravon's warning echoed in my mind: "Speak of this to no one." But hope clung to me like a stubborn ember.

"Sarah," I said, "would you give Dania and me a moment? I need to speak with her privately."

Sarah curtsied low, her expression unreadable, as she slipped out of the room. The heavy steel door closed behind her with a hollow thud.
I turned to Dania, heart heavy with concern. "Dania, what happened to you? You seem so shielded, so closed off."

Her gaze flickered away, lashes trembling as tears gathered in her eyes. "I... I don't want to talk about it," she whispered, voice catching on the last word. She turned from me sharply, shoulders quivering, arms wrapped around herself like she could hold her pain in place.
I stepped closer, cautiously. The stone floor sent a chill into my bare feet. The air between us felt thin, fragile—like one wrong word might shatter her completely. I didn't want to push, but I needed to reach her. I had to.
She was the only one here who might still feel human. And I felt her pain like it echoed inside me—wounded, familiar, and raw.

My voice came out soft, careful, but steady. "Was it Ravon?" I asked. "Did he hurt you?"
Tears threatened to spill over as I stepped closer, my voice low and trembling. "What's wrong, Dania? You can tell me. I'm here for you."

Her lips parted, but no words came out. I could see the war waging behind her eyes, like something fractured inside her was trying to piece itself back together. Her hands clenched at her sides, shaking.

She swallowed hard, her voice breaking through like a whisper torn from the wreckage of her soul.

"Ravon… he killed my family. I…" Her shoulders quivered. "I'm not allowed to talk about it. He forbade it."

Her words hit like a blade to the chest. I could feel the air change—thick with sorrow, with fear. The raw pain etched across her face, the silent scream in her eyes, and the invisible scars Ravon had carved into her spirit gripped something deep inside me.

My chest tightened. I wanted to gather her in my arms, but I also needed to know. I needed to hear it from her lips. Not just for trust… but for survival.

I took a steadying breath and asked softly, but firmly, "Are you loyal to me, Dania? Or to Ravon?"

She wiped her face with the back of her trembling hand, as if trying to erase the truth along with the tears. Her breath hitched. For a long moment, she said nothing. Then, slowly, she lifted her gaze to mine.

There it was. A flicker. A spark of something fragile—but alive. Defiance.
Her voice was quiet, but steady. "I think you know the answer to that, Aundrea."

I let out a breath I hadn't realized I was holding. Relief, frustration, and sorrow tangled inside me, pressing against my ribs. She was with me… but still caught in his grip. Just like I was. I reached for her hand and held it tightly. "Ravon," I whispered, "he has us all trapped in his web."

My voice softened to a murmur as I met her eyes again. "It's okay, Dania. He has us both." Just then, the door swung open, and Sarah re-entered the room, her face etched with worry. "Dania, don't… Ravon warned you not to engage in these types of conversations with Lady Aundrea."

My eyes narrowed as they met Sarah's. She had been eavesdropping. Maybe a spy for Ravon. I glanced down, then looked back up at her as she moved closer. "I'm sorry, Lady Aundrea, but we cannot talk about things like that."

She reached over, her hand gently resting on my growing bump. My eyes met hers again, a question burning in them. "How does Ravon expect me to become friends with you if you cannot even speak of your old lives, or who you are?"

A flicker of surprise crossed her face at my pointed question. She glanced at Dania nervously.
"Lady Aundrea… Ravon said only that we should… focus on your upcoming wedding and your duties as his queen, but I understand what you mean. It doesn't make sense," Sarah said slowly, her hand still on my stomach.

Dania stepped back, eyes wide with alarm, as if silently warning Sarah not to continue.
I covered Sarah's hand with mine, my voice low and deliberate as I turned to both of them, eyes blazing with desperation and anger.

"I'm suffocating… losing my mind in this prison!" My voice cracked as frustration boiled over.

The girls exchanged worried glances, trying to calm me with gentle touches and soothing words. Dania's voice wavered with concern. "Aundrea, what's wrong?"

But I was beyond consolation. I stormed toward the door, flinging it open with such force that it slammed against the stone wall, the sound echoing down the corridor. "RAVON," I screamed, my voice piercing the air.

"I KNOW YOU CAN HEAR ME! I WON'T BE HELD CAPTIVE ANY LONGER!"

I marched toward his throne, my hand raised in defiance. I ripped the golden crest from its place and crushed it beneath my foot.
"DO YOU HEAR ME, RAVON? LET ME GO!"

Tears blurred my vision as desperation consumed me. I collapsed to my knees, screaming again.
"PLEASE! AHHHH!"

Sarah and Dania stood frozen in the doorway—Sarah's face etched with shock, Dania's with heartbreaking empathy. Just as my sobs began to fade... the eastern wall of the throne room began to tremble. Rocks shifted, and a shimmering portal swirled to life, revealing a tunnel to freedom.

Ravon stepped through the glowing threshold, his eyes locked intensely on me, hinting at surprise at my boldness.
"Aundrea... I see the fire in you still burns."

He stepped closer, eyes never leaving mine, as the portal behind him dissipated into nothingness.
"You dare defy me in my own throne room?" His gaze flicked to the crushed crest at my knees, then back to my tear-stained face.
"I am intrigued. Your spirit remains unbroken... even as your wedding to me approaches."

Sarah and Dania exchanged nervous glances, slowly backing away as if they sensed Ravon's wrath still lingered. My attention stayed fixed on Ravon, my eyes burning with desperation and anger. I lifted myself from the unyielding floor, my dress tangled around my legs as I stumbled forward, barely regaining balance.
"Let me go, Ravon," I begged, my voice cracking with anguish. "I am losing my mind."
His gaze met mine—cold and icy. There was no remorse in

his expression. He simply did not care.
"You're not leaving, Aundrea," he stated flatly. "You made a vow to me."

My response was primal, a scream that echoed through the throne room.
"I WANT OUT OF HERE!"

Ravon's amusement vanished, replaced by growing fury as he watched me demolish his throne room. Rage consumed me—blazing like wildfire—as I tore through the space, black tapestries hitting the floor.
His thunderous voice cut through my screams and my rage.
"AUNDREA, STOP! STOP IT RIGHT NOW! ENOUGH!"

But I was beyond reason, driven by desperation and anguish. His massive hands closed around my wrists like vices, spinning me around. I tried to jerk free, still screaming in defiance, but he was too strong. With a violent motion, he slammed me backward. My head snapped against the cold stone wall. Stars burst in my vision, my mouth opened in a silent scream before pain even registered.

My body slid down the wall, my knees buckling beneath me. His grip on my wrists remained crushing. Air returned to my lungs, and with a terrorized shriek, I gasped out two precious words:
"THE BABY!"

His hands instantly relaxed, his face contorting in shock and sudden fear. He dropped to his knees beside me, eyes wide with terror, his voice low and suddenly gentle. How could he change so quickly? Sarah and Dania remained frozen, watching this unexpected tenderness unfold. But Ravon's eyes, still veering into my soul, held something darker beneath the surface.
"You have stayed my wrath, Aundrea… temporarily," he

said. "Tell me… was defiance worth possibly harming our son?"

My body trembled with pain and fear. My head ached from it crashing against the stone wall. I stared up at him, with tears flooding my face. Ravon's voice softened for only a heartbeat longer. Then, like ice forming over water, his expression hardened into cruel indifference. He withdrew his hands from my head, rising with deliberate slowness. His gaze never wavered from mine. His intention was to let me know that he was in control. He was in charge. He stood towering over me, his voice dripped with malice.
"Do not think this moment of concern saves you from punishment, Aundrea. You dared defy me.

His cold eyes burned into my soul. My tears now validated my deepest fears. What had I awoken inside him? Or… is this who he truly was?

I saw his hatred—his malice—escalate beyond comprehension, and in that moment, I knew with certainty: I was no longer safe in his arms. His tone shifted.

"Aundrea, you will be taken to the isolation tower. Reflect on obedience… or face further punishment. Your choice."

My blood ran cold as guards moved to drag me away. My heart sank into darkness as I watched him towering over me. I was dragged to my feet by cold guard hands; my eyes fixed on Ravon's merciless face. His gaze burned with intensity, his voice low and menacing.
"Take her to the isolation tower."

My lips trembled as I whispered, barely audible, "You're killing me, Ravon… slowly. Please," I begged, tears claiming me. "Please don't lock me away. I'm sorry. I will not do it again."

His expression didn't falter, his eyes glinting with cruelty. Then he turned to Sarah and Dania, his voice dripping with malice.

"Ensure all servants know—any kindness shown to her will be rewarded with pain."

I knew that no amount of plea was going to save me from the isolation tower, my plea shifted to anger again. I didn't know how to process his emotional changes, or his escalating anger.

I was pulled away, my feet dragging along the stone floor. I screamed behind me,
"This is because I love him, isn't it? You're tormenting me because Drakon still holds my heart!"

I yelled out words of hate and revulsion. Ravon's head snapped back toward me, his face twisted in rage. The guards pulled me through a portal activated by the power of their magical rings, the air rippling with an otherworldly energy as we stepped through. We emerged on the other side with a disorienting jolt, and I stumbled as they dragged me through the grand council chamber. The rush of footsteps echoed off the high ceiling, and the flickering torches cast eerie shadows on the stone walls as we passed beneath the ornate wooden beams.

The murmurs of councilors and advisors grew louder, then faded into the distance as the guards yanked me along, their grip like ice on my arms. We swept past the long, polished table, where quills and parchments lay scattered, and the scent of ink and parchment wafted through the air.

Then, down a long, dimly lit corridor we went, the damp flagstones beneath my feet seeming to stretch on forever. The guards threw me into the isolation tower's darkness, the heavy door slamming shut behind me with a deafening crash. The scrape of metal echoed through the silence as thick bars locked into place, the sound sending a shiver down my spine. The darkness was absolute, a suffocating blanket that wrapped around me like a living thing.

I collapsed onto the unforgiving stone floor surrounded by utter blackness. My mind raced—Ravon's cruelty, Drakon's absence, my unborn child's fate...
The walls were stone, and it felt like a tomb closing in on me. No bed, no blankets. Just dark, unyielding floor.

***

Days passed, and a faint torchlight flickered outside my cell, casting eerie shadows against the stone walls. Sarah appeared at the bars outside of my cell, she whispered and her voice barely reached me.
"Aundrea... Drakon lives... he will rescue you...just give him time."

My heart leapt at the desperate thread of hope.

I rushed to the bars as soon as Sarah appeared. Desperation surged through me—questions tumbling in my mind faster than I could give them voice. Was he coming? Had she heard from him? Had Drakon broken free?

Her voice was low, urgent. She warned me not to speak too loudly; Ravon had grown suspicious. The number of guards patrolling the palace had increased.

My pulse faltered. I leaned closer, my voice barely a breath. She glanced nervously down the corridor before answering.

Drakon hadn't escaped yet—but a messenger had come. He was searching for a way out, using the power of the Dragon. Sarah believed he would succeed. She had to believe it. And so did I.

Her eyes kept darting toward the hallway. Time was slipping.

Before she turned to go, she begged me to stay calm. To avoid provoking Ravon again. Drakon would want you to stay safe, she'd said. He will come. Just don't give up. I gripped the iron bars with everything I had, forcing myself to believe.

"How did you get here, Sarah?"
While walking away, I heard a faint sound barely from her voice, "You have loyal subjects here."
For the first time in what felt like an eternity, my heart overflowed with hope. Hope stirred—Drakon was coming, and Sarah, once believed to be Ravon's spy, had proven herself an ally.

I let go of the cold steel bars I'd clung to, turning slowly and collapsing to the floor. My back pressed against the cell bars, knees drawn to my chest, arms wrapped around my legs. I buried my face in my lap as tears consumed me again.

***

Time crawled by in silence, swallowed by endless darkness, marked only by the flicker of a single torch and the scrape of food trays pushed through the wicket hatch at the bottom of the door. Time lost all meaning. Only Drakon's promise kept my heart from breaking entirely.

I remembered the ring Ravon had placed on my finger, the one allowing me to enter the garden. With a flicker of hope, I placed my hand over it. A portal began to emerge—but it collapsed with a loud hiss, dark magic crackling through the air. Ravon had sensed it. The noise rumbled through my chest. My heart skipped a beat. My mind replayed every moment with Drakon—laughter, whispers, vows. I clung to the memories, praying to any deity who might hear me.

"Bring him back to me… Let my child and I escape this hell."

Tears soaked my cheeks, mingling with desperate prayers whispered into the darkness. Outside my cell, patrols doubled. Armored footsteps echoed through the corridors, muffled orders signaling heightened alert. Ravon's voice boomed from the tower entrance. I could barely make out his form at the end of the passage.

"Seal all passages. Triple the guards. I sense deception in the shadows."

I yelled out to him, but my voice was dry and cracked,

"Please let me out of here, Ravon, I'm sorry." A lump formed in my throat. I knew he could hear me.

Dark magic swirled around him like a living force. He turned to his captain.

"If Drakon dares break free and attempt rescue—kill him."

My heart shattered at his broken vow, at the cruelty beneath his lies. I waited, terrified with every creak of the tower, every sound in the night. Then came his voice again, cutting through the silence like a knife.

"BRING ME MY BRIDE! Tomorrow night, we wed!"

My world collapsed into utter despair. I screamed silently, my mind breaking beneath the weight of those ominous words. My heart, once sustained by the hope of Drakon's rescue, now threatened to stop beating altogether. Tears dried on my cheeks, replaced by ice as dread set in. Drakon was trapped—perhaps forever. Ravon would claim me as his bride tomorrow night. My child and I would become prisoners to his cruelty. I had sunk deeper into the darkness. No longer wishing for him to let me out. My whisper into the void was barely audible, my hand planted firmly on my stomach.

"No... this cannot be our fate..."

Suddenly, a guard appeared. I rose to my feet, barely able to stand. He grabbed my arm and pulled me from the cell.

"Lord Ravon wants to see you."

Fear burrowed into my chest like a tornado tearing through all hope. I tried to pull away, but exhaustion claimed me completely. We stepped through another portal, opened by his ring. A tunnel formed, leading back to the throne room. The guard yanked me forward. I barely caught my footing. Sarah and Dania were already waiting.

"Get her cleaned up," the guard barked.

"Lord Ravon wants her to dine with him tonight."

My legs trembled beneath me as I stood in the throne room. Sarah and Dania rushed to my sides, supporting my weight as I swayed from fear and exhaustion. Their gentle touches were a stark contrast to the guard's rough handling and Ravon's looming presence. The flickering torches cast eerie shadows as I took in the room's imposing space, my eyes locking onto a shadow cast by Ravon's figure standing before the black stone wall, his back to me—darkness seemed to emanate from his very being, but he wasn't there. It wasn't him.

I stood free now, facing Sarah and Dania, the weight of the cell still clung to me. The darkness hadn't stayed behind—it had followed me, lodged in my chest like a splinter. And now... I was seeing things. Shadows where there were none. Doubt in every corner.

The torches along the walls began to flicker wildly, their flames sputtering as if choking on the sudden shift in the air. Shadows danced erratically across the stone, and a sharp prickle crawled over my skin. I knew this feeling—an unnatural stillness laced with dread. He was coming. He was near.

The dark wall across the room began to twist, the surface rippling like disturbed water. A vortex of swirling shadow took shape, silent but suffocating. From its center, Ravon emerged—his figure cutting through the darkness like a blade, cloaked in power and purpose.

Sarah whispered in my ear, "Aundrea, be strong." Before I could respond, Ravon's low, menacing voice cut through the room. "Leave us to prepare her. Tonight, my bride-to-be will dine with me... alone."

Dania and Sarah exchanged fearful glances before being ushered out by the guards, disappearing into the darkness beyond the wall. Ravon slowly turned to face me, his eyes burning with intensity. My breath caught as he stepped closer, his presence suffocating.

"My bride should shine like the darkness she will soon embrace," he whispered, low and husky. He snapped his fingers, and servants emerged from the shadows to escort me to a luxurious bath chamber hidden behind yet another wall. Ravon himself poured scented oils into the steaming water, his fingers brushing against mine, sending an involuntary wave of emotion through every nerve in my body.

"You will be beautiful for our dinner tonight, Aundrea," he said softly, his tone gentle—but the menace beneath it twisted my stomach. Silent servants bathed and washed me while Ravon watched, his intense gaze crawling over my skin. Afterward, he selected a black gown adorned with delicate silver embroidery and dressed me himself, each movement unnervingly tender.

Fear and passion warred inside me, unaware of anything twisted consuming my soul. His fingers brushed my skin as he fastened the gown's tiny buttons, leaving me breathless and terrified to speak. A tide of sorrow crashed over me, thick and overwhelming, as if my heart had begun to unravel from the inside out. I didn't understand what was happening—only that something deep within me was fracturing. My soul felt like it was splitting along unseen seams.

Without thinking, I surged forward into his arms, desperate for something—anything—to hold me together. He drew me close, one hand cradling the back of my head, guiding my cheek to rest against his chest. The other wrapped firmly around my waist, anchoring me in place.

I tilted my head upward, my voice barely a whisper through the ache in my throat. "I don't want to be alone anymore."

Emotion welled behind my eyes, hot and relentless, spilling over in broken tears. He lowered his head and pressed a kiss to the top of my head—slow, gentle, and hauntingly tender. "I'm here," he murmured, his voice a hush against the storm inside me.

Without releasing me, he guided me back into the throne room, now disturbingly transformed. Candlelight flickered across an opulent table set for two, the air heavy with the scent of roasted meats and spiced wine. It was meant to be intimate, but every detail—each gilded plate, every carefully arranged dish—felt like a performance. A beautifully curated illusion.

Ravon pulled out my chair and seated me with exaggerated courtesy, the echo of his earlier tenderness clashing with the forced civility of this moment. He made a strained attempt at polite conversation, his voice carefully measured, almost rehearsed—like he was playing a part in a scene only he believed in.

I kept my eyes locked on his as we dined, offering nothing but silence. When civility failed to draw me in... he changed tactics.

"Let us dispense with the pleasantries," he continued. "We have... unfinished matters to discuss." His tone shifted from cordial host to menacing captor.

"Your outburst two weeks ago—destroying my throne room, screaming defiance at me..." His voice edged with steel.

"That behavior is unbefitting of a lady of your station... or my future bride." My hands trembled slightly around my glass. I noticed every detail: his clenched fists, the cold set of his jaw, the way his eyes bore into mine.

"Do you think defiance will save you from our marriage, Aundrea?"

His voice cracked slightly, the calm mask beginning to slip. His fists slammed down on the table, making me jump, then slowly opened, fingers splayed on the surface like claws.

"I am tired of your lies. Tired of your attempts to escape. Tired of your heart belonging to another. And tired of your outbursts." His eyes blazed with fury, his voice a silken threat.

"You will be mine, Aundrea. Completely. Tomorrow night will seal that fate."

My breath caught in my throat as he leaned forward, his face just inches from mine.

"Do you have anything to say?" My lips trembled, fear consuming me. I whispered,

"I'm… sorry." Tears welled in my eyes as my voice cracked, anticipating his wrath. But his response was worse than I imagined.

"You will be sorry… because after we are wed—willing or not—we will consummate our union in your bedchamber."

His words landed like a death sentence. Ravon extended his hand to me—a calm, calculated gesture of invitation. I placed mine in his, and he gently pulled me from the chair and into his arms. His hold was steady, almost comforting, and yet I could feel the quiet power beneath it.

He rested his chin atop my head, his breath brushing through my hair as he whispered words meant to sound tender. "You're the only one who can drive me mad. All I require from you is unwavering loyalty... and obedience."

The isolation chamber had taken something from me—left a hollow place in my soul. And somehow, Ravon had found it. That broken part of me was exactly what he had been waiting for. What he had designed.

When he finally let me go, he guided me back to my chamber with silent, possessive ease.

***

The soft glow of candles lit the room—a cruel contrast to the darkness within him. As we stood beside the bed, Ravon reached down and took my hand, his fingers brushing against the black-gold ring on my finger. He turned the ring slowly around my knuckle, his touch sending a deep burning desire through every nerve in my body. I felt guilt swell inside me once again.

"This is my promise to you, Aundrea," he whispered. "You will be my bride." His voice dropped lower, sharp and cold.

"Next time you try to use this ring to escape into the garden I gifted you… when you are being punished… it will be the last time you see the garden."

My body trembled violently. I met his gaze, suffocating in fear. Ravon's eyes bore into mine, demanding obedience. I whispered, "Yes, Ravon."

He released my hand, turned abruptly, and vanished into the shadows beyond my wall.

Alone again, I collapsed against the bedpost, my legs buckling. Slowly, I dragged myself to the dresser—placed in my room while I was imprisoned in the silence of the isolation cell. Tears fell like rain as I changed into a black-and-white nightdress. The soft fabric felt like mockery against my bruised spirit.

I crawled into bed and buried my face in the pillows, sobbing uncontrollably. My tears streamed like a river bursting its banks—unstoppable, unrelenting. My heart shattered into a million pieces. My soul was drowning in Ravon's darkness. My night faded into blackness as anguish consumed me...

Chapter 13

Shadows in Time

Drakon's body trembled with effort as he attempted another dragon shift. Pain seared through his muscles, but his mind raced faster. Something felt off—not just his captivity, but time itself. His inner dragon senses screamed of a discrepancy: days had passed for him, yet his bond with Aundrea hinted that weeks, perhaps even months, had elapsed for her. Ravon's spell was distorting time.

He leaned over the remnants of a long-forgotten stone dwelling—its walls worn by time, roof long since caved in, and ivy crawling like veins through the fractured masonry. Only one partial wall remained upright near the edge of the camp, jagged and leaning with age. Drakon removed a piece of coal from the fire and pressed it to the weathered stone, his eyes narrowing with focus as he brought the riddle from his vision to life—each mark deliberate, born of dragon memory.

"Where shadows dance, footsteps erase. The path unwinds."

Could it mean literally reversing their steps—to walk backward? A spark of hope ignited. Drakon's heart pounded as he grasped the possible solution. "If we walk the path backward," he thought,

"perhaps we can undo the shadow spell's hold on time and space."

With renewed determination, he summoned his guards.

"We may have found a way to break the spell," he said, voice low and urgent.

"We must retrace our exact steps—backward—all the way to the beginning of the trap." The guards exchanged skeptical glances, haunted by failed attempts and dead ends, but Drakon's conviction was infectious.

Without another word, they nodded and fell into step behind him. The army began its backward march, feet moving in synchronized reversal. As they walked, the corrupted landscape around them began to tremble and shift. Shadows wavered and thinned. Light pierced the murky air for the first time in days—maybe longer. Finally, they emerged from the suffocating miasma of Ravon's shadow spell.

Drakon's eyes locked onto their destination: Shadowfort. The fortress loomed ahead, towering and malevolent. Its towers stretched like skeletal fingers clawing at the moon. Walls of black stone absorbed the starlight, reflecting nothing. Gates forged from twisted iron bore the silhouette of ravens. A moat filled with stagnant, dark water mirrored the evil essence of the keep. The army halted, assembling in perfect formation outside the gates. The fortress itself seemed alive—hostile. The very walls seemed to draw the breath from Drakon's lungs. Torches flickered high above, casting grotesque shadows across the ground. The ravens etched into the iron gates seemed to watch with cold, soulless eyes. A foul stench drifted from the moat—rot, magic, and death.

Drakon's pulse quickened, his blood burning with fury. Dragonfire churned inside him, clawing to break free. He would shatter Shadowfort's gates.

He would save her.

Suddenly, the fortress gates creaked open. Ravon descended from the shadows, his form cloaked in swirling dark magic. He stepped onto the battlefield like a phantom rising from a grave. His voice thundered,

"Drakon, fool of Lisona! Your persistence only seals your doom! You are not strong enough to defeat me, brother."

Drakon called out to him, forcing him to pause.

"Ravon, she is not yours to cage. Release her—or I will rip this world apart to take her back, and you will burn in the blaze I leave behind."

The air sizzled with malevolent energy as Ravon raised his hands and hurled bolts of darkness toward the front lines. Drakon's warriors charged, blades drawn.

The two armies clashed with a roar—steel on steel, cries of pain and fury erupting in a storm of chaos. The ground trembled beneath their feet as the battle exploded through the gates. Drakon fought at the forefront, cutting down Ravon's soldiers with the precision of an emperor and the fury of a dragon. The clash of blades echoed through the hollow fortress.

One by one, Ravon's defenders faltered, their lines crumbling beneath the weight of Drakon's wrath. His gaze never left Ravon. He pressed forward through the fray, slicing down anything that dared stand in his way. Ravon raised more shadow to shield himself, summoning arcane forces to hold his crumbling defenses.

The air grew colder. Shadows took on shape— twisted, hungry creatures slithering at Drakon's heels. Then… something stirred inside him. A flicker of dragon power. It surged, awakening like a sleeping beast. But the shift would not come. His body resisted. Ravon's laughter cut through the noise. "You struggle in vain, Drakon. Your power remains chained."

***

I threw off my covers, leaving the warmth of my bed as I stood in the darkness of my chamber, my heart pounding with dread. I felt the walls of Shadowfort tremble beneath my feet, a low rumble rising through the stone like the growl of a waking beast. I stumbled, the ground shifting beneath me, and reached out blindly—my fingertips scraping against the cold, damp wall for balance. The deafening roar of war echoed through the fortress, each clash of steel and cry of fury pounding against the stone like thunder, relentless and near. Horns blared beyond the walls—battle had begun—but I felt something deeper. I felt him., Drakon!

His presence stirred my soul like embers bursting into flames. I sensed his fury, his determination… and his pain. My breath caught—he was close. Closer than he'd been in months. Tears welled in my eyes as I whispered into the silence, "Drakon… is it really you?"

My heart raced like a wild animal in a trap. I rushed to the chamber door, drawn to him like a lifeline. My hand gripped the iron handle—I twisted, pulled, begged—but the door wouldn't budge. Ravon's magic sealed me in. Outside, I heard guards pacing, listening to my piercing screams.

"Drakon, I'm here!" I cried, pounding on the door, desperation clawing up my throat. "So close…" One of the guards barked, his voice sharp and echoing off the stone walls, "Stop that! If you don't stand down, Lady Aundrea, I'll report you to Lord Ravon myself!" His hand hovered near the hilt of his blade, and his eyes darted with nervous tension, as if merely speaking Ravon's name summoned the weight of his wrath.

Tears of frustration streamed down my cheeks. Yet beneath the rising terror, something fluttered inside—hope. Drakon had come for me.

Then, through the narrow bars, a breeze whispered against my skin, soft and familiar. A dragon-scented wind... and with it, an ethereal voice:

"Aundrea, my love... stay strong. I'm here for you."
Drakon's voice echoed through my soul, warm, reassuring, alive. My knees buckled as joy and fear tangled in my chest.
"I'm waiting..." I whispered, knowing he couldn't hear the words, but hoping somehow, he felt them.

***

Drakon's focus never wavered from Ravon as he channeled the mental message through their dragon bond. Aundrea's essence surged in his mind, fueling him with love, fury, and fire. He clenched his fists, bracing himself. The time was now.
Muscles strained, veins bulged, and pain ripped through his frame as he fought to shift. Scales pushed through skin, claws extended from mortal fingers. He roared—half agony, half triumph—as the beast within broke free.
His wings erupted with a deafening crack. His dragon form—massive, gleaming, and full of fury—towered over the battlefield. Shadowfort trembled.
Across from him, Ravon stumbled back, his expression a mixture of shock and disbelief. "No... impossible!" he hissed, lashing out with a barrage of dark bolts. But Drakon retaliated with a roar and a torrent of flame, consuming the shadows and sending Ravon skidding across blood-soaked stone.

With a thunderous crash, Drakon lunged. Jaws wide, teeth like daggers, flames licking his lips. Ravon scrambled backward, tripping over the remains of his own magic shield. He fell, sprawled in the dust, and stared up into the burning eyes of his brother's dragon form. Drakon's voice thundered across Shadowfort, "You have tormented my love, ravaged our lands—your darkness ends NOW!"

He slashed, claws carving through the air, missing Ravon's head by inches as the sorcerer rolled to safety. The ground quaked beneath Drakon's massive paws as he advanced. Ravon leapt to his feet, summoning his final reserve of dark power. Behind him, a monstrous hand of shadow formed, swelling with destruction.

In Drakon's mind, Aundrea's voice whispered again: "Drakon, beware… his last magic is deadly." Drakon's gaze narrowed. Silver light began to pulse from his claws—ancient dragon magic rising in response. The charged air thickened as the two magics prepared to collide. His mind brushed against Aundrea's once more. Her voice trembled: "His magic feeds on destruction… be careful of the backlash."

Drakon gritted his teeth, every sinew focused. Ravon screamed, unleashing the full force of his magic. The colossal shadow hand struck, a comet of dark energy barreling toward him. Drakon raised his claws, the silver glow intensifying. Light met darkness. The ground shattered, sending rocks and warriors flying as darkness descended. Drakon held his ground, silver dragon magic erupting from his claws in a brilliant blaze. When the opposing forces met, the impact ignited a cataclysmic explosion."

Shadows screamed as they were torn apart. Silver light roared in response, cutting through the darkness with searing brilliance. The very air seemed to rip and mend, over and over again.
The backlash was immense.

Shadowfort's gates buckled, crumbling stone walls collapsing as Ravon's warriors fled in terror. Drakon stumbled, his silver magic faltering. Across the battlefield, Ravon's broken form twitched as dark magic coiled around him like a living aura. Slowly, shakily, he rose—eyes blazing with vengeance.

With a guttural cry, Ravon unleashed a brutal counterattack. Bolts of black energy struck Drakon's dragon form again and again, cracking his scales, searing through his flesh. He crashed down onto the stone steps of Shadowfort Palace—wounded, weakened, barely alive. Ravon stood over him, chest heaving, eyes gleaming with triumph.

***

He raised one hand, and dark magic summoned me to his side.
I appeared beside Ravon, my heart shattered at the sight of Drakon's broken body sprawled before the palace. My breath caught as Ravon's voice cut through my grief like a blade.
"Tell him, Aundrea… You choose to stay with me—or I kill him now."
My eyes locked onto Drakon's. Tears streamed down my cheeks as I struggled to speak the lie that might save him. His gaze never wavered, filled with love, trust, and silent pleading. He believed in me.

I forced my shaking feet to move, each step a dagger to my soul. "Drakon," I whispered, my voice cracking. "I love you… and I do this for you. I choose to stay with Ravon."

Pain flashed in Drakon's eyes—raw, agonizing. My soul cried out as I continued the charade, barely holding myself together. "I'll rule Shadowfort… with Ravon. I'll forget you, my love."

But he saw through it. I knew he did. His gaze never left mine, searching the truth behind my trembling voice.

I stepped closer, heart breaking, and gently cradled his massive dragon head in my hands. Leaning forward, I pressed a trembling kiss to his maw, tasting ash and the copper sting of his wounds. My lips lingered, and I called forth my healing power—drawing it up from the core of my soul, where the Divine Light stirred like a sleeping star.

A soft white glow erupted from within me, warmth and brilliance pouring out in waves. It wrapped around Drakon's broken body like silk spun from starlight, seeping into every torn muscle, every cracked bone. The air shimmered with the scent of lightning and lavender, and my skin tingled as the magic flowed.

His massive form stilled beneath me. His eyes fluttered shut—not in defeat, but in fragile peace. His breath, ragged just moments before, began to steady. I felt it—his strength, flickering to life, faint but certain.

But before I could finish, Ravon's magic surged through the shadows like a scream. I barely had time to gasp before it struck—coiling around me like icy chains, cruel and sudden. They snapped tight across my chest, tearing me backward with such force my feet left the ground.

"No!" I screamed. "Drakon, fly away! I'll be waiting for you!"

Drakon's eyes snapped open, locking with mine. In that

fleeting moment, love, sorrow, and determination passed
between us.
With a mighty roar, he launched himself into the sky.
Wings unfurled, powerful and wide, casting shadows across
the shattered battlefield. He climbed into the clouds,
soaring toward freedom.
Ravon's roar ripped through the air. "NOOO! I WILL
STILL BRING YOU DOWN!"
He summoned his dark magic in a final, desperate burst,
but it was too late. Drakon's form vanished into the
horizon, beyond his reach.

Ravon's fury turned on me.
"You haven't seen the last of his suffering," he hissed,
breath cold against my ear. "Because of you, he will soon
be mine to destroy." His magic fell and his grip tightened
around my wrist like iron as he dragged me backward,
portals flaring to life around us. But as I glanced back one
final time, my heart beating with hope.
I knew in that moment that Drakon was free. Ravon's voice
hissed beside me, promising torment. "Your lover will
return one day… and when he does, you'll watch me
destroy his soul." Ravon dragged me through the
shimmering portal, its eerie, pulsing glow shifting the
stones before fading like a dying breath.

***

We emerged into the Shadowfort throne room. The
air was thick with the scent of old stone and malevolence.
Flickering torches cast ominous shadows across the walls,
making Dania and Sarah's faces appear like macabre
masks. Their eyes widened at the sight of my disheveled
state—and at the fury etched into Ravon's contorted face.

My nightdress, once elegant, now clung to my
trembling body like a damp shroud, tattered and stained.

Ravon's grip on my wrist was cruel, his fingers biting into my skin like viper fangs. I winced with each forced step.

He stormed past the dark tapestries, past Dania and Sarah's frozen faces, dragging me toward my chambers. With a sharp pull, he threw the latch and slammed the door open. The crash of iron rang through my skull. Then he hurled me inside and slammed the door shut behind us, the sound reverberating like a death knell.
The rattling iron still echoed as he turned to face me, his eyes ablaze with unholy wrath.
"Aundrea…" His voice was low, menacing. "…you helped Drakon escape."
My heart sank. I knew what was coming.

Ravon slapped me with the back of his hand, hurling me onto the bed. The impact rattled my bones. Dread pressed in around me, thick in the air. His anger crackled like lightning just beneath the surface.

"Tomorrow," he growled, "you will become my bride. What you did tonight burns within my soul."

His dark eyes flashed with fury. "How dare you betray my trust again? I will not TOLERATE such betrayal from my wife!"

The tension coiled tighter, suffocating me. I scrambled back, desperate to put space between us, but Ravon seized my leg, yanking me forward. His grip found my arms, every finger a vice. His breath scraped against my cheek.
Tears streamed down my face as his voice dipped into dangerous calm.
"You deserve punishment, Aundrea, for your actions, but I won't let you ruin tomorrow for us."
I tried to pull away. His grip tightened.
Then, with brutal force, he lifted me off the bed and

slammed me against the cold stone wall.
The impact knocked the wind from my lungs. I gasped, the pain exploding behind my eyes. "Ravon, please… don't hurt me. I'm with child."

His eyes blazed like fire. "Don't test me, Aundrea. I've had ENOUGH!"
He released me abruptly, gesturing toward the dresser. His rage simmered just beneath the surface.
"Change out of those… ruined clothes." His voice was low, even—but menacing.
I felt utterly exposed under his gaze, like prey caught in a trap. My hands trembled as I opened the dresser drawer and pulled out a simple nightgown. The fabric was soft, cruelly gentle against my battered skin.

I changed slowly, every movement weighed down by fear, hyper-aware of his eyes on me.
Once I was dressed, he nodded once. "Get in bed, Aundrea."
There was still command in his voice, but as I lay down, something in his expression shifted—just for a moment. A glimpse of the man I once thought I knew.

He sat beside me, brushing his fingers against my forehead. Then he leaned in, his lips grazing my cheek in a kiss that was far too gentle after the violence he'd just inflicted, but somehow I felt the fire of desire burning my soul, and guilt was left behind. I rubbed the back of my head, wincing as a sharp pain radiated from where I'd slammed into the stone wall. The skin there throbbed, warm and tender beneath my fingertips. My vision blurred with unshed tears as Ravon moved in closer, his shadow falling over me like a second assault.

His fingers slid into my hair—slow, deliberate, and suffocatingly gentle. The contrast made me flinch.

"Why can't you just do as you are told, Aundrea?" he murmured, his voice smooth, almost tired.

Tears stung my eyes, burning hot trails down my cheeks. I couldn't stop them. They weren't loud, they didn't sob—but they ate at me from the inside, hollowing me out.

In a quiet, broken whisper, I replied, "You scared me, Ravon… I thought you were going to kill me."

His expression didn't shift at first. Then, slowly, a small, sinister smile crept across his lips. Something dark flickered behind his eyes—satisfaction, or control.

He leaned in, and in a voice that should've comforted but only unsettled, he whispered, "I would never hurt you like that, Aundrea."

His breath was warm against my skin as he pressed a kiss to my forehead—light, careful, a mockery of affection. The gesture sent a chill through me, more terrifying than the pain. I stayed still, too afraid to move, my body stiff as stone, my soul curling inward.

He sat quietly beside me on the bed, and I leaned into his touch, needing the comfort of his presence. I wrapped my arms around him and began to cry, my tears soaking into his tunic as he held me close, steady and silent. "I don't know what's wrong with me, Ravon," I whispered through broken sobs. He pulled me closer, pressed a kiss to the top of my head, then eased me down gently, laying me back against the pillows with care.

"Tomorrow, we wed. Get rest," he whispered, tucking the blankets around me in a mockery of tender care.
Then he stood and exited the room, leaving me alone with my tears and my torment.

Ravon's anger was escalating. Each day, it grew more volatile, more unhinged—like a storm gathering force with no end in sight. He was becoming darker, shadows clinging to him even in the light. His jealousy burned hotter, his rage more unpredictable. The way he watched me, touched me, claimed me—it wasn't love. It was obsession. Possession.

And I was his prisoner.

I feared for my life… and for the life growing inside me. My hand drifted protectively over my belly, my breath catching as a wave of dread rolled through me. The air around him was suffocating now, heavy with unspoken threats. His presence loomed like a curse I couldn't outrun.

Tears spilled down my cheeks, no longer held back. They flowed freely, soaking the corners of my mouth with salt and sorrow. My feelings for him were a tangled storm—confusion, grief, revulsion… and somewhere, buried deep, something else. Something dangerous.

Love? Is that possible? After everything? Why do I have these feelings?

Gods, what is happening to me?

I laid there as time slipped by, sobbing silently as my mind replayed every moment with Drakon—our love, my betrayal of Ravon, and the storm that waited for me beyond the sunrise.
Tomorrow's wedding loomed like a death sentence.
And after that…
What Ravon would demand of me...
My body shuddered with dread. Exhaustion finally pulled me into a fitful, haunted sleep.

Chapter 14

Thorns of Misery

I woke to gentle voices and the soft flicker of torchlight peeking through my eyelids. My mind was foggy, memories of yesterday's horror slowly resurfacing—Ravon's slap, and his escalating anger.

I opened my eyes to see Sarah and Dania standing beside my bed, a tray of food between them. My stomach twisted with anxiety.

"Ravon instructed us to bring you breakfast... to be eaten in your room," Dania added, her voice carefully neutral.

I searched her eyes, trying to gauge her loyalty—was she truly with me, or had Ravon's brutality broken her spirit?

"Where is your loyalty?" I asked quietly.

Sarah intervened quickly, her voice low and cautious. "Aundrea, let's just focus on getting you ready for tonight. He wants you prepared for the wedding celebration."

My heart sank at the mention of the wedding. I felt trapped, suffocated by Ravon's plans. Slowly, I sat up, threw off the covers, and swung my legs over the side of the bed. Sarah helped me to my feet and led me to the washroom. Dania began preparing warm water and fragrant oils while Sarah assisted me into the bath.

The warmth enveloped me like a soft hug, but my mind remained tense. As Sarah washed my hair, I tried again to test Dania's loyalty.

"Dania, how… how have you been?" I asked casually.

Sarah's warning glance flicked toward me as she interrupted, "Aundrea, shall I add more warm water?" Dania's gaze shifted to meet mine, and in that fleeting moment, I saw something—fear, or perhaps loyalty—flash in her eyes. But her answer was for me, not Sarah.
"I'm nearly finished," she said softly.
I stepped out of the bath, wrapping a towel around my naked body.

***

Just then, the door to my chamber creaked open, and Ravon's voice echoed in, smooth and ominous.

"I've brought a special guest to join the celebration…"

My heart raced. Wrapping myself quickly in a black robe, I turned to watch him enter—with Michelle at his side.

Michelle's eyes met mine, filled with a deep, aching sadness. Her gaze was hollow, haunted. Her skin had paled, her face gaunt—a month of isolation had left its mark. She wore an elegant gown, and her hair was styled immaculately—Ravon's twisted attempt to make her "presentable" for tonight's dark celebration.

"Michelle…" I whispered.

She rushed into my arms, holding me tightly, her voice cracking. "Aundrea… I've been so scared for you…"

Ravon's voice sliced through the moment, thick with menace. "A lovely surprise, don't you think, my bride-to-be? Michelle has been... refreshed during her stay in the isolation tower."

Sarah's eyes narrowed slightly, while Dania looked away, fear flickering across her features. I held Michelle close, heart sickened by what she'd endured.

Sarah gently broke the moment. "Aundrea, let's get you ready..."

My anxiety surged. What did Ravon have planned for tonight?

Michelle clutched my hand briefly, her eyes still clouded with fear. "You look beautiful even in robes, Aundrea... but tonight..."

Her voice trailed off as Ravon stepped closer. His gaze fixed on me with possessive intensity. Michelle trembled beside me. Ravon reached out and kissed her forehead with a grotesque display of mock affection.

"My grateful guest," he whispered. "Enjoy the celebration tonight."

Then he turned to me. His lips grazed my forehead, sending icy shivers down my spine.

"My bride-to-be," he breathed. "Finish preparing. Tonight will be... memorable."

With that, he turned and exited, the door clicking shut behind him.

Michelle exhaled slowly, her eyes still locked on the door. "I feared he'd never let me see you again, Aundrea."

Sarah moved swiftly to my side, helping me toward the vanity. "We should concentrate, Aundrea. Ravon's patience wears thin."

Dania laid out my wedding gown—a breathtakingly beautiful, yet terrifying symbol of my impending captivity. The gown was a fairytale ballgown, with:
– A black silk belt cinched tightly at the waist
– Intricate black embroidery swirling across the bodice
– Matching details trimming the hem of the flowing skirt
– A long, delicate veil attached with a small silver clip, cascading down my back like silk water

Michelle gasped softly as they helped me into it.

"Aundrea, you look stunning… but at what cost?"

"Michelle…" Sarah warned quietly, "We must be careful what we say."

Dania glanced at Sarah, her expression unreadable—part fear, and part caution.

I felt like a bird in a gilded cage, imprisoned inside this exquisite dress. My heart raced as Sarah stepped back to admire their work.

"You're breathtaking, Aundrea."

Dania leaned in for a quick embrace, her arms warm and trembling slightly as they wrapped around me. Her breath brushed against my ear, soft and steady, as she whispered, "I am with you, Aundrea." The faint scent of lavender clung to her skin—a familiar comfort in the chaos around us. In that moment, the weight pressing on my chest loosened, and I didn't feel quite so alone.

I looked down at the ring on my finger—Ravon's ring of promise—its dark gold seeming to absorb the chamber's soft light.

"Girls," I said softly, "let's go to the garden."

I held my hand over the ring, focusing on the peaceful oasis hidden within Shadowfort. Magic pulsed through me. The air shimmered—then we vanished into the garden's serene beauty.

Stone benches surrounded us, draped in flowering vines. Towering columns upheld a glass dome, casting dappled sunlight over our faces.

Michelle inhaled deeply, her eyes closing as she breathed in the sweet scents.

Dania walked silently beside Sarah, eyes darting around the garden as if searching for hidden dangers… or a way out. I felt a fleeting sense of peace wash over me as I gazed at the lush greenery and vibrant flowers of Lisona. For a moment, it felt like the darkness couldn't reach us here.

Michelle gently touched my hand. "Aundrea, this moment… it's like the darkness outside doesn't exist."

My heart ached, knowing that illusion would soon be shattered.

Sarah's eyes met mine, brimming with silent concern—and something sharper. A question lingered in her gaze: Was I still fighting… or had I shattered, just like Dania?
The weight of it settled in my chest, cold and accusing.

Footsteps echoed across the garden path. Ravon appeared suddenly, his eyes locking onto mine with intense admiration.

"Aundrea… breathtaking. The garden suits your beauty almost as much as my ring suits your finger."

He had emerged from thin air, his magic effortlessly transporting him into the enclosed space. Michelle stepped closer to me, while Dania's eyes widened slightly. She glanced toward Sarah—each of us sensing Ravon's ominous presence.

Sarah's hand brushed mine, a subtle, silent question.

Ravon's gaze swept over us before returning to me. His voice was low and commanding. "Time for the celebration to begin. Hold hands, ladies."

He raised his hand, palm upward, magic swirling around it like coiled mist. The energy pulsed and brightened, enveloping us in a blinding burst of violet light.

***

When the light faded, we stood tightly grouped on a massive stone doorstep. Michelle clung to my hand like a lifeline.
We had arrived at Vorga Island's Shadowed Estate.

It seemed like night had already fallen—though I knew it was still daylight back at Shadowfort. The sky above was forever veiled in thick clouds, choking out the sun's rays. Torches flickered along the estate's exterior walls, casting dancing shadows that twisted unnaturally on the ground. The air was heavy with the scent of saltwater and something darker... something foreboding.
Dania whispered barely above a breath, "Where are we?"

Sarah's eyes snapped to mine, warning me silently to say nothing.
Ravon stepped forward, placing his hand on the massive iron door. "Welcome, ladies, to our wedding."
He pushed the door open slowly, revealing a dim corridor lit by flickering torches and lined with his most loyal—and cruel-looking—guards.

Michelle's grip on my hand tightened, nearly to the point of pain. We were trapped.

With a sweeping gesture, Ravon motioned us forward. "Enter, my bride-to-be... and our honored guests. Tonight, we seal our union."

His voice echoed off the cold stone walls as we stepped inside. The heavy door creaked shut behind us, sealing our fate with a finality that chilled me to my core. Guards flanked the entrance, their gazes like twin blades—sharp, unwavering, emotionless.

Michelle clung to my side, her breath coming in shallow gasps. Dania walked stiffly beside Sarah, her eyes scanning every corner of the hall as if trying to memorize escape routes.

The interior was as grim as the exterior: dark wood paneling, low-burning candles, and thick tapestries depicting twisted scenes of domination and conquest. It felt like we had stepped into a villain's sanctum—because we had.

Ravon turned to me, offering his arm. His smile was elegant, but distorted—like a reflection in broken glass. "Shall we proceed to the ceremony chamber?"

I felt cornered, forced to play along just to survive. Sarah caught my eye again. Her gaze burned with urgency. She was waiting for the right moment to act, but that moment would not come.

Ravon's voice cut through the silence again, his tone brisk and exacting. "Dania, Sarah. Take your seats in the back pews. This ceremony concerns only my bride-to-be, her witness... and our special guest."

He motioned toward the dark wooden pews at the rear of the chamber. His eyes gleamed like black coals.

Dania and Sarah exchanged a cautious glance before complying, their footsteps quiet as they moved to the back of the room and sat side by side.

Ravon lifted his hands, palms facing Michelle, and began murmuring incantations under his breath. Power pulsed through the air.

Michelle's eyes widened in shock as her body was gently lifted from the ground, floating toward the front of the chamber. She descended gracefully near the altar, her hands suddenly filled with a bouquet so hauntingly beautiful it made me shiver.

- Dark purple calla lilies

- Velvet black roses

- Midnight blue delphiniums

Their eerie beauty mirrored the tone of the ceremony perfectly. Michelle looked down at the flowers, then back at me with alarm and confusion.

Ravon's smile deepened.

"Our witness holds the blooms of eternal binding—purple for loyalty, black for forever... and blue for my love, your favorite color." Ravon's voice echoed through the chamber. "And now, my bride-to-be shall join me..."

Ravon stepped to the front of the aisle beside Michelle, his eyes never leaving mine. With a slight gesture, he beckoned me forward. The aisle stretched before me, lined with flickering candles that cast eerie, shifting shadows across the icy stone floor. My legs felt heavy as I began the forced walk toward him, every step dragging me closer to a fate I couldn't escape. Michelle stood frozen, her expression a mix of horror and helplessness.

Shadow creatures lurched forward, like dying embers. Their limbs twisted unnaturally, crawling and jerking toward me like beasts born of a nightmare. I screamed, stumbling backward, my breath catching in my throat as cold terror clamped around my chest. My pulse thundered.

Another creature emerged on the opposite side, its gnarled shape dragging across the stone, red eyes locked onto mine. I stopped cold in the center of the aisle. Surrounded.

Their eyes glowed like fire in a void, watching me… waiting. The sound they made defied all nature—piercing and guttural, like a thousand screams buried in one shriek. It scraped against my mind, clawed at my spine, and filled the chamber with a dread I couldn't escape.
I cried out, a raw, broken plea. "Help me… please, Ravon." I couldn't run. I couldn't move. Fear rooted me where I stood.

And then, like a dark flame flaring in the night, he appeared. His hand slipped into mine—cool, commanding—and I felt the trembling in my limbs begin to slow. A low, amused chuckle rumbled in his chest, vibrating against my skin as he pulled me close. My terror… thrilled him. He relished this moment, the fear he had created, the chance to play my rescuer.

With mocking gentleness, he swept me into his arms. I gasped but didn't resist. My body melted into his embrace, weak from panic, disoriented by conflicting emotions. My head fell against his chest—steady, warm, familiar. His scent wrapped around me like a drug.
For a moment, I didn't care that he was the cause of it all.

His touch became everything. My breath slowed. My heart pounded—not from fear this time, but from something deeper… darker. Desire flared in my soul like a flame I didn't understand. I closed my eyes, inhaling him.

He had saved me.
And part of me… wanted him to.

"I've got you. You're safe now, my terrified bride,"
he whispered, his breath cold against my ear. His arms
tightened around me as he carried me down the remainder
of the aisle.

Michelle's eyes widened in horror, the bouquet
trembling in her hands. Dania and Sarah looked on, frozen
in shock. The creatures slithered back into the shadows,
retreating at Ravon's command.
At the altar, he set me down gently, and I felt myself slip
back again, my feelings slowly slipping away, his hands
still lingering on my waist, possessive and controlling.

His voice was low and sweet, tinged with menace.
"Shall we begin our eternal vows?"
He glanced at Michelle, who seemed to remember her role.
Her trembling voice called out,
"By darkness witnessed, this union shall be sealed…"
Ravon smiled and began his vows:

"My darkness to your light,
My power to your surrender,
Forever bound in shadowed night…"

His words sent shivers down my spine.

Then it was my turn.
With forced steadiness, I recited the words I had been
coerced into saying:

"I obey… forever bound to you.
You are my master…
My husband.
I belong to you… only to you.

My voice was trembling with fear. Tears stung at the corners of my eyes as I surrendered to Ravon's darkness.

His eyes gleamed with triumph, his face inches from mine. Michelle looked on, horror etched into every line of her face, the bouquet still clutched in her trembling hands. Ravon's voice was a victorious whisper.
"My wife…"

He crushed his lips against mine in a long, devouring kiss. His grip was possessive, his touch searing, darkness curling around me like chains forged in a flame. My breath hitched, but I kissed him back, lost in the haze of emotion that wasn't mine. His mouth claimed me, forcing my body to surrender even as my soul writhed beneath the weight of it. His kiss was velvet and iron, both a seduction and a prison. I clung to him, my heart trapped in his grasp, my pulse pounding against the invisible walls of love that didn't belong to me.

But the moment he released me, everything shifted.

My mind cleared, like shattering glass, and memories came flooding back… especially one: the kiss I had given Drakon on the Maw. The kiss when he was the Dragon.
That kiss, charged with divine power and Drakon's dragon essence, ignited something deep within me.

A blinding beam of light exploded from my body, illuminating the dark chamber.
My face tilted upward, arms stretched behind me, palms facing down, my very soul unleashing my trapped freedom.
The light—so intense—the shadows screamed, literal blood-curdling wails, as they recoiled in terror.

Ravon stumbled backward, confusion and fear on his face. His dark magic faltered. For a single heartbeat, his confidence wavered, his breath caught.

"No," he whispered, reaching for me as though trying to pull the pieces of his illusion back together. But it was already gone.

The spell that held me began to dissolve, its grip loosening like shattered chains. As the light faded, I swayed, nearly collapsing, but Michelle caught me, dropping her bouquet as she wrapped her arms beneath mine to hold me upright. She helped me regain my balance, her eyes blazing with relief and fury.

I turned to face Ravon, my voice sharp and venomous.

"You had me under a spell, under your dark magic. I saw the truth in the light." His eyes narrowed. I stepped forward, fists clenched, fury burning in my veins. Ravon didn't flinch, but he did not move closer either.

With a swift, angry motion, I slapped him across the face. The crack echoed through the chamber.

Pain shot through my hand as his cheek reddened from the strike. Ravon's eyes widened in stunned fury, his ego wounded.

Without hesitation, he slapped me back, his hand slicing across my cheekbone with brutal force. I collapsed onto the cold stone floor, the sting burning hot across my skin. I raised my hand to the pain, glaring up at him through tears of rage and desperation.

Ravon loomed over me, his face twisted with wrath and possessiveness. Tears streamed down my face—not just from the slap, but from the horror of everything that had just unfolded.

His voice was low and dangerous.

"We will proceed to the reception now, Aundrea. I shall see that my expectant wife is fed… and you will not act in this manner again."

His gaze dropped to my stomach, making my skin crawl.

"A feast… for the mother of my heir," he sneered. "And after… a night you will never forget. You will wish that my spell still held, my love." Then he turned to Michelle, his voice cold as steel.

"If you deny me what is rightfully mine… she will pay the price."

Michelle's face went pale. She took a shaky step back, terror in her eyes.

Ravon's smile twisted wider as he reached down, grabbing my hand and yanking me to my feet. His grip was firm, painful. He pulled me close, wrapping his fingers around my arms with suffocating control.

His breath brushed my ear. "You will submit, my love," he whispered. "I have no patience left tonight for your disobedience." His hand slid behind my back, giving me a gentle yet ominous nudge forward.

"Shall we join our guests?" he murmured.

***

He escorted me toward the reception room. The doors swung open to reveal a grand hall with black crystal chandeliers refracting eerie purple light. Dark velvet curtains with subtle silver embroidery hung from the walls. Tables were draped in fine black lace, adorned with candelabras burning red candles.

Ravon seated me at the head table, with Michelle to my right, pale and frightened. He took the seat to my left, his eyes never leaving mine. With a wave of his hand, he declared, "Let the celebration begin."

The room erupted into activity. Servants brought in a feast beyond imagination. Music floated through the air, dark and eerie.

I leaned towards Michelle, whispering urgently, "I promise you, Michelle, I won't let him hurt you. He has my body, not my heart."

Ravon's expression remained serene, his pleased smile unbroken. But something cold and ancient flickered in his eyes—a brief, knowing intensity that told me he had heard every word I said.

The reception swelled around us with forced celebration.
Guests laughed, drank, and danced in lavish excess beneath a cloud of purple light.

Ravon turned to me, his hand outstretched. "Come now, my wife, let them see who you belong to." Ravon offered his hand like a lover. I struck it away like an enemy, my breath sharp in my throat, shaking my head in defiance. "I don't want to dance with you, Ravon."

His smile didn't waver, but his hand closed tightly around my wrist.
Before I could protest, he pulled me forcefully to my feet. My body dragged behind him like a shadow. He turned to me and bowed theatrically before slipping one arm around my waist, the other entwining his fingers in mine.
I spat in his face.

A ripple of gasps echoed through the room, but Ravon only chuckled. "How feisty you are tonight," he whispered darkly.

A surge of violet light swirled around us, the air crackling with raw magic. My body locked, frozen, and my breath caught in my throat as something unseen invaded me, stripping me of my free will. I was still there, buried inside myself, screaming silently.
He raised our joined hands, and my feet obeyed without my will.

The music twisted—no longer a melody, but a spell—haunting, slow, and dripping with menace. My body moved in perfect rhythm, each step unnatural in its grace. I twirled in his arms, my skirts flaring around me like flames licking at the void.

We spun faster, rising into the air—lifted by Ravon's power. My arms arched around his shoulders, our bodies impossibly close, our movements flawless and fluid, like puppets in a dance crafted by shadows. The chamber blurred into streaks of candlelight and masked faces. Every turn, every step, was dictated by him. He held my waist tightly, dipping me backward as my hair spilled toward the cold air below. I could feel his breath at my throat, hear the murmured incantations that kept me bound to his will.

All the while, I was trapped within myself—watching, burning, hating.
The music built to a crescendo. Our bodies twisted midair in a final sweeping circle, his grip iron-tight as the spell reached its peak.

Finally, we descended. My shoes kissed the floor. The spell broke with a snap like a taut cord cut loose. I staggered slightly, regaining my balance, my body once again my own, yet trembling with the memory of being controlled.

Ravon's magic was not just binding, it was invasive, possessive, consuming. And in that moment, as he kissed the back of my hand with a mockery of affection, I realized: he didn't want a bride.
He wanted ownership.

The music faded into a slow, unsettling hush. Ravon's eyes gleamed with triumph as he turned to address the crowd... "A perfect union, wouldn't you say? Beauty and power, bound by fate. Let our guests raise a glass to submission... and to the Empress who now belongs to me, my new queen. Drink, all of you. Drink to domination."

The crowd erupted in eerie applause as Ravon turned to me, smug satisfaction glittering in his eyes. Ravon extended his hand with a sinister grin. "Time for the night's true celebration... elsewhere." He glanced toward Michelle, Sarah, and Dania. "Shall our closest friends join us?"
Taking my hand, Ravon instructed, "I need all you ladies to join hands."

The girls complied, forming a circle as Ravon conjured a swirling vortex of dark magic. When the shadowy haze dissipated, I stumbled forward, my senses reeling from the disorienting transport.

***

We stood at the threshold of a vast underground hall. The ceiling vanished into darkness above, while torches flickered to life along the walls, casting eerie shadows.
The air was stale and musty, filled with the scent of aged dust and forgotten power. The hall stretched ahead, flanked by towering pillars that seemed to support the abyss above. Polished black stone gleamed beneath our feet, reflecting the flickering torchlight like dark glass.
Michelle clutched my arm tightly. Sarah and Dania exchanged uneasy glances beside us.
Ravon stepped forward, his voice echoing off the stone. "Welcome to the Citadel of Eldarath. Your new home." He gestured down the corridor toward shadowed doorways. "Your quarters await. Aundrea's... has had special preparations."

My heart sank as his eyes met mine, promising nothing but torment.

He smiled darkly. "Let us ensure your companions are settled first, my wife."

A lurking servant stepped into view, holding a torch aloft. "Follow me, ladies," Ravon said, leading Michelle, Sarah, and Dania down the corridor. One by one, the doors creaked open, revealing guarded chambers. Michelle was led into a chamber adorned with soft blue tapestries and a narrow bed, though iron bars covered the window, stripping it of any sense of safety. Just beside it, Sarah's room carried the calming scent of herbs, but chains hung ominously from one wall—a silent threat against her freedom. Dania was guided into the last chamber, dim and unsettling, its stone walls marked with glowing runes that pulsed faintly with restrained magic.

Each woman disappeared behind a separate door. One by one, they closed with a final thud. Guards took their positions outside the rooms, sealing them in.

"Aundrea, you've seen your friends are… comfortable," Ravon said smoothly.

Michelle's voice echoed sharply from down the hall. "Ravon, what kind of monster are you? Why have you brought us here?"

As her words rang out, I used the distraction to survey my surroundings: guards at every junction, flickering torches casting long shadows, and a massive stone staircase curving upward into darkness.

Ravon offered me his arm. "Shall we proceed to your quarters, my wife? A surprise awaits…"

He opened the door for me, gesturing grandly. I stepped inside. Ravon closed it behind us.

The room was lavish—velvet tapestries in rich purple, a massive four-poster bed draped in black silk sheets, a sitting area by a roaring fireplace. A marble washroom with a grand tub branched off to the side.

But what truly caught my eye was the glass door beyond the sitting room. It led into a breathtaking conservatory—an exact replica of the garden from Shadowfort. My sanctuary.

I glanced at the ring on my finger, heart sinking.

"Ravon," I whispered. "That garden was at Shadowfort. How is it here…"

He smiled, gentle and deceiving. "No, my love. This garden is yours—wherever you are. The ring grants access to it, always."

An icy chill ran down my spine as his gaze held mine.

He stepped closer, his intentions unmistakable. With slow, deliberate care, Ravon undressed me, his fingers trailing my skin as he undid each button. I remembered my promise to Michelle. I would not fight it. He laid me on the bed, then removed his own garments, never breaking eye contact.

I shut my eyes and inhaled deeply. The air around me seemed to freeze. Every shallow breath testified to my fear. A suffocating fire burned inside me—panic, grief, rage.

Ravon leaned in, whispering coldly into my ear.

"Aundrea, my love… your body ignites me like a shooting star, lighting my darkest desires."

I turned my head to the side, trying to block out his touch, but he pulled me back, claiming what he believed was his. In the shadows of the room, his scent lingered—a musky blend of cedarwood on a cold winter night. He gently touched my shoulder, hoping to ease my tension, but it only deepened my despair. The intimacy he forced on me was unwanted, and my hopelessness turned numb.

The atmosphere thickened as he drew me closer. I could feel his racing heartbeat as he took me as his wife. Time blurred into a long, dreadful night.

After hours of anguish and silent suffering, Ravon finally collapsed beside me, pulling me into his arms. His fingers stroked the back of my head gently—a cruel contrast to his true nature. He kissed my forehead softly, his lips lingering there as if seeking something he'd never receive. My tears dried slowly as exhaustion claimed me, my head still resting on his chest.

ELDARATH CITADEL

Chapter 15

Escape

I woke to the sound of his steady breathing beneath my cheek, his chest rising and falling in a slow rhythm. His arm remained draped tightly around me. For a moment, I lay still, hoping he was asleep, desperate for a shred of solitude. But as I gently lifted my head, his eyes opened, locking onto mine, intense and fully awake.
"Morning," he whispered softly, his voice low and husky.
I pulled back slightly, and he allowed me to sit up, his gaze never leaving my face. A faint light from the garden filtered into the citadel's chamber, casting long shadows across the stone walls.

"Aundrea, come here."
Ravon's voice coiled through the stillness like a silken leash. He extended his arm, waiting—expecting. My stomach clenched at the very thought of entering his embrace, bile rising with the memory of last night's horror. But I had no strength left—not to resist, not to argue.
I moved toward him, each movement a quiet surrender.
He slid his arm around me, drawing me against his chest with unnatural gentleness. The scent of him—smoke and cedar—lingered on his skin, invading my senses as he lay back down, pulling me with him like a puppet on invisible strings.
His fingers began to thread slowly through my hair, and I shut my eyes, forcing stillness. Each stroke was both soothing and suffocating.

Then came his whisper, low and smug against the shell of my ear. "Everything is exactly how it should be, my love."

I bit the inside of my cheek, tasting blood, wondering how someone could feel love for a woman who loathed him with every breath.
He pressed a kiss to the top of my head.
I flinched and shifted away on instinct.

His eyes darkened, flickering with irritation as they caught mine—sharp, assessing. I reached quickly for my stomach, clutching it with practiced urgency, shielding the recoil with a lie.
"I'm sorry, Ravon," I said, voice soft and strained. "I don't feel well. I think it's the morning sickness again."

His expression softened at once, the predator masking itself behind concern. "Ah… of course," he murmured, nodding slowly.

His hand lingered near me, but didn't touch. The illusion of care draped over the moment like a shroud—thin, false, and cold.
Ravon threw off the covers and stood, towering above me. "Shall I summon breakfast, my wife?"
I nodded curtly, still reeling from the nightmare that had become my life.

He slipped on a velvet robe hanging beside the bed. Though it wrapped around his frame, it did nothing to soften the tension in his posture. He rang a small bell, and a short time later, a soft knock sounded at the door.
"Enter," Ravon called, his voice calm but commanding.

The door creaked open, and Guard Thomas entered carrying a tray. His eyes briefly met mine before lowering respectfully toward Ravon. "Breakfast, milord."
Ravon's gaze sharpened as he caught that fleeting glance.

"Anything else, Thomas?" he asked smoothly, but his voice carried a warning.
Thomas hesitated.

"No, milord. Just the breakfast you requested."
Ravon's stare lingered a moment longer before dismissing him.

"You may go."
Thomas bowed and stepped out, shutting the door quietly behind him.
Ravon turned to me, his expression darker now.

"You seem... familiar with my guard," he said, voice low and edged with suspicion.
My heart dropped. I knew where this was going.
I held his gaze, trying to stay calm.

"What are you implying, Ravon?"
His eyes narrowed further.

"Don't play innocent with me, Aundrea. I saw the way Thomas looked at you, and how you looked back."
My blood chilled. "He was only being polite. That's all."
Ravon stepped closer, his tone dropping to a venomous whisper.

"Polite? To my wife?"
I straightened my shoulders, my heart pounding.

"Maybe because he sees a captive, not a wife." The words came sharp, spiked with attitude I didn't bother to hide.

With a deafening crack, he slammed his fist onto the dresser. I jolted violently, a sharp gasp escaping my lips as the sound echoed through the room like thunder. My heart lurched into my throat, breath caught in my chest. "How dare you!" he roared. "You will learn to respect our bond and fear me!"
He took another step, his hot breath brushing my cheek.
Then he spun around and shouted, "Guard!"
The door burst open. Thomas appeared, alarmed.

"Milord, what's wrong?"

Ravon's voice turned cold. "Remove her lady's maid, Michelle. She is no longer needed. And Thomas… you're reassigned to the outer gates. Immediately."

Thomas's eyes met mine, full of concern. He gave a slow nod, then backed out of the room in silence.

Ravon turned to me, fury etched into every line of his face.

"You've made me realize… you need to be reminded of your place."

"I need Michelle," I pleaded, my voice trembling. "She's my only true friend. Please, Ravon, don't take her away from me."

His eyes glinted cruelly. "Friends are liabilities, Aundrea. You'll learn to rely only on me, and me alone."

My heart dropped. Desperation surged through me.

I spun toward the door to flee, but Ravon was too fast. He grabbed my arm, yanking my naked body back hard.

"You shouldn't have defied me," he hissed, his grip bruising my wrist.

My voice echoed through the room as I cried out, "Ravon, I didn't do anything. Please."

Tears shattered my soul, leaving my heart empty and broken.

I struggled, twisting in his grasp.

He dragged me toward the bed, and panic overtook me. I kicked and thrashed, trying to break free. Summoning every bit of strength, I twisted violently and slipped out of his grip.

I dove for the bed and yanked a sheet around myself, wrapping it like a makeshift toga. Ravon's eyes burned with rage as he lunged again, but I was already at the door. Ravon froze, his momentum carrying him slightly off balance. I seized the moment and tore the door open, bolting into the hallway. The sheet clung to my legs as I ran, the cold floor tearing into my feet.

The corridor was dim, but I saw the guards rushing—not toward Ravon's room, but toward me. Behind me, Ravon's enraged voice thundered, "STOP HER!"

But one of the guards reached me first. He grabbed my arm, not to restrain, but to shield.
"I'm here to help, Lady Aundrea. Thomas sent me, he works for your husband, Drakon!" the guard insisted with a low and comforting voice. I had never met Thomas before but it was music to my ears.

I stumbled beside him, my mind reeling as the chaos exploded behind us.
He whispered urgently, "Milady, my name is Ryder, we have been waiting for a chance to help you escape…"
I trusted him instantly and followed his lead, my bare feet slapping against the cold stone floor as we raced through the dimly lit corridors. Freedom felt close—almost real. But Ravon's rage-filled voice thundered behind us, closer than before.

"YOU DARE BETRAY ME!"
Ryder tightened his grip on my arm and pulled me faster, but Ravon's long strides closed the gap. He tackled Ryder from behind, sending us both crashing to the ground.

I threw my hands out in front of me, instinctively shielding my swollen belly as I stumbled to the hard stone floor.

I screamed as Ravon's hands clamped around my ankles like iron shackles, dragging me back toward him. I searched for something to grab onto, but there was nothing—just smooth stone walls on either side, cold and unyielding.

The corridor stretched in both directions, narrow and dimly lit by torches flickering in iron sconces. Shadows danced along the aged stone, distorting the gleam of rusted suits of armor that stood like forgotten sentinels. The air smelled of smoke, metal, and dust, thick with centuries of silence and secrets. The walls felt like they were closing in, trapping us in this violent moment. No furniture, no alcoves—only bare stone beneath my feet and Ravon's fury crashing down around us.

My knees were bruised and cut from the fall. Ryder struggled, punching upward from beneath Ravon, but Ravon's strength pinned him down easily.
"You…" Ravon spat at Ryder, "…will hang for treason." His gaze shifted to me, eyes gleaming with malice. "And you, my wife… will pay for enticing him."

Ravon's loyal guards pinned Ryder beneath them, and then he seized me. He dragged me closer, his breath cold against my cheek. I twisted my body and sank my teeth into his hand, hard enough to draw blood. He roared in pain and his grip faltered. I ripped my legs free and scrambled backward, but Ravon recovered fast. He pounced like a predator, pinning me beneath him. His wounded hand clamped around my throat, eyes burning with fury… then something changed. His expression flickered, obsession buried beneath a storm of rage.
My voice trembled, and I was barely able to form words. "Ravon, please… don't hurt me. I'll do anything, the baby, please."

His grip loosened slightly, his chest rising in ragged breaths. "Anything?" he echoed, voice low and dangerous, but laced with curiosity.

Tears continued to stream down my cheeks as I nodded frantically. "Yes… anything. Just spare Ryder's life. Don't lock me away alone again, and I'll be your perfect wife…"

Ryder spoke up, "I'm sorry, Lord Ravon. I thought she was in danger. I never meant to defy you."

Ravon was angry and screamed out, "SILENCE!"

His eyes then searched mine, hunting for lies. I continued, my voice raw with desperation. "I'll obey every command, wear the gowns you choose, sit beside you at every meal… and lay with you as your wife. Just don't hurt Ryder, and please… don't lock me away."

Ravon said nothing at first. His grip slackened further. Taking a risk, I reached up and kissed him softly— a submissive gesture. He didn't recoil. His narrowed eyes studied me as though trying to understand my sudden change.

The spell had broken, but this…

this was a performance. It had to be…

Seizing the moment, I wrapped my arms around his neck, pulling myself into him as if clinging for safety. My body pressed to his. I whispered, "Hold me, Ravon… protect me from the darkness in this place. Only you can keep me safe."

His arms closed around me, hesitant at first, then tighter. For a breath, his hold felt almost like an embrace—not a cage.

Pinned beneath a guard, Ryder looked on with horror and reluctant understanding. He knew—I was sacrificing dignity for survival.

Ravon's breath grazed my ear. "Why should I believe this sudden devotion, my wife?"

I pressed my body closer, letting him feel the rapid rhythm of my heart against his chest. His hands slid gently down my back. The sensation made my skin crawl. I forced myself to nuzzle into the crook of his neck, whispering,

"I've realized, my lord husband... you're the only one who truly understands me, and the only one who can protect me here."

His chest rose with a deep breath, arms wrapping around me tighter—possessive. Ryder's eyes widened, but he stayed silent.

Ravon's lips brushed my forehead.

"Perhaps... our marriage won't be so loveless after all."

I swallowed my revulsion and managed a faint, obedient smile.

He drew back and turned to his guard.

"Take Ryder to the courtyard. Give him thirty lashes. Let him be a lesson in loyalty."

The guard bowed and stepped away, gripping Ryder by the arm. Ryder looked back at me—grateful, confused, horrified as I watched the shadows of the corridor swallow him.

***

Ravon turned to me again. "Shall we retire to our chambers, my devoted wife?"

"Yes, my lord husband... I'd like that." I paused and placed a hand protectively over my stomach. "Our child is hungry. I haven't eaten anything yet. May I have something in our chambers?"

Ravon glanced at my belly, and something shifted in his eyes—curiosity, maybe even wonder. His expression softened, and when he spoke, his voice was gentler than I was used to.

"Of course, my wife. I'll have a fresh tray sent right away. You need to stay strong for our child." I exhaled quietly. That tiny moment of distraction might've spared me—for now.

He extended his arm, expecting me to take it. I did, suppressing a shudder as his hand clasped mine. As we walked down the corridor, I added carefully, "A bath would also be lovely, my lord… to refresh myself for you." Ravon's eyes gleamed with anticipation, but he nodded graciously. "Arrange it, servants. My wife wishes to be… presentable."

***

We entered the chambers, and the doors closed behind us. The weight of the room settled over me again. I was still a prisoner—but I had bought time.

In the bath, I lingered, letting the warm water soothe my aching body as my mind raced with escape plans. Afterward, the servants helped me into a deep velvet gown—Ravon's choice.

I sat before the tray of food: roasted chicken, steaming vegetables. I nibbled slowly, delaying time. Before I finished, I clutched my belly with a pained expression.
"Husband… I fear the morning sickness has returned. This baby is exhausting me."
I hesitated, then added softly, "And after our fight… I fear it may have harmed the baby."

Ravon's expression shifted, concern replacing menace. For a moment, he looked almost mortal. "Perhaps you should lie down, my wife," Ravon suggested. "I'll summon the castle healer to ensure everything is well with our child."
I nodded weakly, already stepping toward the bed. "Yes… that would ease my mind. I just need to rest…"

He pulled back the velvet curtains, helping me into the bed before kissing my forehead—a gesture disturbingly

tender. "I'll leave you to rest. The healer will come soon."
The door closed behind him with a soft click.
I waited until his footsteps faded completely… then threw
off the covers and rushed to the door, pressing my ear
against the metal and wood. Silence.

My fingers trembled as I tried to turn the handle,
heart pounding with fragile hope…
It didn't budge. It was locked.
Ravon's gentleness had been a lie—just another illusion of
freedom. He still didn't trust me. I was still a prisoner.

A cold shiver rumbled through my body, as reality
sank its teeth in. I leaned against the door, resting my
forehead against the hard metal wicket hatch, hot tears
prickling in the corners of my eyes. How had I let myself
believe anything had changed?

A soft voice in my mind whispered, because you
wanted to believe escape was possible…

Suddenly, footsteps echoed beyond the door—light
and careful. The healer?
I darted back to the bed, pulled the covers over me, and lay
still, feigning weakness. My breaths came slow and
shallow, mimicking fatigue.

The door creaked open, and Healer Freyan entered,
her kind eyes flicking to mine with a soft smile. A guard
stood in the opening of the door, blocking any hope of
escape.
"Milady," she said gently, "Lord Ravon sent me to ensure
your health—and the baby's."
She set her worn leather satchel down beside the bed. I
nodded weakly, still trying to calm my racing heart from
the failed attempt at escape.
Freyan's hands were steady and warm as she examined

me—checking my pulse, laying a palm gently on my stomach.

"Everything seems well, milady," she said. "Morning sickness is common at almost any stage. I'll prepare a calming draught to help you rest. Is there any other reason you feel ill I should know about?"

My thoughts scrambled, searching for words to veil the truth—
I was afraid Ravon may have hurt the baby during our fight.
"I… I tried to run from Ravon this morning and he knocked me to the ground; his hands were around my neck… I just don't feel well from it."
I could see the growing concern in Freyan's eyes as she pulled my dress away from my neck.
"Yes, you have some bruising on your neck. I will speak with Ravon. This is not good for his child."
She removed a few small vials and herbs from her satchel and quickly mixed the potion. The scent was warm, almost sweet, with a faint floral undertone.
"Here," she offered kindly, holding out a small cup.
I drank it slowly, obediently. The liquid was thick but smooth, coating my throat with warmth. I handed the cup back, the weight in my arms already beginning to fade.
Freyan smiled again, patting my hand. "Sleep now, milady. I'll inform Lord Ravon that you and his child are okay."

She gathered her satchel and exited, the guard closing the door quietly behind him.
The draught's effects spread quickly, soothing my nerves, dulling the ache in my chest. My limbs grew heavy.
Escape… freedom… all of it faded as darkness pulled me under once again.

Chapter 16

The Crimson Veil

As I flew away—Aundrea was still held captive by Ravon—my heart ached with the agony of leaving her behind. Her desperate whisper echoed in my mind: "Drakon, I love you… and I do this for you… I choose to stay with Ravon."

Those piercing words cut the deepest, a wound that still bleeds..., Her lips' gentle brush on my scaled maw lingered, a bittersweet comfort after her goodbye. Her gentle touch had healed part of my broken dragon body—a fleeting solace before our forced separation. The memory of her final cry scorched through my chest like wildfire: "DRAKON, FLY AWAY! I'LL BE WAITING FOR YOU!"

***

Days blurred together as I soared through the skies, my injured body screaming for rest. The feel of the wind against my scales was no longer exhilarating, it scraped like sandpaper, each gust reminding me of how broken I'd become, even with Aundrea's healing touch. Pain clawed its way along my ribs, a reminder of how deeply Ravon's magic had sunk into me. My vision was blurred, not from the altitude, but from the pressure inside my skull, a pulsing ache born of too many battles, too many losses. The memory of Aundrea's touch and whispered promises sustained me. Painful as her words were, they fueled my determination to rescue her.

On the seventh dawn since my departure, the Crimson Spine Mountains finally rose on the horizon. My destination neared—and exhaustion claimed me. I spotted a village nestled at the mountain's base: Ravenhurst.

With the last reserves of strength, I glided toward the village outskirts and landed near a babbling brook. My dragon form collapsed onto the soft ground, weary and wounded. Villagers rushed toward me, concerned faces peering up at their Emperor.
Their healer, Lyra, quickly arrived and tended to my wounds.

"Weeks of rest," she cautioned gently. "Your body is broken, Dragon Emperor, and I do not possess the power to heal such wounds." The bitter sting of salve against open wounds became a daily ritual, followed by the tingling burn of healing magic that seeped into my muscles like hot coals doused in river water. My ribs, once cracked and shifting with every breath, began to knit together beneath tightly wrapped bindings.

Every movement still ached, dull at first, then sharper when I moved too quickly. The air often smelled of herbs and blood, and I grew used to the chalky taste of the potions Lyra gave to me. Sleep came in fragments, broken by fevered dreams and the distant sound of soldiers training outside the tent. But each morning, I rose a little straighter, my breath a little deeper, and I felt the fire return, smoldering slow but steady within me.

***

Weeks passed slowly. Lyra's remedies and time gradually restored my strength. Discreetly, I gathered intel from villagers about two critical matters:

1. The rumored location of the Death Stone.

2. Sabion's presence in Ravenhurst.

Finally, on the twenty-first day of my recovery, a villager whispered, "Sabion returned recently, seeking an ancient map in the village archives."

***

I found Sabion in the dusty archive room, poring over a yellowed parchment. His eyes locked onto mine, relief washing over his face.
"Drakon… thank the gods…" he trailed off, noting the grimness in my expression.

"Aundrea…" I began, my voice low, and urgent. "Ravon still holds her captive." The words burned in my throat. Just saying her name made my chest tighten, as if the very air rebelled against the weight of my failure. I had left her behind. I had promised to protect her, and I failed. Every night since, sleep eluded me. When I managed to drift off, I woke choking on dreams of her cries echoing through stone corridors, of her reaching for me as shadows dragged her away. The Dragon Stone pulsed faintly beneath my ribs, a constant reminder of our bond.

Sometimes, when the night was at its stillest, I swore I could feel her pain thrumming through it, sharp, cold, and like a blade pressed against my heart. I had chosen war over love. Victory over her freedom. And though I'd tried to justify it, though I told myself it was the only way, we had to destroy the Death Stone first, the guilt festered in my soul. How many days had she spent alone in the dark, thinking I had abandoned her? How many times had she called for me… and I hadn't come?
Sabion's jaw clenched, his resolve evident.
"And another prisoner… Michelle," I added.

A flicker of emotion crossed Sabion's face— surprise, concern… and something more. A subtle tension in his posture suggested a hidden affection. He cleared his throat, regaining composure.

"Drakon, this map…" He spread the parchment before us

. "It's inscribed with ancient runes, supposedly revealing the Death Stone's location. But I couldn't decipher them—only those with dragon ancestry can read it."

A strange heat surged through my chest, a familiar fire awakening beneath my ribs. My skin prickled, bones straining as scales began to form along my arms. My fingers elongated, curling into clawed talons that shimmered with a metallic sheen. My breath hitched as the transformation crept further, not a full shift, but enough, just enough to awaken what lingered in my blood and body. The ancient instincts stirred. I could feel the pull of the markings as if they recognized me now.

My heart pounding, I reached out a clawed finger and traced the markings. The runes shimmered, responding to my dragon blood, revealing a winding path through the Crimson Spine Mountains—leading to a hidden entrance, ancient ruins, and deep within… the chamber of the Death Stone.

I read aloud:

"Two passages wait, in endless night,
Yet only one path claims the burning light.
Flame illuminate the fall guiding footsteps,
Through the darkest of them all.
Beneath the ground,
Where shadows are made,
To cast flickers on the cave of stone."

Sabion's brow furrowed. "What does it mean?"
I shook my head. "I don't know yet… but we'll decipher it on the journey."

Turning to more immediate matters, I gave instruction:
"Assemble our men. We leave at dawn for the Crimson Spine Mountains. According to the map, it's a two-day journey."
Sabion nodded and moved swiftly to gather the troops.

***

As the first light of dawn crept over the horizon, casting a pale glow across the rooftops of Ravenhurst, we departed the village with twenty skilled warriors at our side, each handpicked for the perilous road ahead. After a long day's trek, we made camp near a tranquil stream, its crystal waters murmuring softly over smooth stones. The air was cool and fragrant with the scent of pine and damp moss, while the fading light filtered through a canopy of silverleaf trees, casting dappled shadows across the forest floor. Fireflies began to blink to life in the underbrush, and the steady gurgle of the stream blended with the rustling of leaves in the evening breeze, a lullaby of nature that wrapped around our weary group like a quiet promise of rest.

***

That night, Sabion and I sat apart from the others by a crackling fire. I glanced at him, curiosity stirring.
"Sabion… earlier, you reacted strongly to Michelle's name. What bond do you share with my wife's lady? Ravon's captive?"

Sabion's gaze drifted to the flames, his voice low and guarded.
"Do I dare hope she still lives… Drakon?"

He paused, then admitted softly, "My love for Michelle runs deeper than blood loyalty or passing affection. She is the gentle breeze that soothes my soul—the missing piece to my heart."

His eyes met mine, filled with longing and restraint. But he dared not pursue her, for he knew the law. No man may marry a lady who has served as maiden to the Lady of the Realm, Aundrea.

Sabion's jaw clenched, pain etched deep into his face. "I have honored the law, suffering in silent devotion…"

My heart swelled with understanding and affection for my loyal friend. I placed a strong hand on his shoulder, a warm smile spreading across my face. "My friend, you will come with me to save Lady Aundrea and rescue Lady Michelle… and I give you my blessing to marry her."

Sabion's eyes widened, overcome with emotion. Tears of joy welled as he collapsed to one knee. "Drakon, my Emperor, my friend… your gift honors me beyond measure!" His voice cracked with deep gratitude as he bowed his head. "I swear upon my honor, Michelle shall be rescued, and I shall love her until death and beyond!"

I nodded with admiration and approval. "Sabion, my friend, remember Lady Aundrea's law: a woman shall choose her husband. I cannot give her to you, I can only give you, my blessing. You must earn her love."

Sabion's grin spread wide across his face, his eyes alight with admiration and conviction. "Yes," he said firmly, "I will honor Lady Aundrea's decree. From this day forward, no woman shall be forced into marriage, each will choose her own husband, freely and without fear." His words echoed with newfound respect, not just for the law, but for the woman who had the courage to create it.

The camp around us melted away until only the crackling fire and Sabion's vows remained. I raised him up, clasping his forearm in brotherly solidarity. "Tonight, we rest. Tomorrow, destiny awaits."

We retired to our camp, sleeping fitfully until dawn broke over the horizon.

**

The next morning, our group continued onward, traversing rugged terrain toward the Crimson Spine Mountains. Hours into our journey, scouts alerted us to an ambush ahead—a group of thieves, nearly forty strong, blocking our path. Their leader, a burly man marked with cruel scars, sneered, "Surrender all valuables, travelers. Resistance means death."

I glanced at Sabion, quickly assessing our odds: twenty of us against their forty. They had us out numbered but with our skilled worriers, we had nothing to fear.

With a fierce battle cry, I partially shifted. My body remained mostly mortal, but silvery, sun-kissed scales coated my skin. Razor-sharp claws extended from my fingers, and my teeth lengthened into deadly dragon fangs.

Sabion drew his sword, the steel catching the light as he stepped to my side, his eyes burning with resolve. He moved with the grace of a seasoned warrior, every motion crisp and sure. Around us, our fighters surged forward like a tidal wave, a blur of scales, muscle, and war cries. Claws slashed through the air, blades gleamed like lightning under the sun, and snapping jaws tore into armor and flesh. The heat of the midday sun beat down on our backs, mingling with the acrid scent of sweat, blood, and churned dirt.

I was no longer a man; I was fury made flesh. My dragon form surged through the fray like a living tempest. I

tore through the enemy ranks with a savage rhythm, every
swipe of my talons sending bodies flying, every strike of
my blade cracking shield and shattering bone. The wind
rushed past my ears with every lunge, every wingbeat
stirring dust and fear into the battlefield. Sabion fought
valiantly beside me, carving a path through the chaos, his
blade moving in perfect harmony with mine.

His shouts of command cut through the din, rallying
our warriors. Around us, the clash of metal and the cries of
the dying thundered like a storm. Our forces held strong,
disciplined, ferocious. Yet I was the true force of nature,
sweeping through the thieves like a dragon-shaped scythe,
relentless and unstoppable. When the dust settled, bodies
littered the ground, the scent of iron thick in the air. Groans
of wounded echoed among the trees. Silence followed,
broken only by the labored breaths of survivors and the
flutter of leaves disturbed by the passing wind. Only four
foes remained, their leader, a scarred brute with eyes like
obsidian, and three of his fiercest men, still standing amid
the ruin, blood-slick blades gripped in trembling hands.
They had seen the storm we brought…

***

The leader stumbled back, eyes wide with terror.
"The Dragon is the Emperor!" They cowered, backing
away like frightened rabbits.

I stepped forward deliberately, voice low and
menacing. "Flee. Tell others: Drakon, Dragon Emperor,
travels these lands. Cross me again… and perish." They
turned and fled, vanishing into the wild.

We tended to minor wounds and caught our breath.
Sabion approached, nodding in respect. "Your dragon
strength is a wonder, Drakon. We owe you, our lives." I
smiled grimly, still scanning the surrounding landscape.

"Debt will be paid when Aundrea is safe."

I turned my gaze eastward, toward the shadowed mountains where the Death Stone lies. The memory of Aundrea's voice echoed in my mind—strong, defiant, breaking beneath torment she never deserved. My fists clenched. I would not fail her again.

***

With renewed vigor, we pressed on. Our Imperial Guards fanned out ahead, eyes scanning every shadow as we crossed terrain that grew harsher with every step, jagged rocks biting through our boots, the wind sharp with the scent of iron and frost. Eventually, the forest thinned. The trees bent away as if afraid, revealing a colossal stone entrance carved directly into the face of the mountain...

Time had weathered its surface, but the craftsmanship remained—stern and deliberate. Ancient symbols ran like veins across the archway, glowing faintly with forgotten magic. They matched those on our map.

Above the gaping threshold, a single word had been etched—deep and jagged, as though clawed into the stone itself:

"Varð."

Sabion turned to me, his voice barely above a whisper. "Drakon, what does the word mean?"

I stared at it, the letters seeming to pulse with memory and warning. "It is not just a name," I said, my voice sharp with reverence. "It's a warning… to all who enter."

The maw of the cave loomed before us, vast and lightless, a hollow maw waiting to devour all foolish enough to step inside.

Sabion hesitated at my side, then cleared his throat, his tone cautious but resolute. "Drakon... Emperor... the map confirms it. This cave leads to the Death Stone."

"Shall we proceed?"

I drew a deep breath, steeling myself.

"Yes. Aundrea's rescue depends on us claiming that stone, and keeping it from Ravon."

We made camp outside the ominous cave entrance, marked by the warning word "Varð." Sabion and I ventured in alone, torchlight flickering off the damp stone.

"Be cautious, Sabion," I warned, eyes scanning the shadows. "Traps likely await us."

We moved carefully, our senses heightened. Suddenly, the path ahead appeared solid—but I felt the deception. I held up a hand. "Do not step forward!"

Sabion halted, eyes fixed on the illusion ahead.

"This ground is false," I said. "A trap, meant to drop us into darkness."

We carefully circled the danger, pressing deeper into the cave. Then, whispers rose from the walls—clicks, whirs, the ominous prelude to something worse.

"GET DOWN, SABION!" I shouted.

Poison darts shot from the walls, whizzing just above our ducked heads. We scrambled forward, avoiding the barrage.

The air grew quieter as we ventured deeper into the cave, each step muffled by the thick silence that pressed in from all sides. The torchlight behind us flickered and dimmed, swallowed by shadows that seemed to move with minds of their own. Then, faint, music.

The sound was so delicate, it felt like it drifted from another realm. Enchanting. Haunting. The kind of melody that tugged at the heart and clouded the mind, each note soaked in ancient sorrow and seductive promise.

From the veil of darkness emerged a vision, majestic and terrible all at once:

The Siren of Lisona.

Her voice spiraled through the air like spun gold, wrapping around us, pulling invisible threads of longing taut within our chests. Sabion staggered toward her, breath hitched, gaze glassy—utterly lost to her spell.

She stood radiant amid the gloom, a haunting goddess sculpted of starlight and shadow. Her piercing emerald eyes caught ours and held us fast. Skin like polished moonstone shimmered with an otherworldly luminescence, casting faint silver ripples across the cave walls. Crimson strands of silk-like hair lifted and swayed in the breeze that whispered through unseen crevices in the rock, air that carried the scent of wet stone and something sweeter, something almost forbidden.

She was both lure and warning. A beauty born of old magic, and it reached for us like a dream we couldn't wake from.

But I remained unaffected—my imperial dragon bloodline shielding me from her spell.

I drew my blade—Dragonfire—and struck without hesitation. The blade passed through her like mist.

Again and again, I struck—claws slashing, tail whipping—but each swing met only mist and illusion. She danced just out of reach, her presence flickering like candlelight in a storm. My frustration burned, rising like magma.

Sabion drifted closer, his body limp with enchantment, eyes locked on the Siren's. Her song wove around him, threading through his veins like poison wrapped in silk. I saw his fingers twitch—reaching for her.

Panic surged.

With a roar that cracked the silence, I summoned the change. My form exploded outward, flesh to scale, breath to fire. My wings tore open with a gust that scattered stone dust across the cave floor. My chest heaved, the heat building deep in my core, until the blaze could no longer be contained.

Then I unleashed it.

A torrent of fire burst from my jaws, golden and furious, illuminating the entire cavern in a searing bright blaze. The Siren screamed, not a human cry, but something ancient and hollow, as the inferno devoured her illusion. Her once-enchanting voice twisted mid-note, shifting from haunting beauty to a high-pitched, piercing shriek, so sharp and jarring it shattered the illusion and drove Sabion to his knees, hands clamped over his ears in agony.

Her beauty peeled away like paper curling in flame. Her moonlit skin blistered and blackened, hair igniting in strands that vanished into ash. The cavern walls glowed red from the heat, shadows writhing like spirits fleeing judgment.

Sabion was thrown backward by the force, landing hard against the rock, coughing as the spell snapped around him like shattered glass. His eyes cleared, and he scrambled upright, his breath ragged.

"Th-Thank you, Drakon…" he gasped, clutching my scaled forearm. "You saved my life again. I'm in your debt."

I nodded, returning to my mortal form. "Our journey's far from over, Sabion. Stay vigilant."

***

We continued deeper into the cave until we reached a fork in the path. Above each passage were etched ancient Greek words:

Άβυσσος — over the left passage.

Πέτρας Σπήλαιον — over the right.

I studied them for a moment, then translated them aloud.

'Άβυσσος' means 'Abyss',

the left passage likely descends into darkness and unknown danger.

'Πέτρας Σπήλαιον' translates to 'Cave of Stone,'

the right passage might be treacherous as well."

Sabion frowned.

"The riddle from the map echoes in my mind:

'Two passages wait, in endless night.
Yet only one path claims the burning light.
Flame illuminate the fall guiding footsteps
Through the darkest of them all.
Beneath the ground, where shadows are made,
To cast flickers on the cave of stone.'

Which path leads to the Death Stone, Drakon?"

I pondered, then tried the obvious first step. Holding up my torch to illuminate the ground, I examined both passages. But the light cast no special glow, no markings.

"Nothing," I said, disappointed.

Sabion nodded. "The riddle mentions 'burning light' — perhaps not just any flame…"

I reread the line in my mind. "Flame illuminate the fall guiding footsteps…"

Suddenly, the scales on my arms prickled with realization.

"The 'burning light' is not torchlight," I said. "it's dragon fire."

Sabion's eyes widened. "Drakon, Emperor — you're the key!"

With renewed determination, I stepped forward. "Show me the path!"

Shifting into my dragon form once more, I first breathed fire gently toward the right passage marked: Πέτρας Σπήλαιον. Flames danced across the stone, but no markings or glow appeared.

I leaned in. "Perhaps the Ἄβυσσος' path…"

I turned my dragon head and exhaled fire toward the left passage.

The flames caressed the stone — and then… magical footprints appeared, glowing softly along the floor.

Sabion exclaimed, "By the gods, Drakon — the path is revealed!"

The glowing steps led into the abyssal corridor, marking a safe route through otherwise treacherous terrain. I shifted back into my mortal form, a triumphant smile spreading across my face.

"Wait," I cautioned. "The glowing path doesn't guarantee safety. Traps could still lie in wait beyond the marked stones."

Sabion drew his sword and stood ready beside me. We advanced cautiously along the path of footprints…

Then — a click.

The ground trembled, then buckled.
A thunderous crack split the air as a massive stone pillar came crashing down beside me, slamming into the ground with a deafening roar. The edge clipped my legs, crushing pain exploded through me.

I screamed.
"Ahhh—Sabion!" My legs," My voice broke, breath hitching as I clawed at the unyielding stone.

"Drakon!" Sabion's shout cut through the chaos. He dove to my side, hands already gripping the jagged edges. His knuckles blanched white. "Hold on, WITH ME!"

We heaved together, muscles straining, breath ragged. The pillar groaned as it lifted—barely—just enough. Sabion shoved his blade beneath it, the steel screeching against rock, wedging it open.

"GO!" he yelled.

I dragged myself free, pain ripping through my legs like fire, blood surging back into starved muscle. I collapsed beside him, panting, soaked in sweat.

"You… saved my life," I gasped, clutching his arm.

Sabion gave a grim smile and slapped my back. "Let's not make that a habit."

He smiled grimly. "Twice repaid once for the Siren, now this trap."

I nodded, massaging my sore legs. "Our bond is stronger than any imperial tie, Sabion. You are my brother."

We shared a brief, fierce embrace before continuing.

***

The glowing footsteps resumed, guiding us deeper into the Abyss passage.

But between us and the relic yawned a vast, gaping void.
A black hole stretched across the cavern floor—bottomless, silent, devouring light itself.
The ground crumbled at the edge, as if warning us not to try.

Sabion cursed under his breath. "Shite, how are we supposed to cross that?"
His voice echoed into the abyss, swallowed by the void.

I stepped forward cautiously, peering into the dark. The air pulsed with ancient magic. My wings twitched beneath my skin, but I knew the cave was too narrow to shift.
If I transformed here, I'd crush the cavern around us and bury us alive.
I clenched my fists. "We'll need another way."

I looked around the cave, looking for clues. Sabion bent down and picked up a loose stone from the cavern floor. With a skeptical grunt, he tossed it into the abyss.

Nothing.

No thud. No splash. Just endless silence.

A strange unease crept over us, the pit seemingly bottomless—swallowing not just sound, but courage.

Then I noticed the inscription.

Etched into the stone wall beside the drop, glowing faintly in the bluish cave light, were words in ancient script. I moved closer, brushing away dust and webbing to read it aloud:

"Μόνο όσοι βλέπουν πέρα από τον φόβο μπορούν να φτάσουν την Πέτρα."

Sabion raised an eyebrow. "What's it say?"

With a partial shift of my dragon inside, I translated slowly, each word heavy with meaning. "Only those who see past fear can reach the Stone."

We stood in silence, the weight of the message sinking in. Then Sabion let out a soft breath, eyes scanning the abyss again.

"The illusion," he murmured. "Drakon, remember? At the entrance—the ground that wasn't real."

I nodded, the memory flickering back

He continued, more certain now. "This is the same. No bridge, no path, just fear. Maybe we don't need to find a way across... Maybe we need to believe there already is one."

I gave him a skeptical look.

Sabion turned to me, eyes resolute. "We have to walk forward. In faith. If we hesitate, if we doubt—we fall."

I barked a dry laugh, clapping him on the shoulder. "Well, if you're wrong, it's been an honor, brother."

We exchanged a look, half amusement, half terror, and then stepped forward.

One foot over the void.
And solid ground met our steps—though no bridge could be seen.

Each stride forward felt like defiance against reason, against fear. But the path held.

The invisible magic yielded to our faith, and the abyss behind us vanished into shadow.

Heart pounding, I stepped off the last of the hidden path and into the chamber.

***

I approached the pedestal slowly, my boots echoing in the silence, eyes fixed on the Death Stone. It pulsed with dark energy, ancient and angry, as if thirsting for my bloodline.

"Drakon... do we truly understand its power?" Sabion asked warily.

Reaching into my satchel, I withdrew a pair of worn, dragon-scale leather gloves.

"A wise question, Sabion," I said, never taking my eyes off the stone. "To touch it bare-handed would invite disaster. Its power would consume me."

Sabion's eyes widened in alarm. "The ancient lore warned of this..."

I slid the gloves on, feeling their slight magical resistance, a barrier between myself and the Death Stone's corruption.

"These gloves, crafted from dragon-scale, may grant me a moment's protection," I said. "But we must understand what this relic truly is before I risk any contact."

Sabion nodded. "We need to search the chamber for ancient lore, warnings, inscriptions, anything?"

"Yes," I answered firmly. "Let's uncover its secrets before we take the next step."

We began examining the walls and floor of the chamber. Sabion found intricate carvings that depicted dark magic rituals.

Out of the corner of my eye, I noticed a faint light pulsing on the back wall. As my eyes adjusted, I approached an inscription carved in ancient script, glowing softly in the shadows.

Για να μην καταπιεί το σκοτάδι τη γη,
παράδωσε την Πέτρα του Θανάτου στο Στόμα της Ελδρίδα,
μια λίμνη με φλογερά βάθη…

I traced the letters with my fingertips and spoke the translation aloud:

"To prevent darkness from consuming the land,
Deliver the Death Stone to Eldrida's Maw,
A lake of fiery depths…"

I turned to Sabion. "That's two moons' ride from here."

Another line glimmered just below the first:

Μόνο το αίμα του δράκου μπορεί να αναιρέσει τη μοχθηρή δύναμή της.
Ρίξτε την μέσα, και το σκοτάδι θα χάσει το φως του.

I continued reading aloud, each word sinking deeper into the weight of prophecy:

"Only dragon blood can unmake its evil might,
Cast it in, and darkness shall lose its light."

I looked at Sabion, determination etched into every line of my face. "This is our path to saving Empress Aundrea… and Lisona."

With gloved hands, I reached out and grasped the Death Stone. A surge of dark energy pulsed through the leather, but I stood firm.

Suddenly, Sabion shouted, "YOUR HIGHNESS, RUN!"

***

The cave began to collapse, walls shattered like glass, boulders crashing down, clouds of dust rising. The ground shook violently beneath our feet. We sprinted toward the entrance, rocks pounding the stone floor mere feet behind us. Dust choked our lungs; the deafening roar of falling rock drowned out all thought.

We burst out of the cave seconds before the entrance caved in, sealing the passage forever behind us.

A massive plume of dust erupted, blotting out the sun.

Sabion gripped my arm, relief and amazement on his face. "We barely escaped, Drakon…"

***

I carefully placed the Death Stone into a box adorned with magical seals, securing its dark power. Our guards strapped the box to my horse, freeing me of its burden.

With the stone contained, we rode back into Ravenhurst Village , exhausted, triumphant.

As night fell, I turned to my men and shouted, "Tonight, we celebrate! Drink up, men! Your ale is on me!"

The alehouse erupted in cheers and applause as we pushed open the creaky doors. Warm firelight spilled across the wooden floors, welcoming us into the cozy tavern. The air was thick with the scent of roasting meats and fresh bread.

Music started — a lively fiddle tune — feet tapping, hands clapping.

Alewives with loose hair and mischievous smiles greeted us with foamy mugs, seating themselves easily on the laps of our guards, whispering in their ears and laughing.

Sabion and I claimed the center table, surrounded by our warriors. The music swelled, and men spun women across the floor in dizzying circles, cheeks flushed with merriment. Sabion attempted a few clumsy steps, earning cheers and teasing laughter.

I joined in. Despite my size, my dragon-born grace surprised even me, adapting to the rhythm with surprising ease.

Back at the table, mugs clinked and tales spilled. Our men roared as I recounted our harrowing trials beneath the mountain, and of Sabion, our brave knight... who fell under the Siren's spell!

Sabion's face flushed crimson as the teasing began.

"Oh, Sabion," one guard shouted, "charmed by a pretty voice and face!"

"Did you sing back to her?" another laughed. "Off-key, no doubt!"

Sabion rolled his eyes and tossed an ale-soaked rag at me. "I'd rather face Ravon's blade than your mockery, Drakon!"

The alehouse erupted in cheers once more.

As the night wore on, our adventures grew wilder in the telling. Laughter echoed off timber beams. At last call, Sabion and I rose, arms thrown around each other, swaying, eyes bleary with ale and joy.

"Our rooms..." I muttered, voice uneven, "await... if we can make it..."

Sabion and I stumbled outside, singing a slurred Lisonian battle hymn under the stars. But my imperial instincts sobered me slightly.

"Wait," I hissed. "Ravon's spies... we're vulnerable."

Sabion blinked rapidly. "Aye... guards! We need guards!"

I bellowed into the quiet village night, "Imperial escort! Now... for Drakon, Emperor of Lisona!"

Torches flickered as six guards came running. Their leader, a grizzled veteran, gave a quick bow. "Emperor Drakon, sir. Safe escort to the inn assured."

They formed a semi-circle, clearing a path and steadying us as we made our way through Ravenhurst's winding streets.

Sabion leaned heavily on my shoulder. "Tomorrow... Eldrida's Maw... the stone's end..."

I nodded, swaying. "Aye... and Lady Aundrea... will be next...we must free her."

"We've arranged for Your Majesty to stay in the manor house at Ravenhurst, freshly prepared for the Imperial guard."

Guards helped us up the stairs. Sabion collapsed onto one bed, I face-planted onto the other. The guards chuckled as they closed the door behind them.

Just before sleep overtook me, I heard Sabion's soft voice:

"Drakon... tomorrow... will we still be alive?"

I mumbled through a grin, "Hah... dying tomorrow? Only if Ravon can drink more ale than me..."

Sabion's weak laughter mixed with mine, both trailing into snores. Mine echoed through the room, loud as a beast's. The window rattled slightly. The door creaked from the force of it.

Silence returned.

Except... the faintest sound from Sabion's bed: a groggy, half-laughing whisper—

"Drakon... wake up... tomorrow's going to hurt..."

Chapter 17

Bound in Silence

Two moons had eclipsed, and I woke up to Ravon's lips onmine, a touch that once might have stirred something in me, but now only brought revulsion. My skin crawled beneath his gentle kiss. I lay still, feigning the heaviness of sleep, until he pulled away.

Ravon dressed in silence, his gaze fixed on mine—a silent claim of ownership.

"I will send food," he said, voice low and husky.

I forced my tone steady, a spark of defiance flickering in my chest. "No… wait."

He raised an eyebrow, amused by my boldness.

"Please," I added, softening my voice into a plea. "Bring back Michelle. She is my best friend. I don't want to be alone all day…"

His gaze lingered, weighing the request. My heart sank, expecting rejection. But then, his expression shifted—a cruel smile tugging at his lips.

"I will return her… but, Aundrea, if you change your behavior…"

The threat lingered in the air, unspoken but sharp. He turned around once more, his eyes burning with warning. "Every time you make me angry, Michelle pays for it. Remember that."

He exited, leaving me breathless and cold.

Alone, my thoughts betrayed me, drifting to Drakon, his intense gaze, his strong touch. Would I ever be free from Ravon's grasp?

I rose, still in my nightdress, and moved toward the mirror. My hand instinctively rested on my stomach... and then, a

flutter. My heart soared.
My child had moved.
Overwhelming love swelled inside me, tears pricking my
eyes. I clutched the sensation tightly, willing it to stay.

***

The door creaked open behind me. Michelle stood
in the entryway, her face bruised and swollen, tears pouring
down her cheeks.
I ran to her, horror gripping my chest.
"What did he do to you?" I whispered, arms wrapping
tightly around her frail frame.
Michelle trembled in my embrace, her body shaking with
silent sobs. I guided her to the bed, where she collapsed
beside me, burying her face in my shoulder.
"He… he said it was because of you," she stammered.
"That your defiance was… contagious."

Rage bloomed in my chest. Ravon's cruelty knew
no bounds. Her left cheekbone was swollen, a cut above her
eyebrow crusted with dried blood. My throat burned with
helplessness.
"He threw me down the stairs… in the east wing," she
whispered. "Said if you continued to enrage him… next
time would be worse."

I held her tighter, tears falling freely now. The child
within me stirred again, sensing my distress.
Michelle pulled back slightly, her red-rimmed eyes locking
onto mine. "Aundrea, we must escape… or reach Drakon.
Ravon is going to kill us all."

The door creaked again. A servant girl entered
quietly, carrying trays of food with eyes downcast.
My heart twisted at the sight of Michelle's battered face. I
reached out instinctively, brushing her cheek. Closing my
eyes, I summoned my healing light.

A soft, white glow began to pulse from within me, spreading through my fingertips into her skin. The space between us filled with warmth as the healing power surged. Michelle's eyes fluttered shut, her body relaxing. Bruises faded. The cut sealed and the swelling receded.
Her porcelain skin returned. As the light disappeared, I opened my eyes to find Michelle staring at me in wonder, with a smile. She whispered a loving thank you, and we sat together in silence, breaking bread and sipping broth. Her eyes never left mine, filled with gratitude and something deeper… hope.

When we finished, I turned to her, voice firm. "Michelle, I'll handle our situation. Do not speak of escape again. If Ravon suspects anything, he might kill you." Michelle nodded vigorously, understanding etched on her face.
"Now, help me dress," I added, rising to my feet. "Ravon expects me to be presentable."

She assisted me into a silk undershirt trimmed with intricate lace, followed by a fitted, long-sleeved velvet gown in deep crimson with black lace across the bodice, his favorite color. The sleeves clung tightly to my wrists, with subtle slashes revealing glimpses of silk underneath. She brushed and coiled my hair into an elegant updo, securing the loose strands with tiny ruby pins. I slipped on black leather shoes with silver buckles and a slight heel.
Michelle stepped back, studying me carefully, then nodded her approval.
Ravon entered like a storm, dark, abrupt, and suffocating. The velvet drapes swayed behind him as he crossed the threshold, eyes scanning the room.
His gaze landed on Michelle's healed face, narrowing. Then it turned to me.
He strode toward her, graceful yet menacing. His black boots struck the floor in sharp, deliberate taps.

His long fingers gripped her chin—not cruel, but firm—lifting her face.

"Feel lucky, Michelle," he whispered coldly. "Be thankful my wife can heal your wounds… because if either of you act out again, you won't get another chance to recover."

Michelle's eyes widened in terror, darting to me, silently begging for protection.
Ravon released her, his fingers brushing down her neck before falling away.
Then he turned to me. His eyes roamed over my face, my neck, the gown. They burned with hunger.
"You look beautiful, Aundrea…" His voice was husky.
"…But something's missing."

He walked toward the garden's glass door and drew aside the velvet curtain, revealing a moonlit backdrop of flowers and towering trees. As Ravon stepped into the moonlit garden, the soft rustle of his robes and the creak of the door were the only sounds breaking the tense silence. Michelle's wide, fearful eyes remained locked on the doorway, then shifted to me. I tried to offer her a reassuring glance, but my heart thundered in my chest.
Suddenly, a soft knock broke the stillness.

A servant slipped inside, offering a small, folded parchment. He bowed quickly and disappeared as silently as he came.
My heart skipped a beat. I unfolded the note, and my breath caught as I read the hastily scribbled words:

My beloved Aundrea,
I love you.
I miss your touch, your smile, your kisses.
You are not forgotten.
I will come for you soon.
Yours always,
D.

My soul soared. Drakon's words reignited something within me—hope, love, longing. But the euphoria was short-lived.

Ravon returned, a single flower clutched in his fist, presumably to place in my hair. His gaze locked instantly on the parchment in my hand, and his expression twisted into rage. The flower fell to the floor.
He stormed forward and ripped the note from my fingers. "WHAT IS THIS, AUNDREA?"
Ravon's voice thundered through the room, his face purpling with fury.
Michelle cowered behind me, trembling.

Ravon's eyes burned as he seized Michelle's arm and yanked her forward, then slammed her to the stone floor. She cried out, her hands scraping against the unyielding surface and her head hitting the stone wall behind her.
"ANSWER ME!" he roared. "WHERE DID THIS NOTE COME FROM?"
Tears streamed down my face. I stumbled backward in fear for myself and my child. I raised my hands out, in desperate hope of defense.

"I… don't know what it is. A servant just handed it to me and left. Ravon, please—it's not my fault," I begged. "I didn't write the note!"
Tears blurred my vision. My hands instinctively flew to my stomach, seeking comfort from the child within. And then, I felt it.
A flutter.
A gentle, unmistakable movement.
My eyes widened. A sob escaped me.

Ravon's rage faltered. His gaze shifted to my hands resting on my belly.
"What is it?" he asked, his voice still sharp but softened by

curiosity.

I choked on my words, trying to breathe. "The baby… he just moved."

Ravon froze, his eyes searching mine. Slowly, he stepped closer.

"May I?" he asked, reaching out a tentative hand.

Still crying, I nodded. He placed his palm on my belly. For a moment, all was still—his eyes locked on mine, filled with a tangle of possessiveness, curiosity, and a fleeting hint of wonder.

Then his expression hardened.

"I will find out who that servant was," he said coldly, his voice regaining steel. "And deal with them accordingly."

His hand slid from my belly to grip my arm—not painful, but firm.

"But let this be clear, Aundrea," he continued. His gaze drifted down to Michelle, still trembling on the floor. "If you ever receive another note, or even think of responding to him…"

His grip tightened. "Michelle will pay the price. Do you understand me?"

My heart pounded in my ears. I nodded gently, the tears still wet on my cheeks.

"Yes…" My voice was barely more than a whisper.

His grip loosened slightly, but his thumb began tracing slow circles along my skin—a twisted gesture of possession.

Then he leaned in, lips brushing my ear.

"You will forget him, Aundrea. Forget Drakon exists."

His breath sent tremors through me. His lips barely touched my earlobe, making my stomach churn. I turned my head away, defiance sparking to life again.

He caught the motion.

"You dare resist me?" he murmured darkly.

Fear gripped my body as I trembled and whispered, "I'm

sorry, I didn't mean it."

His eyes gleamed with menace. His hold tightened. Tension coiled thick in the air—

I couldn't breathe.

***

Then, a hesitant knock broke the silence. The heavy door creaked open a moment later.

A servant stepped inside, timid and pale. "Lord Ravon, sir… a messenger from the Eastern Realm has arrived."

For a heartbeat, no one moved. The world held its breath. Ravon's grip slackened. His fury cooled into something far more dangerous—calculation.

"Send him in," he said, his voice suddenly smooth as silk.

Then, without turning his gaze from mine, he said with a chilling smile, "Do we have a distraction from your rebellion, Aundrea?"

His laughter sent ice through my veins. The messenger walked in and handed a note to Ravon, and he read it, his expression changing.

"Well," he said darkly, "we cannot have that, can we?"

He bellowed for the guards.

"Send a group of our best men to Eldrida's Maw! Find Drakon, and bring me back my Death Stone!"

The guard bowed and departed swiftly, leaving Ravon's gaze locked on me like a predator watching his prey.

My breath hitched, but curiosity pushed through my fear. "What… what is the Death Stone?"

Ravon's laugh returned, deeper this time, echoing menacingly across the chamber. He released me and turned away, pacing, then faced me again. His eyes were no longer mortal—they blazed with something much darker.

Unholy ambition.

"My Death Stone," Ravon murmured, his voice low and ominous, "is the catalyst for eternal domination. It is the heart of all evil, forged in the deepest caverns of the underworld. Its power will shatter the fragile seal binding the Abyssal Gates… unleashing upon Lisona a maelstrom of unholy terrors: Daemons, darkness incarnate, and souls of the forever damned. With this stone, I will become destruction made flesh. No kingdom, no magic, no god will stand against me. I will devour all!"

My blood ran cold. Ravon's eyes burned with an unnatural light. The baby stirred within me, as if sensing the storm in my soul. Ravon's gaze dropped to my belly, his smile twisting grotesquely.
"Our child," he whispered, "will inherit a realm of eternal shadow."
A scream tore from my throat.

I stumbled back, hands cradling my stomach, horror etched across my face. "No… this can never happen!" I cried, my voice shaking.
Ravon laughed, a sound that chilled the marrow in my bones. He stepped toward me with measured calm, triumph gleaming in his eyes. "Our child will rule the darkness," he hissed. "And I will make sure Drakon fails. He will not destroy the Death Stone."
Michelle, stunned until now, broke free of her fear and rushed to my side.
"Aundrea, we have to stop him!" she whispered urgently.
Ravon's attention snapped to her, his expression darkening.
"Guards!" he barked. "Take Michelle back to her quarters, under heavy watch. She is poisoning Aundrea's mind."
Michelle clung to me, her fingers trembling. "Aundrea, resist him!" she shouted, even as guards stormed in to drag her away.
"Fight him!" she screamed again, her voice cut off as the doors slammed shut behind her. I was alone. With him.

Ravon's eyes fixed on mine, and he began closing the distance. "You will think only of me," he said darkly, "and of our child's future."

He reached out, brushing a strand of hair behind my ear. I flinched at his touch, revulsion rising in me like bile. He smiled, savoring my fear.
"You used to be fascinated by my power," he murmured. "Soon, you'll be obsessed—with it, and with me."
His fingers trailed down my neck. But then... I remembered.
Drakon's letter.
His promise.
A fire sparked inside me.
"Never," I said, my voice low but firm. "I will never be yours."
Ravon's smile faltered, surprise flickering across his face. Then he stepped forward again, menace coiling around him like smoke.
"We'll see about that," he snarled.
His hands shot out, clamping around my wrists like iron shackles.
"We'll see about your loyalty... and your love."
I tried to pull free, but he was too strong. He yanked me close, chest to chest, eyes blazing.
"Drakon is a fool," he spat. "He thinks he can reclaim you?"
My heart screamed for Drakon, but my lips refused to betray it.

Ravon lifted me effortlessly and threw me onto the bed. I kicked and struggled, but he pinned me down. His face hovered inches from mine, his breath sour with hunger.
"Drakon will never reach you," he hissed. "I'll destroy him before he even tries."
Tears blurred my vision as I thrashed beneath him. But my

strength began to fade… my limbs weakening, my screams dissolving into broken sobs.

Ravon's grip slackened slightly, sensing my surrender. He leaned over me, his breath cold against my skin.

"You are broken," he whispered. "Now, you are mine."

His lips descended, gentle, but suffocating. My tears streamed like rain, choking sobs breaking the silence. My body shook beneath his weight, wracked with despair.

My voice, hoarse and haunted, I whispered Drakon's name into the shadows of my mind.

Ravon deepened the kiss, as though claiming what was left of me. When he finally pulled away, his eyes glittered with triumph.

"You are mine, Aundrea," he said darkly. "My birthright. You belong to me. Stop your misbehaving, or you'll only hurt yourself… or our child."

My sobs came slower, dry, broken hiccups of grief. He released me and stood up beside the bed, towering over me like a specter—silent, but satisfied. He turned to walk toward the door and paused, glancing over his shoulder.

"If you need me," his voice slid under my skin, "say my name aloud, and I will come."

He smiled once more.

"I'll be back to take you to dinner tonight."

The door creaked shut behind him with a heavy clang. The lock slid into place.

I lay frozen. Trapped. Alone with despair.

My voice cracked as I whispered one word.

"Drakon…"

It was a prayer, a plea, a whisper of the soul. But silence was my only answer. Tears fell again, hotter than before, as reality settled over me like a shroud. He wasn't coming.

Not tonight.

Maybe not ever.

Ravon's words echoed in my mind like a death sentence: You are mine...

My body collapsed deeper into the bed, defeated. The room spun around me in a dark, hopeless blur. I buried my face in the pillow, sobbing until my throat burned.

My mind screamed silent questions: Would Drakon be able to defeat him? Would our child be born into Ravon's darkness?

My tears dwindled to exhausted whimpers.

***

Hours passed like eternity. The darkness outside mirrored the blackness within. A servant had just left my room, helping me refresh for the night.

The room remained still, broken only by distant footsteps or the faint clinking of silverware from downstairs.

I stared at the door, bracing for the inevitable.

At last, the lock clicked open.

Ravon stood in the doorway, dressed in tailored black. His eyes gleamed with satisfaction as he surveyed my disheveled state.

"Aundrea, dinner awaits," he said smoothly, offering his arm.

I rose, my legs heavy with dread. My gown—no doubt chosen by his servants—was a stunning crimson. A cruel reminder of the life he insisted I now lead with him. I took his arm, my skin crawling beneath his touch.

We walked through the citadel corridors, lined with silent guards, and down a staircase. The guards wouldn't meet my eyes—whether from shame or fear, I couldn't tell. At the grand dining hall, soft music drifted through the doors, mingled with laughter. The sound mocked me.

Ravon leaned in close, his breath brushing my ear.

"You look beautiful tonight, my wife. Smile for our guests."

I obeyed. A fragile, painted smile stretched across my lips.

Dinner passed in a blur. Ravon played the charming host, weaving lies and laughter like silk. The guests ate, drank, and spoke freely—unaware, or unwilling to acknowledge, the horror beside them.
Then… it happened.

A servant leaned in to pour tea. His fingers brushed mine—gentle, brief. Our eyes met.
And in that fleeting glance, I saw it. Kindness. Recognition. Hope.
My heart leapt—too fast. I looked at Ravon, then back to the servant. But it was already too late.
Ravon's eyes locked onto us.
His expression twisted.
His hand lifted.
A dark, swirling void erupted from his fingers. The servant cried out, then vanished into the darkness.

The room froze. Silverware clattered onto plates. Guests paled.
Ravon turned to me, fury contorting his face.
"You dare flirt with another man, under my roof, while carrying my child?!"
I clutched my belly protectively, shaking my head. My voice was caught in my throat.
"ANSWER ME, AUNDREA!" he roared.
I tried to yell out, but I trembled in fear. "I…"

A guest stood abruptly. "Lord Ravon…" he said, bowing deeply. His voice was calm but edged with warning. "Perhaps... wisdom dictates restraint. Tonight."
Ravon glared at him. Gradually, his gaze returned to me, seething. But he lowered his hand.
His voice dropped into a deadly growl.
"Aundrea…"

I met his stare, my eyes rimmed red. His jaw clenched as he spat a single command.
"Eat."

Tears streamed down my face. No sobs. No sound. Just silent despair.
I looked at the untouched food. Protest—and face his wrath… or comply and survive.
I picked up my fork.
Each bite was tasteless. Each swallow forced.
Conversation resumed, awkward, stilted. Ravon's eyes never left me. I finished. Set my fork down. Folded my hands tightly in my lap, my eyes lowered.

I looked up for a brief moment, and the guest who had intervened before glanced at me again. I saw pity in his eyes. For me.
Ravon saw.
His voice sliced through the room.
"The evening is ended. Retire to your rooms… except Aundrea. She will accompany me."

My blood turned to ice.
The guests rose quickly, casting nervous glances my way.
The doors closed behind them.
Only Ravon remained.
"The night is still young, Aundrea," he said huskily. "And desire fills me."
My heart pounded in my chest. He stood—slow and deliberate—rising from his chair like a predator closing in.
I remained seated and frozen. Then, he extended his hand.
Trembling, I rose.

***

The fire crackled softly in my bedchamber as we entered, casting flickering shadows across his face. His eyes burned with intent. He lifted my chin, and our eyes met.

"You want to fight, my love… or be compliant?"

I said nothing, trembling.

He snapped again. "Are you going to fight me?!"

My voice barely rose above a whisper. "No… Ravon."

In one swift motion, he scooped me up and laid me gently on the bed. He leaned in for a kiss, and I closed my eyes. Darkness rose to meet me. I drifted inward, away from the horror, the weight, the pain. I hid somewhere in my mind with only one thought.

Drakon, I need you.

Chapter 18

The Flame Unleashed

The silence was broken by a knock at the door. My dragon-sized snore ceased abruptly as I growled and forced my eyes open. A heavy haze clung to my mind like smoke after a battle. The dim light filtering through the window pierced straight into my skull. My tongue felt thick and dry against the roof of my mouth, and the sour taste of last night's ale still clung to my breath.

Sabion stirred in his bed, his arm flopping over his face with a grunt, still deep in sleep.
I groaned, each movement like wading through mud. My joints ached, and my limbs felt leaden. I threw off the heavy blanket, the rough fabric scraping against my sweat-dampened skin. The cool air rushed over me, stinging like a thousand tiny blades against my overheated body.
Rubbing my temples, I stumbled toward the door. Every step sent a dull throb through my skull, echoing the ache in my chest—the ache that no amount of drink could dull.

Lord Thomas stood on the other side, his expression grave.
"Emperor Drakon, sir..." he began, his voice low and urgent.
My mind cleared slightly, instincts sharpening. I could sense trouble. My chest tightened beneath my singed cloak and torn clothes, and my bloodshot eyes narrowed.
"What news, Thomas?" I demanded, my voice rough from sleep. A cringe rippled through me as my claws half-emerged.

He stepped inside, glancing briefly at the still-sleeping Sabion before fixing his eyes on me.

"Bad news, Your Majesty. I have information about... Lady Aundrea."

My heart skipped a beat.

"She is being held captive at the Citadel of Eldarath by Ravon," he said grimly.

My fists clenched.

Thomas's expression darkened. "Ravon suspected my loyalty. I barely escaped with my life. Lady Aundrea... she is not faring well." My vision blurred with rage and fear. "She fears for your unborn child... and Ravon is using Michelle to torment her."

Sabion stirred awake, sitting up with alarm when he heard Thomas whisper Michelle's name. The bed creaked beneath his sudden movement.

I felt my dragon blood ignite with fury.

"We ride," I growled to Thomas and Sabion. "Mount the horses. Assemble our men. We must destroy the Death Stone at Eldrida's Maw first, to weaken Ravon before rescuing Aundrea."

Sabion jumped into motion, already shouting orders. As the men erupted into movement, I grabbed Lord Thomas's arm.

"Tell me more about Aundrea's condition..." My voice came out low and trembling, barely restrained fury laced through every word.

A storm churned beneath my skin, each breath a struggle against the roar building inside me.

Thomas's expression twisted with anguish.

"Ravon… consummated their union," he said, his voice faltering, "against her will."

Red veiled my vision. The air around me felt thin, like the world itself had shrunk to a single, unbearable point of agony. My heart didn't just break—it tore open in a blinding flash of helpless rage. The room swayed, not from motion, but from the force of what I felt inside—sorrow and fury crashing together like thunder.

Thomas lowered his voice. "Ravon delights in her suffering. He believes his marriage to her, will solidify his claim to the throne."

My hands clenched into fists so tight I heard my knuckles crack, bone grinding against bone. The Dragon Stone pulsed against my chest, hot and furious, reacting to the torment in my soul. I could feel the fire coiling in my blood, begging to be unleashed.

"And there's more," Thomas warned, his voice dropping to a grim whisper. "Ravon is dispatching his elite warriors—the Shadowguard—to intercept you before you reach Eldrida's Maw. They will stop at nothing to kill you and return the Death Stone to him."

I exhaled slowly, mind racing.
"How many?" I asked. "And what route will they take?"
"Five hundred Shadowguard elites, Emperor," Thomas said. "They'll likely travel through Blackstone Pass. It's the fastest route to intercept you."

Sabion stepped forward, hand on the hilt of his sword.
"Blackstone Pass is a death trap, Drakon. Narrow and winding. Perfect terrain for an ambush."
I nodded grimly.
"Agreed. We'll split our forces. I'll lead 300 men through the Pass and confront the Shadowguard head-on. Sabion, take 200 men through the hidden Wyndor Ridge path. Flank them and strike from behind—we'll crush them in between."
Sabion saluted and moved to rally the warriors.

Thomas's voice turned cold.
"One last thing, Emperor. The Shadowguard's commander is Victor Valtor... your former general."
Thomas's voice was grave.
"He knows your battle tactics intimately. He will anticipate your every move."

Victor Valtor—once my most trusted advisor. My brother in arms. A grand warrior whose blade had carved paths through a hundred battles beside me.

His loyalty had been unquestionable… until the day it shattered.

His betrayal had not come from ambition or greed, but grief. His wife, Lasfira, had been executed for treason against the throne—for leading a rebellion in Ravon's name. She had already bound her eternal life to Ravon, body and soul. Her love for him eclipsed her loyalty to Lisona, and she used it to fan the flames of insurrection.

When the truth came out, justice demanded her death.

Valtor never forgave me for it. He turned his back on everything we'd built.

I remembered the moment he defected—his eyes wild with heartbreak, hatred, and something deeper… devotion to a man I now knew was capable of unspeakable horrors.

He didn't just defect.
He pledged himself to Ravon.

Now he leads the Shadowguard—elite, merciless, and bound by shadow.
And he knows me better than any enemy I've ever faced.

My pulse thundered in my ears, the Stone pulsing hot beneath my armor. The air felt heavy, like the past had just walked back into the room and dropped its sword at my feet.

I looked at Thomas.
"Then we'll have to fight smarter. And strike where even Victor Valtor cannot see."

Sabion's eyes narrowed. "Yes. We adapt. Victor will expect a full-force dragon assault."
I nodded. "We'll use stealth infantry. Lure them into the Pass. Trap them. Then strike."

A guard emerged from the trees, leading a familiar figure. Vandros—his coat a striking blend of white and storm-grey—moved with the grace of a creature born for war and wind. His mane, pale as moonlight, rippled with each step.

"Your Majesty," the guard said with a respectful bow. "I found him grazing near us. He'd returned on his own—almost as if he was searching for you."

Relief surged through me. Vandros snorted softly and trotted the last few steps, pressing his muzzle to my shoulder. I rested my palm against his broad neck, the warmth of his skin grounding me.
"You never fail me," I whispered.

In the silence that followed, no words were needed. Only trust—and the steady breath of a loyal companion returned.

***

As the days passed, an uneasy tension settled deep in my bones. Each step forward felt heavier, my instincts whispering louder with every mile—danger was close. I couldn't shake the feeling of eyes watching from the shadows, or the weight of silence pressing too tightly around us.

Sensing something wasn't right on the way to Blackstone Pass, I lifted my hand and signaled for the company to halt, gently reining in Vandros. The others followed suit, the soft clatter of hooves slowing to silence behind me as I scanned the terrain.

"Thorold," I called, "Ready the men. This could be a trap."
Thorold nodded, drawing his sword and issuing quiet orders.

Figures emerged atop the cliffs. Ten. Then twenty. Armed warriors. One of them shouted down:
"Emperor Drakon, welcome to Rispirian Stone Cliff! We are the Saterium Tribe. Come, rest your horses and feet for the night!"

I glanced at Thorold. "Stand down, but remain alert."
We followed the Saterium warriors into their camp nestled between the cliffs. My men mingled with the tribe, exchanging stories, laughter, and even friendly games of Stone Fist. Camaraderie lightened the tension—if only briefly.

Thorold approached quietly.
"Your Majesty, shall we discuss the route to Santonium Centre Pass?"
"Aye," I said. "We'll visit the villagers there. We need a map through the terrain to Blackstone Pass. The Shadowguard lies in wait."

After our discussion, I wandered alone to the camp's edge, settling onto a worn log. My thoughts returned to Aundrea. I allowed my dragon blood to surface slightly—scales shimmered faintly beneath my skin, eyes glowing softly.

Lifting my face to the wind, I let out a low dragon roar, quiet to mortal ears. I breathed my love into the wind. "Aundrea... I love you."

The breeze carried it forth. And then—just for a moment—the wind changed. Violent. Alive.
And I heard it.
"Drakon!"

Faint. Distant. But real.
I froze. For a heartbeat, the world held still. The breeze, which had moments before howled through the cliffs, now quieted to a hush, as if the very skies were listening.

But the echo of her voice—soft, broken, and unmistakably real—lingered not just in my ears, but deep within my bones, like the last note of a sacred song.

My breath caught, chest tightening with the sudden, overwhelming ache of longing and relief. The sound of her whisper stirred everything in me that had been hardened by war and grief. I could still feel her presence—faint and distant, but alive. Real.

Hope flared in my chest like a flame that had refused to die, no matter how long the darkness tried to smother it.

My dragon form trembled, the scales shimmering as they receded beneath my skin. Muscles ached from the shift, but I barely noticed. I dropped to my knees, overcome by the weight of emotion, and stared up at the stars.

The sky above was endless, cold, and glittering... yet for the first time in weeks, I didn't feel alone beneath it.

I remembered the note I had sent her, not knowing if it ever reached her hands, but praying it had.

My beloved Aundrea,
I love you.
I miss your touch, your smile, your kisses.
You are not forgotten.
I will come for you soon.
Yours always,
D.

The words had been etched from my soul, and I could only hope they'd touched hers.

Tomorrow, we ride to war. But tonight, I dream of her voice.

***

Thorold approached quietly, noticing my distant gaze and emotional state.
"Your Majesty, shall we turn in for the night? Tomorrow's journey to Santonium Centre Pass will be challenging."
I nodded, rising from the log. "Yes, Thorold. Ensure the men are well-rested. We meet with the Saterium Tribe's leader before departing. I wish to thank them for their hospitality—and inquire about any news of Ravon's forces."

As we prepared for sleep, I lay awake in my tent, my thoughts lingering on Aundrea...

Suddenly, the silence was broken by a voice just outside.
"Emperor Drakon," came the gravelly voice of Chief Vexar, "may I enter? I bring news that may interest you—about Ravon's Shadowguard and Lady Aundrea."

I granted him entry, and he stepped inside, his expression grim.

"Our scouts have returned from spying on Ravon's forces. The Shadowguard marches toward Blackstone Pass as expected..."

He hesitated, then lowered his voice.

"But there is disturbing news from the Citadel of Eldarath. Lady Aundrea attempted escape with a guard that was loyal to Lord Thomas, secretly placed within the citadel. His name is Ryder. Unfortunately, Ravon's men caught them in the deep tunnels."

My heart plummeted.

"Go on," I said, dreading the next words, I took a deep breath and waited.

"She's been locked in her chambers since then, except for a recent dinner with Ravon's loyalists. I fear for her safety, Emperor. Ravon's jealousy escalates by the hour."

Rage and dread twisted in my gut. My dragon blood stirred, fire crawling beneath my skin.

"Ravon grows more unstable," Chief Vexar added solemnly. "Our scouts can feel it."

I paced the tent, mind racing with fear for my wife.

"We ride at dawn," I declared. "We must obtain that map and reach Blackstone Pass. The Death Stone must be destroyed."

Aundrea, I will come for you, my love, I whispered to the stars. But first, I must destroy the Death Stone. I have to sever any tie Ravon might cling to—and make sure he never wields its power.

Then Chief Vexar delivered the blow that shattered my heart.

"Lord Thomas's guard escaped only because... Lady Aundrea sacrificed her dignity. She submitted to Ravon's desires... to protect him."

The words hit like a sword to my gut. I staggered. My vision blurred with unshed tears, grief and fury battling for control.

"Ravon had her pinned down... hands at her neck," Vexar continued. "She did it to save the guard's life, and possibly her own—and her unborn child."

***

When I awoke, the scent of roasted meats and spiced grains filled the crisp morning air. Campfires crackled softly as smoke curled into the early light, and the soft murmur of conversation drifted through the encampment. Warriors from the Saterium Tribe and my forces sat side by side, sharing wooden plates piled high with hearty bread, smoked fish, and sweet root mash. The clatter of utensils against tin dishes and the occasional laugh added a warmth that had been absent for far too long.

I moved among them, still stiff from the journey but composed, nodding to soldiers and exchanging a few words here and there. I paused beside one of the larger fires where the Saterium chieftain sat surrounded by his kin. I extended his hand in gratitude.
"Your strength, your loyalty, and your welcome gave us more than shelter," he said, voice low but resolute. "You gave us hope."

The chieftain stood, gripping my forearm with a respectful nod. "Lisona must stand united now more than ever."

My head inclined, and I turned to address both armies.

"Eat well. Prepare yourselves. Today, we ride with purpose—not just for battle, but for freedom."

A hush fell briefly, then a cheer rippled outward, echoing off the trees.
I stepped back, my gaze drifting toward the east. The rising sun cast a golden glow across the encampment, but my thoughts were already miles away—with her.

***

By day's end, we arrived at the bustling village near Santonium Centre Pass. My men dispersed to gather supplies for the road ahead. I moved alone, seeking the map we needed.

As I walked through narrow streets, a blur of motion caught my eye. A boy—no more than twelve—darted past me with panicked speed. Shouts rang out behind him.

Guards chased him, armor clanking, their boots echoing on stone.
The boy's terrified screams rose throughout the village.

Within moments, a guard caught him, yanking the boy's collar and lifting him off the ground. The child thrashed in protest. A crowd formed, drawn by the commotion.

I stepped forward, my imperial presence drawing silence.
"You there, guard," I said, voice sharp and commanding. "Why are you arresting this boy?"

The guard bowed deeply, holding the boy before me.
"Forgive me, Your Highness. He is being arrested for theft."

I frowned. "What did he steal?"
"A loaf of bread, Your Highness."

My gaze hardened. A child was being punished for stealing food? I approached the boy, softening my voice.
"Boy, do you know who I am?"
His fearful gaze met mine. He nodded, his voice barely audible.
"Yes… You're the Emperor."
My heart twisted. "Why did you steal bread?"

The boy sighed, defeat etched on his small face.
"I'm sorry… but I was hungry. I haven't eaten in days."

My decision was swift.
"Release him," I ordered.

The guard hesitated, then slowly lowered the boy to the ground and let go of his shirt. The child rubbed his neck, still wide-eyed with fear, trembling, taking a cautious step back.

My gaze remained locked on the guard, every muscle in my body coiled like a drawn bowstring.
Then the bastard muttered, just loud enough for me to hear, "Coddling thieves… like he coddles his rebel wife…"

My jaw clenched.
A low hum pulsed in my ears—the kind that came before the storm.

Heat flared beneath my skin, the fire in my blood rising like a tide. I felt my fingernails dig into the flesh of my palm, trying to keep the dragon within from bursting through.

My gaze snapped to him. He flinched, as if he'd felt the weight of it—the quiet promise of retribution simmering behind my eyes.

But I said nothing—for now.

I would let him stew in his false courage for just a moment. Let him wonder when judgment would fall.

Because it would. Instead, I reached into my pocket and pressed a gold coin into the boy's hand.

"Go. Eat your fill."

His eyes widened at the coin's worth. Without another word, he turned and vanished into the crowd. I stepped closer to the guard, my presence alone making him flinch.

My voice was low, but laced with warning.

"Who do you serve?"

The guard swallowed hard, his eyes wide.

"I—I serve you, Emperor Drakon."

I didn't blink.

"Then remember this—serving me means respecting my wife. Speak of her like that again…" I leaned in, my tone sharp as steel, "and your next breath will be your last."

The guard dropped his gaze and backed away quickly, vanishing around the corner without another word.

The villagers began to disperse, whispering among themselves about the Emperor's unexpected mercy. I watched them go, my thoughts already shifting to the mission—acquiring the map to Blackstone Pass. I approached a nearby village elder who lingered behind.

"Where might I find the cartographer?" I asked. "The one who knows the pass."

The elder nodded respectfully.

"He arrives tomorrow, Your Highness. His name is Master Edwin. He travels from the eastern villages."

Disappointment flickered across my face, but I nodded and thanked him. I retreated to a modest inn, seeking rest for the night.

***

Inside my room, I lay on the narrow bed, staring at the ceiling, my thoughts consumed by Aundrea.
Was she safe tonight?
Did Ravon continue to torment her?

My fingers clenched beneath the blanket, fury rising in my chest.
Darkness clouded my thoughts. Even sleep gave no refuge. Her face haunted my dreams, etched with fear, her voice whispering my name. Chief Vexar's words echoed in my subconscious like a cruel curse:
"Ravon had her pinned down, hands around her neck…"

I tossed and turned, my mind plagued by dark visions—
Of rescuing her,
Of unleashing dragon fire upon Ravon and his Shadowguard.

At last, dawn crept into the room. I rose from bed, eyes burning with grief and purpose. After splashing my face with cold water from the basin, I dressed in my worn traveling gear and armor.

Downstairs, the innkeeper had prepared a simple but hearty breakfast: bread, cheese, and smoked meat. I ate quickly, my mind already racing.

Today, Master Edwin would arrive—the man who held the map to Blackstone Pass.

After finishing my meal, I walked the village streets, asking for directions until I found a cluttered shop

with a sign that read:
Master Edwin, Cartographer.

Inside, the air smelled of parchment and ink. Maps and scrolls littered every surface. At a workbench sat an elderly man with spectacles perched precariously on the tip of his nose.

He looked up as I entered. "Ah! Emperor Drakon," he said with a slight bow. "Word travels fast in Santonium Centre Pass. I've been expecting you."

"I seek a map," I said. "The path to Blackstone Pass."

His eyes twinkled with curiosity. "I possess what you seek. But be warned—few return from that route."

He unfurled a yellowed parchment, revealing intricate markings of cliffs, ravines, and treacherous terrain. "This path will lead your army through Shadowfell Canyon, past Widow's Peak, and into Blackstone Pass— straight into the jaws of Ravon's Shadowguard."

I studied the map closely, committing every mark to memory.
"The details are all I need," I told him.

Master Edwin nodded and leaned in, voice low. "Blackstone Pass is guarded by three Shadowguard encampments," he whispered, tracing the parchment with a thin finger. "Encampment Alpha blocks the main entrance. Bravo and Charlie sit on the eastern and western trails."

He glanced up. "Ravon's commander, Victor Valtor, likely divides his 500 elite troops among these camps." I nodded grimly. "We'll split our forces and strike both flanks."

He pointed to faint X's on the parchment. "These ravines and boulder fields can become traps... or shields, depending on how you use them."

My mind raced with strategy—how to turn terrain into advantage.
"I'll need copies of this map," I said, folding the original.

Edwin immediately began creating duplicates with swift, practiced strokes.
"While you work," I said, "tell me—have you heard any rumors of Ravon's forces beyond Blackstone Pass?"

His quill paused mid-air.
"Yes, Emperor. Whispers speak of reinforcements. Ravon draws power from the temple of Malakar... ancient, terrible magic."

The name hit me like ice. Malakar—home to cursed rituals and forbidden spells.
I clenched my jaw. "Finish the maps, Master Edwin. We march to Blackstone Pass immediately."

Master Edwin nodded swiftly, returning to his work with renewed urgency.

Within the hour, my commanders—Thorold, Smirian, and Vorgan—gathered around me, maps in hand.

"Our strategy remains unchanged," I told them. "We split forces:
• Thorold, take 300 men through the main entrance. Distract Encampment Alpha.
• Smirian, lead 100 elites along the eastern trail. Hit Encampment Bravo.
• Vorgan, flank west with 100. Strike Encampment Charlie.

• Sabion has already moved with his 100 elites along the eastern trail. Smirian and Sabion will meet at Bravo.

Our objective: reach Victor Valtor and crush Shadowguard command."

They nodded grimly, memorizing every route and point of engagement.

With the battle plan set, we mounted our horses and rode toward Blackstone Pass—the first major obstacle between us and Eldrida's Maw.

I rode at the head of our force, wind sweeping through my hair, hooves pounding the rocky trails. The sun blazed overhead, casting long shadows from the jagged cliffs.

"Keep the destination beyond Blackstone hidden from the men," I said quietly to my commanders. "Only we know the truth—Eldrida's Maw and the destruction of the Death Stone await us beyond this battlefield."

Thorold nodded gravely. "Victory here cripples Ravon's forces. Eldrida's Maw will be vulnerable after this."

Our pace remained relentless.

***

Days turned to weeks, the terrain growing harsher, the skies darker as we neared enemy territory. I rode beside Thorold, offering commands and encouragement to the soldiers.
Their faces were carved with resolve.

"Shadowguard scouts likely already know we approach," Thorold muttered.

"They'll be waiting," I replied. "Tell the archers to prepare volleys at Encampment Alpha's gates. We'll soften them before we charge."

Thorold relayed the order. As we crested the final ridge, Blackstone Pass came into view—fortified, narrow, flanked by sheer rock walls. Shadowguard banners snapped in the wind above Encampment Alpha's gates.

Then, a lone figure emerged.

Victor Valtor.

He walked forward boldly, unarmed, armor glinting in the light. I halted Vandros and raised my hand—our entire force froze behind me.

"Drakon," he called, voice dripping with scorn, "Emperor of fools. Still clinging to honor. Where was your honor when you murdered my wife?"

I leaned forward in the saddle. "Say your piece, Victor. What lies has Ravon sent you to deliver?"

He sneered. "Aundrea sends you a message... through me. She says your delay is killing her. Ravon's patience wears thin."

My grip on the reins tightened. I fought the fury rising within me.
"Do you bring proof," I asked, "or just more of Ravon's games?"

Victor smirked and withdrew something from his cloak—a bloodied lock of dark brown hair.

I narrowed my eyes. "Aundrea's hair is black as night," I said flatly. "You expect to deceive me with someone else's suffering?"

His expression faltered for a second. Then he snarled, "You're still blind. Soon, she'll wish she had never known you."

He stepped closer, voice lowering into venom. "Ravon will break her spirit… then her body. You'll be too late, Drakon. And then I will have the revenge I have longed for."

I stared at him, calm on the outside while fury boiled within.
"Enough of this."

I turned to Thorold. "Signal the archers. Unleash hell."

Thorold raised his arm. A moment later, the sky filled with the scream of arrows. The first wave rained down on Encampment Alpha—soldiers cried out, chaos erupted at the gates.

Victor Valtor drew his blade and charged toward me, screaming.

I dismounted, reaching for the hilt at my side—the ancient blade that had served my bloodline for centuries.

Dragonfire.

Forged by my ancestor Tharros atop the molten heights of Drakonian Peak, the sword had been born not in a forge, but in fire itself. Legend told that Tharros, in his dragon form, breathed pure flame into the raw ore and molten steel, shaping it with claw and magic. He quenched the glowing blade in the heart of a rare blazing crystal known only to the mountain, sealing within it both heat and legacy.

The blade shimmered with a molten gleam, its edge engraved with runes long faded from memory. When sunlight or magic struck it just right, it flared like living fire. My father once told me, "A true Emperor must wield fire within… and without."

As I unsheathed Dragonfire, its metal sang—a fierce, ancient tone that rang through the air like a battle cry of my ancestors. The weight in my hand was familiar, yet always commanding. I stepped forward, the sword angled in guard, and met Valtor's steel with a clash that shook the breath from nearby soldiers.

Sparks flew with every clash, steel screaming against steel in a vicious rhythm that rang through the chaos. His blade moved fast—fierce, calculated—but I was faster. Stronger. Fueled by rage and dragon blood, I met each strike with brutal precision.

The air burned with the heat of our fury, the scent of blood and sweat in my nostrils. My heartbeat thundered like war drums, syncing with each powerful swing. Blow by blow, I drove him back, my muscles straining, breath coming in ragged bursts.

Then I surrendered to the storm within. I let the dragon rise.

A surge of power tore through me. My bones stretched, reshaped. Flesh split and scaled over. Wings burst from my back in a blaze of molten fury. My roar ripped through the battlefield—deafening and primal— shaking the very ground beneath us.

Valtor stumbled backward before running for his life. Flames erupted from my jaws, searing the air with blistering heat. The gates of Encampment Alpha splintered beneath the blast, wood and iron exploding into shrapnel.

Shadowguard troops scattered in panic, their screams swallowed by the thunder of my fury.

I soared above the battlefield, fire spewing from my jaws. Infernos consumed their ranks. Screams echoed through the pass as their encampment was reduced to scorched rubble.

Only Victor Valtor escaped, fleeing on horseback, his terrified gaze lingering on me as he vanished into the mountain trail.

I descended, shifting back into my mortal form, Dragonfire still blazing in my grip.

Thorold approached, bloodied and breathless.
"Blackstone Pass is ours, Emperor."
I nodded, sheathing my blade.
"The path to Eldrida's Maw… and the Death Stone… is now open."

But even in victory, my thoughts drifted to her—Aundrea.

I lifted my gaze to the heavens, where stars shimmered through the parting clouds like distant watchers. The scent of scorched soil and smoke still clung to the air, but it was her name that burned in my chest.

My fists clenched, trembling as a surge of power flooded through me. Fire coiled beneath my skin.

I roared—a dragon's cry that shook the sky and echoed across the ravaged land, defiant and full of longing. My hands had shifted, claws glinting in the moonlight, and sunset-colored scales rippled along my neck—a fiery reminder of who I truly was.

"I will come for you, Aundrea!" I bellowed into the night, voice raw with promise. "We are one step closer… I love you."

The wind caught my words, carrying them toward the horizon like a whispered vow.

She was out there, waiting.
And nothing—not shadow, not stone, not Ravon's darkness—would stop me from reaching her.

Chapter 19

Into the Dark

I awoke in a breathless void. Shadows clung to every corner of my stone chamber, broken only by the flicker of torches lining the walls, flames swaying like dancers at a funeral. The scent of cold ash and damp rot hung thick in the air. I couldn't say how long I'd been here—days? Weeks? Time had lost its shape, slipping through my fingers like water swallowed by the void Ravon called a kingdom.

I lay still in the bed he forced me to share, the sheets colder than death, their silk unfamiliar against my skin. I turned slowly, dread curdling in my belly.

He loomed there—Ravon. His breath a chilling whisper, and without warning, his eyes snapped open. Piercing blue, glowing faintly in the torchlight. A thousand unseen knives carved down my spine under his stare. I didn't breathe. My lungs froze, as if his gaze had sucked the air from my body.

"Aundrea… my love…" His voice slithered into the space between us, laced with perverse affection. "I have a surprise for you today."

"I don't want any surprises from you, Ravon." I forced the words out—quiet, but firm. "Something bad always comes from them."

He only smiled. That sick, slow smile stretched unnaturally, like it knew too much. The hunger in his eyes burned not for my body, but for my will—my resistance, my very flame. He thrived on extinguishing it.

"We're going to meet the maker of my magic," he breathed, drawing closer, his breath cold against my ear.

My heart stilled. The maker? My mind tried to rationalize it—perhaps a warlock, some ancient mage. But the dread pooling in my gut told me otherwise.

"What... what do you mean, Ravon? The maker of your magic?" I tried to sound terrified, to mask the question in submissive fear. But the curiosity in my voice was real, and he heard it.

His grip tightened around my wrist. He told me he was barely a boy when curiosity consumed him, wondering about the source of his magic. He revealed that a powerful, ancient entity granted him dominion over the Shadow Lands, and soon Lisona would kneel at his feet. This entity wasn't a sorcerer, nor mortal magic—it was primal, god-born power, forged in darkness itself, older than time." Its gift came with a terrible price: allegiance to shadow, and command over life and death. His eyes gleamed with satisfaction as he ordered me to dress.

"You'll understand soon," he said. "Your place is forever bound to my darkness."

My heart raced with foreboding.

He stood motionless, eyes burning into me as I rose from the bed, legs trembling beneath my weight. My hands faltered, shaking violently as I reached for the corset draped across the chair—another black gown, its silk as cold and unforgiving as the mourning that shrouded my soul.

"Ravon," I whispered as I struggled with the laces, "the baby... my corset doesn't fit anymore."

He approached slowly, like a lion approaching its lamb, eyes never leaving mine. At the wardrobe, he pulled out a different gown—similar in design, but cleverly altered, looser around the belly. Thoughtful, yet chilling in its implication.

He helped fasten it without a word at first, his fingers slow on the ties. My curiosity was a dangerous spark, but I dared to fan the flames.

His fingers paused on the lace as he answered, voice hushed and almost reverent. "One who reigns over realms beyond yours… beyond mortality, where shadows are kings."

His gaze locked onto mine, a wild intensity burning in his eyes—an almost euphoric madness that made my skin crawl.

The final tie of my gown was secured, yet my fate felt sealed even tighter. Suddenly, a soft knock shattered the suffocating silence.

"Enter," Ravon snapped, his voice cold and commanding.

A servant stepped in, trembling visibly, and placed a tray on the small table with stale bread, moldy cheese, and a steaming cup of tea. The moment the door cracked open, a sliver of freedom beckoned. Hope surged in my chest like wildfire.

I moved, legs trembling almost as much as the servant's. I launched myself forward—a desperate bid for escape.

But I was a flicker of motion… and Ravon was a storm.

He caught me inches from the threshold, lifting me off the ground as if I weighed nothing. The world spun violently as he turned me, slamming me back to my feet, his grip crushing, bruises already blooming beneath his fingers.

"Not today, Aundrea... not today."

His hot, foul breath seared my ear—a gesture that turned my blood cold. The servant wisely vanished behind the closing door, leaving us alone again... The room was ours, and I was caged, like a doe in the sights of a hunter.

I really tried. Oh, by the Gods, I tried to reach whatever thread of a civilized being remained.

"Ravon, stop this madness. I have no intention of meeting your God," I said, my voice trembling with a cocktail of fear and fury. "You were once a prince. Beloved. What darkness has consumed you so completely?"

But his smirk only deepened, lips curling with amusement. His reply was silent.

And then, my own defiance exploded.

"You'll never truly rule with darkness as your crown, Ravon! Drakon will destroy you, and I'll rejoice at your downfall!"

His eyes narrowed, glinting with something between admiration and wrath. Silence hung heavily between us, my defiant words still echoing.

His fingers suddenly closed around my chin, gripping tight.

"How delightful," he breathed. And for a moment, I hated how my own strength seemed to please him. "I won't let you ruin this day... You will meet my magic's creator... Eat, Aundrea. Our baby needs nourishment."

I sat, every movement mechanical. Every bite swallowed through nausea. Across the small table tucked against the wall, Ravon watched me, approval and obsession burning like twin torches in his eyes.

"We shall proceed," he said, gesturing to the door.

***

We descended through corridors that twisted like veins carved through stone, deeper and deeper into the underbelly of Ravon's kingdom. The torches burned blue, not orange, each flame casting shadows that slithered unnaturally across the walls, as if the darkness itself recoiled from light. The air grew colder with every step, thick with decay and power.

At last, we reached colossal doors—stone and iron woven together like muscle and bone. Ancient runes carved into their surface bled a dull crimson light, a sour, crackling energy that pulsed through the atmosphere.

Ravon stepped forward, pressing both hands to the stone. The massive doors answered him. They groaned open with a shriek that vibrated in my chest.

Beyond: swirling darkness. A portal, pulsing like a heartbeat. Not just blackness—but a void that pulled at the edges of my soul, whispering threats I couldn't understand.

I stepped back, my arms folded over my chest. "I won't voluntarily walk into darkness with you, Ravon."

My voice didn't shake. Not anymore.

Ravon's smile twisted. "Oh, a challenge. We will see about that."

He reached for me without hesitation, his eyes gleaming with intent—like a predator sensing prey.

In a desperate bid to strike before he consumed me whole, I launched myself at him, reckless and unrestrained.

Fury exploded from me—raw and unchained. My arm lashed across his face, the burn in my palm searing hot. He staggered, surprised, hand rising to his cheek. I swung again. My fist cracked against his jaw.

But he recovered fast.

Ravon grabbed my wrists, twisted, and spun me into the wall. His body pinned mine, his breath flooding my ear again—colder now. Sharper.

"You should have stayed submissive, Aundrea... but you'll learn."

Pain flared as his voice slithered through me.

Then—I bit him. My teeth sank into the edge of his earlobe.

He roared in pain, jerking away. And for the briefest moment—I was free.

I ran like it was the last thing I'd ever do.

My shoes slapped against the stone, heart hammering, lungs burning. I didn't know where I was going. I didn't care. Just—away. Away from that thing that called itself a man. Away from the portal. From the god that waited on the other side.

But Ravon was behind me. Always behind me.

He caught me. Again. As if I'd never escaped at all.

His hand closed around my arm and spun me roughly around to face him. His fury was molten now—no longer veiled beneath silk and seduction.

"YOU WILL COMPLY, AUNDREA!"

I fought him. Fists, knees, whatever I could strike with. I drove into him with every ounce of strength I had left. But his skin might as well have been stone. He blocked each blow, absorbing my fury with maddening calm.

Then… his touch changed.

His hand brushed against my cheek. Not a blow—a caress.

It was worse.

A subtle gesture, yet it coiled unease through my chest like a serpent. Not from fear… but something deeper. Something unwanted. I hated how easily his presence distorted my senses.

"Do you want to play, my queen?" he murmured.

The title dripped with perversion. I spat in his face. The saliva landed on his cheek. He wiped it away with a single gloved finger—slow and deliberate.

"You'll take me through that portal over my dead body, Ravon!"

His amusement died like blood in a grave, leaving only cold, eternal hunger.

"ENOUGH, AUNDREA."

His hand struck me before my mind could catch up.

Agony burst across my cheek, the strike landing with a force that felt molten. As if his hand carried not flesh and bone, but iron straight from the forge. My skin ignited beneath the blow—blistering, peeling in invisible layers. I staggered, a strangled cry caught in my throat as my fingers flew to the wound.

But it wasn't just pain.

It burned deeper, beneath the surface—an unnatural heat seeping into my veins. The sensation crawled like acid through my bloodstream, sharp and biting, turning my blood to fire. My lips trembled. My vision blurred. A bitter, metallic taste crept onto my tongue, and my heartbeat became erratic. Not just bruised. Not just struck.

Poisoned.

I gasped, my legs buckling as the darkness threatened to fold in around me, my breath shuddering as each inhale stung with more than just fear.

He pinned me again, against the corridor wall, harder this time, like he wanted to crush my defiance into dust.

"P-please don't take me there, Ravon…" I sobbed, my voice cracking under the weight of pain. But even through the tears, defiance still stirred.

I screamed. Thrashed. Kicked.

"NOOOO!"

But the fire didn't fade; it curled tighter around my nerves, punishing every flicker of defiance like a serpent striking each time I dared to breathe without permission. Tears overtook me, stripping away resistance. My legs buckled. My arms fell limp at my sides. My voice slipped into a whimper.

"I'll go… just stop the pain," I cried.

The words burned worse than his magic.

Ravon's eyes gleamed.

"What… what did you do to my face?" I whispered through the tears. "Please… it… it hurts."

"A minor spell of agony," he said gently. "It will teach you obedience."

He lifted his hand again—but this time, it glowed.

A blue and purple light shimmered along his palm. He pressed it to my cheek, and like a wave, the fire vanished. The pain dissolved. My skin, blistered moments ago, smoothed beneath his touch.

"You see, my queen…" His voice was soft and smug. "I can both hurt… and show mercy."

Still shaking, I said nothing.

The swirling portal loomed once more. Guards flanked it now, cloaked in robes that matched the darkness itself. He extended his arm.

"Shall we proceed now, my obedient queen?"

I felt… numb inside. Hollow.

"My obedience… for now," I whispered.

His hand folded over mine like a chain. And together, we stepped through.

The portal was not a gateway. It was a maw, a throat of shadow that devoured light, and breath, and time. The moment we stepped through, the world I knew was ripped away. Sound ceased. Gravity twisted. My skin prickled, as though reality itself had been peeled back.

Then—light. But not warmth. Not hope. This was pure darkness.

This was the underworld.

Flickering red lightning cracked across a sky that bled crimson, and a stream of molten lava. A black mountain range loomed in the distance, jagged as broken bones. The ground beneath our feet was gray and lifeless, dry as ash. Each step echoed like a funeral toll. I could hear and feel the crunching beneath my feet as I took each step.

I clung to Ravon—not out of trust, but necessity. I needed a point of stability in this nightmare, even if it was the monster who brought me here. In that moment, I knew that getting out of this dark, evil place depended on my presence with him.

The air stank of brimstone, rotting flesh, something sour and ancient that clung to the inside of my throat. Miasma swirled low around our ankles, pulsing with an eerie glow, like ghostly serpents winding through the dust.

Ahead stood the temple.

It rose like a wound against the sky—massive, black as pitch—guarded by statues carved in the shape of grotesque beasts. Their eyes gleamed red. Alive. Watching me. Judging. Hungering.

Terror clawed at my chest, but I couldn't stop walking. Ravon's grip was iron. My knees buckled with every step toward that looming gate.

As we approached, the doors burst open with a shriek of rusted hinges, exhaling darkness.

The chamber was immense and cold, lit by candles made of black wax. Shadows flickered across walls carved with ancient glyphs—symbols of death, subjugation, sacrifice. My skin crawled with every step.

At the far end of the hall, a throne pulsed like a heart—chiseled from crystal darker than midnight, throbbing with raw power.

And there—upon it—he sat.

Not a man. Not a creature.

The Dark Lord Zha'thik.

His form defied shape—an abyss wrapped in robes of shadow, with two eyes like molten rubies floating in the void. He didn't move. He didn't need to. The air bent around him like a storm held in place.

Ravon bowed. His voice dropped to a whisper I barely heard. "My lord. I present Aundrea... Queen of the Shadow Lands... and soon, all realms."

He pulled me into a forced bow, but my body had frozen. The weight of the Dark Lord's gaze locked onto me, and it was like falling into a pit without bottom or breath.

A voice entered my mind.

Silence reigned, yet the sound thundered from inside me—cold, vast, and irreversible.

"So... this is the source of Ravon's fascination. And the carrier of Divine Light."

I tried to speak, but nothing came out. My throat was raw. My mouth moved, but only a breath escaped. My voice was trapped by fear.

Zha'thik leaned forward. No limbs. No face. Only the pressure of presence.

"Aundrea, daughter of light..."

The voice wrapped around my thoughts like smoke.

"Your silence is… intriguing. Does fear already claim your soul?"

Ravon tensed beside me, his hand tightening around mine.

"My lord," he murmured, "she merely acknowledges your power."

But Zha'thik ignored him.

"No, Ravon. She hides something. Fear, yes… but also defiance."

He lifted a single shadowed hand, and suddenly—I could speak.

The words burst out of me as a whisper. "W-what do you want from me?"

Terror roared inside me. I wasn't ready to hear the answer. I already knew it would be worse than anything I imagined.

"Your Divine Light," the Dark Lord said, his voice like a blade.

"I can harness it… to shatter the boundaries of realms."

The horror was too vast to grasp. He didn't just want to hurt me—he wanted to destroy creation.

"No…" My voice trembled. "You'll never use me for that."

I turned to Ravon, desperate, pleading. "Please… don't let him use me for destruction!"

But something inside me snapped.

Not anger. Not rebellion.

Desperation.

The Divine Light burst forth, uncontrolled—blazing from the pits of my palms. A brilliant gold erupted like a star torn open, hurtling toward the altar. It struck, detonating the stone in a violent eruption. Dark shards flew in every direction, vanishing into smoke.

I dropped to my knees, breathless. The light faded. The power left me weak, vision spinning.

Zha'thik rose.

"NO!"

His voice thundered—fury incarnate.

Dark energy gathered in his hand, like a storm forming in the shape of death. I couldn't move. My limbs refused. This was it.

But Ravon moved first.

He leapt in front of me, shielding me with his body. On one knee, he bowed his head.

"Please! I beg you, my lord… do not take Aundrea from me. She carries my heir."

Zha'thik halted.

The air trembled. The energy coiled but did not strike.

His red eyes narrowed, shifting between Ravon and me. I felt them pierce every wall I had left.

"Punish her, my loyal servant," the Dark Lord said at last.

"Extermination of her spirit… or destruction of her heart. Choose wisely."

Then he vanished—dissolving into the very shadows that birthed him.

Silence fell. In that moment, I knew—Ravon had saved my life. Not for the first time, but this time... it felt different. As if, for a heartbeat, he had a soul. A flicker of something normal.

But the stillness was far more terrifying than the roar. Then Ravon turned to me, his hand sliding around my wrist, squeezing like a shackle.

"Aundrea..."

But I knew—we were far from done.

He dragged me back through the crimson-washed realm, past temples that bled shadow, past statues whose eyes followed like sentient curses. My feet stumbled over cracked ground that seemed to whisper with each step.

I didn't speak. I couldn't.

All I could do was breathe... and try to stay upright.

We returned through the portal and back to the fortress.

Back to the place he called my prison.

***

The stone walls of my chamber closed in around us. The air felt even colder now, as if my defiance had sucked all the warmth from the room. Ravon slammed the door behind us. The sound echoed like a final verdict.

He spun me toward him with a grip that owned me completely.

"You dare destroy the Dark Lord's altar?" he hissed, fury vibrating beneath every syllable. "You leave me no choice, Aundrea."

"I'm sorry, Ravon," I whispered. "I had no control. It just… happened."
My words trembled as they left me, but he didn't answer. He only stared.
A silence deeper than shadow stretched between us. His eyes held no mercy—only calculation, and something far darker.
Then he spoke, softly… like a storm holding back its lightning.

"Extermination of your spirit… or destruction of your heart," he echoed, his voice hushed with twisted delight.
I couldn't move. My breath caught in my throat. My body felt carved from ice.
"I choose…" Ravon leaned in, the words falling like poison.
"Destruction of your heart."

I blinked, confused. What did that mean? What form would that take? He answered with cruel elegance.

"You will lose something precious to you, Aundrea… something that will break your heart."

My voice barely found its way out. "What… what do you plan to take from me?"

He smiled.

"You'll choose what's taken." He turned toward the door. "One of your precious friends… will die tonight."

The blood drained from my face.

"Guards will bring Michelle, Sarah, and Dania here momentarily," Ravon continued. "You will select... which one will die at the stroke of midnight."

"No..." I backed away, the weight of it crashing down. "You can't expect... no!"

But he was deaf to mercy.

"You will watch her final moments, Aundrea."

He stepped closer, voice colder.

"As the clock strikes midnight, one of your friends will take her last breath. You choose which life ends tonight."

He turned and left the room, locking me in the prison I had grown accustomed to. Left alone with my thoughts. My worry. This was it. I couldn't take any more. My knees buckled, and I collapsed to the cold stone floor, sobs wracking my body. How could I choose who would die? What had I become? I had destroyed the Dark Lord's altar...

But at what cost?

***

After what felt like hours, the door opened.

Three familiar faces were forced into the room— Michelle, pale and shaking; Sarah, biting back tears; and Dania—oh, Dania—already weeping, as though her soul knew.

Michelle clutched her stomach, her face contorted in silent agony. Beside her, Sarah's whisper barely reached me—a tremor of fear wrapped in my name. Ravon stepped forward and handed me a small, velvet-covered box. The

meaning was clear. I was to choose. One friend's name…
sealed and surrendered.

On my knees, I broke.

Tears streamed down my face, unbridled emotion
surged through my veins. I begged—wordlessly at first,
then aloud, voice hoarse and trembling—pleading for time,
for mercy, for anything that might delay the impossible
decision.

But Ravon knelt beside me with that familiar calm
cruelty, his presence colder than any blade. There was no
softness in his eyes. No pity.

He stood and walked away, locking the door behind
him.

Midnight was coming.

That echo—the scrape of iron and fate—scratched
deep into my bones.

I clutched the box and looked at the women before
me. My friends. My family in all but blood.

"I can't…" I whispered. "I cannot choose. It will
destroy me."

And then, I heard a whisper on a breeze, gently
brushing my face—Drakon.

Not in body, but in soul.

His voice, as clear and steady as it had ever been,
echoed in my mind through the Dragon's bond between us.

"My love, my heart is shattered… do not choose. I
will bear your anguish."

A deep gasp escaped me, and I caught my breath.

His voice returned, steady and resolute.

"Dania."

"No! By the Gods, no!"

I looked up—and Dania was already watching me. One glance at Dania's tear-filled eyes told the truth. Michelle and Sarah reached for her hands, but their faces mirrored the same horror—the same silent understanding.

I opened my mouth, and the words slipped out, brittle and broken.

Drakon had chosen. Dania.

My chest clenched, and I shook my head in denial. This couldn't be happening. There had to be another way. I looked to Michelle for comfort, but she only sobbed—silently, helplessly—her gaze failing to meet mine, as if the bond we shared now carried guilt instead of solace. Sarah pressed her hand to her lips, frozen between relief and horror, unable to speak.

Tears burned my eyes. I felt like I was shattering from the inside out.

I was Empress of Lisona, bound to my Emperor, bound to his word. My title—my vows—demanded obedience, even in the face of this unbearable truth.

Dania stepped forward, trembling, her spirit stronger than her frame. Her arms wrapped around me, and I clung to her, grief spilling from my soul as if it could pour away the weight of my guilt.

She leaned close, her voice a trembling whisper against my ear. She spoke not just as a subject, but as a sister. Her words cut deeper than any blade.

She had lost everything—parents, brothers—stolen by Ravon's cruelty. And now, she was ready to give what little remained. Not because she wanted to die, but because she believed in something greater than herself. In me. In hope.

I held her tighter. I wanted to scream, to claw time backward. But the clock had already begun its cruel march toward midnight. Every heartbeat was a countdown.

I promised her that Michelle and Sarah would be protected. That her sacrifice would not be in vain. That Drakon would make Ravon pay. Her smile through the tears was radiant—accepting, peaceful, and filled with a love that shamed me.

Dania, brave Dania, gave me her final message for Drakon. For me. She was ready.

The iron door creaked open.

Ravon appeared, a black shadow framed in firelight, his presence choking the room of air. He asked the question I dreaded most. "Have you chosen, Aundrea."

And I answered.

"Yes," I said, though my voice came from a place deeper than flesh. "Dania's life… will be the price."

Ravon took the box from my hand, his smile was sharp and cruel. Guards stepped forward. Dania embraced me once more and whispered her last words—words I would never forget. "Live for me, I love you all."

And then… she was gone.

The door closed with a hollow finality, I sat there on the cold stone floor, unable to stand beneath the burden of it all. The Divine Light inside me pulsed, alive with Drakon's distant rage. But I couldn't harness it—not yet.

Not until the day I would rise and make Ravon pay. Ravon's voice sliced through the tension like a blade.

"The clock strikes eleven… one hour remains until midnight."

He turned away, his cloak dragging behind him like a veil of death.

"When midnight strikes, I will summon you. You will witness Dania's final breath, my queen."

The door slammed shut.

Every inch of my body trembled with grief. Michelle and Sarah dropped beside me, clutching my hands.

"Aundrea, we're here…" Michelle whispered, smoothing the hair from my face.

Sarah's voice trembled. "We'll get through this. Somehow…"

But I knew the truth. Dania wouldn't survive to see the sunrise.

Then, the baby moved.

The stir within my womb was sudden—and sharp. I gasped, pressing a trembling hand to my belly.

Hope stirred like embers in a dying fire.

Would Drakon reach me in time? Would my child be born into freedom… or into this darkness? We sat together silently, consumed by our grief. Time felt as though it had been suspended.

Michelle opened her mouth to speak—

But a black, swirling mist erupted around me.

"No!" I thrashed, reaching for their hands. But I was sinking. The mist wrapped around my limbs like chains. My body grew heavy. Numb, and then darkness.

***

When my vision cleared I was seated beside Ravon on a high stone balcony overlooking the courtyard. Panic surged through me. I tried to flee, but iron cuffs clamped around my wrists, locking me in place.

He sat beside me, smug, eyes gleaming.

Below, Dania stood beneath a lone stone pillar, silhouetted in the torchlight. Her figure was impossibly small... heartbreakingly strong.

Ravon's voice echoed across the courtyard:

"Any last words, Dania?"

Silence fell like snow. A thousand guards, cloaked figures, and specters of shadow leaned in.

Dania raised her head.

Her voice rang out—clear, defiant, beautiful.

"May my blood water the seeds of Drakon's house, Ravon. In death, I join my family... But you, Aundrea, will reunite with yours! You'll always be a sister to me, in my heart... My freedom to you!"

Tears streamed down my face.

I screamed, fighting the restraints, my mouth open in silent anguish.

Ravon leaned toward me, savoring every second.

The executioner stepped forward, sword raised. Firelight glinted along the steel.

I found my voice.

"DANIAAAAA!"

The scream tore from my soul.

The blade fell. Dania's body crumpled. My vision fractured.

Grief howled through me like a storm through shattered glass. I thrashed against the bindings until my skin bled. My cries echoed off the stone.

"YOU WILL BURN FOR THIS, RAVON!"

The courtyard trembled. Torches flared.

He leaned close, whispering his final cruelty:

"Your Emperor will soon join his loyal subject… in death."

Chapter 20

The False Dusk

My vision was still blurred from tears, my throat raw from screaming. Ravon's triumphant smile lingered inches from my face, his eyes gleaming with sadistic delight.

"You will soon learn to obey me, Aundrea," he whispered, his breath cold against my skin.

My body trembled with rage and grief, the restraints biting into my wrists as I glared at him with hatred. Then, a deafening roar shattered the night air. The ground trembled beneath us as a dragon burst from the darkness—its scales glinting like black diamonds in the torchlight. My heart lurched. But this dragon… it wasn't Drakon. Its features were sharper, its aura colder, more ancient. Ravon's eyes glittered with excitement as he rose to his feet.

The dragon swooped low, flames erupting from its jaws in a torrent of molten gold. Guards shouted in alarm, arrows loosed from the fortress walls. But the bolts bounced harmlessly off the creature's obsidian scales. It banked sharply, obliterating one cluster of soldiers with fire, then another—screams tore through the courtyard like a chorus of the damned.

Terror and confusion swirled within me. Who was this being?

It couldn't be Drakon. This dragon exuded no warmth, no familiar grace—only raw, overwhelming power.

As the chaos settled, the beast landed beside the outer stone bridge. With a shimmer of light, it shifted—transformed into a mortal form. An old man stood where the dragon had been, long silver hair cascading over white robes that shimmered with a quiet inner glow. His face was weathered with age and wisdom, yet radiated calm and kindness.

He approached the castle gates, eyes locked on Ravon with something deeper than judgment—grief.

Ravon gestured to his guards, who swung open the heavy doors with a slow, grating creak. The old man stepped through and paused. His gaze swept the courtyard… and met mine.

His eyes softened. Piercing green, ancient and knowing.

"My son," he said gently, his voice deep with sorrow. "Why do you defile our family name? What darkness has consumed your heart so completely?"

Ravon's face twisted in rage, voice snapping like a whip.

"You dare question me?"

The old man stood unmoved. Then he turned to me.

"Aundrea," he said, his voice quiet and full of warmth, "I am Malikai. Your Emperor's father... and Ravon's."

My breath caught. This… was Drakon's father?

He looked again at Ravon, sorrow deepening in his gaze.

"My child," Malikai whispered, "I still see the boy you once were… before darkness claimed you. Aundrea, does not belong to you."

Ravon sneered. "I stole nothing, Father—I claimed what was mine. The throne. My bride. This entire realm should belong to me. I am the firstborn twin!"

My heart clenched. Dania's death still seared behind my eyes, her final words etched into my soul.

Malikai stepped closer, voice steady but pained.

"You know why the throne was given to Drakon. Even as a boy, you turned to forbidden magic. You terrified your mother… and me."

Ravon's rage flared, dark magic coiling in his palm like a serpent ready to strike.

But Malikai moved first.

He shifted instantly—his mortal form dissolving as his dragon wings unfurled. His black-scaled body stretched across the chamber, massive and ancient. With a great gust of breath, he blew a cloud of smoke across the room. When the haze cleared, he was gone.

"Find him!" Ravon roared, spinning on his guards. "NOW!"

Then, he turned to me. His steps were slow, deliberate.

He reached down and unshackled my wrists.

My heart slammed against my ribs. The door was open.

Now.

I bolted.

I ran as if Dania's spirit pushed me forward, her words echoing in my soul.

"May my blood water the seeds of Drakon's house, Ravon. In death, I join my family… but you, Aundrea, will reunite with yours!"

The bridge was just ahead.

But guards blocked my path.

I veered to the right—then left—desperate, breathless. One guard lunged forward, catching my arm. He spun me back.

Right into Ravon's grasp.

His eyes burned with triumph. "You just witnessed your friend's execution, Aundrea. If you don't obey me…" He leaned closer, his voice slick with cruelty. "Sarah and Michelle remain. My choices are delicious."

My heart sank. I felt my soul begin to unravel, like prey devoured slowly by a hungry wolf.

Ravon's voice darkened, sinister and ominous. "Come to me, Aundrea."

Every step I took toward him felt like dragging chains. My legs resisted, but my will had been stripped raw. His hand clamped around my wrist with bruising force, dragging me closer until our bodies nearly touched. His heat seared through me, not with warmth, but with revulsion that crawled across my spine like insects.

Then—his mouth crashed down on mine.

A brutal, punishing kiss. I gasped, struggling to wrench away, but his grip was iron. Only after what felt like an eternity did he release me, shoving me backward. I stumbled, breath ragged, tears in my eyes.

Ravon grabbed my arm again and spun me toward the portal behind him. It pulsed with deep purple light, like a living wound in the fabric of the world. Shadows twisted across the walls, drawn to its pull.

He dragged me through without hesitation.

The air thickened into a suffocating fog as we crossed the threshold. Darkness folded in around us.

***

We emerged into my former prison—cold, familiar, and cruel.

The torches on the stone walls flickered weakly, casting skeletal fingers of shadow. Dampness clung to everything, a scent of rot and despair filling my lungs. This was the room where I had condemned Dania… my sister not by blood, but by soul.

Ravon tightened his grip and spun me to face him.

"Welcome home, Aundrea," he whispered, his breath chilling my skin. "Your new life begins now. You will obey me, or you will watch your other friends die."

His eyes blazed, daring me to resist.

Tears spilled down my cheeks like a flood. Dania's death haunted every heartbeat. Her lifeless body—her strength—her sacrifice. My soul trembled under the weight of it all.

"How could you?" I choked, my voice shaking. "She served you faithfully. For years, she was loyal to you… Is that what I have to look forward to, Ravon? Will you throw me away when you tire of me?"

His face twisted in fury.

His hand lashed across my cheek. A white-hot burn exploded across my skin. I stumbled backwards, crashing to the floor. I clutched my face—then my stomach. A pain tore through me, sudden and sharp.

"No…" I gasped. "Something's wrong."

Ravon moved faster than I'd ever seen, one moment distant, the next at my side, his knees hitting the ground as if the world had tilted.

Panic darkened his eyes, his breath shallow, almost frantic. A sharp cry tore from my throat as another wave of pain rippled through me. My body shook uncontrollably. Seven months was too soon, far too soon. My child wasn't ready. I wasn't ready.

The realization struck him like a blow. Color drained from his face, leaving him pale beneath the torchlight. Without hesitation, he shouted for the guards, his voice echoing with desperate, uncontrolled authority. Feet scrambled on the stone as orders scattered like birds into the air.

Then, his arms folded around me, shockingly careful, as if I might break. He lifted me with a reverence I didn't expect, laying me gently on the bed. His fingers swept across my brow, wiping away sweat already beading at my hairline.

"It will be okay," he whispered. The words were quiet, almost tender, but the tremor in his voice betrayed him.

For the briefest moment, something flickered in his eyes—something mortal. Not kindness… but perhaps a ghost of it.

My voice cracked. "Ravon… please. Michelle and Sarah… bring them."

He hesitated.

Then nodded.

With a flick of his wrist, a guard vanished down the corridor. Another stationed himself silently at the open door.

Ravon looked down at me, his hand brushing my cheek. Then Freyan entered, her long hair flying behind her, eyes locked on mine.

"Lord Ravon," she said firmly, "step aside." Ravon moved aside without hesitation, giving Freyan room to examine me as he spoke, his voice low and steady.

"She has merged with the Dragon Stone. You said she is… complicated."

Freyan nodded grimly. "I cannot heal her directly. But I'll do what I can."

Ravon backed away.

Freyan pressed her palms to my abdomen. Magic shimmered faintly from her fingertips as her eyes closed in focus. I cried out, another sharp wave of pain wracking my body.

Michelle and Sarah burst in, rushing to my side.

"Oh gods—Aundrea!" Michelle's voice broke as she climbed onto the bed, gripping my hand.

I clung to her.

Another spasm. My back arched.

Freyan leaned over me. "Breathe, Aundrea. Breathe through it."

I forced air into my lungs, my chest aching.

"This is not true labor," Freyan said gently. "Your fear has gripped you so tightly, it's tricking your body into believing it's time." Tears spilled down my temples. My whole body trembled. "It feels so real…"

Michelle wrapped both arms around me. "You're safe. We're here."

I caught a glimpse of Ravon watching Michelle's hand in mine. A flicker of jealousy flashed in his eyes before he turned away.

Freyan's hands never left me. "It will pass. Just keep breathing."

I held on. To Michelle. To Sarah. To life.

And somewhere deep inside… to hope.

Freyan turned to Ravon, her voice serious yet laced with concern. "I need to speak with you privately, Lord Ravon."

He gave a curt nod and followed her to the far corner of the room, their hushed voices barely audible. Sarah slipped onto the bed beside me and took my other hand in hers. Their gentle presence grounded me, helping ease the tremors in my chest.

"Aundrea," Sarah whispered, "what happened to... is Dania dead?"

Before I could answer, Ravon's head snapped toward us, his face purpling with fury.

"DO NOT SPEAK TO MY WIFE ABOUT THAT RIGHT NOW!"

Sarah recoiled in fear, tears welling in her eyes. She looked at me, silently pleading for truth.

My voice trembled. "She is gone."

Ravon stormed toward us, seizing Sarah by the arm. "Remove her from my sight," he barked at the guard by the door. Without hesitation, the guard pulled Sarah away. She cast one terrified glance at me as she was led out.

Michelle's grip on my hand tightened, her eyes blazing with defiance.

"If you want to stay," Ravon growled at her, "this subject ends now."

Michelle gave a single sharp nod, her jaw clenched. Ravon turned back to Freyan, his fury still simmering.

Freyan returned to the bedside, her tone calm but firm. "Lord Ravon, perhaps you should sit. Aundrea needs a peaceful environment."

His glare lingered on Michelle before he finally nodded and sat beside me, his hand brushing against mine. I flinched inwardly. Though I remained still, my skin crawled at his touch. Michelle's gaze never wavered, holding a protective warning in her eyes.

Freyan spoke gently. "Aundrea's episode has passed, but her emotional state remains fragile. Lord Ravon... your outburst may have deepened her distress."

Ravon's jaw tightened. His eyes flicked toward Freyan in irritation, but he reeled himself back. Turning to me, he spoke in a low, almost contrite voice. "Aundrea... forgive me. I lost control. I never intended to hurt you."

The words stunned me. Ravon, ruthless, brutal, remorseless, was apologizing?

Michelle's grip on my hand tensed again, as if to say: Don't be fooled.

Freyan stepped in again before I could respond. "Perhaps Lord Ravon should allow Aundrea to rest."

He nodded stiffly and stood.

"Guard," he said quietly, "escort Michelle out as well."

Michelle hesitated, her eyes locking with mine. I gave her a faint nod.

The guard gestured, and Michelle reluctantly stood. "I'll be close," she whispered.

The door closed behind her, leaving only Ravon and Freyan.

Ravon turned back once more, pausing at the threshold. "Aundrea," he said softly, "sleep. Freyan will stay with you."

His gaze lingered for a moment too long before he stepped out, and the heavy door closed behind him. Freyan's voice was gentle, but it carried the weight of command. She guided me into a nightdress—soft and silken, simple yet elegant. The fabric whispered against my skin, a strange contrast to the raw ache inside me.

Freyan moved to my side and gently tucked the blankets around me. Her touch was warm, reassuring.

"You should rest now, Aundrea. Your body and mind are still recovering."

I nodded, though my body moved like it no longer belonged to me. My eyelids drooped with exhaustion, yet sleep hovered just out of reach. Every breath I drew was thick with ghosts—Dania's final embrace, Ravon's twisted love, and the echo of Drakon's voice, so far away it felt like a dream slipping through my fingers.

Freyan's voice, soft as wind through leaves, whispered beside me. "Sleep, Aundrea. I'll be right here."

***

Hours blurred. Time unraveled like thread through trembling fingers. I drifted in and out of sleep, weighed down by grief, my chest aching with sorrow that would not fade.
Then I felt it—movement beside me.
Freyan shifted slightly, her breath warm against my cheek as she leaned close. Her gaze was focused, piercing— watchful in the dim light. I stirred, slowly pushing myself up on my elbows. The silk sheets rustled beneath me like whispered memories. The space beside me was empty— Ravon was still gone. I let out a quiet sigh of relief.

Golden torchlight flickered across the walls, casting shadows that danced like restless spirits. A quiet relief spread through me. For once, he wasn't looming nearby. Freyan remained seated, ever watchful. She brushed a loose strand of hair from my face with fingers soft as a breeze. I could see the love building behind her eyes. I could feel a subtle change of loyalty. Would Freyan become my ally? Would she betray Ravon? I wondered, but I didn't dare ask. "How are you feeling this morning, Aundrea?" she asked gently.
Morning felt like a foreign concept, as if I'd been trapped in an unending night.
"I feel better," I said, my voice rough from sleep, like a flame flickering low.

Freyan helped me to sit up. I reached for the black silk robe folded beside the bed—its cool, elegant fabric cloaking me like a veil of shadow. I tied the sash around my waist, slipped into my velvet slippers, and walked toward the door leading to the garden.

***

The air outside was thick with the scent of jasmine. For a brief moment, I felt transported—untouched by grief, even if only in illusion.

I wandered past the marble pillars, fingers brushing their cool surfaces, and found my way to a wrought-iron bench in the garden's center.

Turning to Freyan, I spoke softly. "Could I have some time alone?"

She bowed her head, her eyes full of understanding. "Of course, milady."

With graceful steps, she returned inside, leaving me in the stillness.

At last, I exhaled. Alone. Free, if only for a moment.

The warm sun kissed my face through the huge dome that surrounded me. I closed my eyes, trying to find a moment of peace amidst the turmoil brewing within me like a storm-tossed sea. Dania was gone—and nothing could bring her back. The truth pierced my heart like a dagger. Tears pricked the corners of my eyes as I silently vowed to protect my friends from the same fate, my heartbeat pulsing with new resolve.

I placed my hands over my stomach and felt the baby stir within—a gentle flutter that drew a bittersweet smile to my lips. And a memory that left my heart aching for Drakon.

For a fleeting moment, I imagined myself back in his arms, surrounded by the warmth of his kisses and the safety of his embrace...

"Aundrea!"

My eyes flew open, startled, to find Ravon standing before me, his gaze locked intently on my face.

"You look beautiful this morning," he murmured, his voice low and husky.

I turned away, my eyes fixed on the ground. My stomach churned at the sight of him—the man who had orchestrated Dania's brutal fate. The last face I wanted to see.

He stepped closer, his long strides swallowing the distance before he sank onto the bench beside me. One arm slid around my shoulders, pulling me into his chest.

I didn't resist.

The moment felt like betrayal to my own soul. For the briefest heartbeat, I wished desperately that he were Drakon—my love, my protector.

His warm breath whispered against my hair. "You seem troubled, Aundrea. What weighs on your mind?"

My heart thudded with suspicion. He already knew. And yet, he waited for me to say it, his piercing eyes burning with something unspoken.

My voice came out as a whisper. "You know why I'm devastated, Ravon… You stole Dania's life. She was barely more than a girl…"

Tears flooded my cheeks, unstoppable rivers of grief. I wiped them away with shaking fingers, my voice cracking. "Why?"

Ravon's expression softened slightly—an illusion of concern that made my skin crawl. He reached out, brushing a lock of hair behind my ear with fingers like ice.

"Aundrea," he said gently, "stop fighting me. You don't have to suffer. I can bring you joy—or plunge you into misery. The choice is yours."

I recoiled from his touch as if burned, pulling away and walking quickly down the garden's stone path. My eyes remained downcast, as if escape could be found between the cracks of the stone. I stopped at a vibrant bed of peonies and lavender. Their scent filled the air—sweet, delicate. I sank down among the blossoms, letting their quiet beauty offer me a moment's reprieve. But Ravon followed. His tall figure loomed over me like a shadow, his eyes gleaming.

"Why do you torture yourself like this, Aundrea?" he asked, voice low and curious.

I looked up, fury flashing through me like lightning. "I'm not torturing myself, Ravon. You brought me here. You forced me into this marriage."

My voice rose. Passion and desperation tangled. "I don't want you! Why can't you see that? I will never want you."

Ravon's expression twisted into amusement. My defiance only entertained him.

"Oh, poor Aundrea," he said mockingly. "Do you think I need your love? Do you think I care?"

He stepped closer, voice sharp and venomous.

"You are my wife. You belong to me."

He grabbed my wrist like a shackle, yanking me to my feet with a sudden jerk.

I yelped in pain, trying to pull away. "Ravon, you're hurting me."

He loosened his grip—but only enough to wrap his arm around my back, holding me firm. Then his lips came down on mine, brutal and punishing. I tried to turn away, but his hand locked behind my head, forcing me still. The kiss deepened, overwhelming, crushing, as if he sought to smother my resistance. My body remained rigid with defiance. When he finally pulled away, he lingered close, breath ragged, eyes blazing.

"One day," he whispered, "you will surrender to me." His gaze bored into mine, a threat disguised as a promise. "But for now… I will take what is mine."

He gripped my wrist again, fingers curling tightly around it, and began dragging me toward the palace doors. I dug in my heels, refusing to move.
"Not another step, Ravon," I said through clenched teeth. My voice was low, venomous. My eyes burned with defiance. He stopped and turned to face me. For a heartbeat, something like surprise flickered in his expression. Then he smiled—a slow, cruel smile that chilled me to the bone.
"How adorable," he said. "You think you have a choice." He yanked me forward again, our faces inches apart. Suddenly, he released me—only to seize my chin, his fingers bruising the skin.
"Walk. Now."
I slapped his hand away, my palm stinging from the impact. "Take your hands off me, Ravon."

His eyes narrowed, his face darkening with fury. But he didn't touch me again—at least, not yet. Instead, he stepped closer, his voice low and menacing.
"You're pushing your luck, Aundrea."

I stood my ground, my heart pounding like a war drum, bracing for whatever would come next. And then he lunged—his hands reaching for my face. That's when I did it. My eyes locked onto his, and I spat directly into his face. He jerked back, stunned. For a moment, he just stood there, silent, as the spittle glistened on his cheek. Then his expression twisted into a feral snarl.
"You. Are dead."
I stepped back slowly, heart racing, a twisted smile spreading across my face.
"Finally," I said, voice laced with sarcasm, "something we

agree on."

But even as I smirked, fear clawed at the edges of my resolve. Ravon's rage gave way to something colder—calculation. His eyes narrowed, voice dropping to a dangerous whisper.

"Perhaps some time in isolation will do you good. Time to reflect on your hospitality... toward me."

He wiped the saliva from his cheek, then turned and called out.

"Guards!" Two massive guards appeared instantly, their gazes fixed on me with grim anticipation.

"Escort my queen to an isolation cell," Ravon ordered. "Immediately."

Their hands clamped down on my arms, unyielding. I struggled as they dragged me backward, screaming at the top of my lungs, my voice ricocheting off the hard stone halls.

"YOU HAVEN'T WON, RAVON! THIS ISN'T OVER!"

He didn't flinch. He took one step toward me, lips curling in a mocking smile.

"Oh, but it is over... for now. You'll rot in isolation until you learn obedience."

I twisted in their grasp, my heels scraping across the stone floor as they hauled me down the corridor toward the dungeons. Just before the shadows swallowed me, I turned my head and met his gaze one last time.

"I'LL ESCAPE... AND I'LL KILL YOU!"

His laughter echoed after me—a cold, menacing sound that clawed its way into my bones.

"You'll kill me?" he called, voice dripping with mockery.

"I doubt even your spirit could survive my wrath, Aundrea."

The guards hurled me into the cell. Darkness swallowed me whole—a thick, suffocating thing. A single torch flickered beyond the bars, casting erratic shadows that danced like specters on the walls.

***

I blinked, straining to see—but the blackness clung to everything. It was like staring into a void. The floor was wet, rough stone beneath me. The air reeked of mold and ancient decay.

I sat down, curled against the far wall, arms wrapped around my knees. I rocked gently, letting despair crash over me in waves. Hatred seethed in my chest.

"Why did he do this to me?" I whispered to no one, tears streaming down my cheeks.

And then came the memory—Dania's radiant smile, her fierce loyalty.

"Oh Dania… I miss you so much. I wish you were here to escape with me."

I thought of Sarah. Of Michelle. Still inside the walls of the Citadel. Still in danger.

"Please… stay safe," I whispered. "Don't let him hurt you."

My heart felt extinguished, hollow, but my hatred burned on.

Ravon's victory would be his last mistake.

Chapter 21

Fall of Eldrida's Maw

Days later... Blackstone Pass lay scarred but victorious behind us. Our army marched onward, morale bolstered by conquest. I rode atop my black stallion, Dragonfire's sheath empty at my side—a silent reminder of the battle just won. Thorold trotted beside me, scanning the horizon and updating our scouts' reports.

"All quiet ahead, Emperor," he said. "Greenhaven Plains stretch open—perfect terrain for swift advance."

My gaze drifted northward, toward Eldrida's Maw and the destruction of the Death Stone. Yet my thoughts lingered on Aundrea—her smile, her strength, her fate forever entwined with mine.

As we crested a gentle hill, a village came into view: Nazima.

Smoke drifted lazily from chimneys. People bustled about their daily lives, oblivious to the army approaching their doorstep.

Thorold leaned in, voice low. "Nazima Village, Emperor. Reports indicate loyalty to our cause... but also rumors of Ravon's influence lingering."

I nodded, eyes scanning the village.

***

Suddenly, a commotion erupted near the square—guards dragged a woman toward a makeshift gallows.

Villagers cried out in protest, held back by armored men. The woman's eyes locked onto mine—pleading, desperate.

A banner above the gallows read: Blood betrayal.

I spurred my stallion forward. Thorold and a handful of guards followed close behind. The village square fell silent as I dismounted, my presence alone commanding attention.

The woman's gaze never wavered from mine—a silent cry for mercy.

I approached the gallows, turning to the village elder—a frail man trembling beside the executioner.

"Why does this woman stand condemned?" I demanded, my voice firm but controlled.

The elder swallowed hard. "Emperor... she is Kaelinna, daughter of our blacksmith. Accused of treason against her lawful husband—blood betrayal. Her husband is Mantakai, Lord Victor's cousin."

My eyes narrowed. "Explain. What treason?"

The elder glanced nervously at the guards before continuing. "She was forced into marriage with Lord Mantakai—a cruel man. He beat her mercilessly, but last night, she defended herself and struck back. Mantakai lives... barely. But he accuses her of blood betrayal."

Blood betrayal is no small accusation in these outer provinces. The penalty is death.

I shifted my gaze to the guards holding Kaelinna— tight grips on her trembling arms. Then to her face—tears streaming, but defiance still burning in her eyes.

"By whose authority was she condemned to death?" I asked, voice sharpening.

The elder's voice barely rose above a whisper. "Lord Mantakai's petition was granted by Ravon's magistrate, Emperor... citing laws that contradict your decree granting women the right to choose their husbands."

My anger ignited. The executioner moved with cruel precision.

The noose was tightened around Kaelinna's neck. The platform beneath her feet creaked upward. She stood on tiptoe, eyes wide with terror. The villagers gasped as her body began to sag...

I drew my bow from my back—silent, unnoticed by the guards. My fingers released the arrow.

THWACK.

The rope snapped inches above Kaelinna's head. She crumpled to the ground, gasping.

Gasps turned to cheers as I approached. Kaelinna rubbed her neck, stunned, eyes locked on mine— shock and gratitude mingling in her expression.

I extended my hand. "Why didn't you defend yourself against Lord Mantakai sooner? What did he do to you?"

Still coughing, she took it, her gaze steady. "He beat me daily, Emperor—since the day Ravon's magistrate forced me to marry that monster. Last night, he threatened to kill my sister. I tried to get away, but he kept locking me up."

Her words hung in the air like a death sentence—for Mantakai. My grip tightened slightly, urging her to continue.

"He said if I didn't obey him completely, my sister would suffer the same fate as our mother... who died at his father's hands. I struck back to protect her—and myself."

The square fell into solemn silence. Thorold's low growl rumbled behind me.

I released her hand, my voice thundering: "Lord Mantakai will face my justice. Thorold—summon him. Now."

Thorold nodded and dispatched soldiers. Kaelinna's gaze followed them before returning to mine, surprise softening into gratitude.

"Thank you, Emperor... my life is yours."

I met her gaze. "Your life is your own, Kaelinna. I simply upheld my decree. Tell me—are you skilled in combat? Because to take on a man the size of Mantakai... that's no small accomplishment."

Her expression brightened. "A skilled warrior, Emperor. My father, the blacksmith, trained me alongside my brothers. I fought in secret tournaments against village men... and often won."

Thorold returned, his expression tinged with amusement.

I nodded, impressed. "I think you'd be a valuable addition to my army. Will you ride with us to destroy Ravon and bring justice to men like Mantakai?"

Kaelinna's eyes blazed with determination. "I would ride into hell itself with you, Emperor."

I smiled. "Then it is settled. Thorold, see that Kaelinna is given quarters among the warriors. Armor. Weapons suited to her skill."

Thorold bowed and led her away, discussing army protocol as they disappeared into the crowd. Moments later, Lord Mantakai was dragged into the square—pale, trembling, flanked by soldiers. He dropped to his knees.

"Mercy, Emperor. I acted under Ravon's law!"

I stepped forward. "Ravon's laws are worthless to me. You will stand trial—for abusing your wife and conspiring against my decree."

His face drained of color. "And if found guilty," I added, "your punishment will be... death."

I summoned Thorold to bring Kaelinna back to the square. She returned, armor already fitted, sword at her side—a warrior transformed.

I gestured to Lord Mantakai, still cowering on the ground. "Kaelinna, do you wish to confront him before we depart for Eldrida's Maw? His trial will be held tonight, at our camp."

Kaelinna's eyes blazed with intensity as she stepped toward him. Her voice was low and venomous. "You once told me my spirit would be broken. Instead, you unleashed my wrath."

Mantakai trembled, glancing up at her with fear.

Kaelinna spat at his feet. "I'll witness your execution tonight, Mantakai. Not because you beat me... but because you underestimated me."

She turned to me, chin lifted high. "I'm ready to ride with you to Eldrida's Maw, Emperor."

I nodded, admiring her fierce spirit. "Ride beside me, Kaelinna. Your presence will send a message to my army—about courage and loyalty."

She mounted a black mare provided by Thorold and took her place at my side.

Then I turned to face the villagers still gathered in stunned silence.

"Hear my decree, people of Nazima Village. From this day forward, you are under my protection and jurisdiction. Ravon's tyranny ends here: • Taxes will be reduced. • Justice will be fair. • Women's rights will be upheld."

"Thorold," I called, "assign a squad to remain behind and ensure a smooth transition."

Thorold bowed and began issuing orders.

With Nazima secured, I looked to Kaelinna and nodded toward the road ahead. "To Eldrida's Maw. The Death Stone's destruction awaits."

Kaelinna drew her sword slightly, her eyes burning. "For Aundrea, Empress of Lisona, let us march."

We lunged forward and led the army onward.

***

Days turned to weeks as we marched relentlessly toward Eldrida's Maw. The terrain shifted beneath our horses—lush forests gave way to rugged hills, then to barren wastelands that surrounded our destination. We made camp beneath a cold, starlit sky. Fires crackled across the encampment, and I walked among my men, boosting morale with promises of victory and freedom.

Later that evening, I sparred with Kaelinna. Her skills were sharp, her movements fluid. Our blades clashed in near-perfect rhythm, and she landed a clever strike across my shoulder.

I stepped back, laughing softly. "You would have bested many of my guards, Kaelinna. You've earned your place among us."

She bowed slightly, pride and sweat glinting on her brow.

That night, I returned to my tent. Alone again with my thoughts, my mind drifted to weeks past... to Aundrea's voice whispering through the Dragon Stone's magic:

"How do I choose, Drakon? Which one dies—Sarah, Michelle, or Dania?"

My heart clenched again at the memory. I had answered her in silence: "You won't choose, my love. I will spare your heart that pain."

I had chosen Dania.

Because: • Sarah was my loyal informant and trusted ally. • Michelle was Aundrea's dearest friend and confidante. • Dania... Dania had no one left to mourn her. I could feel it, deep, intertwined in Aundrea's heart.

The weight of that choice still pressed against my chest. I'd condemned one life to preserve another—and I would carry that burden to my grave. Yet I felt no regret for saving Aundrea from that impossible pain.

Sleep came slowly. I closed my eyes, and visions seized me: Aundrea's tears falling like rain. Dania's face, frozen in a silent scream. • The towering cliffs of Eldrida's Maw, sealed with dark magic.

My dragon roared within me in my dream—an echo of grief and fury. Then the vision shifted. Kaelinna appeared before me, her eyes shining with inner fire. She extended her hand, and my dream-self reached for it. Her touch was warm and strong... but then her face shifted into Aundrea's—tears carving paths down her cheeks.

"Drakon... come for me," she whispered. "Ravon's cruelty never ends." The dream shattered.

I sat upright, gasping for air, drenched in sweat. The tent around me was still and dark. Outside, faint light crept over the horizon. Sabion's voice echoed in my thoughts: A dark seal surrounds Eldrida's Maw—strong enough to repel even your dragon form. I threw off the blanket and stood, my resolve hardening like steel. The Death Stone could not be allowed to fall into Ravon's hands. If he claimed it, his darkness would spread unchecked.

My jaw tightened. My course was set. I called into the predawn hush: "Sabion."

The tent flap opened at once. He had been waiting.

"Emperor, the mages and Thorold are ready. Shall we discuss the plan to breach Eldrida's Maw and destroy the Death Stone?"

I nodded grimly. "Yes. But first… any word of Aundrea's fate?"

Sabion's expression darkened. My heart plummeted into shadow as his words cut through me like ice.

"Ravon's cruelty knows no bounds, Emperor. Aundrea was driven into false labor after relentless torment over Dania's death. She recovered… only to face a new nightmare: solitary confinement in utter darkness. Her cell lit solely by the faint flickering of a single torch in the hallway beyond her door."

Sabion's pause hung heavy in the air.

"Thirty days of silence have passed," he continued softly. "My source confirms Aundrea remains unbroken… but barely. Her spirit still resists him. Yet the darkness is taking its toll. He fears her mind may begin to slip soon."

My vision blurred with rage and fear for her sanity. I clenched my fists, nails digging into my palms.

"We destroy the Death Stone and reach her before Ravon breaks her," I growled.

Sabion nodded. "Our mages believe they can dismantle the dark seal protecting Eldrida's Maw with a powerful spell. But they require a rare ingredient— Starheart petals. They grow only near the Maw's entrance, which is heavily guarded."

Thorold had proposed a solution.

"A stealth unit," Sabion said, "led by Kaelinna. They'll extract the petals under cover of night."

I nodded decisively. "Assemble the team. Kaelinna leads. Brief her—and make sure she understands: This is not just about the spell. This is about saving Aundrea's life and Lisona." Sabion bowed and left to make the arrangements.

My mind burned with images of Aundrea, trapped in that cold cell… suffering, waiting, enduring. I would oversee this personally—at least until the petals were secured. Afterward, I'd return to command via messenger bird coordination with Sabion.

I armored in dark leathers and strapped my dagger to my thigh. Kaelinna led the team: herself, five elite scouts, and me. Sabion's voice was quiet and urgent as he delivered final instructions.

"Starheart petals glow faintly in moonlight. Gather quickly—leave no trace."

***

We vanished into the night, crossing the blasted terrain that surrounded the Maw. At the perimeter, the faint silver shimmer of the glowing petals appeared in the distance.

I raised my hand. "I'll provide overwatch from here. Kaelinna—go."

She nodded and led the others silently into the glowing field.

Suddenly, torches ignited along the Maw's walls. The guards had noticed something.

"Now!" I hissed. "Just the petals—hurry!"

Kaelinna responded instantly, directing her team to snatch the glowing blooms. They moved quickly, expertly—pouches filled in moments.

"Done, Emperor—retreating!" she signaled.

They slipped into the shadows, the guards swarming only moments behind them.

Once safely away, Kaelinna turned to me, breath steady, eyes alight. "Mission success, Emperor. The petals are ours."

"Return to camp," I ordered. " We strike at dawn."

***

At first light, the mages gathered around a runed circle inscribed into the soil. Lyra, our lead mage and healer, held a vial of Starheart essence—glowing like captured moonlight. She poured it carefully over the symbols and began her chant, the air humming with ancient power.

The seal protecting Eldrida's Maw rippled... then collapsed in silence.

But Lyra had been clever—her deception spell made it appear intact to any of Ravon's magical sentries. His forces believed their defenses still held.

I turned to Thorold and Sabion. "The seal is down, but Ravon doesn't know. We strike with stealth. Ready the army—quietly. Battle formation." Thorold nodded and disappeared to issue commands.

As we approached the Maw, I studied the massive stone gates. Still locked. Still dangerous. I turned to Lyra. "Any wards or magical traps?"

She closed her eyes, searching the weave of energy with her senses. "Yes. Deadly wards line the main halls and chambers... But also... there's something else. A network of tunnels beneath the Maw."

Thorold leaned in, pointing. "Tight passages. Only someone small and agile could pass through."

My gaze drifted to Kaelinna. Her slender build... her courage...

"We have no other choice," I said quietly. "Kaelinna. You must enter alone. Reach the gate chamber. Unlock Eldrida's Maw for us."

She blinked—but only once—before squaring her shoulders.

Kaelinna met my eyes, determination etched into her features. She didn't need to say it—I saw her resolve. She would do it. For Aundrea. For justice.

I clasped her arm firmly. The instructions were clear: navigate to the gate chamber, disable the traps, unbar the doors… and come back. I pressed a pouch of protective charms into her hand along with the map Lyra had scribed earlier. Her nod was silent but sure, lips drawn tight with focus.

She turned toward the narrow entrance, inhaled deeply, then drew her dagger. With quiet resolve, she vanished into the shadows beyond.

Beside me, Thorold's unease was visible, but I gave him a curt nod, grounding us in the mission.

Her risk was calculated, and worth it. If Kaelinna succeeded, we would breach Eldrida's Maw and shatter the cursed Death Stone. Ravon's power hinged on it—without it, his dark ambitions would crumble. Lyra agreed, her jaw set with grim determination.

I addressed the soldiers, voice raised and steady. The moment Kaelinna gave the signal, we would move. All eyes were on the tunnel, my breath held for a moment.

Then the whisper tube crackled in my hand.

"Emperor… gate mechanisms disabled. Main gates creaking open…"

Kaelinna's voice, though faint, carried triumph.

I brought the tube close. "Well done. Status?"

Her reply came swiftly. Minimal guards patrolled the entry; the outer seal had given them false confidence. The Death Stone chamber lay at the heart of the citadel—third level up. Traps lined the stairways, magical blades swung in rhythmic intervals down narrow halls, and Ravon's elite guarded the passage with lethal precision.

We had our opening. The time had come.

I relayed the intel to Thorold and Lyra, who began positioning our forces. I drew Dragonfire, its blade catching the dawn light.

"Lyra, handle the magical traps. Thorold, clear the stairway. We go now."

Our army surged through the opened gates, overwhelming the entrance guards. Inside, the structure pulsed with dark enchantment.

Lyra began chanting, weaving dispelling magic to neutralize the swinging blades and hidden sigils. Thorold's unit engaged the elite guards, blades clashing with brutal rhythm.

I activated the whisper tube. "Kaelinna, path to the chamber is secure. Meet us there—we end this together."

"Already in route," she replied, breath tight with resolve.

***

We met at the heart of Eldrida's Maw, standing on the edge of a churning lava pit. Kaelinna and Lyra flanked me, eyes locked on the dark stone box held in my hands. I pulled on protective gloves—woven from dragonhide—to shield me from the artifact's corruptive essence. Slowly, I opened the lid.

The Death Stone.

A pulse of cold darkness radiated from within, as if it sensed its freedom—and its doom.

Carefully, I lifted it. The power screamed through the gloves, trying to corrupt, to twist.

Everyone held their breath as I raised the Stone over the lava pit. Its surface writhed, shadows clawing at the air.

With a cry of finality, I hurled it into the molten abyss.

The Death Stone hit the lava—and exploded in a blast of black fire. But the inferno swallowed it whole. Golden light erupted from the pit, dispelling the darkness with a wave of purifying heat.

It was done.

***

Back at camp, the air rang with cheers, but I raised my arms, silencing them. "Aundrea is still captive," I announced. "Our mission is not complete. We ride again." I summoned Thorold, Lyra, Kaelinna, Sabion, and my trusted commanders to the central tent.

"Our victory over the Death Stone is only a milestone," I said, unfolding a weathered map. "Aundrea is still in Ravon's clutches." Gasps broke out around the table as I pointed to a mark deep in the mountains. "The Citadel of Eldarath." Even the bravest among us shifted uneasily.

Eldarath was infamous for: Treacherous mountain passes • Layers of dark magical wards • Ravon's personal Shadowfort guard

Lyra spoke first. "Our scouts estimate one to two moons' journey, Emperor. The terrain is perilous." Thorold nodded. "We must be swift, yet precise. Ravon will anticipate vengeance."

Kaelinna leaned forward, eyes alight with tactical fire. "We split forces:

1. The main army with you, Emperor.

2. A magic disruption unit led by Lyra.

3. A stealth vanguard—myself and five elites."

I nodded solemnly. "Then we ride."

***

I stepped out of the tent into a dawn kissed by fate. Sabion fell into stride beside me, his presence steady and loyal.

"We will save Aundrea," I said softly but firmly. "And we will bring Michelle home... together, brother."

Sabion clasped my hand, pulling me into a fierce, wordless embrace. His other hand gripped the reins of his horse—and mine.

"Together we ride," he whispered, voice trembling with passion.

We locked eyes—twin flames of unbreakable resolve.

"Together," he repeated, "we'll shatter Ravon's darkness. We'll cut down his shadows and bring our loved ones home—alive and free."

The camp fell silent, the very ground holding its breath. Even nature seemed to acknowledge our oath. One to two full moons lay ahead, heavy with peril and shadow...

And at the end—blood, battle… and destiny.

Chapter 22

Fractured Mind

For weeks, I sat alone in the cold silence of my cell, the damp stone walls pressing in around me. Only a single torch flickered dimly from the corridor beyond the bars, casting shadows that danced like ghosts across the floor. The air reeked of mold and rot, choking what little hope I had left.

Cut off from Michelle, Sarah, and the outside world, the isolation gnawed at my sanity. I felt helpless—adrift in a darkness that seeped not just into my cell, but into my soul. There was no sound except the eerie dripping of water in the distance. My mind began to fracture. The chill of the stone floor crept into my bones, numbing my fingers as I pressed myself against the unyielding iron bars. My thoughts blurred and tangled, shifting from rage to crushing sadness to waves of panic I couldn't explain.

The only thing that kept me holding on was the love I carried for Drakon—and for the life growing inside me. I didn't know who I was anymore. Pieces of me were slipping away, eroding into a quiet, consuming void.

Desperate, I looked down at the palm of my hand, barely visible in the shadows. I focused what little energy I had on the Divine Light—the power I knew lived inside me. Just once, I begged. Just let me feel it. And for the briefest moment, I did. A soft golden glow bloomed in my hand, illuminating the cell like a fragile promise. Then it vanished.

I tried again, reaching deeper—but nothing came. Another failure.

Still, I refused to give up. Day after day, night after night, in the cold and the dark, I pushed through the fog in my mind, willing the light to return. To control it. To reclaim something of myself from the grip of this cursed prison—and from the Divine power I still barely understood.

With each passing day bleeding into the next, the light grew stronger. No longer flickering and elusive, it began to respond to me. It pulsed within me, no longer a whisper but a force I could feel rising—sharpening, becoming mine.

At last, I could summon it at will. I had found the strength to command what had once overwhelmed me. I turned that power on the cell door, channeling the Divine Light to break free. But Ravon's magic still held fast— dark, tangled, and deeply rooted. The lock didn't yield.

***

A sharp pain tore through my stomach, stealing the breath from my lungs. It vanished—then returned, sharper, deeper. Again. And again.

Something was wrong.

I pressed my hand to my belly, trying to steady the tremble in my fingers, but the agony only built—wave after relentless wave. Panic surged through me.

"Guards!" I shouted, my voice echoing against the stone walls. No answer.

Another surge of pain sent me collapsing to my knees. My palms hit the cold floor, rough and unforgiving, while my breath came in short, ragged gasps. I called out again, louder this time. Still nothing—only distant laughter. Cruel. Indifferent.

They'd heard me cry out too many times before. Thought I was lying. Manipulating them.

But this was real.

The pain ripped through me like fire, tightening around my abdomen until I thought I might split apart. Tears welled in my eyes as I clutched my stomach, rocking with the waves of pain. My body was trembling now—no, breaking.

Oh gods… no. No. This couldn't be happening. Not here. Not alone.

I tried to stand, but my legs gave out and I collapsed against the cold, unyielding cell bars. Then it happened— warmth spilled down my legs. My water had broken. Panic seized me as the pain sharpened, becoming harder, more rhythmic, each wave crashing with relentless force.

A realization hit me like a thunderclap: I'm having the baby.

A scream tore from my throat, raw and desperate. "Ravon!" I cried out, forcing my voice to rise above the agony. "I know you can hear me!" My tears streamed freely now—hot trails down my cheeks, burning with fear, fury, and pain.

"I'm having the baby," I sobbed. "Help me… please."

And with one final shred of hope, I reached inward, past the fear, past the pain, searching for that flicker of Divine Light I knew lived within me.

I felt like I was going to pass out.

My body gave in, curling against the freezing stone floor as I clung to the hope that Ravon had heard me. My sobs echoed off the cell walls, raw, broken sounds swallowed by the darkness.

Then, footsteps.

Faint at first. Distant. But growing louder with every heartbeat. My heart pounded in rhythm with them. I lifted my head just enough to see Ravon approaching, flanked by several guards. Ravon waved his hand, releasing the locking spell, and Valtor stepped forward to open the cell. Ravon entered alone, kneeling beside me with a strange expression that twisted concern into something almost… possessive.

"Did you hear me calling you?" I whispered through trembling lips, eyes brimming with tears.

A smile crept onto his face—gentle, yet laced with something darker.

"Yes, my love," he said softly. "I heard you."

And for just one breath, I was grateful. Grateful that someone had come. That I wasn't alone anymore. For a heartbeat, I let myself forget who he was, what he had taken from me. My life. My love. Dania.

But then the pain returned with a vengeance, slicing through my belly like a knife, forcing a scream from my throat. My body felt like it was being torn in half.

Ravon didn't hesitate. He scooped me into his arms, holding me tightly against his chest. His heartbeat pulsed beneath my cheek—slow and cold, too cold—and yet I clung to him out of instinct. He moved quickly, carrying me through dim corridors and up endless stairs. The castle was quiet, lit only by flickering torchlight that cast long, shivering shadows on the walls.

He carried me into my chambers. After so long, I barely recognized them. The scent of my old perfume lingered beneath layers of smoke and damp. Ravon lowered me gently onto the bed, and the feel of velvet beneath me nearly brought me to tears. It was the first softness I'd known in weeks.

***

He turned toward Valtor. "Get Freyan. Now," he barked. Valtor gave a sharp nod and disappeared through the door.

Another wave of pain tore through me. I arched against it, my teeth clenched, breath ragged. Ravon hovered beside me, his expression softening into something that might've looked like worry—if I didn't know him so well.

His hand brushed my cheek, then threaded gently into my hair. I flinched at his touch, but I was too weak to pull away. His voice dropped to a hush.

"It's going to be okay, Aundrea," he said. "I promise."

His words were meant to soothe, but they only made my skin crawl.

Just then, the door opened and Freyan entered, with Valtor close behind. Valtor moved silently to stand guard by the wall, his expression cold and unreadable.

Freyan rushed to my side, dropping to her knees and opening her satchel. The scent of dried herbs and tinctures filled the room as she began pulling out tools, cloth, and vials.

She glanced toward Ravon. "I need hot water and clean towels. Now."

Without hesitation, Ravon turned to Valtor. "See to it."

Freyan leaned over me, her voice calm but firm. "Aundrea, I need to examine you. It may be uncomfortable, but you have to try and relax."

I nodded through the pain, my body trembling, her hands on my abdomen, poking and prodding.

She turned toward Ravon. "It's time. She is ready," she said.

A scream ripped from my throat as another birthing pain surged through me. My body felt like it was splintering from the inside out.

"Ravon," I sobbed, "please, I need Michelle and Sarah."

His jaw tightened. His expression turned cold, defensive—his old bitterness rising like smoke.

"Aundrea, you don't need them. You have me."

But I shook my head, fresh tears blurring my vision. The pain was too much. Their absence felt like a void I couldn't breathe through.

"Please, Ravon," I begged, voice hoarse. "I beg of you…"

Something shifted in his eyes.

That icy wall, so carefully maintained, began to melt. I saw it flicker there—the war within him. Guilt, maybe. Or doubt. Something real.

Freyan added softly, "She'll relax more if they're here. It will help her."

Ravon stood motionless a moment longer, then finally gave a curt nod to Valtor. "Bring them."

A servant slipped in, placing a basin of hot water and a stack of folded towels near the bed before disappearing again. Steam rose gently from the basin, curling through the air, mixing with the scent of lavender and blood.

Freyan looked into my eyes and touched my forehead gently.

"Aundrea," she said, her voice steady and kind, "I need you to breathe. Slow, deep breaths. It's almost time to push."

I tried. By the Gods, I tried. But the pain felt like it was tearing me apart, ripping through my abdomen like a blade. My cries echoed through the chamber despite everything in me trying to hold them in.

Then, I heard the slight sound of footsteps approaching. Valtor returned, this time with Sarah and Michelle behind him. They looked terrified, but their eyes went straight to me. They waited for permission, and Ravon gave a subtle wave of his hand. Then they moved. Michelle climbed onto the bed and gently lifted my head into her lap, brushing the hair from my sweat-drenched forehead.

"It's going to be okay, Aundrea," she whispered, her voice thick with emotion. "I'm here."

Sarah moved quickly to Freyan's side, staying low at the foot of the bed, ready to help but careful not to get in the way. Surrounded by them, I felt the first threads of strength return to my body—frayed and fragile, but real.

I wasn't alone anymore.

***

Hours passed in a blur of agony and fire. Birthing pains came in relentless waves, each one stronger, longer, more brutal than the last. I lost all sense of time—no day, no night—only the tightening grip of pain and the pounding of my own heartbeat in my ears.

Then I heard Freyan's voice, urgent but steady. "Push." I did. Again. And again.

My body screamed, wracked by exhaustion and searing pain. The urge to bear down was primal now, uncontrollable. I could feel myself shaking, muscles trembling, every inch of me on the verge of breaking.

Freyan leaned close, eyes locked with mine. "Aundrea, one last big push," she said. "You're doing great. I can see the baby's head."

But I couldn't breathe. I couldn't think. The pain was like wildfire, burning through every part of me. Tears spilled down my cheeks, my voice cracking as I gasped, "I can't…"

Michelle pressed a warm cloth to my forehead, wiping away the sweat. Her hand was gentle, steady.

"Yes, you can," she said softly, firmly. "Just breathe. Deep breath, and push. One more time." Her voice anchored me. Somehow, I found something left, buried deep beneath the pain, beneath the fire. I clenched my teeth, drew in the breath she asked for, and pushed with everything I had left.

A rush of release. Silence.

Then—a cry. High and sharp and impossibly small.

I opened my eyes, vision swimming with tears and flickering torchlight and disbelief. Freyan was holding him, wiping him down, wrapping him gently in a coarse brown blanket.

"It's a boy, Aundrea," she said, her voice trembling slightly. "Congratulations."

My heart clenched and stopped—but only for a moment. Then, she stepped forward and placed him into my arms.

Ravon stood nearby, his eyes wide, lit with something between admiration and awe. But I couldn't focus on him. All I saw was my son. His tiny body nestled against my chest, skin warm against mine. His cry quieted as he breathed me in. Tears streamed down my face.

And all I could think about was how much I wanted Drakon. By the Gods, I wanted him here with me. I wanted him to witness the moment that should have been ours.

Out of the corner of my eye, I saw Ravon step closer. His hand reached toward the baby, barely touching him, but I pulled him back instinctively. Fear gripped me—not knowing what to expect.

"I want to hold my son," he said quietly. "You don't have to protect him from me, Aundrea. I am his father."

I clutched the baby tighter, my instincts flaring. But I was too tired. Too fragile. This wasn't a battle I could fight—not now. And so, slowly, cautiously, I let him go.

He cradled the baby in his arms, eyes shimmering with pride. But even as he smiled, my heart pounded in my chest. What did he see when he looked at my son? What did he want from him? And what kind of future had just been born into Ravon's hands?

Ravon's eyes gleamed with something close to joy—twisted, consuming. "He shall be named Ravon," he declared, holding the baby high as though making an offering to the gods. "Ravon Jr."

A chill rolled down my spine. "Wait," I whispered, my voice still hoarse from labor. "Let's not rush. Let me hold him a while longer before we decide."

His expression shifted, darkening instantly. He let out a sharp, bitter laugh. "Do you think me a fool, Aundrea? His name shall be Ravon Jr."

Something inside me shattered. Not just at the name, but at the weight of it. The claim. The legacy Ravon wanted to wrap around my son like chains.

I was afraid—afraid of what this man would offer my child, what he would shape him into. Afraid of being separated. Of never holding him again. Of losing the only piece of Drakon I may have left. I hoped, I wished… My heart swelled with optimism that my son was Drakon's son. But I didn't have the strength to fight. Not now. Not yet.

Ravon leaned over and returned the baby to my arms. "Ravon Jr. it is," he said with finality.

I held my son tightly, pressing a soft kiss to his tiny forehead. His fingers curled weakly against my chest, and my heart ached with love and helpless fury.

That will never be your name, I thought. Not truly. Not in my heart.

Freyan approached, her voice measured. "Ravon, I need some time to clean the baby and tend to Aundrea."

He nodded, distracted already by his fantasy of triumph. "Get my wife out of those filthy clothes and clean her up. I have a celebration to plan in my son's honor."

I watched Ravon go. Celebrating, while I lay there, in pieces. Consumed by his own wants and desires, his own obsessions.

And with that, he turned and swept from the room, his cloak catching the torchlight as it vanished into the hall. Valtor closing the door behind him, then, the unmistakable sound of the lock.

***

Michelle and Sarah remained close, their presence like a fragile shield. Freyan moved quickly, quietly, her touch gentle but focused as she took the baby from my arms with care.

Freyan gently bathed the baby in the basin near the firelight, her voice a soft murmur as she cooed to him. His tiny limbs kicked at the water, splashing weakly, his skin still pink and wrinkled with newness. He was so small... so perfect. A miracle cradled in the chaos.

Michelle and Sarah moved to my side, helping me sit up. My legs trembled beneath me, the weakness setting in fast now that the urgency had passed. They steadied me, holding on tightly as they led me toward the washroom.

***

The scent of rose petals met me first—faint, comforting, almost unreal. A basin had been filled with warm water, steam curling into the air like breath. My nightdress and robe, once beautiful, were cut away. The fabric was stiff with age, stained and clinging in places it shouldn't. I sank into the basin slowly, the heat wrapping around me like an embrace. I hadn't felt warmth like this in so many weeks—maybe longer. It melted into my bones, unlocking something inside me I hadn't realized had been clenched shut. I let out a shaky breath and leaned back. Michelle and Sarah worked silently, with tenderness and care, washing the blood and sweat from my body as if wiping away the entire past month. I closed my eyes. For a moment, I allowed myself to forget the cell. The cold. The silence. Even Ravon.

For one fragile breath, I let myself be cared for. As I sank deeper into the warmth of the water, the heat cradled my aching body like a lover's embrace, and with it, memories began to rise—unbidden and relentless.

Drakon's hands… the way they moved over my skin, reverent and sure. His lips pressed against mine, full of hunger and promise. I could still feel the weight of his touch; the last time we were together before Ravon tore us apart. His hands gripping my hips, grounding me in a world that had made sense only when he was near. His kiss— firm, desperate, full of the kind of love that didn't ask for permission.

I would've given him anything.

And now, I would give anything just to be in his arms again.

Back where I belong.

Drakon didn't love the power in me—he loved me. Entirely, without question. He saw the cracks in my soul and held them together. He was my heart. My soul, and my destiny.

Every moment without him has scraped me raw, like time itself is digging its claws into me. Every hour apart has been a wound left open.

The water lapped gently against my skin—pale, untouched by sunlight, delicate and bruised from too many days in the dark. The heat soothed me, but it couldn't reach the cold grief carved into my chest.

Still, I closed my eyes and let myself believe. One day, we would be together again. I knew it as surely as I knew how deeply I loved Drakon.

And for me, that day could not come soon enough.

Once my bath was complete, they helped me into a nightdress unlike anything I had worn in what felt like ages. It was soft as moonlight, black silk that clung delicately to my skin, with silver leaves embroidered beneath the bodice and along the hem. The fabric shimmered faintly in the low light, whispering of a life that once felt like mine.

***

They helped me back to bed, gently lowering me into the freshly prepared linens. My body ached, but the pain was distant now, drowned by the love swelling in my chest. I closed my eyes for a moment, as I saw Drakon's image in my mind, a moment I wanted to live in. My eyes slowly opened and Freyan approached, lifting the baby from his bath. She wrapped him in a soft blanket and placed him carefully in my arms. I whispered softly into his ear. Drako, that will be your true name, my son.

The moment he touched me, I felt whole.

Utterly, devastatingly complete.

A love unlike anything I had ever known surged through me, pure and deep, almost too large for my heart to contain. As I held him close, his tiny face nestled against my chest. He turned his head instinctively, nuzzling softly against my skin.

Freyan gave a small, knowing smile. "He is hungry."

I nodded, though a flicker of nervousness passed through me. I'd never done this before. Would I be able to feed him? Would he know how? What should I do?

Freyan's hands were gentle as she helped me shift, guiding my arms and lifting my gown with quiet grace. The silk fell away from my shoulder, and I held my breath as he found his way.

And then, he latched on.

A soft gasp escaped me.

It wasn't just the sensation, or even the relief, it was the intimacy of it. The overwhelming connection. This little soul, born of love and chaos and impossibility, was now tethered to me in the most natural, primal way.

Tears filled my eyes again, but they were different now. Not from fear. Not from pain. But from love. Fierce. Raw. Undeniable. He nursed peacefully, his tiny fingers resting lightly against my skin. I stroked the back of his head and closed my eyes, letting the rhythm of his breath steady mine. For this moment, at least, I wasn't a prisoner. I was his mother.

I cradled him close, his warmth seeping into me, healing something I hadn't realized was still broken. His tiny hand reached up and wrapped around my finger, so small, so strong, and I smiled. A true, unburdened smile.

Then… something shifted.

He opened his eyes.

And they weren't just blue. They weren't Ravon's dull steel or even my pale grey. For one breathtaking heartbeat, they blazed.

A brilliant orange glow flared within them—fierce, radiant, almost blinding. Like fire. Like embers. The glow lit the space between us, and in that light, I saw him. Really saw him. I gasped softly. And then, just as suddenly, the glow faded, leaving behind bright, blue eyes. In that moment,

I knew, bone deep, soul deep.

He was not Ravon's son. He was ours.

Drakon's and mine.

The room had gone still. Silent.

When I looked up, I saw Michelle frozen in place, her hand still resting on the edge of the bed. Sarah stood beside her, wide-eyed. Freyan's mouth was slightly open, her gaze fixed on my son as if the air had been knocked from her lungs.

Tears stung the corners of my eyes. My voice broke in a whisper. "Freyan…"

She looked at me slowly, her eyes full of fear and dawning horror.

"Please," I whimpered, "don't tell Ravon."

Freyan swallowed hard, her expression torn.

"You have to help me," I continued, voice trembling. "We need to get him out of here. If Ravon finds out… if he even suspects… he might kill him."

Freyan's face shifted, uncertainty, fear, and then something deeper. Resolve.

Though her loyalty to Ravon had never wavered before, I saw it then—in her eyes. She knew. And in her heart, she already understood what had to be done. She nodded once, almost imperceptibly.

And with that, everything began to change.

We all knew what we had to do.

Chapter 23

Broken Chains

My body felt impossibly heavy, drained not just from childbirth, but from the hours of pain, the weeks of caivity, and the crushing weight of everything still to come. Every muscle ached, every breath felt like it had to be pulled from deep within my chest. My skin was still flushed from the bath, tender where the warmth had seeped into me, now cooling against the silk of my nightdress.

I lay back against the soft pillows; their scent faintly laced with lavender and old stone. My son was tucked beside me, wrapped snugly in the blanket Freyan had given him. His breath was steady and light, rising and falling against my arm like the flutter of moth wings. I couldn't stop looking at him—his tiny fingers, his impossibly soft cheek, the miracle of his presence.

Michelle moved near the foot of the bed, tidying the basin. Sarah adjusted the curtains to dim the torchlight. Freyan remained close, watching the baby with quiet intensity.

But the peace couldn't last.
Not here. Not under Ravon's roof.

A chill slipped through the room, even with the fire crackling low in the fireplace. The shadows on the walls seemed to dance with the flickering of the torches.

"I need to talk to you," I said quietly, my voice rough, still hoarse from hours of screaming but steady.

The three of them paused, and the room shifted. The warmth faded into stillness. That feeling of dread crept in, settling in the hollow behind my ribs.

They came closer, gathering around the bed, eyes heavy with knowing.
We all felt it. The unspoken urgency.

"I've been thinking about how to get the baby out of the palace," I said, brushing my fingers gently along his cheek. His skin was soft and warm beneath my touch—so real, so fragile. "And how to get all of you out too."

Michelle's breath hitched. Her eyes widened, lips parting in disbelief.

"I'll distract Ravon," I said, forcing myself to shift upright. My arms trembled with the effort, but I pushed through it. "While you make your way out. Freyan knows the passages; she can lead you."

Michelle stepped forward, her hands twisting together at her waist. The candlelight flickered across her face, drawing out the worry etched in her brow. "But the palace is sealed with Ravon's magic. That dark barrier—it's everywhere. How are we supposed to get through that?"

I nodded, slow and heavy. "During my time in isolation… I learned to control more of my power." I took a deep breath and continued. "Not all of it. Not yet. But enough to call it when I need it. I'll try to bring the barrier down."

Silence wrapped around us like a second skin. The fire popped softly, the only sound for a long moment.

Then Sarah whispered, "What about you, Aundrea?"

The question sliced through me. I turned to her, then to each of them. The baby stirred at my side, a soft whimper escaping his lips as his hand curled tightly around my sleeve.

"I'll stay," I said, my voice quiet but sure. "At least for now. If I run with you, he'll come after all of us. But if I stay… and he still believes the baby is his… it'll buy you time."

Michelle blinked rapidly, her eyes glassy with tears. "You'd be giving yourself up."

"No," I whispered, placing a hand over my chest. My heartbeat thudded beneath it, slow and heavy. "I'd be protecting him. Protecting all of you."

A long silence passed. Then Michelle reached for my hand.

"We won't waste the time you give us."

With their hands still wrapped around mine, and the weight of my decision pressing down on all of us, I felt the truth rise in my chest like a wave I could no longer hold back. I knew someday, I would be with Drakon again.

I looked down at my son—our son—and brushed a trembling finger across his cheek. With a voice heavy with love, sorrow, and something unshakable, I exhaled the words like a vow:

"I would do anything for my child, Drako."

The silence that followed wasn't empty. It was reverent. Because they all knew—I already had.

Just then, the door opened. Ravon stood in the entrance, his eyes locking onto mine.

"Leave us," he told the guards and the women. The women exchanged nervous glances, then filed out quickly with the guards, leaving me with Ravon and my son. The door closed behind them with a soft click.

Ravon's eyes never left mine as he moved closer, his presence still a dark shadow, filling the room. My heart quickened, my skin prickling with unease. But I forced myself to remain still, to meet his gaze.

The baby stirred again, his tiny hand tightening around my finger. Ravon's eyes flicked to him, then back to me. He stepped closer, his presence filling the space like a storm about to break. His eyes burned with that familiar intensity—controlled, but dangerous just beneath the surface.

"Aundrea," he said, his tone deceptively gentle, "now that you're recovering, I think it's time our son had his own quarters."

My fingers tightened around my son's tiny hand without thinking. The warmth of him against my skin grounded me, even as a rush of dread rose in my chest.

"No," I said quietly, forcing calm into my voice. "Not yet."

Ravon raised a brow, unamused. "He needs his own space. And a nursemaid. I've already chosen one, but perhaps you'd like to meet her first?"

I shook my head. My mind was already racing.

"I don't want him to leave my side. Not even for a nursemaid."

He watched me, gauging my resolve. For a brief heartbeat, something in his expression softened—perhaps a feigned tenderness, or maybe a calculated concession.

"Aundrea," he said, stepping beside the bed, "he'll only be down the hall. And I'll ensure the nursemaid is trustworthy. But perhaps... you'd feel better if you chose her yourself?"

I hesitated.
A trap? Or a thread of mercy?

Either way, I seized the moment. "Freyan," I said, lifting my chin. "I want Freyan to care for him."

His eyes narrowed, the flicker of resistance flashing across his features. But after a pause, he gave a short nod. "Very well. Freyan it is."

I drew a breath, steadying myself for the next step—carefully, deliberately.

"And I want Sarah and Michelle to stay with him too," I said, meeting his gaze. "In the nursery. Please. It would make me feel better about him being away from me."

The room went still for a heartbeat.
I saw the calculation behind Ravon's eyes, sizing up my request, weighing the risk against the illusion of control.

After a long, loaded silence, Ravon finally spoke.

"Fine," he said, his voice clipped. "They can stay—with him. But only for a few days."

My stomach twisted, but I kept my expression still. A few days. It wasn't enough, but it was something. It had to be enough for my son. Time to prepare. Time to plan. Time to act.

"Thank you," I murmured, lowering my gaze to hide the fire behind my eyes. I stroked my son's cheek, his warmth reminding me what I was fighting for.

Ravon called for the guards standing outside my quarters. They stepped in without hesitation, their boots soft against the stone floor. "Take the child to the nursery. Freyan, Sarah, and Michelle will attend him. See it done."

One of them reached for my son, and I instinctively pulled him a little closer before forcing myself to let go. His warmth slipped from my arms as they lifted him carefully. I felt the ache instantly—a hollow pang in my chest—but I pushed it down.

This is only the beginning, I reminded myself. Every moment counts.

Ravon watched them carry the baby out, his expression unreadable. When the door shut behind them, sealing us in, he turned to me.

Without a word, he unfastened his black cape and hung it neatly on the hook by the fire. Underneath, he wore a simple black shirt and matching pants, the fabric soft and fitted to his form. Slowly, deliberately, he pulled the shirt over his head, baring his chest to the firelight.

Muscle and shadow. Control and power. A predator in silk.

My heart quickened, a knot forming low in my stomach. I fought the instinct to recoil.

He slipped beneath the covers beside me, his movements slow, intimate, deliberate. His eyes stayed on mine—burning, heavy, invasive.

My body tensed.

I felt the mattress shift beneath his weight, the warmth of him radiating behind me. I forced myself to inch closer, every movement practiced, careful. The performance I had no choice but to give.

He lifted one arm and drew me in, wrapping it around my waist. His bare chest pressed against my back, and I could feel the steady beat of his heart against my spine.

His breath touched my ear—warm, deliberate. Possessive.

"I see isolation has helped you, Aundrea," he murmured, his lips brushing my hairline. His voice was low and rough, coiled like a serpent.

I closed my eyes, willing my heart to slow. Willing my body not to betray the storm within me.

Ravon leaned in close, his breath warm and deliberate as it traced the curve of my ear.

"Tomorrow, Aundrea," he whispered, "we will introduce our son to the world… with a celebration fit for a king."

My chest tightened.

I turned my head just enough to offer a faint nod—measured, careful. My mouth shaped the response he wanted, but inside, the words turned bitter on my tongue.

Deceit, I thought. It tastes like ash.

But Ravon seemed content. His eyes gleamed with satisfaction, the glint of a man who believed he had won.

I shifted slightly, just enough to add a thin edge of weariness to my voice. "I'm very tired."

His expression softened, his fingers moving to my hair. He stroked it slowly, the touch gentle—dangerously gentle.

"Sleep, my love," he murmured. "Sleep."

I let my eyes close, my heart pounding beneath my ribs.

I had to survive this night.
Because tomorrow… the mask would crack.
And everything would begin.

***

I gently opened my eyes, still heavy with sleep. For a moment, I couldn't breathe. The walls felt like they were closing in, thick with silence and the weight of Ravon's presence. He was already awake, sitting upright beside me on the bed, fully dressed, his back straight and his gaze fixed on the far wall.

As my vision adjusted, I blinked a few times and raised a hand to wipe away the last haze of sleep.

"Ravon," I murmured, voice hoarse. "I need to feed the baby. Can you—"

He cut me off before I could finish.

"I've already sent for him, Aundrea."

A flicker of eagerness stirred in my chest. My heart quickened. I longed to see my son's face again, to feel his warmth, to hold him where no darkness could reach. There was a light inside me, burning, persistent, and only he could feel it. Only Drako stirred it to life.

Ravon stood and adjusted the cuffs of his sleeves. "Once you've fed him," he said evenly, "he'll return to the nursery. Call for the guard when you're done, and he'll take him back to Freyan." I gave a small nod of agreement, masking the knot in my throat.

Silence lingered between us. Then I cleared my throat softly, cautious. "May Sarah and Michelle help me prepare for the celebration?" His head tilted slightly. Suspicion flickered in his eyes—he was always watching for betrayal, always waiting to catch the lie behind the smile.

But after a pause, he gave a slow, wary nod. "Very well."

***

A knock at the door interrupted him. He strode over and opened it. One of the guards stood just beyond the threshold, cradling my son in his arms.

The guard instinctively held the baby out to Ravon, but Ravon stepped back, waving him off. "Give him to his mother," he said. And in that moment, I could have cried.

The guard placed Drako in my arms, and everything else—Ravon, the walls, the fear—it all faded for one precious breath. I clutched my son gently, drinking in the sight of him. His soft skin, the weight of him nestled against me, the tiny yawn escaping his lips. The light he brought into my soul was more than magic. It was life. The guard bowed and exited.

Ravon lingered by the door, turning back one last time.

"Call the guard when you're done. I'll send Michelle and Sarah to help you dress." His voice dropped lower, colder. "But beware, Aundrea. Don't cross me. If I even suspect betrayal, I'll throw you back in that cell. And this time, you'll stay there until Ravon Jr. is old enough to walk."

His words hit like a blade, sharp and deliberate. He wasn't bluffing. I knew that.

But I also knew something he didn't. I would risk everything for my son.

***

An hour passed in strained silence before Michelle entered the room with the guards, her eyes flicking nervously between Ravon and me. Sarah followed close behind, her expression tighter, more guarded. One of the guards stepped forward, reaching for my son.

My heart clenched as Drako was lifted from my arms.

The guard cradled him carefully, then turned and left without a word, the door clicking shut behind him.

The moment we were alone, I straightened. My voice was low but urgent. "We need to talk. Quickly." Both women leaned in. Sarah's brow furrowed with concern. Michelle's face was pale, fear swimming just beneath the surface.

"You need to leave tonight," I said. "When the baby is returned to you during the celebration, don't wait. Go. Take him and run."

Michelle opened her mouth to speak, but I shook my head. "There won't be time. When the moment comes, you have to move fast."

Sarah nodded slowly, piecing everything together. "The barrier?"

"I've been practicing," I whispered. "I should be able to open it, but not for long. I'll hold it open as long as I can, I'll keep Ravon distracted..."

A beat passed between us, one heavy with unspoken fears and a shared understanding of the risk. But they both nodded. They knew what they had to do.

Michelle helped me into the deep emerald gown that had been laid out for the celebration, her fingers moving quickly through the laces. Sarah brushed my hair, weaving it back from my face with trembling hands, trying to hide her worry behind the familiarity of routine.

Then, I heard it.

Footsteps.

I turned quickly toward the door, trying to still my breath as the latch clicked.

Ravon stepped inside, the firelight catching the silver trim on his sleeves. He swept the room with his gaze before settling on us.

"Girls," he said, his voice smooth. "Return to the nursery with the guard." Without protest, Sarah and Michelle slipped past him and followed the waiting guard into the corridor. The door closed softly behind them.

Ravon turned back to me.

I forced a smile, wide and full of deceit, and took a step forward. Then another, spinning once, slowly, with my hands planted gently against my waist.

"I can wear my dresses again," I said, feigning delight.

Ravon's eyes drank me in. He stepped closer, that familiar eerie smile creeping onto his face. His hand slid around my waist, pulling me against him.

"You look very beautiful, my love," he murmured.

He leaned in, and I stilled myself. My stomach twisted in protest, but I didn't pull away. For Drako's sake, I leaned into him, kissed him back.

The moment dragged, long, suffocating, heavy with disgust I didn't dare show. When it ended, I tasted only bitterness.

Ravon studied me, suspicion just behind the softness in his gaze.

"You seem different, Aundrea." I dropped my eyes to the floor, careful to keep my voice fragile.

"Drakon is not coming for me," I whispered. "I know that now. And I want to be happy again. For the baby's sake. I want to stop fighting."

He watched me for a long, silent moment. Then he leaned down and kissed my forehead.

"Good choice, Aundrea."

He offered his arm. "You will stand beside me tonight, Aundrea. Our son deserves a proper celebration." I placed my hand in the crook of his arm and let him lead me from the room.

The corridor stretched ahead, lit with golden torches and lined with velvet banners. Valtor waited halfway down, holding my son in his arms.

The moment I reached for him, Ravon slapped my hand away, not hard, but enough to jolt me, and pulled me firmly back to his side.

"You'll have your time with him," he said under his breath, smiling as if nothing had happened.

But my heart was already burning.

Soon, I promised myself. Soon, I will have him again... and we'll be free.

**

Ravon led me to the long table at the head of the great hall, each of his steps measured, regal, practiced. The hall buzzed with hushed anticipation. Nobles in dark silks and polished armor filled the space, their eyes flickering toward us with reverence and fear.

He pulled my chair out, and I sat down, hands folded in my lap, doing my best to appear composed.

He joined me at my side, his presence looming. I scanned the room, heart racing.

Where was he?

Then, Freyan appeared.

My breath caught. She wasn't in the nursery. She was here.

The plan.

She approached with grace, carrying Drako in her arms. She had taken him from Valtor. My son. My precious boy. Relief swelled in my chest.

Freyan reached our table and curtsied. "Milady," she said quietly, "after the baby's introduction, I'll return him to the nursery. Would you like to hold him for a moment?"

I didn't hesitate. I gathered him into my arms, my body instantly relaxing against his tiny warmth. Ravon looked down at us, his pride nearly radiating off him like heat. His expression glowed with ownership, not love, and it made my skin crawl.

Then—

The torches flickered. The air thickened. A glowing purple haze began to spread through the room, shimmering across the stone floor like a living mist. A rift began to open, wide and deep, tearing through the very fabric of the hall.

The creatures.

Just like the wedding.

Those foul, unnatural things—eyes like voids—twisting through the breach as though crawling from a nightmare. My heart felt as though it would jump from my chest.

Ravon rose swiftly from his seat and reached for the baby. I hesitated, but he pulled Drako from my arms before I could stop him. Fear coiled around my throat like a noose.

I grabbed his arm, my voice sharp. "Ravon."

He looked down at me, his eyes glowing with dark delight. "It's all right, Aundrea," he said, the calm in his voice more terrifying than a scream.

He raised the baby high, turning toward the rift.

"My child!" he declared, voice echoing through the stone hall. "Born to darkness, he will be my heir to this world. Welcome my son, Ravon!"

A cheer erupted—not from the nobles, but from the creatures. Eerie, jagged, otherworldly sounds that scraped the inside of my skull. The rift pulsed with energy, casting flickering shadows that danced across the walls like fire made from flesh.

Ravon handed the baby back to Freyan and gave her a sharp, knowing nod. My chest seized. This could be the last time I ever saw him. I stood up to watch, my eyes never leaving Freyan and my son. A single tear slid down my cheek as I watched her vanish through the double doors. Then one of the shadow-creatures lunged toward me with a hiss that rattled through my bones. I gasped and staggered back, another one closing in—drawn to something inside me.

My light.

The last one struck fast, nearly grazing my skin. I fell backward into Ravon's arms, my heart slamming in my chest.

"There's nothing to fear, my love," he said with a low chuckle, clearly entertained by my fear, as he guided me back into my chair with unsettling gentleness. I said nothing, keeping my head low, breathing through the panic.

Deep within, I called to my Divine Light, not to reveal it, not yet. Just enough to act. I closed my eyes briefly and felt it pulse. There. The barrier dropped. I felt it.

Quietly. Silently.

Ravon, too consumed by his own spectacle, never noticed. He basked in the attention, reveling in his own delusions. I had to hold the barrier open as long as I could.

Dinner passed in a blur of tension and shadow. Ravon led me back to our chambers when the evening was done, smiling as if the night had been perfect. He helped me out of my gown, his hands brushing my skin. I fought the instinct to flinch, my body shivering under his touch. But I held on.

***

Then I felt it—the barrier surge back into place. It was done. My strength faltered. My legs gave out. I collapsed at the foot of the bed. Ravon reached for me, concern flashing across his face.

"Aundrea?"

"I—I think I'm still weak from the birth," I whispered, the lie slipping easily from my lips. He turned as if to leave the room, his hand already reaching for the door.

"I'll call Freyan," he said.

"No... no," I said softly. "It's okay... I'll be fine."

He dressed me in my nightdress himself, then lifted me into bed and pulled the soft velvet blanket over me, tucking it around my shoulders.

He slid in beside me, pulling me close again. His lips found mine, lingering far too long. I let him. Because I had to. My thoughts spun wildly.

Did they make it?

Were they safe?

Were they gone?

My heart pounded with the questions I couldn't ask. I stared into the darkness behind my closed eyes as Ravon held me.

One last kiss. Then the cold settled in. I held on to hope.

And I let the night take me.

Chapter 24

Unbroken

The wind howled across the mountain ridge, sharp as a blade, tearing through the long grass and battering the folds of Drakon's cloak. I watched from a distance in spirit alone bound by love, by blood, and by the ache of everything I had left behind.

Drakon stood at the edge of the wind-swept ridge, his silhouette rigid against the gray sky. The Citadel of Eldarath loomed in the distance, its black spires rising like dark fangs to pierce the clouds. Lightning shimmered faintly in the distance, and the air stank of damp soil, cold iron, and the raw bite of ozone

Beside him stood Sabion, his jaw clenched against the chill. His eyes narrowed, scanning the bustling camp below, where soldiers prepared for war, sharpening blades, oiling armor, and checking saddle straps. The clang of metal and murmurs of strategy filled the air, a constant hum beneath the wind.

Then, movement.

Three shadowy figures emerged from the mist-thickened edge of the forest, their cloaks soaked through, feet barely making a sound over the sodden ground. Drakon and Sabion drew their swords in one fluid motion, the silver flashing like teeth in the fading light.

"Who goes there?" Sabion called, voice hard and steady.

Then, relief.

A familiar voice answered, breathless but unmistakable. "Emperor Drakon, it's me, Michelle."

The wind howled across the mountain ridge, sharp as a blade, tearing through the long grass and battering the folds of Drakon's cloak. I watched from a distance in spirit alone—bound by love, by blood, and by the ache of everything I had left behind.

Drakon stood at the edge of the wind-swept ridge, his silhouette rigid against the gray sky. The Citadel of Eldarath loomed in the distance, its black spires rising like dark fangs to pierce the clouds. Lightning shimmered faintly beyond the horizon.

Sabion froze. His heart thundered in his chest as he dropped his blade and rushed forward. He reached Michelle and swept her off her feet, spinning her once before lowering her gently to the ground. Her damp cloak billowed as she landed, her eyes wide, stunned.

He leaned in, his voice low, filled with the weight of sleepless nights and unspoken prayers. "I thought I would never see you again."

Michelle's heart raced as their lips met, brief, heated, forbidden. Her cheeks flushed as she stepped back, breath catching.

"Sabion?" she whispered, her voice tight. "Why did you do that? You know what I am… my position in the court,"

"I'm sorry," he said quickly, glancing away. "I've been so worried. We'll talk about it later."

Behind them, two more figures stepped forward from the trees, Freyan and Sarah, cloaks heavy with mist.

They approached with purpose, dropping to one knee before Drakon.

Drakon's voice was tight with command. "Who is this?"

"This is Freyan," Sarah said, rising and casting a glance toward the woman beside her. "She is a healer. She aided Aundrea while she bore the child... and risked her life to help us flee the palace."

At the sound of her name, the world narrowed. Drakon's breath caught, his chest rose, then stilled. He knew who she was. He had heard her name spoken before. A healer turned dark, but somehow-brought back to...

"I am in her debt, and what of Aundrea?" he asked, voice barely audible.

Michelle lowered her gaze to the muddy ground below. Her lips trembled. "I'm sorry, Your Highness," she said. "She didn't make it out."

Drakon turned away, his cape whipping behind him as the pain overtook him, raw and sudden, like an arrow through his ribs.

"Your Highness, wait!" Michelle called out.

Freyan stepped forward, her arms cradling something wrapped in a thick, woolen shawl, small, quiet, alive.

Michelle's voice shook as she continued, "Aundrea told us to flee. She used the power of the Dragon Stone, and the Divine Light. She brought down Ravon's seal on the Citadel so we could escape. She gave everything..."

She turned toward Freyan, gesturing with her trembling right hand.

"This… this is your son, Drako."

Drakon's entire body stilled.

The storm seemed to hush around him. Slowly, almost reverently, he turned.

His eyes locked onto the child in Freyan's arms.

His son.

He stepped forward, each movement like stepping through a dream, disbelief, fear, wonder all warring in his gaze.

I felt it then. From beyond the veil of shadow and time. I felt him reach for the part of me that still lived in our child.

And I knew, He would protect him. No matter what.

Drakon approached Freyan with ease, the wind tugging at his cloak as he slid his sword back into its sheath. His steps were cautious, reverent, as if afraid this was all a dream that might dissolve if he moved too quickly.

He stopped in front of her, his gaze falling to the tiny figure nestled in Freyan's arms. The child was wrapped tightly, barely moving, but so undeniably real.

"This is my child?" he asked softly. "My son?"

Freyan smiled, her voice warm and steady. "Yes, Your Highness. He is yours."

Drakon's heart thundered inside his chest. Pride swelled so fast it nearly knocked the breath from him. Love, instant, fierce, and overwhelming, rose in his throat.

He took a shaky step closer, eyes never leaving the bundle. "May I...?"

Freyan nodded. "Would you like to hold him?"

"Yes," he breathed. "Yes, oh by the gods, yes."

She gently transferred the baby into his arms, and Drakon cradled him like something sacred. He eased the blanket back from the child's face with trembling fingers, revealing soft skin and the faintest trace of gold in the baby's lashes.

Then,

The baby's eyes opened, locking with his father's. And for a moment, they burned.

Bright orange, molten, powerful, alive. A glow flickered within them like fire beneath glass. Drakon froze, awe-struck.

He saw it. The Dragon Fire. His fire.

Alive and burning inside his son.

Emotion swelled like a tide. He leaned in and pressed a kiss to Drako's forehead, reverent and full of wonder. A moment later, the child's eyes shifted back to a clear, brilliant blue.

Drakon let out a breath he hadn't known he was holding.

Then, with a fierce grin, he lifted his son into the air and turned toward the waiting camp.

"Here!" he shouted, voice ringing with pride. "Here is the next heir of Lisona!"

A thunderous cheer erupted across the ridge. Soldiers raised swords and fists, their voices carrying through the wind.

Drakon lowered the baby and carefully handed him back to Freyan. His joy didn't dim, but it sharpened into purpose.

"Guards!" he called. "Gather a team, our best men. Escort Freyan, Michelle, Sarah, and my son back to the palace. Keep them safe."

A nearby guard bowed deeply and barked orders, gathering his unit at once. Drakon turned, lifting his sword once more, the fire now in his eyes.

"No more waiting," he said, his voice a blade. "Now let's go get my wife." He looked to the horizon, wind catching his cloak like wings behind him.

"Let's ride to the Citadel and bring back Lady Aundrea," he said with absolute conviction.

***

I woke in the dark. No sunlight. Only the flickering torchlight along the chamber walls, casting long, wavering shadows that danced across the stone. My body ached, the heaviness of sleep still clinging to my limbs, and my mind scrambled to reconstruct the night before.

Ravon was already awake, seated beside me on the edge of the bed, his figure outlined in gold by the firelight. I pulled myself upright, wincing slightly, trying not to betray the fear pressing down on my chest.

He turned to me and kissed the top of my head. I forced myself not to flinch, though my stomach twisted at the contact. I couldn't let him see it, what I had done.

"Good morning, my love," he said, his voice low and velvety, but laced with that twisted possessiveness I had come to dread. "How are you feeling today?"

Love—this wasn't that. Not from him. What Ravon felt was control, obsession, and ownership.

"I'm feeling better," I answered, my voice carefully even.

He pulled me into his arms, and though my pulse quickened in panic, I forced myself to lean into him. If he even suspected…

Had Michelle, Sarah, and Freyan escaped with Drako? Or had everything I sacrificed been in vain?

Ravon called toward the door. "Bring me my son," he ordered the guard outside.

Then he turned to me, eyes narrowing. "What's wrong, Aundrea?"

I took a breath, choosing my words carefully. "I'm just eager to see him… I miss him."

He leaned in, pressing an unwanted kiss to my lips. My skin crawled, but I didn't pull away. Not yet.

"This is our new beginning," he murmured.

I nodded slowly, the lie bitter on my tongue. "That's all I've wanted… a new beginning."

A sinister grin twisted across his face, satisfied by the answer he wanted to hear. I had said nothing false, but the truth he heard was not the one I meant. I did want a new beginning… but not with him. With Drako. With Drakon.

Just then, the door swung open.

The guard stepped in, panic on his face. "Forgive me, Lord Ravon," he stammered, "but... the baby is gone."

Ravon rose like a shadow erupting from the ground. "Gone?" he bellowed, fury igniting in his voice.

Terror crashed through me, but I had to act. "WHAT DO YOU MEAN GONE?" I cried, standing quickly, matching his anger with my own.

His hand lashed out, not a strike, but a silencing motion, warning me to be quiet. I obeyed instantly.

"Where is my son?" he roared.

The guard trembled. "I... I don't know, Your Highness. Sarah, Michelle, and Freyan, they're missing too."

Ravon's voice cracked through the air. "FIND THEM!"

He signaled to the guards behind him.

Valtor entered the chamber like a vulture drawn to a carcass.

"My lord," he said, bowing slightly. "Drakon has been spotted. He approaches the citadel gates with his men."

Ravon stiffened. "Ready the Shadow Guard."

Valtor and the guards nodded and exited swiftly, the doors slamming shut behind them.

Then the room turned to ice.

He pivoted back toward me, and with each step he took, I felt smaller beneath his looming shadow.

"If I find out you had anything to do with this…" he said, his voice a quiet growl, "you will live to regret it."

My mouth went dry. I could barely speak.

"How, how could I?" I choked out, forcing the words past my fear. "I've been with you since yesterday… every moment." He stared at me, eyes digging into mine like knives. My heart thundered in my chest.

"Then why do you tremble, Aundrea?" he whispered. "What are you hiding?"

"I…" I paused, forcing tears to the surface, letting them tremble on my lashes. "My baby is missing, Ravon. How do you think I'd be acting? Find him. Please… find my son."

He studied me for a long moment. Then, with a strange softness, he kissed me once more.

"I intend to."

He turned and dressed quickly, pulling his dark cloak over his shoulders before striding to the door. With a flick of his hand, I heard it, searing magic etched into the lock, sealing me in.

Then he was gone.

I sat frozen in place, listening to the stillness.

They made it!

A full day's head start, enough. It had to be.

But I couldn't wait for Drakon to find me.

I had to go. I had to go now!

I rose to my feet and dressed with purpose, slipping into a red and black gown. I twisted my hair back into a simple braid, each movement steady, deliberate. I pulled on the black leather boots Ravon had left for me and stood tall.

I approached the door.

I could sense the guard on the other side, standing, still, unaware.

My hand hovered near the seal, heat rising in my chest. My power stirred.

I closed my eyes and summoned the Divine Light, focusing it into my palm. A warm ball of energy swelled in my hand, pulsing like a heartbeat.

The lock screeched softly, metal grinding as the enchantment released.

The guard turned just as I flung the door open, light pouring from my body like sunlight breaking through storm clouds.

He covered his eyes, stumbling back, but I was not fast enough. He lunged, grabbing my arm.

I struggled, twisting, but his grip held firm. My pulse spiked. I closed my eyes,

And let go.

An explosion of light burst from my core. The blast threw him backward with such force he slammed against the stone wall and crumpled to the floor, unmoving.

I stood alone in the corridor, breath ragged, my skin glowing faintly from within.

I knew where I had to go.

The path was burned into my memory, every hallway, every hidden turn, from the last time I had tried to escape.

Only this time, I wouldn't fail.

***

I reached the end of the corridor, heart hammering, breath shallow. The only visible exit was blocked, by two guards, armored and alert, standing at their post. I pressed my back to the cold stone wall, hidden just beyond their line of sight.

My eyes began to glow, soft blue light pulsing gently as I reached out with my senses. The Citadel's seal, Ravon's dark enchantment, hung over the castle like a suffocating curtain. My vision flickered back to normal.

I could do this, I knew I could!

I closed my eyes and drew a deep breath, feeling the Light stir inside me. I stepped out from behind the wall, calm on the outside, fire on the inside. I walked straight into their path, my head held high, feet firmly planted.

They turned, laughing as if I were a joke. That was their mistake.

I raised my chin and summoned the Light.

It roared through me, radiant, golden-white, exploding from my skin like a star born in the night. The guards' laughter died instantly. Their smiles fell into fear as they stumbled backward and ran, their boots echoing wildly off the walls.

The barrier fell, and I bolted through the open door. The front gate loomed ahead, massive, iron-bound, but I couldn't go that way. There was too many soldiers.

Then, movement to my left.

A servant girl, crouched behind a cluster of ale barrels, her body trembling.

I darted toward her. Her wide eyes met mine, and she gasped.

"Aundrea?" she whispered in shock. "What are you doing here?"

"I'm trying to get out," I told her. "Do you know another way?"

She exhaled in relief. "There's a hatch," she said, pointing to a small iron door embedded in the ground, half-hidden by crates. "It leads to an underground tunnel, but… there are too many guards near it."

I nodded. I'd seen her before, delivering food trays to my cell, though I'd never known her name. I placed a finger to my lips.

"Quiet."

Her head nodded in obedience. We crept low around the barrels, toward the execution platform. The air there was thick with blood and memory, stains still clinging to the wood. I waved her behind the structure and knelt beside her.

"Stay here," I whispered. "Wait for my signal."

She obeyed instantly, staying alert.

I stepped out from behind the platform. The guards saw me and started forward. I didn't hesitate.

I threw a wave of Divine Light from both palms, a torrent of power that crashed into them like a tidal wave. They dropped where they stood, unmoving.

I waved to the girl and rushed to the hatch.

It was iron, rusted, and heavy. I struggled with the latch until she joined me. Together, we forced it open with a groan of metal on metal, the sound painfully loud.

We climbed down the ladder into utter darkness, sealing the hatch behind us with a soft thud that echoed in the stillness. There were no torches, no hint of light, only the suffocating cold and the damp scent of stone closing in around us.

Beside me, she whimpered, barely noticeable, but trembling with fear.

I opened my palm, summoning a faint ball of light that bathed the narrow corridor in a warm, golden glow. The walls appeared slick, almost weeping with moisture. My other hand found her shoulder, light but steady. Her name surfaced in a whisper: Altra.

She was frightened; but still moving.

A quiet reassurance passed between us, unspoken. I gave her a gentle nod, guiding her forward into the depths. We had a long way to go—but she wasn't alone anymore.

"It's going to be okay, Altra,"

I told her gently.

"My husband, Drakon, is just outside these walls. He is close. We just need to reach him."

She nodded, still trembling, but comforted. We began to walk, boots splashing softly through the shallow stream that trickled beneath us. The air smelled of damp stone and wet dirt, and the tunnel's ceiling arched low over our heads.

Eventually, we reached a second ladder.

I signaled for Altra to go first. She climbed the ladder to the top, opening the hatch slowly. The glow of the moonlight spilled in.

I followed, climbing into the night air. We emerged outside the palace walls, the trees surrounding us like sentinels. I grabbed her wrist.

"Run."

We didn't stop. I didn't know where I was going, only that I had to keep moving. We burst through the underbrush until we reached a small clearing.

I paused at the tree line, heart pounding, scanning the shadows.

Then, there. A flag, Orange and gold, flapping in the wind.

Drakon's sigil.

One of the guards turned, spotting something moving through the trees. I stepped into the open, Altra close behind.

Sabion.

He ran toward us. I didn't stop myself, I threw my arms around him, joy overtaking my fear.

"Where is," I gasped, catching my breath, "Where is my husband?"

Sabion looked stunned, then elated. He pointed toward a large command tent on the far edge of the camp.

"There," he said.

But I was already running.

I flung the tent flaps open, and there he was.

Drakon stood over a battle map, his soldiers at his side. He turned the moment he saw me and closed the distance between us in a heartbeat.

He caught me in his arms and lifted me from the ground, holding me so tightly I could barely breathe, but I didn't want to breathe, I wanted to live in that moment.

When he set me down, his hands cradled my face. He kissed me, deep, desperate, and real.

Tears clung to my lashes as I looked up at him. "The baby… I had the baby. I sent Michelle and…,"

He pressed a finger to my lips, his eyes shining. "It's okay, my love. They're safe. I sent them to the palace with our best guards."

Relief crashed over me like a wave. I collapsed into his arms, burying my face against his chest.

The feel of him, the warmth, the strength, the way his heart beat beneath my cheek, I never wanted to let go.

But I had to.

I shivered beneath his touch, the chill seeping into my bones as the wind whispered against my skin. Without a word, Drakon unfastened his cloak and swept it around my shoulders. The fabric, still warm from his body, cocooned me in his scent—smoke, spice, and something purely him. His gesture was silent, but the meaning was unmistakable: I see you. I feel your need. I am here.

"Drakon," I whispered, pulling back. "Ravon knows you're here. He is preparing his men, but I took down his protective veil that sealed the Citadel."

Drakon nodded with a silent understanding.

He took my hand in his, holding it tightly as if he'd never let me go again.

I turned to Altra. She stood quietly nearby, her face pale, eyes wide like a lamb lost in a storm.

"Altra," I said gently, "go to Sabion. He'll find a place for you to rest."

She nodded, bowed, and disappeared into the camp. And I stood there, beside Drakon. Ready for what came next.

***

We moved swiftly toward the front lines, the night thick with wind and war drums. Smoke from the fires curled into the sky, mixing with the mist that clung to the battlefield like breath over a grave.

Without a word, he reached for me, lifted me onto a waiting steed, and mounted Vandros. He turned to his army, his voice rising like a clarion call across the trembling ground.

"Brothers!" he cried. "Tonight, we take the Citadel of Eldarath, and we feast on Ravon's blood! His darkness ends here. Now! And our legend begins."

The soldiers responded with a deafening roar.

"Every shadow he casts," Drakon continued,

"we burn. Every soul he's taken, we avenge.

For you. For our people.

For Aundrea, and for your Emperor!

We march with honor!"

He drew Dragonfire and lifted it to the sky. The blade lit with a flash of blue fire, gleaming under the moonlight like a lightning bolt trapped in steel.

The charge began.

I held the reins as tightly as I could while the army surged forward like a wave of fury. Drakon rode beside me, his armor dark silver. Our horses thundered over the ground, the sound like drums from the deep. I could feel the heat of the Dragon Stone pulsing within me, waiting, ready.

The Citadel gates exploded open.

Ravon's forces poured out like molten tar, his shadow Guard in jagged black armor, creatures not entirely mortal, howling like wolves, eyes glowing with malice.

I dismounted mid-charge, nearly losing my balance, but caught myself on a soldier's shoulder and found my footing. I sprinted into the chaos, light already crackling through my veins. I moved through the fray, striking down soldiers one after another, my hands radiating power that sent them flying backwards like ash on the wind.

Beside me, Drakon roared to life, his dragon form unfurling.

His scales burst through his skin, the black, silver, and orange gleaming like starlight. Wings snapped open with a thunderclap, and he launched into the sky, rising higher with every beat of his massive wings. The battlefield froze as his roar tore through the heavens, shaking the very bones of the land below.

Ravon's beasts screamed as Drakon's fire descended upon them.

Walls crumbled. Siege towers collapsed. The flame carved rivers of light through the darkness. I could hear the awe, the fear, the hope rising in our men.

Sabion fought near the front, his blade flashing like a mirror of Drakon's. A Shadow Guard tried to flank him, sword poised for the kill.

I raised both hands and blasted the enemy with a wave of raw light. The man flew backward, his body limp, and Sabion turned, driving his sword into his heart. He looked at me, nodded once, then threw himself back into the fray.

Explosions rocked the courtyard as Ravon's magic cracked the stone.

From the gates, the Shadow Guard emerged in ranks of disciplined evil, unnatural things that had once been men, now twisted and loyal only to Ravon. They moved in tight formation, pressing our front lines back.

I ran toward them, feet slamming the stone, and let my light burst outward in every direction.

The first rank collapsed.

The second hesitated.

The third turned and ran.

I moved forward again, light blazing from my body like a star's heart.

Then,

He appeared.

Ravon stepped through the shattered main gate, flanked by his personal guard, cloaked in deep purple flame. His eyes met mine, and the crowd seemed to dissolve into mist. Time slowed.

We walked toward each other, drawn like opposing forces in the center of the storm.

"You've made a big mistake, Aundrea," he said, his voice unnaturally calm. He raised his hands, and a cyclone of dark magic whipped around him, turning the dust into a twisting pillar of power.

I felt my inner light building as Ravon lifted his hand again. A surge of shadow lashed out—thick, serpentine chains of magic coiling around my body. The restraints tightened with searing heat, and I gasped as the spell burned into my skin, branding me with the same darkness that once stopped me from healing Drakon.

But I fought back. I dug deep—past the fear, past the pain—and found the fire still buried within me.

In that moment, a blast of light erupted from my core, brilliant and blinding. It cracked through the air like thunder, shaking the ground beneath my feet.

Ravon's magic faltered.

I was free.

Drakon saw us.

He turned in the sky, roaring.

Then dove deep.

His fire struck Ravon full-force, hurling him into the Citadel stairs. He screamed, scrambling to his feet, throwing a massive blast of shadow straight up. It struck Drakon mid-air, his wings folded, his body crashed down near me in a storm of flame and dust.

"Drakon!" I cried, running to his side.

He shifted back into mortal form, crumpled, blood smeared across his chestplate. Sabion and the guards closed ranks around us. Steel rang on steel. Arrows whistled overhead. I fell to my knees beside him.

"No," I whispered. "Not now. Not you."

I placed my hands on his chest and summoned everything within me—every spark, every flicker of light, every thread of power the Dragon Stone and healing magic had ever granted. Light poured from me into him." His eyes fluttered open. Glowing.

He stood, transformed once more, as the dragon rose within him This time, no fear, only awe. Even Ravon's personal guard began to back away, their courage shattered.

Drakon flew into the sky again, circling above us like a storm.

I turned to face Ravon alone.

He rose from the rubble, face twisted in fury, magic surging around him like a hurricane. I stepped forward, light pulsing outward with each step, wrapping around me in waves. The sky seemed to darken except where my light burned.

Then I did what I was born to do.

I lifted my arms and poured every ounce of My Divine Light into Drakon.

The sky exploded.

The fire he released lit up the battlefield, burning through Ravon's magic like dawn through thorough the mist. The blast hit Ravon directly, he screamed, fell to his knees, he tried to hold the flame back but his fire overtook him, his cloak ablaze. His power crumbled.

Drakon landed with a quake beside me, shifting back to his mortal form, smoke rising from his shoulders.

I approached Ravon.

He brought this upon himself. Just as I had shattered the altar of his dark god, I would now break the last of his power.

Ravon lifted his head weakly, desperation flickering in his eyes—a final plea buried in fear—as his voice came low and shaky. "Aundrea, my love... our child."

But my resolve was steel. The child he tried to claim was not his. A Dragon Prince was born, bearing the unmistakable mark of Drakon. I gazed down at Ravon's broken body, my breath steady, but the fire within me raging. The pulse of my Divine Light surged through my veins—alive with the essence of the Dragon Stone, bright and undeniable.

"Ravon," I said, my voice low but unshakable, "the baby is not yours. My child belongs to Drakon. His eyes unmistakably bare the mark of the dragon."

For a moment, everything stilled.

I saw it then—the exact second Ravon's soul shattered. His gaze lost focus, the weight of truth crashing through him harder than any blow I could deliver. There was a crack in Ravon's pride, a silent scream in his gaze. It was as if his very soul was being torn from him, unraveling everything he thought he owned. I placed my hands on him. My Light erupted like a supernova.

Ravon screamed as the dark energy tore free from his soul, rising like black smoke into the air. It twisted and

writhed above us, shrieking one last time before dissolving into the night.
I stepped back, the ground steady beneath me, unlike the man before me.

Ravon staggered upright—a shell of who he once was. He clutched his scorched arm, eyes wide with disbelief, as if the weight of his loss had only just begun to crush him.
Drakon moved beside me, his presence calm and unyielding. The unspoken judgment in his gaze said more than words ever could: Ravon would never harm another soul again.
Grief twisted Ravon's features. He trembled, as if trying to make sense of the emptiness left behind. But the truth was clear—what he claimed to possess had never belonged to him. And now, it was gone.

Then,
A thunderous crack split the sky. The ground behind Ravon broke open, yawning into a chasm dark as eternity.
Shadow creatures burst forth—howling, gnashing, the ones that were born of nightmares.
They seized him.
"No!" he screamed, thrashing in vain. "No, please!"
But they did not yield.
They dragged him to hell, their shrieks echoing as the rift slammed shut behind them. Sealing not only his fate, but the curse he unleashed upon the world.

And silence fell.
The battlefield stilled.
Smoke curled toward the stars. The wind whispered.

***

Relief crashed over me like a wave as I turned toward the one constant in my world—my husband, my mate, my home. His presence drew me in like gravity, steady and sure. The moment our eyes met, Drakon opened his arms, and I rushed into them, the wind still stirring around us, heavy with smoke and ash. His embrace closed around me—warm, unyielding, familiar—and for the first time in what felt like forever, I could breathe. The battle was over. The darkness had passed. In his arms, I felt the world realign. I felt safe. I felt whole.

In his arms, I found my throne.

Not made of gold or forged by crowns, but of love, and fire, and fate.

his breath trembling against my hair. "It's over," he whispered, though even he seemed afraid to believe it.

He leaned in, and our lips met in a deep, searing kiss—one that lit fire through every corner of my soul. His warmth poured into me, steady and consuming, like the blaze of dragonfire awakening something ancient inside my chest. I melted into him, tasting ash and wind and the salt of lingering tears.

When he finally pulled back, his breath mingled with mine. His eyes—molten, golden, and fierce—locked onto me with a love that could shatter kingdoms. "You are a powerful one, my love," he murmured, his voice thick with reverence.

A slow, knowing smile spread across his face.

I brushed my lips against his once more, softer this time, a spark in the aftermath of the storm. "Only together does our power ignite," I whispered.

His arms loosened, just enough for us to breathe, but our gaze held fast in the smoky twilight.

Then Drakon's voice, low and full of promise: "Let's go home."

Without a word, he stepped back. His body shimmered with light — not harsh or searing, but radiant, alive. In a flash of brilliant fire and shifting shadow, he transformed. Where once stood my husband, now stood the dragon — mighty, majestic, and mine.

His wings spread wide, catching the rising wind, his scales glinting with embers of Silver, gold and crimson. He lowered himself to the ground, head bowed, inviting me forward.

As the smoke cleared and the wind stilled, I stepped forward, my heart pounding. The enormous beast before me was no stranger—he was mine. My husband. My love. My Drakon.

His silver-and-sunset scales shimmered like a living flame, catching the light of the burning horizon. Every movement of his massive body radiated power barely held in check. The heat rolling off him was fierce, yet familiar— like the warmth of a hearth I had always belonged to.

I reached up, placing both hands on either side of his massive, scaled cheeks. The skin beneath my palms was smooth and hot, alive with a hum that vibrated through my bones. His great head lowered, slowly, reverently, until his golden eyes met mine.

They burned with ancient fire.

But beyond the fire… I saw him. Truly saw him. The man who had walked through agony and war to reach me. My Drakon, stripped of every mask, every doubt— glorious and wild and free.

My eyes filled with tears as I leaned in and pressed my lips to the warm, ridged curve of his maw. His breath stirred my hair, and a low rumble vibrated through his chest—a sound of recognition, of love.

Then I stepped onto his foreleg, the scales slick beneath my boot. I climbed with care, clutching the ridge of his back as I pulled myself upward. My legs locked around his powerful shoulders, my fingers gripping the firm curve of his neck. The muscles beneath me rippled like coiled lightning, and his body thrummed with restrained fury and flight.

And then, with one mighty beat of his wings, we rose.

The ground fell away in a rush of wind and heat. Below us, the world was smoke and shadow—but above, the stars opened like a promise. I held tightly, heart hammering with joy and awe.

We were fire and sky.
We were homebound.
We were free.

The wind tore at my hair, my cloak billowing behind as Lisona stretched below us — bruised, battered, but whole. Fires flickered. Fields were flattened. Yet I saw people rising from the wreckage, holding each other, weeping, living.

Drakon soared higher, wings cutting through the clouds. The stars blinked above like watchful eyes. I pressed my face to the side of his neck and whispered, "Let's return where our story began."

And he roared — not in fury, but in triumph.

The sound echoed across the land, a promise that darkness had not won.

Chapter 25

No More Chains

Οἶκος Δράκων

HOUSE DRAKON

The wind rushed past my face, sharp and clean as it swept over the highlands of Lisona. I clung to the ridges of Drakon's shimmering scales, the muscles beneath them flexing with every beat of his wings. For more than a month, we had flown this way—soaring far above the world we'd saved, the armies that marched below, the broken lands left behind by Ravon's darkness. Sabion and the guards traveled beneath us, their banners rippling in the breeze as we kept vigil from above. My husband—the dragon, the emperor, the soul I had nearly lost—was no longer just Drakon in name, but in flesh and fire.

The sun dipped low as we approached the Lisonian Palace, gilding the towers in hues of rose and gold. A thousand memories stirred in me as we descended—the time I first arrived here as a stranger, the nights I cried myself to sleep, the aching hope that one day Lisona might feel like home. And now, I returned not as a prisoner or pawn, but as the Divine One, with my true mate beside me and our future nestled safely in the arms of those waiting.

Drakon's vast wings slowed, then folded inward with a final, graceful sweep. He landed with thunderous precision at the palace steps, stone cracking faintly beneath his talons. He crouched low and turned his massive head, waiting. I slid from his back, my hands briefly brushing the warmth of his scales before he shifted.

Light burst outward in a ripple of gold and fire. The air shimmered around him. Within a heartbeat, my husband stood before me again in his mortal form—his bronze-tinged skin glowing in the waning light, his expression softened by something unspoken. Without a word, he extended his arm. I took it.

***

The palace doors burst open with a bang.

Michelle's voice broke first. "Aundrea!" Her feet pounded the steps as she ran toward us. Sarah followed close behind, skirts flying, her usual composure utterly undone. And then Alissia—her eyes already brimming—reached me first, throwing her arms around me with such force it nearly knocked the air from my lungs. I didn't care. I held my sister as tightly as she held me, tears finally slipping down my cheeks.

Around the corner, a familiar figure appeared. Jasper—stoic, solid, and for once, visibly shaken. His voice cracked as he said, "Brother... I feared the worst." He stepped forward and embraced Drakon in a rare, fierce hug, clapping him on the back like a man afraid to let go.

And then—I saw her.

Freyan.

She stood near the colonnade, a soft bundle cradled against her chest. My heart forgot how to beat. She stepped toward me slowly, reverently, as if each footfall carried a world's worth of care. I reached out, trembling.

And then he was in my arms.

My son.

Warm and solid and real.

He nestled against me with a tiny sigh, his dark curls pressed to my skin. My entire being folded in on him, protecting, loving, marveling. So much love. So much pride. So beautiful.

Drakon moved in behind me, wrapping his arms gently around mine. We stood that way for a moment—just the three of us—his chin resting near my shoulder, his presence anchoring me.

Then... it happened.

Our son's tiny hand uncurled and wrapped around Drakon's finger like it had always belonged there. And as if stirred by that single connection, his eyes fluttered open. A brilliant orange glow pulsed from his irises—majestic, like the colors of a Lisonian sunset. But not just any sunset. A rare one. The kind that only appears once in a generation, when the light bends just so and the skies catch fire.

A Dragon Prince.

Right here in Lisona.

And already putting on a light show.

Drakon leaned close, his breath warm against my ear. "I think he has your eyes," he murmured with a grin.

I swatted him lightly. "Oh, shut up," I said with a laugh, tears still sliding freely down my cheeks.

He turned me gently to face him, careful not to disturb the child nestled between us. His lips found mine in a kiss that tasted of salt and hope and everything we had survived. When he finally pulled back, his gaze never left mine.

"Still worth it," he whispered.

I rolled my eyes, but couldn't help smiling. My heart overflowed.

I turned back to our son, brushing my fingers across his glowing cheek.

"Drakon," I whispered. "He looks just like you. I love you. I love you both."

Just then, I heard the thunder of boots behind us, and Sabion swept in through the palace entrance like a force of nature. His eyes scanned the hall until they landed on Michelle—and everything else seemed to vanish for him. Without hesitation, he crossed the distance in long, purposeful strides. In one fluid motion, he lifted her into the air, spinning her around. Michelle's delighted laughter rang through the grand marble hall like chimes in a summer breeze, lifting the heaviness of our recent memories.

He set her gently back on her feet, but his gaze didn't leave hers. His expression shifted—no longer playful, but full of love, urgency, and reverence. Slowly, Sabion dropped to one knee and pulled a ring from his pocket. A breath caught in my throat.

"Michelle," he said, voice steady and heartfelt, "from the moment I first met you, I knew. I've known every day since. But until now, it was forbidden." He glanced briefly at Drakon and me, then returned his eyes to hers. "I love you. Will you be my wife?"

Michelle blinked, her bottom lip trembling as tears filled her eyes. She turned to look at us, her gaze searching. Drakon gave a single nod—silent, powerful, and full of approval. It was all the answer she needed.

Tears spilled over her cheeks, joy radiating from her in waves. "Yes! Oh, yes!" she cried, bouncing slightly on her toes, laughter tangled in her sobs.

Sabion slipped the ring onto her finger, then rose. His hands cradled her face like she was the most precious thing in all of Lisona. Their lips met, and the room erupted into applause. The kiss lingered, timeless and beautiful, as if sealing more than just a promise—it sealed healing, and a future.

Drakon leaned close to me with a grin, his voice low. "Let's eat. I'm starving."

Everyone chuckled, and the joyful procession moved into the dining hall.

***

A long table was already set with platters of roasted meats, fruits, golden bread, and warm spiced wine. As we sat and ate, laughter and stories spilled through the room. The men recounted their fearless stand on the battlefield, each tale grander than the last. I told of the escape—how I helped Michelle, Freyan, Sarah, and the baby avoid danger, and then of my daring flight to freedom.

But then, the mood shifted. A hush settled over the table as I began to speak of my final moments before liberation—of the shadows, the spell, the fear. I faltered. The words stuck in my throat. Images flooded my mind uninvited—his voice, the darkness, the weight of what had been stolen. Silence stretched, heavy and raw.

Drakon, sensing it immediately, gently reached beneath the table for my hand. Then he stood and raised his voice.

"Kaelinna," he called.

From the shadows near the archway, a woman stepped forward. Her armor gleamed under the hall's golden light, a sharp contrast to the softness in her expression. She moved with grace and strength, and as she approached, she dropped into a respectful bow.

"Aundrea, my love," Drakon said, his voice proud, "I want to introduce you to your new personal guard."

I looked up at her, my throat still tight, and nodded with gratitude.

"She is Kaelinna," he continued. "We met her on the way to Eldrida's Maw. She helped us destroy the Death Stone."

I managed to find my voice. "Thank you for helping us, Kaelinna."

She straightened, her eyes steady. "No, milady. It's I who owe you my life. If not for your proclamation giving women the right to choose their own husbands, I would be dead. And your husband saved me. I am in your debt, now and always."

A small, genuine smile broke across my face—one that reached all the way to my chest, warming the cracked places inside me.

Drakon stood and moved behind me, helping me to my feet and sliding my chair back with care. He turned toward the others in the room, bowing his head with a quiet reverence.

"I believe it's time for my wife and I to retire," he said.

He offered me his arm, and I slipped mine through his as we made our way down the candlelit corridor. Each step echoed softly off the palace stone walls. When we reached our chambers, he opened the door and guided me inside. Only then did he turn to face me, the flickering light casting soft shadows across his features.

***

Without a word, he pulled me into his arms. His lips brushed my forehead, then the corners of my eyes, and finally—soft and lingering—my mouth. I melted into him, letting the warmth of his body and the strength of his arms take hold.

He removed the tie from my hair, letting the strands tumble freely down my back. His kiss followed, soft but hungry—everything I had yearned for during those long, aching months trapped in darkness. Slowly, he turned me around, his fingertips trailing down the row of delicate buttons along the back of my dress. Each one came undone with reverence, not haste. When the last clasp fell open, his hands came to rest gently on my shoulders, and the fabric slipped from my body, pooling at my feet like a whisper.

He lifted me effortlessly into his arms, cradling me against his chest. My heart beat wildly, yet I felt utterly safe. He carried me to the bed, laying me down with a tenderness that broke me open all over again. Then he undressed before joining me, his skin warm against mine as he drew me into a kiss that spoke of longing and devotion. His mouth moved over mine—slow, consuming—a testament to the love that had endured through so much.

He brushed the hair from my eyes and gazed down at me, his voice low and awestruck. "You are beautiful, my love."

Behind him, the flames in the hearth rose higher, as if stirred by our passion. Shadows danced across the stone walls. Heat glowed over our skin.

"You're trembling," he murmured, concern softening his voice. "Why?"

A breath shuddered from my lips. "I just never knew I could feel this way."

He kissed me again, and the fire I felt inside surged to match the one crackling in the fireplace. His hand sought mine beneath the covers, his fingers twining with mine in a silent vow. The world slipped away around us, time losing meaning, until there was only the sound of our breath and the rhythm of our hearts.

Pleasure bloomed in me, slow and bright. I clung to him, overwhelmed by sensation, our bodies woven together like threads in a tapestry too sacred for words. When I caught my breath, I leaned in close, my lips brushing his ear.

"I love the way the firelight shines in your eyes."

He looked at me then—and in that moment, his gaze changed. The flicker of his dragon soul surged to the surface, orange flames dancing in his irises like a reflection of the fire that raged within both of us.

He kissed me again—deeper this time. Fierce. Worshipful.

His power flowed into me, igniting wildfire beneath my skin. The world tilted. Passion exploded, rich and consuming, a sensual storm that swept us away. I gasped, overwhelmed by the sweet surrender of it all—the touch of his hands, the warmth of his breath, the way he knew every corner of my soul.

Our love was a dance—fierce and slow, wild and tender. A symphony of sensation that built, until only breathless moans remained. In his arms, I found more than desire.

I found where I belonged. Drakon collapsed beside me, breathless, and gathered me into his arms. I curled into his chest, my ear pressed against the steady rhythm of his heartbeat. It echoed through me, grounding and sacred. I'd never felt so breathless, so completely consumed by another soul. There was a power in our connection—intoxicating, magnetic—pulling me closer as if the universe itself demanded we never part.

His warmth enveloped me. My fingers traced lazy patterns across his skin, not out of restlessness, but reverence. I couldn't stop touching him. I didn't want to forget the feel of him—solid, real, and mine.

I lay there, wrapped in his embrace, refusing to let go. The room was quiet except for the soft crackle of the fire and the quiet hum of our breath. Time faded. Nothing else existed beyond the rise and fall of his chest beneath my cheek.

Eventually, sleep claimed us—gently, like the closing of a beloved book.

***

One year had passed, and Lisona had changed in ways we once only dreamed possible. Today, the people gathered not in fear or mourning, but in celebration—of life, of love, and of a new future. And of her—our daughter. Clarissia was born with more than just the Divine Light.

She was light!

Her eyes, the softest shade of blue, carried the calm of still skies and the promise of peace. To look into them was to remember hope. She was divine in every way, a dragon princess not forged by the stone, but born of it— complete, whole, radiant from her very first breath.

The courtyard teemed with thousands, their cheers rising like waves. Banners danced in the breeze, streaks of crimson and gold against a clear blue sky. The scent of blooming marentha petals filled the air, carried by warm winds and hope.

Sabion stood proudly at the edge of the grand staircase, his voice carrying over the murmuring crowd. "People of Lisona," he proclaimed with strength and reverence, "I give to you: Your Emperor Drakon, Empress Aundrea, Prince Drako, and Princess Clarissia!"

Drakon stepped forward, regal and glowing in the sun, with Drako nestled proudly in his arms. I held Clarissia close to my heart, walking at his side as our cloaks trailed behind us like flames of honor. The crowd erupted—voices crying out in joy, hands raised high, tears streaming freely from faces both old and young. The sound of it washed over me, pure and electric.

Drakon leaned in, pressing a kiss to my temple as he pulled me tighter into his side. His warmth, his strength—it reminded me that no matter what had passed, no matter what trials were still to come, I would never face them alone.

We descended the marble steps slowly, with Michelle and Freyan just behind us. As we reached the foot of the stairs, I turned and gently handed Clarissia to Freyan. Drakon passed Drako into Michelle's waiting arms. Both women accepted them with reverent joy.

Together, we moved through the throng. The people parted before us, hands reaching out to brush our garments as if our presence alone could bring healing. At the raised platform, two thrones awaited. As Drakon climbed the steps, he raised a hand—music began to play, swelling with string and voice, cascading like sunlight through the land.

I looked up into Drakon's eyes, those fire-kissed eyes, and saw not just a ruler, but a man who had earned his crown through blood, mercy, and unwavering love. There were laws to rewrite, wounds to mend, a future to forge. But with him beside me, I knew it was all possible. We were no longer two. We were a united force.

Michelle lowered Drako to the stone beneath our feet, his chubby legs wobbling uncertainly. And then—he stepped. One foot, then another. My breath caught. I dropped to my knees and gathered him into my arms, tears of joy blurring my vision. He looked up at me, his face the very reflection of his father's strength and my own stubborn hope. My heart exploded with love.

A soft coo drew my gaze. Clarissia, nestled in Freyan's arms, reached out tiny fingers. Her presence was like starlight—gentle but full of power. I smiled so wide it hurt.

Then, Drakon rose.

His form shimmered, the air around him trembling. I stepped back instinctively, my heart pounding in awe. Silver light rippled across his skin, turning his flesh to molten metal kissed by the last rays of a dying sun. His body elongated, limbs stretching, spine arching. With a mighty crack of magic, he transformed—scales bursting forth, wings slicing the air open wide. His roar shook the sky, primal and righteous. The crowd gasped in reverent silence.

Drakon—the dragon—lowered his enormous head. Firelight danced across his eyes, and with the utmost care, he lifted Drako in one massive claw. Freyan stepped forward with Clarissia, kissing the child's forehead before placing her gently in Drakon's other claw.

The two little ones nestled safely against his armored chest, bathed in the glow of ancestral fire.

I stepped forward, trembling not with fear but with something more profound—liberation.

I climbed onto his back, my fingers gripping the warm ridges of his scales. The moment my feet left the ground, a weight I hadn't realized I still carried fell away. With one breathtaking leap, we soared. The wind kissed my face, wild and free.

Below, the crowd erupted, weeping, cheering, collapsing to their knees in reverence. The sky opened above us, welcoming its children home. Drakon unleashed a stream of fire into the heavens—not destruction, but blessing. The flames painted the sky with streaks of gold, like a second sunrise.

We circled, majestic and slow.

Victory was ours, carved from the edge of despair and lit by the fire of love, not with strength alone, but with our hearts that refused to yield.

Then, wings angled downward, we descended through the parted sea of people. As Drakon landed in the heart of the crowd, silence fell again—deep, sacred, waiting.

I slid from his back, stepping forward beside him. My hand rested against his gleaming side. And I spoke.

"No more chains.
No more fear.
From this day forward,
we rise together…
and we
Free Lisona!"

About the Author

Οἶκος Δράκων

HOUSE DRAKON

Trish Martinez is a former restaurant owner, event planner, and mobile DJ with over two decades of experience bringing stories to life through celebration and connection. She has served on the board of her local Chamber of Commerce and has worked closely with domestic violence survivors and foster youth, offering support and advocacy.

Now living in a small rural town in Oregon, Trish shares her passion for storytelling with over 133,000 followers on TikTok. *Free Lisona* is her debut novel.

***

Next in the Series
Free Lisona: The Oath That Chained the Light

The prophecy was only the beginning.
Aundrea must descend into shadow, forge an unholy alliance,
and risk everything to save the child who may one day destroy them all.

***

Follow her on TikTok: **@TrishMartinez32**

Website: http://www.freelisona.net

www.ingramcontent.com/pod-product-compliance
Lightning Source LLC
Chambersburg PA
CBHW052330110726
47901CB00005B/1182